THE FIVE WILD SONS OF RANDOLPH RANCH BOX SET

CLEAN COWBOY ROMANCE

TERRI GRACE

PUREREAD.COM

CONTENTS

KENDRICK'S BRIDE ON THE RUN

MAYNARD'S SCARRED SECOND CHANCE BRIDE

CALLUM'S BROKEN BRIDE ON A MISSION

DEAR READER, GET READY FOR
ANOTHER GREAT STORY...

A CHRISTIAN WESTERN ROMANCE

Turn the page and let's begin

QUINTEN'S WILD CHRISTMAS ROSE

THE WILD WEST

*T*he middle-aged man with distinguished features was taking a stroll through the lovely rose garden. This beautiful, well-landscaped garden lay on one side of his sprawling ranch house. Unknown to him, his eldest son was watching him from the brow of the hill on the far end of the vast ranch.

Quinten Randolph, twenty-nine years old, wondered what was going through his father's mind. Come rain or sunshine, twice a day, his father walked through the rose garden that his mother had planted fifteen years ago. Mama had loved her rose garden and had tended it lovingly, making her family enjoy it with her.

At the time, Quinten, who'd been fourteen then, hadn't understood why his mother spent nearly all her mornings in the garden.

"I'm making it ready," she would say whenever he asked her why she spent so much time on her knees. "My son, you see these roses that I'm growing? The rose is the universal flower that depicts love, and each time you and your brothers pluck a rose for the lapels of your coats or fill a vase with them or even just take a stroll through this garden, remember that your Mama loves you very much. This is the symbol of my love for you."

Quinten was to recall his mother's words a year later when she fell from her horse on Christmas Day and broke her neck. The horse got spooked by a rattler as his mother had been on her way back from visiting a friend of hers on the neighboring ranch. She'd decided to take a short cut so she could get home before dark, and that was when disaster had struck.

To this day Quinten felt the tears smarting at the back of his eyes whenever he thought of his mother's painful last moments on earth. She'd lain in the ditch where she'd fallen, all alone for over an hour before her riderless mare had returned to the ranch. The horse's agitated state had alerted everyone that all wasn't all right. Though his mom had informed them about her visit to her friend's place, no one knew which route she'd taken, for there were many different ones.

So, Quinten's father had dispatched people in all directions to search for his missing wife. In the end, it was Quinten who'd found his mother lying half-conscious in the ditch and held her broken body as she took her last breath.

"Take... care... of... your... father... and... brothers..." were the last words she'd ever spoken. Within seconds she was gone.

Quinten felt the dampness on his face, and he lowered the binoculars from his eyes as he wiped the tears away with the sleeve of his plaid shirt. Before losing his mother, Quinten had always wondered why people mourned a loved one for so long and never seemed to get over their grief.

He'd lost both sets of grandparents when he was small and had often noticed that his parents were sad at certain times, especially when the anniversaries of their deaths came up. He would do all he could to cheer them up during such times and he hadn't understood their need to lock themselves up in their bedroom for a few hours to deal with their pain.

Now he knew better because fourteen years later the pain of losing his mother was as fresh as if it had just happened that morning. Do people ever recover from such loss?

Once again, he raised the binoculars to his eyes, and this time, he trained them on his father's face. His father was only sixty, but the grooves of sorrow made him look much older. Pa had been this way ever since that fateful day when he'd found his wife of fifteen years had fallen off her horse and broken her neck and back. When the cowboys had carried his mother's lifeless and broken body home, everyone had been weeping, for she'd been well loved. His father had broken down, and it had hurt Quinten to see the strong man reduced to a weeping and blabbering man. The quick actions of one of the ranch managers had saved the mare's life because Abner Randolph had come to the house carrying a rifle with which he'd intended to shoot the horse. That same manager had arranged for the horse to be sold on Quin's instructions because the teenager had feared that his father would eventually harm it.

Being the oldest at fifteen years, Quinten hadn't once shed a tear in public for his mother, nor really grieved for her. He had to be strong for his father and brothers and couldn't afford to fall to pieces. His great fear was that if he started crying, he wouldn't stop, and his family needed him.

Quinten saw his father stop and stare at the roses that his wife of fifteen years had planted and hoped to enjoy, but the cruel hand of death had cut short those plans.

It seemed as if from that day onward, laughter had gone from his father's eyes. While he went through the motions of merriment once in a while, the pain and shadows lurked in his eyes.

"Dad, what are you thinking now?" Quinten muttered as he watched his father pull out a small pair of shears from his dungarees pocket. He plucked fifteen roses, all red and Quinten knew where he was taking them.

Every Saturday for the past fifteen years, his Pa cut fresh roses, always fifteen: one for each year that he and his wife had been married. He would then carry them and walk slowly to the family cemetery and lay them on his wife's grave.

On the anniversary of their wedding which fell on Christmas Day, his father would carry two different bouquets, one white and the other red, still fifteen in each bunch. Then on his mother's birthday his dad would place a mixed bouquet of roses to commemorate what her age would have been that year. This year he'd placed fifty roses for she would have been in her Jubilee year.

Watching his father walk slowly to the family cemetery, Quinten purposed that he would never fall in love with a woman. The pain of losing her would drive him mad. Quinten knew that it was the grace and mercy of God that had kept his father alive until now.

In the early months after his mother's death, Quinten had been terrified that he would one day wake up to find his father dead from a broken heart. So deep was his father's grief that there were days he wouldn't even get out of bed.

"I can't love a woman like that," Quinten lowered the binoculars and patted his horse's neck. "Thunder, can you imagine giving your whole heart to a woman and then losing her?" He shook his head. His age didn't bother him at all, even though most of his friends who were his age were married with two and some even three children. No, marriage and love weren't for him, not if it meant having his heart ripped out should anything happen to his beloved.

"Let my brothers fall in love and get married," he muttered. "They can give me all the nieces and nephews I need. My life is this ranch and that's the way it will always be," he told himself, suppressing all feelings of the loneliness that sometimes assailed him.

ABNER RANDOLPH SAT on the small marble seat he'd built close to his wife's grave and sighed deeply. This was his peaceful spot, and he retired to it every single day unless the weather was extreme.

His wife had been dead for fifteen years, and he still missed her every single day. He felt that no one understood why he'd never remarried, especially when the boys were still very young. It certainly wasn't for lack of suitable companions. A number of women inside and even outside church had tried their best to find their way into his heart and his home but to no avail. His heart was completely closed to love. Only one woman had ever occupied the space in his heart and not even death had removed her from that position.

Abner leaned forward and laid the fifteen long-stemmed roses on his wife's grave and then, like he did every Saturday when he came here, he let his eyes roam over the large headstone, also made of marble like the seat. It was inscribed in gold lettering.

"Mrs. Barbara Naomi Randolph, beloved wife and mother, gone too soon. You are dearly missed by your beloved husband and sons. The generations after you are bereft, for they will never know what a wonderful and outstanding woman you were."

With another sigh Abner leaned back on the seat. As his eyes remained fixed on the gravestone, he allowed his memories of the past to take over.

Barbara had been new to Cedar Hill when they met in church for the first time thirty years ago. For Abner, it was love at first sight, though it had taken some convincing before Barbara even agreed to go out for coffee with him. It was another full year before they tied the knot on Christmas Day.

"I love Christmas," Barbara had said when Abner had asked her why it was so important for them to wed on that particular day and not any other. "Christmas Day has always been very special to me, and from when I was a little girl it was my dream to get married on the day itself."

And Barbara had given him fifteen wonderful years and five strapping sons, and then just like that, without warning, she'd gone away from them forever.

"Oh Barbara," Abner whispered, turning the ring round and round on his finger. He'd never once taken it off during his marriage or even after Barbara's death. He just couldn't get rid of the ring, even though friends urged him to do so.

"Abner, taking the ring off is the only way you'll be able to move on with your life," his longtime friend, Dustin Buck Knerr, always told him. "Barbara would be brokenhearted to see you like this."

Abner always brushed his friend's urgings aside. He'd loved Barbara with his whole heart, and it was as if it had been buried with her. He sighed and held his head in his hands just as he felt the vibration of his phone in his shirt pocket.

"Must be one of the boys," he muttered impatiently, though it touched him that his sons were always checking up on him. He couldn't stay out of sight for more than half an hour before they started calling to ask him where he was and if he was all right.

But the caller identity said it was Dustin calling him. "Buck," he said as he received the call.

"Abner, where are you? I passed by your house, and no one seems to know where you are."

"They all do but think that I don't want to be disturbed. I'm at Barbara's grave."

"Give me a few minutes and I'll be there with you."

As Abner waited for his friend to join him, he pondered over their friendship that had lasted years and was still going strong. Both of them had been raised by single mothers after their army fathers had died overseas during the Vietnamese war. The two of them had still been impressionable teenagers, and the following years had been quite tough on them.

Abner was always quick to admit that but for Buck he might have gone down a terrible path. And Buck also said the same thing about Abner.

It took Buck almost twenty minutes to get to Abner. He was sweating and panting, and his shirt was damp.

"How are you?" Abner made room for his friend on the marble bench.

"Give me... a moment... to catch... my breath," the other man sat down heavily.

Abner smiled as he looked at his friend. Buck had put on a lot of weight these past few years. "My dear man, you're going to have to reduce your intake of too much sugar, fatty foods and those delicious pastries that you have a weakness for."

"I blame it on the woman I married," Buck grumbled good-naturedly. "I can't help it if she's turned me into her culinary guinea pig."

"So, the restaurant and bakery must be doing well."

Buck nodded, "So well that Abby has taken on two more new staff. And she hasn't stopped inventing new dishes and pastries, and guess who is her chief taster?"

"You could always say no to the new dishes, Mr. Taster," Abner was laughing.

Buck scowled at him, "What? And get my woman all riled up? Some things are worth the pain."

"You're out of breath after walking for a short distance and that's never good for the heart."

Buck waved a dismissive hand, "Are you now trying to take the place of my doctor?"

"Oh no! Not at all, but I like you, Buck, and I'd like to have you around for a long time."

"Have no fear, my friend, there's longevity in all branches of my family so you can count on my being around for as long as you want."

The two men fell into companionable silence. Abner enjoyed Buck's company very much because he wasn't one who was a chatterer. And in all the years that he'd known him, Buck never said anything unkind about anyone. Such friends were rare, and as he'd said, Abner wanted to have Buck around for the longest time.

Then Buck made an impatient sound and Abner turned to him questioningly.

"Has Mrs. Matheson been by the house lately?"

Abner shook his head. The woman his friend spoke of was his sons' former high school principal. "The boys have been out of school for years now so I don't see why she should still be coming around."

"It's not you she's after," Buck leaned forward. "Her interest lies in your sons."

"Do tell, my friend."

"Mrs. Matheson's three daughters have come of age, and she seeks spouses for them."Abner threw his head back and laughed out loud. "And the poor woman feels that my sons meet the criteria to be her daughters' spouses?" Buck nodded. "Poor deluded soul," Abner said. "If I can't get my own sons to take an interest in any women whether in church or outside, how does she think she'll do it?"

"The woman is determined, and I for one don't envy your sons. A mother who wants to see her daughters married and settled will stop at nothing to see that she succeeds."

Abner smiled, "Then Mrs. Matheson should be prepared for disappointment because I know my sons very well. She's wasting her time. What haven't I tried, Buck? Is it throwing endless parties and inviting all the eligible young women in Cedar Hill? Is it taking my sons on forced trips where I've arranged for them to meet beautiful young women? Nothing seems to work."

"Try a dating agency or something. These youths of today believe in finding love on the Internet."

"That's all a hoax if you ask me," Abner easily dismissed his friend's suggestion. "Cindy, one of the interns said that most people on those dating sites are conmen, murderers, and serial killers, including women. I wouldn't want my sons to end up in trouble because I'm desperate to get them married."

"What about marriage agencies then?"

"Buck, you're priceless. How do you know so much about these things, and do they even work?"

"You won't believe me when I tell you this, but these marriage agencies and matchmakers have been there since time immemorial," Buck told Abner who stared at him in disbelief.

"And the marriages lasted forever or got cut short at some point?'

"Most marriages worked and I'm living proof of that."

"What do you mean, my friend?"

"My great, great grandfather was a good man whose name was Jethro Knerr. He had seven sons who were just like your boys, each having their own reasons for not wanting to marry and settle down. He'd lost his wife and also his youngest son, who happens to be my direct great grandfather. You see, the two supposedly drowned. My great, great grandmother's body was found but not that of her son. Anthony was my great grandfather, and after he went missing, he lived among the Nez Perce Indians for a full year before some trader recognized him and he was reunited with the rest of the family."

"Buck, that all sounds like a folktale."

"Be cynical all you want, but I'm telling you that my great grandfather Anthony found his bride through a bridal agency."

"That's all fine but what does any of it have to do with me wanting to find wives for my sons?"

"This is where the interesting part comes in. Do you remember when my wife visited her sister in Denver some few months back?" Abner nodded. "While she was at Dallas airport waiting to board her flight to Denver and complaining as usual about the restrictions caused by the Corona virus, she happened to start chatting with a young lady. When Abigail introduced herself as Mrs. Knerr, she noticed that the young lady looked excited."

"That's rather odd, especially if they were strangers. Had they met before?"

"Not at all, and when they got onto the plane, the two of them managed to talk their respective seatmates into allowing them sit together. That's when the young lady, her name is Sally-Jo Manning, asked Abby if she was perhaps the descendant of someone who lived in the eighteen eighties and his name was Jethro Knerr. Having an unusual name like that makes people pay attention. When Abby answered in the affirmative, the young lady told my wife something very interesting. That it was her great, great grandmother who had made matches for all seven sons of Jethro, including my own great grandfather, Anthony Knerr."

"You're pulling my leg on this one, Buck," Abner stared at his friend in disbelief. "What are the chances that a descendant of a matchmaker meets the descendant of one of those who benefitted from their services?"

"You can call it coincidence, but I say it was well planned by the Lord. That Abby should meet with Sally Jo, the descendant of the woman who was responsible for my great grandfather and his brothers finding their brides. Just so you know, all those ancestors of mine—all seven of them—lived well into their nineties with the wives of their youth. So, I believe that this is a godsent opportunity."

"For whom?"

"Your sons, of course," Buck said. "Why don't you engage the services of Miss Sally-Jo Manning? She runs an exclusive agency for modern-day cowboys and cowgirls who are looking for true love and romance wherever they can find it. The young lady is providing the same services that her great, great grandmother did, but this time it's even better."

"How?"

"With Internet, phones and Skype and all the other communication platforms, dating and finding love has become very easy. No more unnecessary waiting or sending letters that could even go missing and never get to their destinations. How did we survive without the Internet and cell phones?" Buck shook his head. "You and I grew up with landlines and phone booths. Now I walk around with this thing," he held his handset up. "And sometimes it's even a nuisance because anyone who is looking for me can get me as long as the phone is on."

"Stop complaining! I've seen you playing with your phone. But back to Miss Manning, do you think my sons can benefit from her imaginary services?"

"Stop mocking me, Abner. If you don't want Miss Manning's help, then so be it. But you don't need to mock what works for others."

"Pardon my humor, my friend. But it all sounds like one of those Internet fraud games. I bet the woman asks for payment before she can match a man to his supposed mate," Abner's voice was dry.

"Remember I said it was an exclusive agency, right?"

"Right."

"The fees Miss Manning asks for are a bit high, but she delivers on her promises."

"If you had proof of even one single couple she's united in holy matrimony, I would believe you. Otherwise, all this sounds like a hoax and a bid for some clever young lady sitting behind a laptop to make money by exploiting the loneliness of people."

"Abner, there is proof, and right here in Dallas."

"Seriously?"

"Yes. Don't you remember me mentioning that Abby met Miss Manning at Dallas Airport? She had come to attend the wedding of one of the couples she'd brought together."

"That sounds interesting, but how can we tell that it's true? If Abby travelled a few months ago then these people are still on honeymoon and will only say nice things about each other and the person who brought them together."

Buck gave his friend an exasperated look. "Cut it out now, will you? You have to start believing that the Internet is the new mode and means of people meeting their future spouses."

"Well, I need references before I can commit to anything."

"I'll call Sally-Jo and ask her to give us the name of the couple, and then you can visit them and find out the truth. Perhaps there are others who have been together for a little bit longer and I'll ask her about that too."

Abner didn't want to further offend his friend by continuing to express his disbelief. "Well, Buck, if you can get me some references, I'll consider your suggestion," he said, but was sure that he wouldn't be making any follow-ups.

However, in the days to come, Abner got to thinking that using a marriage agency might not be such a bad idea after all. And the high fees made sense if the agency was able to weed out the fake and false people from the real ones who were genuinely in search of true love.

"Lord, could this be the way in which you'll help my sons find their brides?" He prayed for many days. Finally, he got the conviction that he should speak with Buck and called his friend up.

"Buck, I'd like you to give me Miss Manning's number," he said after they had dispensed with the niceties of knowing how each one was faring on.

"Why?"

"I'd like to use her services to find brides for my sons."

Buck chuckled. "What changed your mind, my friend?"

"I just got to thinking and prayed about the whole idea and when I finally felt peace within my heart, I decided to call and ask you for Miss Manning's number."

"I hope you know what you're doing. Miss Manning is a serious person, and I wouldn't want you to waste her time."

"I promise you that I'll have a chat with her and see what she has to offer."

"Fine then, let me send you the number."

As soon as Abner received the number, he dialed, and a sweet voice came on. "This is Hitch Your Wagon Romance Agency, how may I be of assistance to you today?"

"My name is Abner Randolph, and I'd like to speak to Miss Sally-Jo Manning."

"Miss Manning is on another call. Would you like me to call you later or will you hold on the line?"

"I'll hold," Abner said, praying that he wouldn't have to wait for long.

A few minutes later he was connected to Miss Manning. "My name is Abner Randolph of Randolph Ranch in Cedar Hill, Dallas County, Texas. I was given your number by my good friend Dustin Knerr. You met his wife Abby a few months ago on a flight from Dallas to Denver."

"Oh yes, the delightful Mrs. Knerr," Sally-Jo laughed, a deep and pleasant sound. Abner felt that he could trust her. "We were both complaining about the restrictions brought about by the Corona virus and just hit it off. Then we had a good chat and laugh all the way from Dallas to Denver. It surprised me, very pleasantly I must admit, to find out that my great, great grandmother actually got wives for all of Mr. Knerr's ancestors."

"I believe that you have proof of this?"

"Oh yes, documented and well preserved. Great, great grandma Molly White's legacy for finding romance for wild and crazy young men out on the frontier continued for many years. She was widowed at an early age and later married my great, great grandfather who was a veteran of the American Civil War. My great, great grandpa had one daughter, who bore my great grandfather and his sisters, then down to my grandfather, my father and now me. Throughout those generations, women in our family continued running that agency but we moved from Philadelphia to Denver with time, and finally it was left to me."

"Buck told me the agency was called Cozy Brides or something like that."

"Yes, in earlier years. But my aunt who ran it before I took it over changed the name to *Hitch Your Wagon Romance Agency*. She didn't want to deal with just any ordinary clients, but cowboys and cowgirls who were searching for love. I think she wanted to continue Molly White's legacy because she helped frontier people find love and romance."

"This Mrs. Molly White must have been quite a remarkable woman."

"History doesn't lie, and the documents say that she really was. Do you know that she was also an amateur detective?"

"No, I had no idea. But the reason I'm calling is because I have five sons who don't want to find love, get married, settle down and give me grandchildren."

"I'm sorry to hear that. Have they been through some form of trauma that caused them to shun romance? I've had a few clients like that but with therapy and patience they eventually opened up their hearts and found love again."

"Not really," Abner sighed. "I lost my wife fourteen years ago and I must say that it was a really dark time in my life. My boys must have picked up on my pain and decided that love hurts too much."

"I understand and I'm happy to help in any way that I can. If you would send me their contacts, say email and phone numbers, I could give them each a call and find out exactly the kind of women who would interest them."

"I'm afraid that won't work. You see, if my sons feel that they're being set up in any way, they won't stand for it, and you'll get no further than saying 'hello' to them."

"I have a number of eligible ladies in my books. These are virtuous young women because I insist on references from their pastors, church teachers and even one or two close relatives. As well, I invite the ladies for a face-to-face chat and if that can't be done, we Skype. In this way I'm able to get to know them very well before matching them with eligible male partners."

"I know that nothing can be one hundred per cent perfect but what is your success rate like?"

"Ninety-eight per cent," there was pride in her voice and Abner smiled at her confidence. "Of course, one or two fall along the way but we're very careful when it comes to matching people up."

"How can you help my sons? I'm looking at a scenario where none of them has any idea that they're being set up, but you send a lady down to the ranch."

"I see what you mean. Well, I have some discreet young ladies who might actually fit what you want. I'll speak to them, and then if they're in agreement, I'll send them your way and they will present themselves as workers on the ranch. In that way they will get to meet your sons without revealing the true reasons for being there. They will also be able to size the men's hearts up and see if they even want to be married to them. If they win their hearts, then we'll proceed with the next step of revealing the truth."

"Let's pray that this works."

"It will work because I believe in the women who come to me searching for love. I would never send you a person who will cause trouble, so you can trust me on this."

"I understand that there's some payment involved."

"Yes, we charge agency fees to the men only. The women register with us for free, and all expenses are then paid for by the man who wants them to go to him. In your case, since this is an arrangement between you and this agency, we'll expect the payment from you."

"Thank you for your discretion. And I promise that if you should succeed in getting all my five boys hitched, a generous bonus awaits you at the end of it all."

Sally-Jo laughed loudly, "I must say that history is somehow repeating itself. I read through Molly White's journals, and there's a notation somewhere that Mr. Jethro Knerr said those exact words to her. And he was very generous and gave her a huge bonus once she'd found wives for all his seven sons. But you know what was even better?"

"No, I don't."

"At the end of it all, Molly even found a bride for Mr. Jethro himself."

Abner chuckled. "You can rest easy, young lady, that won't be happening to me. All I want is for my sons to find brides. I've done my time and already had the one true love of my life, so I'm content."

"If you say so, Sir, but life is complex."

Abner didn't want the young lady to get any ideas about matchmaking for him. He was here to find wives for his sons, period!

"Mr. Randolph, please have no fears at all. We won the western frontier, wild as it was in those days of the pioneers and now hundreds of thousands of people have settled down there and are living their dreams. But the real frontiers worth fighting for are the frontiers of the heart, and we pride ourselves on being one of the best in this industry. I'll find wives for your sons, Sir; you can count on me."

"Thank you. And just a quick question before you go, what if I want to meet with the young ladies before you send them down to Texas?"

"That can easily be arranged though it will have to be over Skype because of the current lockdown due to the corona protocols that are in place."

"Perfect. I'd like that very much. So, if you could please send me your invoice I'll see that this gets paid as soon as possible."

"Start with one and let's see how things go."

"Aah, yes! I want the first person to be Quinten. He's my firstborn, and the others look up to him. If we can get him hitched, the others will be a walk in the park."

"You'll need to send me a dossier on him. I'll email the template over to you. It's fairly simple and easy to fill in, and once I get all the information I need, this dance will begin."

"I'll text you my email address so you can forward the forms and the invoice to me. Miss Manning, I have faith in you and thank you."

"Thank you, Sir, for choosing to engage our services. We promise you excellent service."

Once he'd hung up, Abner texted his email address to Sally-Jo and then looked up to heaven. "Please Lord, let this be the start of a journey that will see my sons get good Christian wives who are virtuous women, hardworking, God-fearing and loving."

THE LONELY COWBOY

Shortly after noon the next Saturday, Quinten answered his father's summons sent to him via text message. He found his parent in the smaller den perusing through one of the many monthly ranching magazines to which Randolph Ranch subscribed. Quin and his brothers had left this office for their father while they shared the larger one on the other side of the house.

"You sent for me, Sir," Quinten hovered in the doorway hoping that his father would send him on a quick errand. Lately he'd been avoiding the old man because all he could talk about was yearning for the sound of little feet pitter patting all around the large house. And woe unto Quin and his brothers if their father was invited to the christening of one of the newborn grandchildren of his friends. They never heard the last of it, so they did all they could to evade his company.

"Come in and sit," his father waved a hand at him and indicated one of the chairs in front of his large desk.

Quinten's steps were heavy as he dragged himself across the room and sat down. "Yes, dad?"

Abner took his time and Quinten got the feeling that he wasn't going to like what he was about to hear. Abner placed both elbows on the desk and steepled his fingers under his chin.

"I understand that you've been seen around town with Miss Yvette Matheson. Is there something I should know?"

Quinten's lips tightened. His instincts had been right, and he didn't like what his father had just said, nor the insinuations.

"Dad, it's never good to believe everything you hear. I ran into Yvette a couple of times last week and had coffee with her, that's all. That hardly counts as being seen around town with her."

"Well, her mother hasn't been silent about the situation at all. She's practically tolling the wedding bells herself. If you're not careful you'll find yourself standing at the altar exchanging vows with one of Mrs. Matheson's three daughter," Abner's eyes danced with laughter. "Don't say that I didn't warn you."

Quinten grimaced, "The woman is delusional if she thinks I can marry any of her daughters," he noticed his father's frown. Dad had instilled it in them to never disrespect women. "Dad, it's not that Yvette and her sisters are bad people or troublemakers. The thing is that all three of them want marriage, babies, picket fences and puppies in the backyard," he shuddered. "That's not for me, dad." He saw the disappointment in his father's eyes. "I respect women and that includes Yvette and her sisters too, but that doesn't mean that I want to marry any of them. We may meet up for a cup of coffee as old friends since we were in the same class in high school, but that's all. You've taught us to treat all people, and especially women, with kindness. That's what my brothers and I always do. We can't help it if the ladies and their ambitious mothers take that the wrong way."

"I really don't see why you shouldn't give Yvette or her sisters, Lenah and Paris, a chance. They're good girls and from a good family."

Quinten shook his head, "Dad, like I said, those girls have been brought up believing that marriage and children are the ultimate prizes for women in life."

"And aren't those things what every woman longs for in her lifetime?"

"How can you even think that, Dad? I believe that there's more to life than just marrying a woman and producing offspring with her. What about ambitions, what about self-fulfillment and actualization, the things that make a person grounded in their lives? Having a woman with no ambition apart from being a wife and mother is dangerous, dad. Children eventually grow up and leave home and if a woman has tied up all her life in them, then she begins to nag her husband," he shuddered. "I wouldn't want to be married to a woman who will eventually nag me to an early grave. I'd rather remain single for the rest of my life, dad."

"When did you become this cynical about the oldest institution in the world? Marriage started in the Garden of Eden and the Lord wants godly offspring so His divine purposes will be fulfilled here on earth. I know that there are a number of marriages which leave a lot to be desired. But that doesn't mean that we reject that noble institution altogether."

Quinten snorted and then coughed to cover up the sound. It was rude, and he didn't like being disrespectful to his father. But his father sometimes said the strangest things.

"If you have something to say then just go ahead and do it instead of grunting," Abner fixed his eyes on his son, who fidgeted. "Well?"

"Dad, if you think marriage is so good and noble why didn't you remarry when Mom died?"

QUINTEN SAW his father's face spasm with pain and the deep sorrow in his eyes and was immediately remorseful. "I'm sorry dad; I have no right to ask you such a question."

Abner smiled sadly, "Not at all, and that's a reasonable question. You see, between taking care of you boys and running this ranch after your mother's death, there was barely any time left for anything else, let alone a new wife."

"You could have done with the help. My brothers and I could have done with a woman's gentle hand from time to time."

"That's why Mrs. Brian was there. Hasn't she been like a mother to you over the years? Hasn't she provided for all your maternal needs and continues to do so?"

Quinten shook his head. "Dad, it wasn't the same thing having a housekeeper and nanny. We needed someone to take care of us full time and Mrs. Brian had her own family needing her attention. It wasn't fair for her to also take on five randy and rowdy boys."

"But she loves you as if you're her own children."

Quin nodded, "We all truly appreciate the part she's played and continues to in our lives. That she refused to move to Georgia with her children after her husband died means a lot to us. She stayed to take care of us, and even though we're all grown up now, we still love her very much. But we also worry about you, Dad."

Abner frowned. "Why?"

Quinten bowed his head for a long while, saying nothing. Finally, he raised his head. "We saw your pain and lived with deep worry that we would one day wake up to find that you too had gone and we were orphans. You were so broken up after Mom died that we despaired of you ever coming back to us. Thank God for Mrs. Brian who pulled you back from the brink so many times."

"Oh Son, I'm really sorry that you all had that burden to bear. But I had good memories of your mother to keep me going. And the Men's Fellowship in church stood by me, and the Lord gave me strength. I loved your mother deeply, and it's as if I gave her my whole heart. The reason I never remarried is because I don't have anything to give another woman, and it wouldn't be fair to her."

"You have the biggest heart I know, dad. But I understand about you loving our mother so much and not being able to give your heart to another woman in that way," and he really did.

ABNER SAT DEEP in thought in his den long after his son had left. He was glad he'd had the conversation with Quinten. Of all his sons, Quin was his biggest problem because his four younger brothers all looked up to him. From when they were small, the younger boys had always followed Quin's lead.

Abner was worried that if his oldest son continued being stubborn about finding a woman and settling down, all the others would do the same. Love was beautiful and he wanted that for all his sons. He believed that it was better to have loved and lost than never to have loved at all. Even though losing Barbara had nearly broken him, he didn't want his sons to go through life without experiencing what he'd had with his wife. He didn't want them to live and die as old and lonely bachelors.

"Please Lord," he prayed. "Don't let that happen to my sons."

"KELSEY, PLEASE DON'T DO THIS," her lastborn sister, Tina begged with tears in her eyes. "It's not safe."

"Tina, this is the only way for me now," the twenty-five-year-old woman said. She briefly paused from tossing clothes into one of two suitcases that lay open on her bed. She didn't want her sisters to worry, but she was terrified of what the future held. She was going out to the unknown to meet a stranger and hopefully they would get married at some point. It had all seemed so exciting in the initial planning stages. But now that it was about to become a reality, she wondered if she was making a mistake or not. At least her mother had no idea of her plans and she'd sworn her sisters to secrecy. Her mother thought she was going to work on a ranch in Dallas, Texas. "And remember, not a word about this to Mom. She knows that I'm going to work and that's all. I don't want her to worry about me."

"But you don't have to go to the other end of the world," Tina's eyes brimmed with tears. The twenty-two-year-old was the most sensitive of the three sisters. "I know that you don't like the people our father has been bringing around and hoping you'll marry them. But it doesn't mean that you should fall into the arms of a total stranger. What if he turns out to be a bad person?'

"Come here," Kelsey pulled her sister into her arms. Twenty-three-year-old Jeannie pretended not to be concerned about whatever was going on around her. As the middle child, Jeannie always behaved as if she had no emotions, but Kelsey knew that it was all a way of coping with their bully of a father.

"Tina, Texas isn't the other end of the world. I'm only about two to three hours away by flight. Last I checked, Texas was still a state in the United States of America," she joked, and her sister gave her a watery smile. "That's my girl, now smile and be happy for me."

Just like their mother, Kelsey's two sisters were tenderhearted, and their fragile emotions got easily bruised. It was the reason why Kelsey always protected them from their father's wrath and unreasonable demands.

She would have left home as soon as she'd graduated from engineering college three years before but for her concern for her mom and sisters. Kelsey knew that if she'd left at the time, their father would have bullied them into bowing to his will.

Mr. Jonathan Brooke's will and desire was that his three daughters be married to men that he approved of, regardless of whether love was involved or not. Arranged marriages weren't the worst idea according to Kelsey. It was the men her father chose that she had a big issue with. They were either as narcissistic and controlling as he was, or else they were fawning sycophants.

And now the only reason that Kelsey was finally leaving home with a clear conscience was because both of her sisters had been accepted to Stanford University in California. That was thousands of miles away from Denver and out of reach of their domineering father's control. Both girls were going to study Biomedical Engineering, something that irked their father no end.

"Women are only good for two things," he'd shouted, almost frothing at the mouth when he'd been presented with their admission packages. "Marriage and producing offspring to perpetuate a man's lineage is what you should be thinking about. Not making a nuisance of yourselves by going in for courses that are only suitable for men. What are you trying to prove? That you're as good as any man?"

To make matters worse, he had cast the papers aside and declared that he would only pay for his daughters to go to the nearest community college to learn the skills needed for housekeeping in their husbands' homes.

It was the same fight he'd had with Kelsey when she'd declared that she wanted to do mechanical engineering. He wouldn't pay her fees, but she was a hardworking girl and had won scholarships all through her years of being in college.

Tina and Jeannie had wept when it seemed as if their dreams were about to die, and Kelsey had felt very helpless. While they all had healthy trust funds, they had no access to them until they got to the age of thirty. In that mood of despair and hopelessness, Kelsey had told her sisters that they needed to turn to God for answers. And their mother had surprised them by paying the two sisters' annual fees for the first year of their studies in full.

"Mom, where did you get the money from?" Even Kelsey was shocked when she looked and saw the payment slips. Stanford was one of the most expensive universities in the world and her mother had paid every single penny required for that year's fees, both tuition and accommodation. *Where had her mother found nearly two hundred thousand dollars from?* Kelsey wondered.

Mrs. Eleanor Brooke smiled at the shock on her daughters' faces. "You can't be the wife of an oil magnate for over twenty years and not learn a trick or two about stocks and shares." And that was all she would say on the matter. Kelsey had no idea how her father would react when he found out that her sisters had left for Stanford. She nearly cancelled her plans, but they were at an advanced stage for her to back out now. Perhaps she would settle down and then convince her mother to come and live with her out in Dallas.

Kelsey would be leaving home on the same day as her sisters. She was taking them all the way to California before proceeding to Cedar Hill in Dallas, Texas.

"I don't feel so good about leaving Mom here all alone," Tina said, wiping her face. "What if our father vents his anger on her?"

"Well, he can scream all he wants but in as far as I know, he's never laid a hand on Mom. She won't let him bully her; that much I know."

"Are you sure?" Jeannie put in, biting her lower lip nervously.

"Mom is a strong woman, even if she comes off as being fragile. The only reason she's been putting up with our father's bullying is because of us. But now that all three of us will be gone from home, I know she'll come into her own and stand up for herself."

"I have a bad feeling about all this," Tina said.

Kelsey knew that the only way her sisters would find peace was by reassuring them that their mother would be all right. "If Mom didn't think she'd be all right, she wouldn't have come up with your college fees." Kelsey looked at her sisters. "Remember that Stanford is very competitive, and it's a great blessing that you both got in. I don't think Mom still has much money left. Father's rules and regulations tied up our trust funds, so we have no access to the money until we're thirty. So, you both have to promise me that you'll work hard so you can be awarded full scholarships for the remaining years."

"We promise," Tina spoke sincerely.

"Good. Texas isn't that far from California, and you'll get to spend holidays with me. Once I settle down in my new home, I'll invite you to come over for a visit so you can get to meet my husband and his family. And if I feel that Mom isn't all right here, I'll convince her to come and live with me in Dallas."

Tina was shaking her head, "Kelsey, I still don't like this. You're going to some ranch out in the wilderness of Texas. If you were really going for a job, I wouldn't protest too much. But here you are, going out there to become the wife of some cowboy you've never met before. You've never even exchanged as much as a phone call or a text message with your intended husband. How do you know if he's a good man or another tyrant just like dad? I still don't understand how it is that in this day and age of modern technology, that you and your husband to be haven't even communicated. What kind of relationship is that?"

Kelsey sighed and sat on the bed, all packing abandoned for the moment. She was scared and had been asking herself the same questions. But Sally-Jo at the Bridal agency where she'd registered had been very clear.

"This is a special case, Kelsey," the agency director had told her. "There can be no communication between you and the gentleman in question."

"I don't understand this."

"Mr. Quinten Randolph or Quin as his father calls him isn't aware that such plans are underway. His father, a delightful gentleman, told me that his sons have refused to find women to marry and settle down with. So, the only way he can make sure that his sons settle down is by finding them wives. He doesn't want his sons to know what he's doing or else they'll resist."

"How then will Quin and I have the chance to know each other and eventually get married?"

"Some position will be created for you at the ranch so you can go out there as a worker. Once there, you'll need to find a way of getting Quin to notice you so he can eventually propose to you. It will also give you the chance to find out what kind of a man he is and if he's the person you'd like to spend the rest of your life with."

"But how did you choose him for me?"

"Your data matched his needs according to the information Mr. Randolph sent us. The two of you stand at ninety-eight per cent compatibility, which is the highest score any of our clients have ever

attained. Most stand at eighty to ninety per cent, and yours is almost a perfect match if you ask me."

"But computers can't be that accurate."

"I know that, but the parameters we set are there to ensure that each person finds their perfect match."

"Is there really anything like a perfect match?"

"At Hitch Your Wagon Romance Agency, we believe in happily ever after, but are also quite realistic. Life isn't all rosy and perfect, but we expect any couples that we match to work on their relationship. I must admit that while we have a very high success rate in matching people to their prospective spouses, we've also suffered a few setbacks when the couples ran into trouble. Thankfully those are few. So no, there's no perfect match but just two imperfect human beings coming together, falling in love then going on to build their happily ever after."

"I feel like I'm taking a really big risk. I know that with Internet dating and matchmaking, at least the man and woman get to meet, even if it's over Skype. That I can't even get a photo of my prospective groom makes me rather uncomfortable."

"Mr. Randolph requested that it should be so. He has five sons and doesn't want to influence your decision. What if you go out there and decide that the man we've selected for you isn't the one, but are able to fall in love with one of the other four?"

"That would be odd, don't you think? If your computers have matched this Quin gentleman with me and we came off as an almost perfect match, why would I then choose someone else?"

"Kelsey, the heart is very strange, and it wants what it wants. Just rest assured that you'll be in good hands with Mr. Randolph and his sons. If after this whole exercise you don't fall in love with any of them, it's all right. Nothing is etched in stone, and even I want to see you settle down with a man who is passionately in love with you."

Kelsey had even used Google to try and find out more about her intended spouse, but found nothing about him and nothing about his brothers either. It was as though the men had no online footprint, and that made her the more wary. In this day and age, what person didn't even have a Facebook or Twitter account?

"Kelsey, you're not saying anything," Jeannie was shaking her, and she blinked and returned to the present. "You're taking a great risk with your life, and it makes us very scared."

"Well, my dear small sisters, life is a risk, and I'm willing to take this one to find true love. I'll never accept a tyrant for a husband and if I find that this Mr. Quinten Randolph is such a one, I won't give him the time of day."

"Please just be safe. It's a terrible world out there and there are so many dangers like human trafficking or people wanting to use others for their own evil motives."

"Don't worry," Kelsey smiled at her sister while she ruffled her hair. Jeannie squealed and moved away. "I'll be all right because the agency I used is a reputable and respectable one," yet even as she reassured her sisters, she was praying that she hadn't made a terrible mistake.

HOMEWARD BOUND

When Kelsey got to the large gate with the sign that read *'Randolph Ranch,'* it was coming up on four o'clock in the afternoon. Though the flight from Denver to Dallas had taken slightly less than three hours, all the Covid Nineteen protocols in place at both airports had made the process of clearing very slow. Despite not wanting to get one, she had reluctantly succumbed to getting her vaccination certificate. Some of the other passengers clearly had not and were turned away. She sure would be glad when all of this was over, she mused.

Kelsey pulled her mask off and tossed it with relief on the passenger seat as she drove through the large gates which stood wide open. She was surprised to see no buildings in sight. All around her was green vegetation but no buildings. She didn't meet anyone as she drove through on the asphalt-paved road. It was another fifteen minutes' drive downhill before she spotted the large ranch in the valley below.

She stopped her rental car on the brow of the hill and gazed in awe at the spectacular sight that met her eyes. Having never visited a ranch before, she'd really had no idea what to expect. When Sally-Jo at the agency had told her that Randolph Ranch was one hundred and fifty thousand acres, Kelsey had been amazed. She had no idea that one single family could own so much land.

The homestead below looked like a small town, and it was clear that the one-story ranch house was the center of it all. Even from this distance Kelsey could tell that the house was beautiful.

"This looks like a small paradise," she muttered to herself. Being from Denver and having seen how the wealthy lived, she should have been used to such glamor. But the place she was seeing blew her mind. All the buildings were either new or at least had received a fresh coat of paint. Or maybe she was lost, she thought, then shook her head. This was Randolph Ranch because the sign at the large gate said so. This was the home of Quinten Randolph, the stubborn cowboy who refused to marry and settle down.

"That one and his brothers are like wild stallions," Sally-Jo had remarked. "That's what their father says, and all the old man wants is to find suitable cowgirls to lasso in those stallions."

Amidst much laughter and joking Sally-Jo had told Kelsey not to expect to be welcomed with open arms. After all, she was here incognito to the five men, and she really wasn't expecting a red carpet to be rolled out in her honor. If this ranch belonged to Quinten Randolph's family, was it any wonder that the man was arrogant and stubborn? His kind probably felt that they were American royalty!

The sound of a car approaching alerted Kelsey to the fact that she was about to get some company. A large Bronco pickup, gleaming black in color, slowed down and came to a stop a few feet away from her own rental car. The windows, including the windscreen, were tinted, and she couldn't see the driver inside the large vehicle. Her curiosity was aroused, and she leaned against her car and watched to see who would emerge. Kelsey loved big cars, and this one, though not new, seemed to be in very good condition. Its owner no doubt handled it with much love and care.

The driver's door opened, and the first thing Kelsey saw were shiny black boots. Then the person emerged and rose to his full height.

Kelsey felt a whoosh that made her breathless. She felt the impact of the newcomer's eyes even though they were hidden behind dark shades, the kind worn by cowboys in the few Western movies that she'd watched. The man looked like he'd just stepped off the set of a western movie. He was tall, broad shouldered, and his thick brown hair fell to his shoulders.

His lips curled in amusement, and she hastily turned away. Then she felt, rather than saw, him moving toward her and turned again. He took his shades off.

"Good afternoon, Miss," his voice was very deep and polite. "Are you lost? It sometimes happens when people miss the turning that should take them to Dallas City. So, they often end up here and we have to give them proper directions."

"I'm sorry," was all Kelsey could get out at first.

The large, handsome man had beautiful gray eyes, and they twinkled in merriment. He smiled, "Don't worry about a thing because no harm has been done. If you drive back the way you came, you'll soon get to the junction and can be on your way again."

Kelsey shook her head, "No, I'm actually expected at the Randolph Ranch, so I'm not lost."

The man looked surprised. "Really?"

Kelsey smiled, "I got here and couldn't resist stopping to admire the great view. This place," she waved a hand towards the homestead, "I've never seen anything so beautiful and well planned."

"It's just a ranch homestead," the man smiled but looked pleased. "Are you visiting one of the cowboys or their families?"

"Something like that," Kelsey said, "But in this case it's Mr. Randolph that I'm here to see." She was surprised when the man chuckled softly. "What's so funny about that?"

"You see, there are six Mr. Randolphs, so you'll have to be specific about the one you want to see."

"Oh!" Kelsey felt flustered. "I'm actually here to see Mr. Abner Randolph, the ranch owner."

The man grinned, and she admired the neat rows of perfectly formed, white teeth. Her own were a bit crooked and she felt a little embarrassed about showing them to such a man.

"Welcome to Randolph Ranch, and I'm glad you like what you're seeing. Come, let me take you Mr. Abner Randolph."

"Thank you, Sir," Kelsey was surprised when the man walked up to the car and opened the driver's door for her. Clearly, chivalry was still very much alive in these parts of the country.

"Would you like to drive ahead or behind me?" He asked. "The homestead looks close from here and in days gone by when cowboys rode on horses, one could actually take a shortcut straight down the hill. But now you have to travel another five miles of curving roads to get to the ranch. If you don't pay attention, you might take the wrong feeder road and end up on the other side of the highway to Dallas."

"Then I think I should follow you," Kelsey quickly said as she slid into the car. Though the journey from the airport to this place wasn't long, she was still tired. It was only when the man went back to his car and drove past, hooting as he did so, that she realized she didn't even know who he was. Then she shrugged, the only way to find out was to follow him to the homestead. Maybe he was one of the cowboys, and she wondered if all of them were this handsome.

"Movies really exaggerate," she smiled. "This is cowboy and cowgirl country and maybe they all look this good."

It took them about ten minutes of driving slowly down the road before they got to the homestead itself. She'd seen large herds of cattle behind the barbed wire on either side of the road. Though they had fascinated her, she was glad they were locked up on the other side of the fence where they couldn't stray to the road. One butt from a steer could have overturned her vehicle with her in it.

Her guide drove toward what seemed like a lot where gleaming large jeeps were sold. Her own Toyota Corolla looked like a toy car among the monster trucks.

The man appeared before her, then used hand motions to guide her to a parking spot. Once she'd turned the engine off, Kelsey rested her head briefly on the steering wheel. The door opened and she looked up.

"You look beat," her guide said, "Like you've driven a long way to get here. Do you have anything you wish carried into the house?"

"Yes, I have two trunks in the trunk."

"We'll get to them later. Why don't you come with me so I can take you inside?" Kelsey gladly reached for her mask and slipped it on, then picked up her handbag and followed the man into the house.

QUIN FELT like he hadn't caught his breath ever since he'd come upon the woman standing on the brow of the hill. She was stunning even without trying too hard. Her face seemed devoid of makeup, but it didn't matter. Her natural beauty shone through. She had the most expressive green eyes and thick dark hair that fell to her waist.

He was really curious, because the only women who ever drove themselves to the ranch were sisters from church or else companions of the workers. He'd never once seen a woman come to ask for his father, and for some reason, he felt that she was here to stay. Why would someone bring along luggage unless they intended to be here for a while?

Who is she? Quin wondered even as he led the way to his father's den. He knocked briefly, then opened the door and ushered the guest in.

"Dad, I brought someone to see you," Quin said, and his father looked up and smiled.

"Aah, glad to see you again, Miss Kelsey Brooke," Quin saw the broad smile on his father's face, and it surprised him. It was as if his father was very happy to see the visitor. Could this be a distant relative that they'd never met?

"My dear," Abner came around the desk and shook hands with Kelsey. "I'm so pleased that you made it safely. I was worried when you declined to have someone come to pick you up from the airport."

Kelsey smiled at the kind-looking gentleman. "The best way to learn how to move about a new place is to get there by oneself," she said. "The drive from the airport was spectacular and refreshing."

"I hope you didn't have too many problems being cleared because of this corona issue."

"It was quite strenuous getting cleared at the airport in Denver and then again here in Dallas. But it's better now that the lockdown has been lifted."

"We thank God that life is slowly returning to normal all over the world. The lockdown affected so many operations of businesses and even ranches, and life was tough for a while. But the Lord has preserved and spared us and for that we're grateful." He turned to Quin. "This here is my firstborn son, Quinten Randolph, but everyone around calls him Quin."

Kelsey felt her face turning red. So, this was the man she'd so confidently declared would be eating out of her hand in no time! "Don't worry," she'd said to Sally Jo, "I'll lasso that wild stallion like a skilled cowgirl and bring him to his knees," she'd bragged. Now she felt tongue-tied before him. Sally-Jo should see her now!

"Quin, this is Miss Kelsey Brooke and she's our new mechanic."

"New mechanic?" Quin's eyes widened. He couldn't have heard right. A female mechanic that looked like a model, even though she didn't have the height that went with that profession? Was his father serious or was this some kind of a joke? His eyes immediately went to the well-manicured, long, beautiful fingers that he'd noticed out on the hill and liked. "Dad, I wasn't aware that we needed a new mechanic." Something struck him as being odd. "Even if we needed a new one did you have to go and get someone from Denver? Don't we have many skilled mechanics right here in Cedar Hill and even Dallas itself?"

Abner shook his head. "Kelsey isn't just an ordinary mechanic, Son. I placed an advert in one of our magazines because we need someone who is quite familiar with the new technology being rolled out frequently. Kelsey's was the best response, and I got to interview her over Skype. Since I was highly impressed by her presentation and skills, and her references came through, I offered her this position."

"No one told me that we were hiring," Quin still felt that his father wasn't telling him the whole truth. "I thought we'd all agreed on a temporary hiring freeze. With all the craziness happening in the world right now it's all become way too complicated!"

Quin rubbed his chin thoughtfully, "And I still don't understand why we had to hire someone from out of state. I mean no offence, Miss Brooke, but my father knows what I'm talking about."

"No offence taken," Kelsey said, wondering whether this man was going to give her marching orders before she was even offered a drink of water. Kelsey was quickly revising her opinion of the man she'd earlier thought of as being polite and welcoming. She gave him a look that dared him to ask her something else.

Quin looked at his father and was surprised to see the gleam in his eyes. It was as if his father was enjoying their exchange. Then his parent blinked, and the look was gone.

"I'm sorry," Quin realized that he was coming off as being unwelcoming. "It's just that all this has taken me by surprise. You see, my father always consults me on any changes that are taking place on the ranch. That he didn't let me know about you is rather troubling."

"Quin, I'm sorry if you feel offended that I didn't consult you about hiring Miss Brooke, but you've been rather busy. I remember mentioning to you that one of the mechanics was leaving and waited for your response."

Quin shifted from one foot to the other, clearly uncomfortable, and Kelsey lowered her eyes so he wouldn't see the glee in them. His father seemed to have the upper hand in this matter.

"I didn't think we needed someone so soon."

"Well, we did, and I've gone ahead to hire Miss Brooke. My dear," the kindly gentleman turned to her. "May I please call you Kelsey?"

"Yes, Sir."

"Good. We don't stand on ceremony around here, and I'd like you to feel at home. This is now your home, and I hope you'll be happy here. But you need to work really hard and prove to my son here that your employment is warranted."

"I understand," Kelsey was relieved. The last thing she wanted was to sabotage her mission before it even began. She was glad that Mr. Randolph had silenced his son because she'd felt her ire rising. She told herself that she had to learn to curb her temper before it got her into trouble.

"Well, now that you've met and I've made everything clear, why don't you show Kelsey around the ranch, Quin? She needs to familiarize herself with the place that will be her home for the unforeseeable future."

"Dad, the poor woman has only just arrived. At least, let's give Miss Brooke a chance to freshen up and even be served with some refreshments. Denver is a long way off, and she must be exhausted and hungry after all the waiting at the airport and then the drive down to the ranch." Quin smiled, and Kelsey felt that he was trying to make up for his earlier rudeness. "If Miss Brooke, er, Kelsey is anything like me, she doesn't enjoy the food served on the plane."

"It's true that I don't," Kelsey wanted her time here to be smooth, and she would have to be amicable to this man even though she had a feeling that he still wasn't quite satisfied about her presence here on the ranch. Well, his father could deal with him.

"So, it's settled then," Quin turned to his father. "Dad, I hope it's all right with you that Kelsey should get some rest before I can take her around or find someone to do it."

"You're right," his father nodded. "Why don't you have Cindy show her to her bedroom in the guest wing? Kelsey, I'll see you at dinner time. My son will get one of our ladies to show you to your room, and if you need anything, please let Cindy know. Dinner is usually served at eight and I'll send someone to get you."

"Thank you, Sir."

"Why don't I get your trunks from the car?" Quin held out a hand. Kelsey absentmindedly placed hers in it, thinking he wanted to shake hands with her since they hadn't done so before. And shaking hands also signified that two parties had come to an amicable agreement like they'd done. The amused look on his face made her realize that he'd been holding his hand out for the keys.

"Oh!" She blushed, feeling embarrassed as she pulled her hand away. She handed the keys to him and wanted to cover her face with her palms.

"Think nothing of it," Quin said as he walked to the door, then stopped and turned around. "Wait here while I go and bring the trunks from your car. I'll send Cindy to get you."

"Thank you."

Abner waited until his son's footsteps faded away then he turned to Kelsey. "Does he suspect a thing?"

She shook her head, "We didn't talk much out on the hill, and like Sally-Jo told me, I haven't had the chance to mention anything to him."

"Good," Abner grunted in satisfaction. "Of all my children, Quin is the most stubborn. If he even gets a hint as to the real reason that you're here, all our plans will fall apart."

"I'll be very careful," Kelsey promised.

"And I'll be praying that things will go according to plan. So much is at stake here and we must not make any mistakes."

"Yes, Sir."

Light footsteps were heard coming down the hallway. "That must be Cindy now."

Cindy turned out to be a young woman of about twenty-one years of age, and she reminded Kelsey of Tina.

"I'm here on internship," she said as Kelsey followed her out of the den after excusing herself. "I'm studying Food Management at Texas Christian University, and this ranch provided me with the best opportunity to practice what I've been learning."

"That's wonderful. How long have you been here?"

"This is my second month and I'm here until spring of next year. The beauty of it all is that this is a paid internship, and the money I get will help me during my final year. I've also been saving for a trip abroad."

Cindy led Kelsey down another wing. "This house is huge," she commented as they crossed into yet another hallway. "I saw it from the hill when I was driving down, and it looks like a school building because of its many wings."

"Randolph Ranch was originally an army barracks way back during the Mexican and American war in the eighteen hundreds. After Texas became part of the United States of America, a larger barracks was constructed on the other side of town and Mr. Randolph's great grandfather bought the whole place. This house had only one wing then, and over the decades, the people who lived here have added all the rooms they need. Right now, there are four wings. This is the one exclusively for women guests since the family has no girls. There's the South wing which belongs to Mr. Randolph and his oldest son, Quin. The West wing is for Kendrick and Maynard and the East wing is for Waylen and Callum."

"You seem to know much of the history of the place."

Cindy grinned at Kelsey as she stopped outside a door. "This is the Princess wing, as Mr. Randolph calls it. He's such a sweet man and treats us all like princesses. No males are allowed to come here, not even Mr. Randolph or his sons unless they're bringing in furniture or luggage or something like that, and we feel very safe, all of us."

"How many is 'all of us'?"

"There's me, then Marion who is away in Mexico visiting her family. She's the ranch nurse. There's Roselyn who is doing animal husbandry at some university in Arizona. There are two extra rooms since this wing has six bedrooms, all of them ensuite. Actually, all the bedrooms in the house are ensuite to ensure our total privacy. Mr. Randolph gives many students the opportunity to do their internships here and he pays us for it."

"He sounds like a good man."

"That he is, but you have to watch out for his sons."

Kelsey was curious but didn't want to be caught gossiping about the family. She knew that Quin was about to put in an appearance with her luggage, so she followed Cindy into the room and gasped.

"This looks like a hotel room," she told her companion.

Cindy grinned, "This is the work of Teresa, another intern who is studying hotel management and hospitality. Teresa doesn't stay here since she recently got married to one of the cowboys and Mr. Randolph gave them their own house. We all pull our weight here and work together,"

The room's walls were painted lilac and the large windows brought in plenty of light. Her four-poster bed reminded her of the one at home, and she knew that she would be comfortable here.

"All rooms have study desks because mostly it's students who stay here. I must say I'll be sorry to leave this place."

"You sound really content."

"That I am, but after my time on campus is over, I plan on travelling to Europe for a whole year of backpacking with some friends. I'd like to get as much experience as I can get working for different establishments before I decide to settle down."

They heard heavy footsteps, and Quin appeared with her trunks. "Where do I place these?" He asked.

"Beside the closet," Cindy directed. "I'll help our guest to unpack."

"My name is Kelsey," Kelsey told her new friend. "And thank you."

"I'll be on my way now," Quin said. "I'll send someone to bring you some tea."

Once he'd left Cindy sighed and placed a hand over her heart. "There's five of those fine specimens wandering around this house, and then out there, you'll meet many more. Why do cowboys have to be so gorgeous looking?" She giggled. "Teresa told me that she took one look at Pierce and her knees didn't stop knocking each other. Good thing is that he also fell in love with her, and we had a beautiful wedding here during my first week in this place. Mr. Randolph footed the whole bill for the wedding and there was so much food. Those cowboys can make a normal and sane woman turn into a blabbering idiot."

Kelsey laughed as she reached into her purse and pulled out the keys to her trunks. "Cindy, you're really funny."

"Dear Sister, you won't be laughing when you have to sit at the dinner table with nearly ten handsome men and your heart is thumping as if it wants to race out of your chest. And your mind is confused because they all look so good," she sat on the bed. "But don't fall in love with any of them," she said.

"Why would I want to fall in love with any of them?"

"Girl, those men are not only handsome and wealthy, they're so well behaved and treat us all like their sisters, protecting us and being very helpful. But if you make the mistake of falling for any of them, Mr. Randolph will give you your marching orders. What are you studying on campus?"

"I'm not on campus. I finished three years ago and worked as a firefighter for two of those. I'm the new mechanic here."

"What?" Cindy sat upright. "You look so dainty and delicate. How did you manage to hoist those heavy hoses and climb into burning buildings looking like that?" Cindy waved a hand up and down indicating Kelsey's figure. "You're built like a model, and I bet those firemen got quite distracted whenever you were on duty with them."

"Looks can be deceiving. I had to make a good impression on my new employers, so there was no way I could show up dressed like a mechanic. And yes, I'm strong and easily carried those hoses up and down burning buildings."

"What happened, for I sense a story unfolding?"

"A bad injury at work put me in hospital for weeks and my mother was beyond herself with grief. When I got better, I promised her that I would never again do such a dangerous job. So, I instead decided to sharpen my mechanical skills and here I am."

"I truly admire women who do such tough jobs."

Footsteps came down the hallway and a lady appeared at the doorway carrying a tray. "Cindy, Mrs. Brian is looking for you and here you are chatting like an idle magpie."

"Roselyn, I don't know what has irritated you, but don't take it out on me, please," Cindy rose from the bed. "Besides, Mrs. Brian knows that I'm here to show our new guest the ropes."

"You better hurry up then," and without glancing in Kelsey's direction, Roselyn left.

"Don't mind her," Cindy said as she poured Kelsey a cup of coffee. "Do you like it with milk or strong?"

"A little milk and sugar, thank you."

"That's the mighty Roselyn. She's always in a mood because none of the Randolph men has looked her way. She's especially after Quin but the man treats her like a little sister; that's all. I've warned her, and Mrs. Brian has done the same, but she doesn't listen. She's been here for too long is what I think, and whenever a new female joins the household, she goes out of her way to make her as uncomfortable as possible, as if she's marking her territory."

Kelsey's heart sank. The last thing she wanted was any kind of drama and especially where it concerned Quin. If Roselyn was after Quin, then the days ahead were going to prove to be a challenge.

Cindy and Kelsey took the tea and scones Roselyn had brought. "Do you want to rest?"

"Not really, I'd like to see a bit more of the house and meet everyone I'll be interacting with."

"Good. Come and let me take you to meet Mrs. Brian."

Kelsey insisted on carrying the tray as Cindy locked her room for her and slipped her key into her dungarees. "We have to keep our bedrooms locked at all times. Those are Mr. Randolph's instructions."

"Why?"

Cindy shrugged, "There are some questions that I don't have answers to. Come, let's hurry."

Mrs. Brian turned out to be a beautiful woman and Kelsey admired her thick locks. "Are those real?" She asked, staring at the woman in fascination. She was middle aged but had those ageless looks.

"This is my real hair," Mrs. Brian said with a broad smile.

"And you keep it natural like that?"

"Oh yes. No chemicals or funny products on my head, thank you. You're a beautiful girl, and I understand you're the new mechanic around here."

"Yes, Ma'am."

Mrs. Brian clapped. "I love it when girls take on challenging jobs and even do better than men. But I'm no feminist so don't take it the wrong way."

"You're kind for saying that.

Thank you for the tea and scones."

"If you want more there's plenty."

Kelsey stood in the large kitchen and stared in fascination at the large shiny pots and pans lining one wall.

"Have you ever lived on a ranch before, Girl?" Mrs. Brian asked.

"No, Ma'am," Kelsey grinned. "Does it show that much?"

"Yes. Your eyes widened when they lit on those pots. Believe me, this ranch has males who enjoy their food. Cindy will bear me witness."

"Do you do all the cooking?"

Mrs. Brian nodded. "Cindy and the other girls help me, and there are two days a week when it's the men's turn to prepare dinner."

"Seriously?"

"You should see those handsome hunks in aprons," Cindy moaned and earned herself a light tap from the ladle in Mrs. Brian's hand.

"Behave yourself, Child. No need ogling men who have their sights set elsewhere."

Her comment made Kelsey wonder. Could all these men be having secret partners? And if so, what did that mean for her—and she was here to win Quin's heart?

"Mrs. Brian, I'm only giving credit where it's due. Those brothers are fine!"

"Cindy, stop being so cheeky?"

"Yes, Ma'am."

"Now, I have to prepare dinner."

"It's burgers and fries tonight," Cindy was almost dancing.

"This child eats like a horse but never gains a single ounce of fat on her," Mrs. Brian looked fondly at Cindy. "Are you bringing the potatoes?'

"Yes, Ma'am."

"Is there anything I can do to help?" Kelsey asked.

"Oh no, you've just arrived and must be exhausted. Mr. Randolph said you should rest."

"Cindy, I'm fine. If I rest now and fall asleep, I won't be able to sleep tonight, and that will throw my whole system into disarray. What can I do to help?"

FLYING SPARKS

"*T*here's a reason many ranches don't employ women in any other capacity other than as housekeepers and cooks," Quin said, and Kelsey felt her hackles rise.

"Deep breaths," she told herself, counting to twenty so she would calm down. As Mr. Abner had said, there was a lot at stake, and she wasn't going to jeopardize their mission just on her second day on the ranch. Even though it wasn't her fault that two calves had bolted out of the barn and been restrained by Quin and one of the other cowboys, Kelsey felt responsible. Quin had rushed in and secured the calves before turning on her. He naturally assumed that she was the cause of it all because she was the only one inside the barn when he came in with the animals, and she'd been standing beside the door that was hanging from its hinges.

"Slow down, Brother," another voice called out. "Miss Kelsey had nothing to do with this mess and you owe her an apology." A tall man, almost the same height as Quin came into view. Kelsey guessed that it was Callum, the last born of the family. She'd met Waylen, Kendrick, and Maynard at dinner last night, but Callum hadn't been around. Kelsey had recalled Cindy's words about the men being very courteous and well behaved. And they were all very handsome, but she felt that Quin beat the whole crowd.

"What do you mean?" Quin turned to his brother. "I found Kelsey holding the broken door while the calves ran around the yard. It's a good thing I arrived when I did, or they might have strayed to Mom's rose garden and trampled it. And you know what that would have done to Dad."

"Again, I say to you that it wasn't Kelsey's fault that the calves ran out. It's that reckless cowboy wannabe you insist on keeping around here even though he's now getting out of hand. How many times have I warned you that Frank is just a disaster waiting to happen? Will you pay attention when he finally burns down the house or hurts someone while carrying out one of his stupid pranks?"

"I'll talk to him," Quin said. He turned to Kelsey. "I'm sorry for the misunderstanding."

Kelsey's lips tightened. "I don't accept your apology," she looked him straight in the eyes. "Just because you found me holding the door, you naturally jumped to the conclusion that the newbie must have destroyed it and let the calves out. Just so you know, I was checking to see how I can repair this door.

And your comment about women only being fit to be housekeepers and cooks is so offensive from one befitting your status."

Quin felt his face warming up. What was happening to him? He respected women and was always careful about how he spoke to them. Why then had he shot his mouth off like that with Kelsey?

"That was totally uncalled for, and I sincerely apologize," he held out a hand which Kelsey ignored.

"If you're done ranting and insulting me, can I please get on with my work?" She folded her arms across her chest. She had no idea that she looked so pretty even though she was wearing thick and very shapeless dungarees.

"My name is Callum," the brother came over and Kelsey shook his hand. "Ignore this bully here. If he dares to bully you, just tell me and I'll soon put him in his place."

"Thank you," Kelsey gave him a dazzling smile. "It's nice to see that there are still gentlemen left on this earth."

Callum chuckled, and Quin felt like boxing his brother's ears.

"Carry on with your work," he told Kelsey, choosing to ignore her jibe. He couldn't get out of the barn fast enough and sensed his brother hard on his heels.

"What was that all about?" Callum asked. "You didn't handle Kelsey very well and it's not being fair. It was Frank who crashed the old SUV into the barn door early this morning. I was thinking of making repairs to it when I saw Kelsey heading in that direction. She'd barely touched the door when the calves sprang out."

"What? But Frank can't drive so why would he be behind the SUV's wheel?"

"You have to control that boy, Quin. I know you feel responsible for him because his deadbeat father is in prison and his mother is dead. But if you don't put your foot down, we'll soon have a delinquent running around the ranch causing problems."

"Point noted," Quin entered the house through the kitchen door. Their housekeeper, Mrs. Brian was stirring something in the large pot on the stove. It smelled delicious and his mouth watered.

"Mrs. Brian, Quin just insulted housekeepers and cooks," Callum said and earned himself a deep scowl from his brother.

"You're such a tattletale," Quin said and turned a charming smile on Mrs. Brian. "Mrs. B, please ignore this juvenile delinquent. It was just a slight misunderstanding with Kelsey out in the barn."

"Call it whatever you like but I can say for sure that Kelsey was quite offended by your words," Callum reached for a carrot and got his knuckles rattled by a wooden spoon. "What is that for?" He asked Mrs. Brian.

"For touching food with dirty hands," she said. The African American woman turned her gaze to Quin, but her words were meant for Callum. "What was this one saying about housekeepers and cooks?"

"That those are the only positions fit for women on ranches."

"Is that right?" Mrs. Brian walked slowly towards Quin, and he felt sweat running down his back. He always thought of himself as fearless but never in the presence of the woman who had taken on the role of their mother fourteen years ago. "So, you believe that women are only good for being cooks and housekeepers?"

"I'm sorry that I was out of line," Quin had quickly discovered that admitting his mistakes to Mrs. Brian always got him out of trouble. And he had no defense because he'd actually uttered those unkind words.

"I thought you were better than that, especially given that we have many female interns in various capacities on the ranch." The disappointment in her voice cut him deep. She turned away and he felt like he'd been cut off. He stood there for a while, wondering how he could make things right. He also realized that the cheeky Callum had left him to face the music alone.

"Mrs. Brian, you taught me better, and I'm sorry that I disrespected Kelsey. I promise that you'll never hear such words from me again."

She shook her head, "You may not say them out loud but if that's what you think, then your apology is of no use. Now leave my kitchen before I use my ladle on you."

Quin quickly gave her a peck on the cheek, and when she chuckled and touched his arm, he knew that all was forgiven. She was that sweet, and more than once he wished his father would open his eyes to see this beautiful woman and make an honest woman of her. He wandered into the living room where he found his four brothers. They were getting ready to play a game of Scrabble.

"Join us for a game, dear brother," Waylen said as he moved on the couch to create room for Quin.

"I'm not interested in playing with the likes of some of you," Quin glared at Callum who merely shrugged and went about setting up the table for the game.

"Wait a minute," Kendrick held his hand up. "What's going on between the two of you now? You always seem to be at loggerheads for one reason or another."

"This one has a mouth that never closes," Quin said angrily.

Callum merely grinned at his older brother. "Don't blame me for your own folly." He turned to his other brothers. "Frank took the old SUV and crashed it into the barn door, the one that has the month-old calves. Your clever brother here found our new mechanic about to repair the door and blamed her for the mess caused by Frank because two calves ran out into the yard and were trampling the lawn. But that's not the worst part of it. Quin here told our Kelsey that women are only good to be housekeepers and cooks on ranches."

"Ouch!" Kendrick shivered dramatically. "You're a dead man, Bro!"

"Dead man walking," Waylen echoed, and he shuffled around the living room like zombies did in movies, both arms held out in front of him and eyes blank, much to the amusement of his other brothers except Quin.

"Dead and buried," Maynard made the sign of one slitting his own throat. "Do you realize that the woman can slip under the hood of your car and slightly adjust a valve or wire, and you're toast? When will you learn not to insult women who hold your life in the palm of their hands?"

Quin glared at his brothers. "The whole lot of you are sick and I won't stay here and listen to your nonsense. You should be somewhere on the ranch doing chores and not playing Scrabble like high school kids. Wait until Dad catches you in here."

"We're on late afternoon duty so we're taking some time off to recharge our dead batteries," Callum announced. "You should play a game with us and lighten up your mood."

"Don't talk to me," Quin pointed at him.

"What did you do to this fellow now?" Kendrick picked up his tiles and aligned them on the rack.

"Can you believe that his fellow reported me to Mrs. Brian? And she wasn't at all happy with me, but I've appeased her."

"Only a bunch of roses will do for both women that you offended," Maynard said. "I could go out there and help you pluck the roses if you're scared of getting your dainty hands pricked by thorns."

"Why are you all giving me a hard time now?"

"You offended the woman who prepares your meals and the one who takes care of your car; go figure," Callum said.

"I told you not to talk to me."

"Go and get the roses already," Kendrick said. "We're playing a game here and you're wasting our time. I want to get some money from these fellows, so please leave."

"I'm going, and you'll miss me when I'm gone," Quin walked toward the door.

"Dead man walking away," Callum said and the four howled with laughter as Quin left the room in a huff.

There were times when Quin felt like knocking his brothers' heads together. He loved them very much, but they could also be a pain in the neck. Yet he knew that their teasing was never malicious, merely fun. It irked him sometimes, but he bore it like the big brother that he was.

He found himself wandering out of the house and toward the rose garden. Maynard was right; he needed to appease the women he'd offended, and getting them roses would do the trick. Women loved receiving roses, and he would do that. Since he didn't have any scissors with him, he decided to get a pair of shears from the workshop. There were heavy clanging sounds coming from inside the workshop, and he found the three regular mechanics, including the supervisor, repairing a broken-down combined harvester.

Mark Keith, the supervisor, and Quin's old schoolmate sauntered over to him. "Boss, is there anything you need us to do today?"

"Not really," Quin's eyes roamed around the workshop. "Miss Kelsey was repairing the barn door and might need help. Would you send someone to assist her please?"

Mark snickered, "What does a woman know about such things. I already sent Bill to take over from her."

"And where is she now?"

"I sent her to clean the cars out in the yard," Mark said, unaware that his boss was barely

holding onto his temper.

"You did what?" Quin turned on him. "Isn't that one of the tasks assigned to Frank? And where is he now?"

Mark shrugged, "I figured that the lass needed something to keep her busy rather than have her running underfoot. And as for Frank, I have no idea where he is right now."

Quin took a deep breath, not wanting to lose his temper. The man sounded so smug, and it irritated him. "Kelsey is a qualified, professional mechanic and not an errand boy, Mark. Why would you allocate such menial tasks to her?"

"I thought..." Mark's face turned red.

"You thought wrong," Quin snapped. He felt guilty for having his own prejudices and it irked him that there were many other men out there who thought in the same way.

My sins look bad on others, he thought to himself. He was going to have to organize a workshop for all staff to deal with such matters and nip them in the bud before they got out of hand. It wasn't fair on female members of staff to have to deal with prejudiced men.

He looked up at Mark. "From this moment and going forward, you need to understand that my father interviewed Kelsey and found her to be qualified enough to be one of the ranch's mechanics. She's not a casual laborer."

"Yes, Boss," Mark looked suitably chastened.

"See to it that she always receives all the help she needs."

"Yes, Sir."

"Thank you." Quin looked around. "I need to borrow a pair of scissors or shears," he said and one of the other mechanics brought him the latter. After thanking the man, he walked to the rose garden and stood at the side. The roses were in full bloom, and it never ceased to surprise him that at no time did the stalks ever dry all at once. His father took twelve roses to his mother's grave every Saturday and yet one would always find a rose if they needed it. He plucked six roses each and removed the thorns. Then carrying the two bunches, he made his way back to the house.

"Mrs. Brian, these are for you," he handed her one bunch. "Please accept my sincere apology for offending you."

"Oh, Child!" Mrs. Brian looked emotional as she received her flowers. "Thank you so much."

"It's the least I could do."

He was smiling as he left the kitchen because his world felt right. He hated offending Mrs. Brian but with his offering of roses, he was back in her good books. Now to find Kelsey and make things right with her!

KELSEY WAS angry as she stared at the row of beautiful SUVs that she'd been ordered to wash. There were about ten of them. She'd been repairing the barn door when one of the other mechanics walked over and told her that the supervisor was calling her.

She'd expected to be allocated to repair one of the machines or vehicles in the workshop. Instead, she'd been handed a bucket and rag and told to wash all the vehicles in the yard.

"If I go ahead and wash these vehicles and don't speak up for myself then I'm allowing these men to turn me into a doormat," she mused. "I'm not a doormat and never will be one. But if I refuse to do as I'm told, then that supervisor will report me to Mr. Randolph. I don't want to lose my position even before I achieve what I came here to do."

She bent down and wrung out the extra water from the rag and moved to the first car. Then she shook her head and dropped the rag back into the bucket. She came to a decision to stand up for herself. In times like this she needed to take a stand and make it clear that she wasn't going to bow down to any form of discrimination or prejudice. If she didn't do that, it would be easy for her supervisor to think that he could get away with treating her differently from her counterparts. She'd lived through the scorn of one tyrannical man and wasn't about to let history repeat itself. As she approached the garage, she heard Quin's voice.

"Kelsey is a mechanic and I expect you all to treat her like an equal. She deserves our respect. Is that clear?"

"Yes, Boss," Kelsey heard Mark reply. She was quite surprised because, less than an hour before, Quin had told her how women were only good as housekeepers and cooks. Yet now here he was defending her to the supervisor and her other counterparts. She shrugged and stepped into the garage. Quin stopped talking as soon as he spotted her.

"Miss Kelsey," Mark called out and she turned her eyes to him. "I apologize for my earlier treatment. It wasn't fair, nor was it right."

His words sounded sincere, but his eyes were cold, and Kelsey shivered involuntarily. Without intending to, Quin had just earned her an enemy. She noticed that the other two mechanics were keeping their heads bowed as if they didn't want to be a part of whatever was going on.

Kelsey's resolve hardened. She'd lived with a bully of a father for most of her life and wasn't going to take such treatment from another man. While she respected authority, for she'd learned that in Sunday School, she refused any further tyranny directed toward her. She noticed the roses in Quin's hand and wondered who they were for. They were beautiful, six long red stems.

"These are for you," he approached her and held them out to her.

"Thank you," she blushed when the two mechanics exchanged a knowing glance.

"Please accept my sincere apology for offending you earlier, and I promise that it won't happen again."

"Thank you, Sir."

"Good. Now let me give you the chance to carry out your duties." After Quin had left, Kelsey turned to her supervisor. She felt odd holding the flowers.

"Mr. Keith, I was just returning to let you know that I'm a good mechanic. Please allow me to do what I do best."

"Go ahead," Mark waved a hand around the workshop. "There are three projects awaiting our attention this morning. This combined harvester, Mrs. Brian's car, and the fire truck. Take your pick."

Kelsey smiled inwardly. She was sure Mark expected her to choose to work on Mrs. Brian's car.

"Thank you, Sir," she said as she made her way to the fire truck. She wanted to ask what the trouble with the vehicle was but then decided to run her own diagnostics. She'd been taught all these things in college and then during her two years working as a fireman for the city of Denver.

She looked at her roses and smiled. It was nice to receive fresh flowers from someone even if they were an apology gift. She placed them on a small side table and then opened the truck door.

The keys of the truck were still in the ignition, and she started it. It coughed and spluttered then fell silent. She turned the key three times and smiled when she was finally able to identify the problem.

"Never be too overconfident about your findings," Hector Connor, the fire chief had always warned them. "Go through every step thoroughly and meticulously and don't be given to making assumptions. Mistakes can be costly in our line of work when it's a matter of life and death."

An hour later when Kelsey drove the large truck out of the garage, the engine was purring like a contented kitten. She stopped at the workshop door and climbed down, carrying the written report with her.

"Sir," she addressed Mark. "May I deliver the truck back to the fire station?"

"Sure, go ahead," and this time the smile he gave her reached his eyes. "When you're done, please come back here so you and I can have a little chat."

"Yes, Sir," Kelsey handed him the report. "My report, Sir."

Kelsey found Maynard at the small ranch fire station when she drove the truck into the shed. He was inspecting the second truck, and when he caught sight of her a smile broke out on his face.

"You sure are a sight for sore eyes," he said, walking towards her.

"This is all done," she said, looking around the small fire house with interest. "This ranch is self-sufficient and quite impressive."

"Dad told me that you used to work at a fire station back in Denver."

"Yes, for three years until an injury on the job put paid to my plans to become fire chief someday," she said. "How many people do you have working in this station?"

"I can't really say that there are permanent staff for this place. Most are volunteers but we like to keep the trucks well maintained and ready for any eventualities."

"If you like, I could come around when I'm free to check all your equipment and make sure that it meets the required standards."

"That would be wonderful, and I owe you dinner for that."

"Not really necessary because I like doing it." She handed him the truck keys. "I have to get back to the workshop," she said.'

"If you give me a minute, I'll drive you back."

"I don't want to bother you," she said and then groaned when she spotted Roselyn walking toward the firehouse. "Besides, I think you're about to get a visitor."

When Maynard looked up and spotted Roselyn his countenance changed. "The more reason why I need to drive you back to the workshop," he said. "This woman is trouble, and I don't want to be alone in this place with her."

Kelsey took pity on him because she knew that women like Roselyn were trouble. The woman might corner Maynard while he was alone in the station and if he rejected her, she could then cry out and claim that he'd attacked her.

"Let's go before she gets here," Kelsey said, and Maynard emerged with the keys to his truck that was parked outside the fire station. But he was polite enough to wait for Roselyn to get to where they were.

"Roselyn," the smile on his face was genuine. "I hope you weren't coming to look for me."

"I actually was, but I can see that you have company," she glared at Kelsey.

"Oh, Kelsey came to return the truck that was in the workshop for repairs. Was there something you wanted?"

"I need to ask you to help with one of my assignments," Roselyn said. "Perhaps I could come back later."

"Or we could do the assignment at the house," Maynard suggested as he entered his truck after Kelsey. "Can I drop you off at the house?"

Roselyn shook her head. "Do you know where Kendrick is?"

"He and Waylen rode to the other side to check on some of the horses."

"Oh!"

"Well, we'll see you around."

Kelsey watched Roselyn though the side mirror as they drove away and was troubled at the expression on her face.

"What are you thinking?" Maynard asked.

"Something about Roselyn is troubling me but I can't tell what it is. I met her for the first time yesterday, but she makes me uneasy."

"Huh!"

"What does that mean?"

"Mrs. Brian mentioned something like that to me a few weeks ago and I thought she was just being fussy. I'll have someone look into Roselyn's background and find out more, seeing as she's the longest-serving intern on the ranch. I mean, she's been here for over a year."

Maynard's words troubled Kelsey, and she purposed to ask Cindy more about Roselyn.

UNEXPECTED REMEDIES

Kelsey lowered the lid of her laptop, letting her gaze linger on Quin. She quickly glanced away before he could notice her watching him.

"So, were you able to find out what's wrong with the cream separator, and can the problem be fixed?" Quin asked.

"Yes and no," she replied.

"What do you mean by yes and no?"

"Don't scowl at me," Kelsey found herself saying. "Whoever repaired the separator last time used a wrong part and forced it to work. That wrong part has affected the whole circuit system of the separator. And no, the problem can't be fixed."

"Why not?"

"The circuit board is fried and buying a new one is of no use. Opening the machine up to repair it will require too much time and effort and it may or may not work. This is an older model and I'm not sure that the parts for it are still in stock. You could try but the best thing to do would be to get a new one. I would advise that you don't waste money or time trying to repair this machine. Just get a new one."

"Mrs. Brian will throw a fit if we can't get this thing to work," Quin muttered.

"What are you muttering about?" Abner walked into the workshop with Mark.

"The cream separator broke down yesterday and I was asking Kelsey if she's been able to find out whatever is wrong with it."

"And did she?" His father asked him.

"Yes. The circuit board is fried, and I think that has affected many other parts as well. I don't know all the mechanics of the machine but the long or short is that it's badly broken down."

"I could get a new circuit board and we can work on it with Miss Kelsey," Mark offered quickly.

Quin shook his head, "Kelsey says that the last repairs done caused more damage to the gadget. The wrong part was fitted in, and it has now caused more problems."

"She could be right," Mark gave Kelsey a sharp look. "Sheldon was the one who fixed it last time. It's a good thing we got rid of him because he was causing much damage to whatever he worked on."

"You should have supervised him more closely." Mr. Randolph told the supervisor.

"Well, we now have to get a new one," Quin announced. "Kelsey, would you like to come to town with me to get a new separator?"

"Me?" She gave Mark a quick glance to see how he was taking the news. He didn't seem pleased at all.

"Miss Kelsey has been here only a few days. She might not know what works for the ranch. I think I'm in the best position to come with you to choose a new machine."

Quin once again shook his head, "This will be a good experience for Kelsey. She needs to learn how to do some of these things, after all."

Kelsey saw Mark's lips tighten and groaned inwardly This man was always creating situations that caused friction between her and the supervisor. Ever since he'd given her flowers in front of Mark and the other mechanics it seemed as if they had many questions about her. But she shrugged the feelings off. She'd done nothing wrong and if someone wanted to have issues with her, there was nothing she could do about it. She was here on a mission and didn't want small things to derail her. And much as she didn't want to make Mark angry, she was excited about finally being able to go into Dallas even if only for an hour or two.

So, she turned to Quin, "Should I go and change?"

He observed her, then shook his head, "You look perfectly all right to me. Shall we go?"

It turned out to be a whole morning of searching for the perfect cream separator.

"We've spent the whole morning searching for the machine, but you refuse to make up your mind about which one you want," Kelsey said. She hadn't felt this happy and relaxed in a long time. It reminded her of the happy times she'd shared with her mom and sisters. She really missed them.

Quin saw Kelsey's countenance change suddenly and wondered what had caused it. A lot about her life filled him with curiosity. She'd been living on the ranch for close to three weeks now, but not once had he heard that she'd gone out on a date. While it was true that she was new in Dallas, he also acknowledged that these days many meetings were arranged via social media. The other young women living in their house often went out with one cowboy or the other but not Kelsey. And another thing was that she treated her phone with indifference. Not once had he seen it blowing up with calls and text messages. Cindy and the other ladies always seemed to be on their phones or else they would spend hours on the laptops that were provided for staff to use.

"Why are you looking at me like that?" Kelsey's voice penetrated through his thoughts.

He smiled. "Why don't we get lunch before going around once more? We can spend that time talking about the merits of each separator that we looked at."

"Nothing fancy, I hope," Kelsey said. "A burger and fries will do for me."

Quin leaned forward and touched the tip of Kelsey's nose. "Eating while driving isn't at all healthy. I promise that I won't take up too much more of your time than is necessary. I've kept you out past lunch time and it's an hour's drive away to get back home. The least I can do is feed you and I promise that the diner where I'm taking you has good food and their service is very fast too."

Kelsey looked down at her coveralls. Though the white garment was spotless and clean, she still felt uncomfortable walking into a diner dressed so casually.

"I'm not exactly dressed for proper dining," she said.

"And neither am I," Quin indicated the pair of jeans he had on and his red plaid shirt. "Have no fear dear girl, we both look the same. The place I'm taking you to is known for its casualness and we'll fit right in."

Kelsey hoped he wasn't just saying that to make her feel better about herself.

The Spurs and Whips Diner was a new experience for Kelsey. There seemed to be cowboys and cowgirls everywhere, people dressed in all manner of ranching regalia and Kelsey's eyes lit up with interest. The moment they entered the diner, it seemed as if all eyes turned to observe them. Kelsey noticed that the women were especially eyeing Quin and she felt both proud to be with him and a little jealous. She even found herself glaring at one or two cowgirls before deciding that she was being rather silly. She laid no claims on Quin, and it wasn't his fault that he was a very attractive man.

One daring cowgirl even sashayed over to where they were standing as they waited to be shown to their table and placed a hand on Quin's arm. "Sugar," she drawled, and Kelsey wanted to roll her eyes. "Are you taken?"

Kelsey found her respect for Quin growing even more when he didn't rudely brush the woman aside but made a joke of the whole issue. "Oh yes, Sugar," he drawled right back then took Kelsey's hand. "This is my cowgirl and she's the jealous type," he said looking intensely into her eyes. "May I just say that she's a sharpshooter and I wouldn't like to get on her wrong side?"

"Why is it that the good ones are always taken?" The woman said and dropped her hand. "Honey, keep your man close or someone might just be tempted to grab him."

"Oh, believe me, I never let him out of my sight at all," Kelsey joined in the jesting, and they all laughed as the woman walked away.

Even though it was all a joke Quin was rather pleased that Kelsey had held her own with the cowgirl. She was the most beautiful woman among all those he could see, and he was glad that she was with him.

"Do all these people work on ranches?" Kelsey asked.

"Nothing of the sort," Quin laughed, retaining her hand in his. "Many city dwellers only get to experience what ranch life is like in places like this. It's a pity that we have to dine and run. Mr. Froth, the owner, usually puts on a show in the backyard where he demonstrates whatever happens on a ranch. He's a retired ranch cook who turned his experiences into this," Quin waved a hand around, indicating the diner. "A few daring souls also try the lassoing and roping and even bull riding. If you like we can stay for a little while longer and you can see what I mean."

Kelsey shook her head, "I live on an actual ranch and I'm sure that I'll get to see what happens there at some point. In any case, we need to go back and purchase a separator because we promised Mrs. Brian we would bring her one." She was anxious because she knew that Mark wasn't happy that Quin had overruled him first by agreeing to buy a new separator instead of just replacing the broken-down parts. And, Quin had showed that he preferred her company to Mark's. "There's some work that Mark needed me to finish by the end of the day."

"Then we need to hurry if we're to enjoy our meal."

A smiling hostess led them to a table for two at the back of the diner. She could hear loud thumping and cheering through the walls and knew that some demonstrations were going on.

The hostess's name tag said Carrie and she quickly seated them.

"Will you have your usual Mr. Randolph?" Carrie asked, a pen and notebook in her hand ready to take their order.

"No, I'll try something else. Maybe a plate of cowboy steak today."

"Sizzling?"

Quin cast a glance at Kelsey who nodded, her eyes glowing. She could see waiters carrying plates that were piled high with aromatic ribs and meats and when they got to a table would make the platter sizzle as the patrons cheered loudly. It was a noisy place, but Kelsey felt right at home.

"Would you like something to drink with the steak?"

"Mineral water for me, thank you," Quin said. "Kelsey?"

"Same here."

"Add some baked potatoes and green vegetables."

By the time lunch was over, Kelsey was dozing off. She was stuffed and sighed with contentment.

"That was really nice, and now I'll spend the afternoon dozing off and earn myself an earful from Mark," she said.

"I'm glad you enjoyed the experience," Quin reached for the folder that had their bill. He motioned for Carrie to come over and he handed her his credit card. "Add the usual takeaway package," he said.

Carrie returned a few minutes later with Quin's card and receipt and a large sack. Kelsey looked inquiringly at Quin.

"There's an unwritten rule back on the ranch that anyone who comes to Spurs and Whips for any meal must bring back short ribs for those at home."

"Oh!" Kelsey reached for the sack. It was heavy.

"I'll get that, have no worries."

They were walking out of the diner when Kelsey heard someone call out to Quin.

"What…" she saw Quin's countenance when he saw whoever was calling out to him. A strikingly beautiful woman came up to him. She ignored Kelsey and placed a hand on Quin's arm.

"Why haven't you called me back?" she pouted prettily. "I've been waiting for your call for days now, darling."

"Yvette, good afternoon to you," Quin gently extracted his arm from hers. "This is Kelsey." But Yvette barely glanced in Kelsey's direction, and she was amused. The woman was acting all territorial, as if she owned Quin.

"Why haven't you called me?"

"I've been rather busy at the ranch. Christmas is around the corner, and you know how busy we get at this time." He didn't want his irritation to show. "Please excuse us as we have to leave now."

"Can I ride back to the ranch with you? I'd like to see Mrs. Brian about one of her recipes," she gave him a coy smile and Kelsey wanted to roll her eyes at the woman's blatant flirting. "It's your favorite and I'd like to know how to make it for you."

Quin shook his head, "There will be no one to bring you back later."

"I could sleep over."

"Yvette, we've talked about this before," Kelsey now heard the impatience in Quin's voice. She realized that she was eavesdropping in on a private conversation, so she walked away.

Kelsey wondered how serious things were between Quin and Yvette. He didn't act like a love-smitten man, but then again, she didn't know him well enough to form an opinion about him and his relationships. Yet Yvette seemed to be very familiar with him. She felt jealousy begin to stir up in her heart but quashed it.

Yvette was a beauty; maybe she was a model. Everything about her was sleek and in place. From the tip of her hair down to her toes, everything reeked of class and expensive grooming. Kelsey felt that she didn't stand a chance against such competition.

"There you are," Quin sauntered up to her and using his free hand, took hers. "This way please. Let's drop this package in the truck then we can carry on with the business that brought us to the city."

The drive back to the ranch was done in silence and Quin was amused to see that Kelsey had fallen asleep. He'd enjoyed himself right until Yvette had come to spoil the mood. From then onward, Kelsey seemed to withdraw into herself.

She woke up just as the truck rumbled into the homestead. Quin beckoned to some ranch hands to help offload the large separator.

"Will you need any help getting the equipment installed?" Quin asked Kelsey. "The salesperson said it needs some configuring and all that jargon. I could ask Maynard to come in and help because he understands all the jargon involved in configuring this thing."

"Thank you," Kelsey said. The old separator had been taken away and now the new one stood there in all its glory. She stood back to admire it. It was twice as big as the previous one. According to the saleswoman who'd sold it to them, this one worked much faster, cutting the production time into almost half.

Quin left, and Kelsey wondered why she suddenly felt bereft of his presence. She was reading through the manual when Maynard appeared.

"This one looks like it belongs inside a large milk production factory, rather than a ranch," he commented, walking around it. Kelsey smiled. She was the one who'd picked this separator and had argued that it was far more cost effective than getting a smaller one. Quin had explained that the ranch supplied milk to a number of small bakeries and eateries around Dallas. Most of them preferred the milk to be skimmed and devoid of any cream, for they catered to a certain type of customers who were very fussy. So, the ranch sold both cream and processed milk. Mrs. Brian ran the unit and when Quin had explained how many liters of milk were processed every day, Kelsey had urged him to get a larger piece of equipment.

"This one makes sense because it will save Mrs. Brian a lot of time," she explained to Maynard.

"You have a point there. Now let's see what this baby can do."

It didn't take Maynard long to have the cream separator configured and up and running. He called for milk to be brought and some cowhands brought in about one hundred liters of freshly produced milk.

"Let's test the new equipment and see what it does."

Kelsey was amused at how excited Maynard was when the different spouts began to churn out milk and cream separately. In no time the one hundred liters of milk had been separated and the product stood ready in different containers.

"It's ready for packaging," Maynard said happily. "I can't wait to show Mrs. Brian what this thing can do." Then he impulsively hugged Kelsey and kissed her on the cheek. They were both laughing happily like two children who'd just shared a wonderful experience.

"What's going on here?" Quin's voice broke through their laughter. Kelsey turned and saw a deep scowl on his face. He seemed angry for some reason.

"We just finished installing this machine and have tested it. It's very fast and efficient and should save a lot of time," Maynard still had his arms around Kelsey. "So, I was just congratulating my beautiful assistant here for choosing the right equipment for this work."

"Do you always congratulate those who help you install all the gadgets on the ranch by hugging and kissing them?"

Maynard grinned and finally released Kelsey. "None of them have been as beautiful as Kelsey and in any case, those I work with have been men. I can't go around hugging other men," he grinned at his brother.

"Stick to being professional," Quin growled.

Kelsey excused herself and left the dairy barn. Quin couldn't believe that he wanted to punch his brother's face. When he'd walked in and found Kelsey in Maynard's arms it was all he could do to restrain himself from throwing a few punches at his brother.

"Don't give the woman the wrong idea," he said instead.

"Oh Brother, you should see your face," Maynard teased. "I wasn't aware that Kelsey is your woman. From the way you're behaving one would be excused for thinking that Kelsey belongs to you."

Quin glared at him but said nothing.

PUBLIC AGGRESSION

Kelsey sat in her leather chair gazing out into the courtyard. Her phone, vibrating in her shirt pocket, roused her from her thoughts. She fumbled in the pocket, and the caller ID revealed it to be Sally-Jo.

She was alone in the workshop because there wasn't anything left to repair. Mark and the other mechanics had left for somewhere, and it was upon her to act as receptionist in case someone needed help.

She answered the call and they exchanged niceties. "How are things going?" Sally-Jo rarely wasted time beating about the bush.

Kelsey sighed, "I'm not sure that things are going anywhere at all," she finally got out. "I don't think Quin is interested in me as a woman at all."

"Don't worry, it's only been four weeks."

"Maybe I'm just wasting my time here," Kelsey said. She hated that she sounded whiny. At the time she'd been in Denver preparing to come out to Dallas, she'd been very confident about making Quin notice her as a woman. Now she felt foolish because love wasn't a switch that could be turned on and off at will. All her preconceived ideas about love were fast fading.

"I think I got caught up in all the humorous stories about your great, great grandmother and how she helped men and women on the frontier find true love and their happily ever after," Kelsey said. "That was over a century ago and I should have known that things are very different now."

"You sound like you're ready to give up."

Kelsey laughed shortly. "I shouldn't have started it at all in the first place. I feel rather foolish for claiming that I would get Quin Randolph attracted to me within a very short time."

"Let me call you back," Sally Jo said. "Something is happening in the outer office that I need to attend to."

"That's all right," Kelsey said and immediately the call was disconnected. She looked down at her Galaxy phone and sighed. She wasn't like her sisters who changed their handsets every few months. Much as she was a mechanical engineer, electronic gadgets held no fascination for her. These were just gadgets and useful for performing certain functions for her. This handset was over two years old, and her sisters had teased her mercilessly about living in the past. But the thought of having to lose a few contacts when switching phones is what made her stick to what she called her 'Old and Faithful Companion.'

As she put her phone back in her pocket, she knew that she was projecting her grouchiness, which was rather childish. Sally-Jo had sounded very enthusiastic, but Kelsey had clearly dampened her mood. No wonder that she'd wanted to get away as fast as possible. Yet Kelsey could no longer pretend to herself. She'd failed in her mission to lasso the stubborn and wild cowboy. Why had she though that winning a man's heart was easy?

I blame Sally Jo's romantic stories of the nineteenth century, she said inwardly.

In her desire to leave home and find a new life away from her father's influence, Kelsey had turned to the Internet. The search for a dating agency had led her to Sally Jo's establishment.

Hitch Your Wagon Romance Agency had caught Kelsey's eyes. That was because Kelsey had decided long ago that being all feminine and girly wasn't for her. The kind of men her father wanted her to marry were after a woman who over-pampered herself. Trophy wives is what they wanted, women whose mission in life was to spend thousands of dollars to make themselves look young and good. And then all they were good for was to stand or sit pretty beside their partners, just to boost their men's egos. That wasn't the kind of life Kelsey wanted for herself, and it had long been a bone of contention between her and her father. He'd tried to turn Kelsey's mother into one of those trophy wives but to no avail. Eleanor Brooke was a well-grounded and spiritual woman. Yet while she refused to be treated as a chattel and show pony, she was still very submissive to her husband and allowed him to exert his tyranny over her.

Sally-Jo's agency had provided the solution Kelsey had sought. They helped cowboys and cowgirls to find love. Because of the lockdown, it hadn't been easy to get a face-to-face appointment, and Kelsey didn't want to Skype. She needed to see evidence of the agency's claims that they had tens of clients who were now enjoying life with their spouses. Matches made in heaven was what the agency claimed to be responsible for. But eventually Sally-Jo had made time for Kelsey, and she'd visited the agency's posh offices on Maple Avenue.

"You see all those old newspaper cuttings dating back to the nineteenth century," Sally-Jo pointed at the various framed clips and old photos adorning the walls of her sleek offices. *"All those are the testimonies of the people, both men and women who found love out on the frontier. And it was my great, great grandmother Molly Smith who made it possible in the eighteen eighties."*

"This is truly remarkable," Kelsey walked around the gallery stopping at each framed photo or newspaper clip. *Some photos showed the couples with their children and grandchildren and even great grandchildren. And the testimonies were very moving.* *"These stories are so real and down to earth, and it makes me wonder how they did it in the era when there were no phones like now."*

Sally-Jo smiled. "You could say bridal matchmaking runs in my family line. My ancestor's agency was called Cozy Brides. As you can see, that lovely woman was responsible for tens of marriages. And the beauty of it all is that great, great grandma Molly matched godly women and men out on the frontier and made it possible for people to enjoy their lives together. Apart from one or two here and there whose relationships failed, nearly all those marriages lasted until the couples were well into their advanced years."

"That's really remarkable but that worked very well in those days because men genuinely wanted wives to help them build up the West. Can such matchmaking tactics work even now? All I know about dating sites and romance agencies these days is that many people use them for just temporary attachments, and nothing is ever permanent. A good number of men claiming to be searching for love are actually not serious. They want temporary and ungodly unions and that has made me a bit wary of it all. Does Internet romance really work?"

"Kelsey, there are hundreds of dating sites all over the Internet and one really must be careful. Ours is a Christian Romance agency and we're very strict about signing people up. If we get even a slight hint that a man or woman isn't who they claim to be, we immediately freeze the account until they can clear themselves. If not, we take their profiles down and blacklist them. You won't believe how many men and women who aren't even Christians pretend to be believers just to get godly and virtuous partners. People nowadays are too busy to use the methods that worked before like introduction by family and friends or even meeting during social gatherings and so turn to the Internet for that. It's sad that some unscrupulous people take advantage of people's need and yearning for love to con them. But also, I can say with all confidence that there are still good agencies out there, and ours is one of them. Can I tell you something?"

"Ye, please."

"Do you know that even as the world was on lockdown because of the corona virus, love blossomed on the Internet?"

"Really?"

"Yes. Public places where people could meet were shut down and people got lonely. So, they turned to the Internet dating sites. While many, of course, are the usual scammers, many others also found love in that way too. I know of a couple of folks who got married once the lockdown was lifted. They met during the lockdown and used the Internet to keep in touch and build up their relationship. Now they're married and get to spend the rest of their lives together."

"It all sounds like a fairy tale," Kelsey said laughingly. "I know that people spend a lot of time on the Internet trying to find love, and this is the first time I'm trying it. I hope it works."

"Believe me, Internet dating works, and this is one of the ways in which you get to meet people from all over the world. Gone are the days when finding a mate meant searching around your neighborhood, asking friends to introduce you, or attending social gatherings. Now women and men from all over the world can meet online, communicate by whatever channel they feel comfortable with and if they're compatible, arrange for a face-to-face meeting. Then the rest becomes history for them."

Kelsey sighed as she returned to the present, rose from her seat, and started pacing. Sally-Jo's words had caused excitement to mount in her heart and when the woman had told her of a wild cowboy down in Dallas who needed taming, Kelsey had believed that she was the one to do it.

What pride, what arrogance! Then she slowly walked back to her chair and sat down once again. The sermon preached on Sunday flashed through her mind.

"Trust in the Lord with all your heart and lean not on your own understanding," Reverend Garden of Cedar Hill Independent Church had preached. *"In all your ways acknowledge the Lord and He will make straight your paths."*

Kelsey shook her head as she felt convicted in her spirit. She'd trusted in her own abilities as a woman to win Quinten Randolph over so he would end up marrying her. She'd thought that she was attractive and intelligent enough to win the man's heart, yet all her efforts were now proving to be futile.

"Please, Lord," she murmured, "forgive me for being so arrogant. I leaned on my own understanding and didn't seek for your guidance before coming out here." She'd done everything out of defiance toward her father, yet the Bible clearly instructed children to honor their parents. Was it any wonder then that nothing was working for her?

She'd guarded her salvation and virtue even in college where anything goes. Kelsey, like a few of her other friends, had stood firm and they'd made what they called the 'six pack pact.' Six of them who'd met in their first year of college had become accountable to and for each other. They'd prayed together and purposed that they would live godly lives in these wicked and evil times. They had looked out for each other, never putting themselves in temptation or harm's way. They had all graduated among the top students and now, five years later, five of the six were happily married to godly men, and their testimonies had stood the test of time.

"What happened to me?" Kelsey asked herself. She'd attended the fifth wedding last summer and seeing all her five friends so happy with their spouses had struck a chord in her heart. Her five friends had taken time to sit with her and encourage her to continue trusting in God and holding on to His promises. She'd smiled through it all but walked away feeling very lonely.

That's when it had all started, the yearning for a mate. Since none of the men in her family circle had met the criteria she sought, she'd turned to the Internet.

Now here she was, four weeks later and no closer to getting Quin to even notice her as a woman. He treated her in much the same way as he treated Cindy and the others, like a little sister.

She'd also noticed that lately he went out in the evenings, returning quite late to the house because she would lie awake in bed listening for his truck. Kelsey believed that Quin was probably visiting the beautiful Yvette and spending time with her. Her heart melted within her because she felt that she'd lost.

What right did she have to come between those two, when clearly, they had something going on between them? She felt ashamed of herself because she'd tried to play God and ensconce herself into Quin's life, but that plan had failed. All she had to do now was to cut her losses and move on, because clearly the Wild Stallion of Randolph Ranch had already been tamed by another!

A MEASURE OF SENSE

Quin woke up to Saturday morning sunshine streaming through his bedroom window. He'd forgotten to close the drapes last evening so light poured into his room, and he groaned. He could hear the merry chimes of church bells in the distance as they ushered in Christmas.

It was the day before Christmas Eve, and he groaned as he got out of bed. Though it was winter, the weather was beautiful, and he didn't want to waste a single moment in bed. He'd signed up for range duty for the next few days so the cowboys and other workers who had families out of state could travel and be with them during the holidays.

Quin knew he was running away from home as he'd always done these past few years. His mother had loved the Christmas season because she and his father had been married on Christmas Day itself. On a day like today, the aroma of freshly baked ginger and cinnamon cookies would be wafting through the air. And with the cookies there would be delicious eggnog.

Quin walked to the wide windows and threw them open, then frowned. "I must be dreaming," he said to himself. For the delicious aroma of his mother's ginger and cinnamon cookies filled the air, wafting into his bedroom.

It had been years since such had happened and it was even stranger because the only other person who knew his mother's recipe was Mrs. Brian. And she wasn't around, having travelled to Milton, Georgia, to be with her son and his family for the holidays. She did that every year without fail so she couldn't be the one baking his mother's cookies. In fact, he was the one who'd driven Mrs. Brian to the airport to catch her flight to Georgia two days ago.

The other female interns had also travelled to be with their families for Christmas and only Kelsey was still around. Quin had wondered why she wasn't leaving for Denver to be with family, but since she hadn't offered any explanation, he'd let matters be.

During such times when Mrs. Brian and the other female interns were away, Quin and his brothers prepared their own meals, yes, but that is as far as their culinary skills went. None of them could bake very well and since his father also couldn't bake to save his life, that only left Kelsey.

His lips tightened. What was she up to, and how had she gotten a hold of his mother's recipe? Perhaps Mrs. Brian had given it to her, but he had his doubts. The woman jealously guarded all the recipes that had been handed down to her by Quin's mother. He needed to get to the bottom of this holiday mystery.

Quin hastily threw on some clothes and walked to the kitchen. Even before he got to the kitchen door, he could hear his brothers chattering like magpies on a warm spring morning. It was as if they were trying to outdo each other with their talking. Quin pushed open the door and everyone in the kitchen turned to look at him. Even his father was present.

"What's going on here?" He demanded, feeling angry when he noticed that Maynard had his arm around Kelsey's shoulders. The two of them were standing at the kitchen island where Kelsey was in the process of mixing another batch of dough. His other three brothers had their mouths stuffed full of cookies.

"Kelsey found Mom's old cookbook," Waylen said, reaching for yet another cookie. "And she's really outdone herself. These are really good," he said as he took a bite and closed his eyes to savor the taste. "You should try one, Quin."

"Mom only had one cookbook and it's up in the attic with the rest of her things," Quin said angrily. He couldn't understand how his brothers, and even his father, were here in the kitchen indulging themselves when it was clear that their mother's privacy had been tampered with.

Kendrick shook his head, "Not anymore. When Kelsey and Maynard were up there searching for Christmas decorations, she stumbled upon the book."

"Mom's trunk was locked, so it's clear that Kelsey was snooping," Quin said. "She should have left it alone," he said forcefully, and everyone fell silent, staring at him in shock. "There's a reason I locked those things away years ago. You had no right to go poking your nose into matters that don't concern you."

"Quin!" His father's voice rang out.

Kelsey felt the rebuke and stopped whatever she was doing.

"I'm sorry," she said, taking the apron off.

"Kelsey," Mr. Randolph called out, but she ignored him. Quin's harsh words were unwarranted since it was Maynard who'd opened his mother's trunk and told her to dig in and find anything useful. She'd found the book and showed it to Maynard. He told her that she could have the book because those were the dishes his mother prepared for them when she was still alive.

Kelsey felt the tears stinging her eyes. All she'd wanted was to make this a very special Christmas Day for the family. Maynard had mentioned that not only had their parents wedded on Christmas Day, but his mother had died on that day too. They all had mixed feelings about the day and Kelsey had decided to help them make new memories through Mrs. Randolph's cooking

"I was only seven when Mom died but I still remember the delicious ginger and cinnamon cookies she baked for Christmas, and the delicious eggnog," Maynard had said sadly, perusing through the old cookbook that had lain untouched for fifteen years.

"What about your Dad and brothers, do you think they remember your mom's Christmas cookies and eggnog?"

"And her mince pies, sweet and savory turkey and all the other delicious dishes she prepared for us on Christmas Day. All her recipes are in this book. Once in a while Mrs. Brian bakes cookies for us, but she never quite gets it right." He handed the book to Kelsey, and she held it close to her chest, for she felt that it was rather precious. "There in your hands you hold the secrets to opening the hearts of the Randolph men," Maynard had joked.

Filled with excitement, Kelsey had set out to bring Christmas cheer to the Randolph men. But Quin had just crashed her enthusiasm and made her feel like an outsider.

Wiping her eyes, she entered her room, locked the door, lay on her bed, and wept. She wished she was back home in Denver with her mother. Tina and Jeannie had Skyped with her last evening and told her that they would be travelling home during the few days' holiday break they'd been given at school.

"You should also come," Tina had urged. "Now that you're still not married, there's no one to stop you from coming to Denver for Christmas."

But much as Kelsey had wanted to go and join her family, she couldn't just walk away from the responsibilities she had on the ranch. Though Mr. Randolph hadn't made her sign a contract for her position, she was conscientious enough to know that an employee didn't deserve to ask for any leave when they'd only been working in a place for a month. And with Mark and the other mechanics being away from the ranch over the holidays, someone had to be present in case of a mechanical emergency.

Now she wished she'd asked Mr. Randolph for permission to travel home. She sat up and wiped her face. It wasn't too late for her to get a flight to Denver, and she wouldn't be returning to Cedar Hill. Her plans of getting Quin to fall in love and marry her had failed. There was nothing left for her and especially not when Quin went out of his way to make her unhappy.

With this new resolve, Kelsey reached for her laptop and powered it on. She was dismayed to discover that almost all flights from Dallas to Denver were fully booked and she nearly wept in frustration. But she refused to give up and finally she caught a break and got herself a seat on a red eye flight.

Then her eyes went to the six roses that Quin had given her on her second day on the ranch. They had long dried up, but she just couldn't bring herself to throw them out. At the time, they had given her hope that Quin might be getting attracted to her. But now she felt foolish for keeping them and with a slight cry she swept them off the table and into the dustbin.

"What was all that about?" Callum turned to Quin. "Did you have to humiliate Kelsey like that and make her cry?"

"I don't like it when people don't respect Mom's things," Quin said defensively. The aroma of the cookies still baking in the oven was tantalizing and his mouth watered. He reached for a cookie, but Waylen pulled the large dish away.

"None for you and no eggnog either," he was told in no uncertain terms.

"What's wrong with you, Waylen? I only want a cookie."

"You came in here riding on your high horse about nobody having the permission to touch any of Ma's things. Yet now you want to eat the cookies that Kelsey baked. Double standards if you ask me."

"Keep them," Quin fumed. "See if I care."

"Be silent!" Their father ordered. "Look at you, bickering over a plate of cookies like five-year-olds. Now, Waylen put the dish back on the table."

"But Dad..."

"Do as you're told. You're no longer five years old, so stop all this," their father said. "There's much work to be done around the ranch, yet here you are behaving like tantrum-throwing toddlers and all because of a plate of cookies." He glared at them in turn. "You didn't give Kelsey the chance to prepare breakfast. Mrs. Brian and the other ladies are away so I expect all of you to pull your weight around the house. Just a warning now, let me not catch any of you leaving all the chores for Kelsey to do. Even if the workshop is shut down for now, she isn't here to cook and clean up after us."

"Yes Dad, we'll do all our chores," Maynard spoke on behalf of his brothers.

"Good. Now Quin, a word with you in my den please."

"Yes Dad." He stared longingly at the cookies until Kendrick took pity on him and held the dish out. Quin grabbed four of them and then followed his father out of the kitchen.

"What a fruitcake," he heard Callum saying, and he tightened his lips but didn't stop.

"Son, what's going on with you?"

"Dad, I don't understand what you mean."

Abner stared at his firstborn, a slight crease on his brow. "This is what I mean. I've noticed that you're very hard on Kelsey. The poor girl is trying her best to fit in here, but I understand that you're always in the workshop picking on her."

"That's not true," Quin bowed his head, face flaming. "I'm only trying to help her settle in."

"That's not how your brothers see it. According to them, you're making that young woman's life very unpleasant, and I don't like it. Either you're prejudiced toward Kelsey because she's a woman or something else is going on with you. Talk to me, Son."

"Dad, really, nothing is going on."

"Then why the unwarranted attack over your mother's cookbook? The last time I checked, the woman who owned that cookbook was my wife and she had four other sons apart from yourself. If the five of us see no problem with Kelsey using my wife's cookbook, then I don't see why you should."

Quin collapsed onto a seat. "I miss her so much," he whispered hoarsely. "I wish she was still here."

Abner cleared his throat. "Not a day goes by that my heart doesn't weep for your mother. But she left those things behind for us to have good memories of her. Kelsey was only trying to cheer us up because you know the effect that Christmas Day has on all of us."

"I'm so sorry that I snapped at Kelsey."

"Son," Abner came around the desk and placed a light hand on his son's shoulder. "I know that you, more than your brothers, were affected by your mother's death and felt her loss the greatest. I acknowledge that I also didn't handle myself very well at the time. My grief didn't give you the chance to mourn for your mother. You were the one who held us together when you needed me to be strong for you. You were but a child, and I left all the weight to fall on your shoulders." Abner sighed deeply. "Quin, I'll never stop regretting how I absconded on my fatherly duties, forcing you to take over. Please forgive me."

"Dad, I was glad to be there for all of us." Quin placed his cheek on his father's hand. "I shouldn't have snapped and caused tension all around. It's just that Christmas doesn't bring out the best in me. I just wish that the years would come and go without Christmas."

"My son, don't ever say that again. Much as we either celebrate or weep on Christmas Day and during these holidays, remember what the day stands for. It's not about what we have lost or gained over the years We celebrate Christmas as the time when the dark world was illuminated by the light of the love of God. He sent His son to be born as our Savior and the redeemer of mankind. He brought us out of the darkness of sin into the light of His glory and love. Remember this, Christmas should always be about Christ and not us."

"Yes, Dad."

"Even though it's a painful time for all of us I think it's time that we created new memories. Your mother is gone, and we need to pick ourselves up and live. That's what she'd have wanted us to do"

"I don't know how to do that, dad. Moving past all this is so hard." Quin closed his eyes tight so the tears wouldn't fall. He was afraid to let go and cry even though a therapist he'd seen a few years ago had told him that it was the first step for him to heal from the pain of losing his mother. "I keep thinking that if I'm just a little bit more hopeful and prayerful, Mom will walk back into our lives."

"Quin," his father groaned. "This is all my fault for holding onto things that I should have let go of years ago. I built a shrine for your mother and let you children worship at it, and may the Lord forgive me. But all that ends today."

Quin gave his father a sharp glance. "What do you mean by that, Dad?"

"All the photos and mementos placed all over the house have to go. The closet where her clothes and shoes and jewelry are stored needs to be cleaned up. The attic which holds her belongings and which we guard so jealously must be cleared of all those things. These things have turned into a shrine of worship to your mother and now I see things very clearly. It was wrong of me to hold on tightly when I should have let go years ago."

"Dad, we need these things so that we can remember Mom. In future when people ask about her what are we supposed to tell them?"

"Yes, we need to remember your mother but not like this. That's why families have photo albums. Today I'm going to strip my room bare and the attic too. You boys each get to choose something of your mother's to keep and everything else will be donated to charity. We have to make a clean break and start living in the future; otherwise, we'll forever be stuck in the past."

"I don't know how I feel about all this, and I don't think I want to be here when you're doing all that. It will feel as if I'm getting rid of Mom and saying goodbye forever."

"Well, I have a suggestion, and please hear me out and don't snap my head off."

Quin looked up at his father and smiled, tears shimmering in his eyes. "Dad, go ahead and I promise not to snap your head off."

"Good, good," Abner scratched his chin. "Well, the weather seems rather pleasant today and very good for having a picnic up on the hill right at the spot where I liked to take your mother whenever she felt overwhelmed by everything on the ranch, including raising five robust sons."

"Up by the falls?'

"Yes, where you and your mother also spent a lot of time. Many years ago, your mother said she would love to be buried in that peaceful spot. I shut her down and didn't want to listen to her talking about matters of death. Little did I know that she was preparing me for whatever was to come. She was so full of life, and it never once crossed my mind that I wouldn't get to spend the rest of my days with her."

"So, Dad, you want me to take you up the hill for a picnic?" There was laughter in Quin's eyes. "We haven't done that in a long time."

"Me? Of course, no! I stopped going on picnics when your mother died."

"But Dad, I can't go up the hill for a picnic alone."

"I never suggested that you should go up there alone."

"With whom then? One of my brothers or all of us?"

"Kelsey is who I want you to take up there."

"But..."

"You owe her an apology and what better way than to take her on a picnic at your mother's favorite spot?"

OUT OF BREATH

Kelsey raised her hand to knock on the den door and paused midway when she heard Mr. Randolph mentioning her name. She was here to inform Mr. Randolph that she would be leaving on the early morning flight.

"Kelsey has been cooped up here in the workshop and then the house all these days. This would be a good break for her, don't you think? And it will also give you the chance to apologize for being very boorish to her."

"Boorish, dad?"

"Or like a bear with a sore head, take your pick of whatever idiom you want to use. Take a break and go on a picnic with Kelsey. She'll enjoy the fresh air up on the hill."

"But what if she refuses to come with me?"

"You're a man and by now should have learned how to be persuasive enough to get a young lady to listen to you. Taking her up the hill will also give you the chance to show her around the ranch. She's only seen small portions of it, and it's about time that she got to know more of the place."

"I don't know..."

"Stop muttering and quivering like a nervous teenager about to ask a girl out on prom night. Kelsey is a delightful girl and I want to see a smile on her face when you bring her back."

"I'll try."

"That's all I ask."

Kelsey heard a chair scraping the floor and realized that someone was about to come out of the den. She didn't want to be caught eavesdropping, so she tiptoed away and returned to her bedroom. It was clear that Quin's father was trying to push things along. But she'd accepted defeat and didn't want to get humiliated by holding on. There was no way that Quin could ever be attracted to her, and even though he'd accepted to take her on a picnic, Kelsey felt that he was only doing it to please his father. In any case, she'd already booked her ticket out of Dallas early tomorrow morning.

But she'd always wanted to go up the hill and explore. Cindy had warned her that it wasn't safe for her to go out there alone. This was her chance to go up there and then she would take away good memories when she left.

She was brushing her hair when her phone rang. It was Quin and she half smiled because she knew what he was about to ask her.

"Yes?" She made her tone sharp. "Are you calling to shout at me again?"

"Kelsey, I'm sorry," Quin sounded subdued. "It wasn't fair or right for me to shout at you. You were only trying to cheer us up at this time. And may I say that you got both recipes right, just how Mom would have done it."

The words of praise made Kelsey's heart flutter. "So, you tasted the cookies and eggnog?"

"As we speak, I'm in the kitchen devouring whatever my greedy brothers left. And we've fixed the remaining dough and put it in the oven, though I don't know if that batch with come out as good as the ones you made."

"Thank you. You're so kind for saying that. Your mother's recipes are so easy to follow because her instructions are very clear."

"Thank you for giving us that special memory and I wish you would keep the cookbook and use it whenever you want."

"You're welcome." They both fell silent. "You must be busy..." Kelsey started.

"Kelsey, wait. There's another reason that I called you."

"Do you need me to do something in the workshop?" She held back a giggle.

"No, I don't need anything from the workshop, and I happen to know that there's nothing you're working on right now. I realize that apart from the day that you and I went into town to purchase the cream separator, you really haven't had the chance to see much of anything. We've kept you so busy."

"Oh!"

"I'd like to take you out for a ride but that's only if you're willing. Call it a peace offering from me."

"Thank you, I'd love to come."

"You don't ride much around here. Will you be comfortable riding your own horse or should we use one?"

"I'd like to ride on my own," Kelsey said, heart beating very fast. "I actually know how to ride, but as you say, we've been rather busy these past few days and I haven't had the chance to take a horse out."

"That's wonderful then. I know that you're from Denver, the city of many things but ranches. I didn't think there were any ranches or large farms out there."

"There are a few but that's not where I learned how to ride," Kelsey was smiling. "I've always loved horses and been fascinated by them. Whenever I had the time, I would beg my mother to take me and my sisters to a stud farm that wasn't too far from our house."

"Kelsey, do you realize that this is the first time you're mentioning your family to me?"

"We've never had the chance to talk about anything else except work," she answered.

"That's true," Quin admitted. "Why don't you get ready and meet me at the front of the house in an hour's time?'

"I'll be there in fifteen minutes," Kelsey said, feeling the excitement flowing through her. She couldn't believe that she was going to spend the day with Quin.

And just as she'd promised, she was standing outside the front door with two minutes to spare from her fifteen.

Quin stood a few feet away holding the reins of two saddled horses. The larger one, a black stallion had a wicker basket tied to its rump. Kelsey's lips twitched in amusement, and she wondered what Quin had prepared for their picnic. He must have done things in haste, and she didn't expect much.

It's the thought that counts, she told herself.

"Are you ready?" Quin called out as he studied her. She had on one of her usual dungarees but this one was made from denim material. Her bright red blouse made it the more attractive, he thought. Her hair was caught up in a ponytail, and as she walked toward him, their gazes locked on each other.

Kelsey broke the gaze first and looked down at Quin's boots. "I'm afraid I don't have cowgirl boots, though I've been meaning to get myself a pair. I would have borrowed Cindy's, but she wears a smaller size," she was blabbering like an idiot and her face brightened.

"You look fine to me," Quin said. "When we get back, remind me to take you to Old Matthew the tanner and he'll fit you with a pair." He reached into the wicker basket and pulled out a pretty hat.

"This hat belonged to my Mom," he said. "It will shield you from too much sun."

"Thank you," Kelsey held out a hand for the hat, but Quin dropped the reins and placed it on her head. She looked up at him and suddenly felt shy at his intense gaze.

"You look really beautiful," Quin's voice was husky.

Someone cleared their throat, and their small private moment was lost. It was Maynard, and he swaggered toward them.

"I'm here to help the little lady onto her horse," he announced.

Kelsey giggled when she heard the growl from Quin's throat. Someone was clearly being very territorial.

"Maynard, keep off," Quin warned his brother. "I'm well able to help Kelsey onto her horse," he said, and to prove his point he helped her up and then made sure she was properly seated. "Are you all right?" He asked, ensuring that the saddle was secure and she was comfortable.

"Yes, I am," Kelsey said as she shifted in the saddle. "I hope I'm riding a gentle creature and not a skittish one."

"Black Beauty here is one of the best horses on the ranch. She's gentle and careful, and you'll enjoy riding her."

Kelsey patted the horse's neck gently and murmured soothingly, reassuring the mare that she would be a considerate rider. The horse neighed softly as if she understood whatever Kelsey was telling her, and Quin grinned.

"Black Beauty already likes you."

"She's adorable, and I like her too."

Quin walked up to his own horse and easily got on.

"If you two wait for me I can quickly saddle a horse and come with you," Maynard said.

"You have work to do right here on the ranch," Quin glowered at his brother. "Hop to it."

"Please, I'd like to come with you."

"Maynard, would you go away, please?" Quin was very cross. What was his brother up to now? Kelsey was about to say something when she caught the gleam in Maynard's eyes. Clearly, he was teasing Quin, who wasn't getting it.

"All I want is to spend some quality time with my favorite brother and his beautiful companion," Maynard sounded like a child who was about to throw a tantrum.

Quin raised his voice and called out. "Dad, didn't you say that you needed Maynard for something?"

Their father came into view. "Maynard, to heel," he barked but he was grinning broadly.

"Aw, Pops!"

"You're not too old nor too big for me to turn you over my knee."

Maynard winked at Kelsey before stomping off like a temperamental child. Kelsey burst out laughing.

"What is it now?"

"You've got to stop being such easy prey for your brothers, Quin. You're so rigid and serious all the time that you never realize when your brothers are teasing you," she said.

"Oh!" Quin's face turned red, much to Kelsey's delight. So, the man could be demure!

"Shall we leave before another one of your brothers decides to abscond from his duties and grace us with his unwanted presence?"

BURSTING FORTH

*U*sually when Quin made trips up the hill, it was more for work than anything else, and he always avoided this particular route they were taking today. During his childhood years he and his mother had taken long rides up this path together. She would take him deep into the forest, pointing out various plants to him. That's how he'd learned which ones had medicinal properties and which ones were poisonous. He, in turn, had done the same for his brothers so they would stay safe all the time, especially while they were out in the forest.

"Quin, you're my first born and that makes you very special to me," she'd told him on their last ride together just a few days before the tragic accident that had taken her life. *"Make no mistake, I love all my five sons equally but in a mother's heart is a special place for the child that opens the matrix."*

Kelsey noticed that Quin had fallen silent. They were riding side by side on the wide path that even a truck could pass over. She was shocked to see tears on his cheeks. Much as she wanted to speak, she knew that he was caught up in a very private moment.

They rode for a while, then entered the small forest that was visible from the house. The horses were surefooted and picked their way carefully up the stony trail. The trail led to a small waterfall, and Quin wiped his face with his hanky.

He suddenly felt eager to show Kelsey the falls, which they had named Barbara Falls in honor of their mother. He'd spent many hours out there with his mother, diving into the waters below from the top of the falls. It wasn't a long drop, and he missed those days. His mother had taught him to swim, and he'd taught his brothers. All his life he'd taken his firstborn duties very seriously.

As they rode up the hill and emerged from the forest to a landscape with shorter shrubs, Kelsey smiled. "This is really beautiful," she said as she stopped her horse and looked toward the valley below. "The first day I came here and stood on the brow of the hill where you found me, I thought Randolph Ranch looked like a small town."

"It used to be a barracks and my great, great grandfather kept it exactly the same. The only improvements we've done over the years have been expansion to the house and the barns as our herds grew. My grandfather told me that there used to even be a fully functioning post office on the ranch, but that was shut down."

"If it was a barracks no doubt it had housed hundreds of soldiers."

"Those barns used to be the soldiers' sleeping quarters. Remind me to show you a book written by someone years ago on the history of the barracks at the time."

Kelsey remembered Cindy telling her about the property.

"Roughly how many staff work on the ranch?"

"We employ sixty fulltime cowboys who live in those houses over there," Quin indicated an area which had neat picket-fenced houses. He handed her a pair of binoculars, and she was able to see things more closely. She saw a woman hanging out her laundry while another was washing her car. There were children running around. She could see the general store that served the ranch families, and someone was offloading goods and carrying them inside.

"It looks so homey and peaceful," she lowered the binoculars. "What about the other staff?"

"During branding and culling seasons, we also take in about thirty to fifty casual laborers. The exercise takes about a week or two, depending on the weather, so we turn one of the barns into sleeping quarters for the casuals who need accommodation. But since most of them come from around here we only need to provide for their meals."

"This is like a small town. Don't you think you should have maintained the post office to serve all these families?"

"Oh no. These days the mail man delivers all mail for the ranch, and it is sorted out in the office which Kendrick runs." Quin looked around. "Shall we continue with our ride?"

"Yes."

"May I confess something to you?"

"Sure."

He looked slightly guilty, "Well, I may have exaggerated things when I said I wanted to show you around the ranch."

"Really? Then where are you taking me?" Kelsey wasn't at all concerned. Spending time with Quin was like a dream come true. She couldn't believe that, even if it would be only for a brief moment, she would have him to herself.

"I'm taking you to my mom's special spot. It's close to a small waterfall, and she loved coming out here. Sometimes she would bring all of us out here and we would swim while Mom caught trout, which we then roasted over an open fire. Once in a while we would camp for a whole day and night. She always said that we needed to learn how to live off the land in case we ever got lost in the wilderness."

"She was a wise woman."

"That she really was," Quin said.

Kelsey looked around and noticed that she could no longer see the homestead. Instead, she noticed what seemed to be hundreds of black rocks in the distance. Quin noticed where her gaze was trained.

"Those are some of our animals."

"Oh!" Kelsey felt slightly foolish. "They're lying so still, for a moment I thought they were rocks."

Quin threw his head back and laughed. "Those are just our fat and lazy Angus cattle. They eat so much and lie around a lot."

"Why did you choose to breed the Angus specifically? I noticed the few dairy cows are also very black."

"Their meat is very tender and good for barbecuing. And the milk is very creamy. Mrs. Brian is able to make a lot of butter for sale. Many restaurants prefer the meat and milk from Angus cattle."

"I know that the dairy part of the ranch has nearly one hundred cows. And I noticed many calves too, but I haven't seen the steers."

"We have different paddocks around the ranch."

"Are you able to tell how many animals you have on the ranch at any given time?"

Quin nodded, "Down to the last calf and foal that dropped last night," he said confidently.

"That's quite a feat."

"We have roughly ten thousand steers, two hundred dairy cattle and fifty quarter horses."

"No wonder you need so many people to handle them."

"Our outfit is small if you compare it to some of the other ranches in Texas."

"Really?"

"Oh yes. One day I'll take you to visit King Ranch. It's the largest ranch in the United States of America, and they keep about thirty-five thousand cattle or thereabouts. When I was still in school, we visited the King Ranch. A good portion of the school tour was done by helicopter. Before that, I used to think that ours was the largest ranch in the world," Quin laughed at his childish ignorance. "I came away feeling very humbled."

"I never realized that ranches can be very huge."

"Because of the large numbers of animals kept on ranches, most of them grow their own fodder. We also grow our own corn and wheat for local consumption and sell off the surplus. We've separated the herd into four groups."

"Why? Doesn't that make the workload too much?"

"Even though it's much work, doing that protects the herd in case of a disease outbreak. We always say that even in the worst-case scenario, at least one herd out of the four will survive and we can then build up our stock again."

"Have there been any disasters where you lost many animals?"

Quin nodded, "Just three years ago when a terrible tornado hit Dallas. We lost a quarter of our herd but have been able to build it up again. We were lucky that the herds had already been separated or else the losses might have been worse."

Kelsey digested all the information given. She gained new respect for ranchers. It wasn't easy running a successful ranch.

"I feel guilty for taking you away from your work when it's evident that you have so much to do."

"Dear Kelsey, all work and no play makes Quinten a dull and grumpy fellow that no one wants to be around. Besides that, we have enough people covering for me today."

"I feel humbled and honored at the same time."

"Don't be. Coming out here is my way of apologizing to you for being really hard on you these past few days." He recalled his father's words. "I'm sorry for making your stay at Randolph Ranch rather unpleasant."

"Think nothing of it," Kelsey said quickly. "Well, yes, there are times when I feel like tossing a spanner at your head, but then I remember that everyone needs to pull their weight in order for things to run efficiently and effectively on the ranch."

"You're such a generous soul," Quin reined in his horse. "We're here," he announced.

Kelsey was surprised to find that indeed they were on flat ground and the clearing ahead had four picnic tables and benches.

"I haven't been up here in a while," Quin said in a quiet voice and Kelsey turned to look at him. He got off his horse then helped her down. After tethering the horses and giving them enough slack to graze he carried the basket to one of the tables.

"I'm really curious to see what's in that basket," Kelsey said teasingly so as to break the somber mood that had descended on Quin. She sat down at the table. "I'm surprised that these tables are as clean as if they were used just recently."

"There's someone who comes up here every few days to clean up. All the families on the ranch are allowed to use this place for relaxation. My mom had the first tables built, and over the years we've been replacing the worn-out ones. Anyone who needs a break from the ranch down in the valley is free to come up here for times of refreshing. Waylen is a scout and often gathers the little boys on the ranch and brings them camping."

Quin took his place on the bench next to Kelsey instead of sitting across from her. "Kelsey, there's something I've been wanting to say to you from the moment I first saw you," he turned to face her. "You remind me so much of my mother."

"How is that?" Kelsey felt both honored and humbled.

"Mom was a tough and strong woman who never let anything hold her back. She would have loved you."

"You really miss her, don't you?"

Quin nodded, "So much," his voice broke, and Kelsey put her arms around him. A deep groan and sob broke out from his lips, and he wrapped his arms around her, holding on as if for dear life. They stayed that way for a long time as Quin finally allowed the tears to fall. Fourteen years of holding back and it was as if a dam had burst open. He wept for the loss they had suffered and how his father and brothers still lived with the pain. He wept because his children would never get to know the wonderful woman his mother had been. He wept for all the good times that he'd enjoyed with his mother. He wept until he felt completely drained.

Kelsey rubbed his back from time to time, murmuring soothing words of comfort. He was trembling with emotion, and she kept repeating that he would be all right. Finally, he calmed down and took a shuddering breath. "Quin, are you all right?"

"Yes," he pulled away and reached into his pocket for his hanky. "Thank you, I really needed that."

"You've never really grieved for your mother, right?"

He shook his head, "Not until now," he admitted. "I was only fifteen when she died, and my father fell apart. I was scared that if I ever allowed myself to cry for my mother, I wouldn't stop. My brothers were scared and all of them looked up to me. I thank God that we have good managers both now and in the past. They handled things very efficiently while I held my family together until my father was strong enough to take over again."

"I'm so sorry for your loss."

"It's never easy but we'll eventually get there," Quin cleared his throat. He reached out a hand and took her chin and raised her face. "You're a very special person, Kelsey, and I'm so glad that you're up here with me."

"I'm happy to be here," she said shyly.

Quin reached into the basket and pulled out a large loaf of freshly baked bread. Next a chunk of ham followed as well as lemonade in cans and fresh red apples. Finally, he brought out the plates and cutlery.

"There's a tap by that tree," he pointed in one direction. "We need to wash up; then we can have our picnic." He winked at her as he waved his hands dramatically over the table he'd just set. "What do you have to say now, young lady? Still doubting me?"

"My hero," Kelsey placed a hand over her heart. "At least there's no risk of me starving today."

"I would never let my woman starve," Quin found himself saying and Kelsey blushed. Quin was delighted that she was so shy.

After washing their hands in turns, they dug into their food and ate in silence for a while. Then he turned to her. "What about your family? Are your parents still alive and do you have any siblings?"

"Yes, both parents still alive and living in Denver. I also have two sisters, Tina and Jeannie who recently joined Stanford. But for now, they're at home because of the Christmas break."

"Brains run in the family," Quin said.

"Try telling that to my father," Kelsey scoffed. She looked at Quin. "My father believes that women are only good as wives, mothers, housekeepers and cooks."

"Ouch!" Quin raised both hands in surrender. "I'm sorry I ever said those words to you. Trust me when I say that I must have been out of my mind that day because I believe in a woman being able to achieve whatever she sets her mind on. My mother taught me that."

"Are you sure you're not just saying this to please me?"

"My mother was so strong as I told you before and she proved to us time and time again that a woman can be as good as a man. Do you know that my mother once flew the ranch helicopter to rush my father to hospital? And she didn't have a pilot's license at the time."

"What?"

"Oh yes. Our regular pilot was away on some errand and dad got badly injured as he was branding calves. Mama refused to wait for an ambulance. She had us strap dad onto a stretcher and we carried him to the helicopter. We loaded him on, and she took Callum along to watch him. Then she made my father instruct her on what to do until they finally touched down at Cedar Hill Hospital. Needless to say, Mama got her pilot's license to fly helicopters and light planes soon after. My father honored her by ensuring that by the time each of us turned eighteen we not only learned how to drive cars and trucks, but we also got our pilots' licenses as well."

"You're forgiven then," Kelsey said, feeling glad that this man she had fallen in love with respected and honored women.

Then she gave a start and resignedly accepted that she was indeed in love with Quinten Randolph.

TAMING THE STALLION

Kelsey found herself having a wonderful time with Quin. He was so easy to talk to and she didn't feel judged at all when she poured her heart out to him.

"I had to leave home or go crazy," she said as she helped him pack the plates and cutlery back into the basket once they were done with their simple meal. "My father was bent on getting me married to one of his cronies. Some power couples thing," she shuddered. "I wasn't going to let myself be used in that way."

"That seems to be the norm in American now," Quin said. "Wealth attracts wealth, and families hope to make such unions for their personal benefit."

"What do you feel about such unions?" She really needed to know.

"Your father was only looking out for you, I guess."

"No, I don't believe that. It was to fulfill his own interests that my father tried to get me married to one of his friends or acquaintances. The men my father introduced me to were either domineering and tyrannical like he was, or else they had sycophantic tendencies and practically prostrated themselves before the mighty Jonathan Brooke."

"Wait, are you telling me that your father is the Jonathan Brooke of Jobro Oil and Gas?"

"I can see that you know of him," Kelsey didn't know what to make of all this. "Everyone knows about Jobro Oil and Gas, how the owner was a man who dropped out of college because he couldn't raise the fees. How he started working at a gas station filling people's cars. Then he scrimped and saved, buying shares and stocks and it seemed as if he had the touch of gold. Within ten years he had his own gas stations all over Denver and beyond and now he's counted as one of the wealthiest oil barons in America. Is that your father?"

"Yes," Kelsey said in a quiet voice. "That is my father."

"I read about him and found out that he has a very high IQ. No wonder his daughters take after him."

"No, I like to believe that I got my brains from my mother. You see, she's a neurosurgeon but not a practicing one."

Quin looked confused. "Why wouldn't your mother be practicing her career? The world needs all the neurosurgeons we can get. That is so much skill lying dormant when the world needs it."

Kelsey gave him a sad smile. "My father made Mom give up her dreams and career for motherhood and to be his trophy wife. Well, he let her work until my small sister turned five. Imagine, sixteen years of studying and four of being a fully-fledged neurosurgeon all down the drain just like that. Instead, he turned her into a housewife."

Quin placed a gentle hand on Kelsey's arm. "I feel your frustration," he said. "Maybe now that you've all left home she can return to her career?"

Kelsey shook her head, "Over the years my father's domineering attitude and manipulative ways have eroded Mom's confidence. She has remained subservient to him and is the reason I lived at home until recently when I came to Texas."

"Please tell me that he wasn't physically abusive towards her."

"No, he believes that he's too much of a gentleman to hit a woman. But it's the emotional and psychological abuse that worked for him. And denying my mother the chance to work and do what she loves so much is what crushed her. That's the kind of man my father is and why I had to stay at home and protect my mother and sisters."

"You're a strong woman, and you'll be surprised to find that your mother is too. Some women lie low just so they can bring their children up. Then when the last one leaves home, she rises up and takes over."

Kelsey tilted her head to one side. "I would never stay in an abusive marriage, not even for my children's sake. Seeing my mother going through all my father did made me do the opposite of what he wanted a daughter to be. I decided to follow a different career than one he'd chosen for me."

"What did he want you to become?"

"A teacher of all the things."

"What's wrong with being a teacher?"

"Nothing, if that's what a person's calling is. Mine wasn't. I actually wanted to become a nuclear physicist but didn't get the marks required. So, I settled for my next interest which was mechanical engineering. When I was done with college I trained for a year and became a fire fighter."

"What?" Quin was quite impressed. "You truly are a remarkable woman, Kelsey. How then did you end up working as a mechanic?"

She bit her lower lip, "Over a year ago I got badly injured in a burning building and had to be in the hospital for many weeks. My mother was distraught and devastated, and I promised her that I would never again do anything so dangerous. My father, of course, was happy to say, 'I told you so,' and that only made me the more determined to prove him wrong."

"It sounds to me like you're still very angry with your father."

"I am," Kelsey decided to be very honest. "That's why I'll never agree to become the wife of a man who doesn't respect and honor women. I saw what it did to my mother, and I can't live through such pain."

"People can change, Kelsey. Or don't you believe that your father can become a better man?"

Kelsey snorted, a very unladylike sound, then quickly apologized. Quin laughed. "You needed to hear my mother when she was fed up with someone or something. Her words would make your hair stand on end and even if she didn't use bad vocabulary, she had big words that always hit the mark."

Kelsey was laughing, "I can imagine the five of you getting into all kinds of mischief."

"One time we decided to play with empty oil barrels. So, Waylen, Maynard and I stuffed Kendrick and Callum in empty barrels and rolled them down the hill. The boys were having fun until one barrel went rogue, hit a rock and went flying in the air. By the time it landed Callum was concussed."

"Oh no!"

"Let's just say that the five of us didn't sit down comfortably for a week."

"Even Callum?"

"Yes. Mama said he willingly allowed himself to get injured because he was a participant in the sport. We were called miscreants, and Mama said she wasn't going to raise delinquents."

"What did your father say or do?"

"Dad has always been the mild-mannered one, and he always left matters of discipline for Mom to handle. And boy, did she take her responsibilities seriously!"

"But she was a very loving mother, or else you wouldn't have turned out to be the man you are right now."

"Your father in his own way did a good job too."

Kelsey pursed her lips, "When it comes to my father, let's just say that I gave up hoping for any change in him years ago. He's a lost cause. While it's true that he came from very humble beginnings, he's become someone who looks down on those who are struggling in life, as if he wasn't once like them."

"Kelsey, you've got to give your father a break. Don't you believe the Lord when He promises to save us and our households?" She remained silent and he was encouraged to go on. "It's never over until one is in the grave. We sing the hymn that says, *'The vilest offender, who truly believes, that moment a pardon from Jesus receives.'* And I believe with my whole heart that if Saul of Tarsus could have an encounter with Jesus and be changed on the road to Damascus, then anyone else can too. For God so loved the world that He gave His only begotten Son, that whosoever believeth in Him should not perish but have eternal life."

"It's been so hard to hold onto faith that my father can change."

"I know that, darling, but you're the only children your father has. Your children after you will carry his blood in their veins. If you give up on him then you're also condemning your children and generations after you to be lost forever. When your children one day ask you if their grandfather knew the Lord, what will you tell them? Do you think they'll be happy to hear that you gave up on praying for your father? Sometimes we have to keep pressing on and begging for God to be merciful to our loved ones and snatch them from the jaws of hell. Can you in all honesty tell me that it will rejoice your heart to see your father going to hell because he refused to believe in the Lord Jesus Christ?"

"No," Kelsey said hoarsely. She'd never thought of it like that. Would posterity blame her for giving up on her father and seeing him end up separated from the Lord forever?

"There's a reason that salvation came into your family. Were you the first one to know Christ?"

"No, it was my mom. She got so frustrated in her marriage that she decided to seek for answers and help and thankfully ended up in a good church that has nurtured and strengthened her. She made sure that we went to church every Sunday, and when we were old enough, she preached the Gospel to us, and we accepted Christ. Her salvation is the one thing my father was never able to take away from her. When he realized that her faith was so strong, even during persecution, he began to mock and taunt her. I don't understand why she put up with him all these years."

"She loves him, and her faith is strong. That is what will change your father."

"It will take a miracle, and a great one at that," Kelsey scoffed.

"Anything can happen. I still believe in miracles, and why don't you hope for one this Christmas? The Lord is still in the business of performing miracles for His children whose faith is immovable and unshakeable."

"If the Lord should save my father, I'll be one of the happiest people on earth."

"Then begin to prepare yourself for a miracle—and never give up."

"You're such a wonderful man and thank you for inspiring hope in me. All my life I prayed that my father would love us for who we are. I always felt that if we had been boys then he would have loved us."

"Kelsey," Quin took her hand in both of his. "Your father loves you; I believe that strongly. There's no bad person on earth, only those who've taken the wrong paths. That's why a man can be a murderer and persecutor like Saul of Tarsus one minute and the next he becomes one of the world's greatest apostles. We hear of thieves and other terrible people one day coming face to face with the saving grace of our Lord and their lives then change forever. Nothing is impossible with our God, and I want you to stand on that conviction."

"Thank you for giving me hope."

"Just promise me that you'll continue to pray for your father."

Kelsey nodded. "I will."

"That's all I ask, and I promise to pray with you for as long as it takes." He rose to his feet. "It's getting late, and I need to take you home before Dad sends out a search party."

Kelsey also rose to her feet and took a deep breath. "Quin, wait."

"What is it?"

"I have a confession," she said, looking very serious.

"I hope you're not about to tell me something that will give me a heart attack."

"I don't know, but please hear me out. You won't like what I'm about to tell you, and I start by asking for your forgiveness."

Quin sat back down and pulled her to him. "What is it, Kelsey, you're scaring me."

"I came to Randolph Ranch under false pretenses."

"Explain," Quin seemed to withdraw from her. He folded his arms across his chest.

Kelsey told him everything and didn't leave anything out.

"So, you thought that you would come out here and win my heart and marry me just like that?"

Kelsey nodded, feeling too ashamed to look at him. "I'm so sorry that I got carried away."

Quin observed her for a while, then to her surprise, a chuckle broke out from his lips. "And all this time I've been praying that I would find a way of telling you how I feel about you."

"You're not angry with me?" Kelsey was shocked. It was the last reaction she'd expected from him.

"Why do you think I was always picking on you? You see, I told myself that I would never fall in love, not after I saw what it did to my father after my mother died. When Mom died it was just the grace and mercy of God that preserved my father's life. Even now I know that Dad still lives with so much pain and especially around this time of the year. My parents got married on Christmas Day and then fifteen years later, Mom lost her life on the same day."

"Maynard told me all that."

"That's another one who raises my hackles," Quin muttered.

Kelsey laughed out loudly. "Your brothers know you well and have learned which buttons to push to get you all riled up."

"So, you're saying that there's nothing going on between you and Maynard?"

"He's a good friend, that's all and he did that to tease you."

"And you, little imp, have been having fun at my expense, right?" He pulled her close.

"I, too, had to hide my feelings from you. Cindy warned me on the first day that I arrived that it would be dangerous to fall in love with any of you Randolph men."

"Why?"

"She said your father would give any woman who fell in love with his sons their marching orders."

"But wasn't he the one who brought you here?"

"Still, it's not very encouraging to be falling in love with a man who only sees and treats you like a sister."

"So, are you saying that you love me, Kelsey?"

"I'm in love with you, Quin," Kelsey said. "I felt that I was getting nowhere with you, especially when I saw you with Yvette. And then you started going out and staying till late. I believed that you were with her and didn't want to continue holding onto hope."

"Yvette?" Quin frowned. "You thought that I've been visiting her in the evenings?" Kelsey nodded. "Dear girl, I'm glad it made you jealous, but that's not where I've been spending my evenings."

"Where have you been going?"

"One of the cowboys lost his wife, and he was falling to pieces. She left two sweet daughters and I've been going over to his place to encourage him."

"She died?"

"No, she ran away with some man. A few of us have been going over to his house to encourage him to stay strong. He still loves her and believes that she will return. So, a few of us in the Men's Fellowship at church have been standing with him."

"I hope things work out for him."

"Pedro is a good person and I know the Lord will remember him. He's asked his sister from Mexico to come and help with the children. She's expected any day now."

"Like I said, you're a good man. But when I thought that you were going to see Yvette, it filled me with so much despair. So, this morning after you snapped at me, I gave up completely." She chewed on her lower lip. "I decided to go back home and even booked myself a seat on a red eye flight leaving at two tomorrow morning."

"I feel sorry for that seat."

"Why?"

"It's going to go empty all the way to Denver because there's no way I'm letting you walk out of my life, my darling."

"Oh, Quin!"

"My father was right when he said that we need to make new memories over this season. It's two days to Christmas and the future begins here and now with you, Kelsey."

"I'm just happy that there was nothing going on between you and Yvette."

"Were you jealous?" He teased.

"I just told you I was."

"And I'm so happy to hear that you were jealous because now I know that you love me," he pulled her close and kissed her forehead.

"Now who is rejoicing at my pain?"

"I am," he grinned. "And I love you, so that should make you happy."

"You're a cheeky man."

"As long as my beloved loves me, nothing else matters."

"Your father will be so happy."

"That cunning old fox deserves some good news. This will also be the start of new memories for him. So how about we go home and give him the good news?"

"Can we do it just the two of us, without your brothers being present?"

"But of course."

ABNER DIDN'T HOLD back his tears when his son told him that he'd found the woman of his dreams and fallen in love with her.

"Your Mom would have loved Kelsey," Abner said, weeping unashamedly in the den. "You've both made me so happy today. And to think that I was about to give up. Sending you two up the hill was surely by the unction of the Holy Spirit. You needed to get away and spend time with each other, so what's in your hearts could be revealed."

"Thank you for interfering in my life, Dad," Quin hugged his parent. "You brought this beautiful woman into my life, and I'll love her forever."

"But please let this be our secret," Abner begged. "Let your brothers believe that you and Kelsey fell in love when she came to work at the ranch. You see, I want your brothers to also meet good women and settle down. Sally-Jo did a good job and I'd like to ask for her help to do the same for your brothers. If your brothers get a hint that I had a hand in your meeting, then they'll put up walls as high as the Tower of Pisa."

"Consider it our secret," Quin held Kelsey close.

EPILOGUE

*C*hristmas Day - Early Morning.

The ringing phone startled Kelsey, and she quickly sat up when she saw that it was a new number. She was seated at the kitchen table having some cereal because she was so hungry.

"Yes, who is this?"

"Kelsey, this is your father," the person at the other end said and she fell silent with shock. "Kelsey, are you there my child?"

Her father sounded funny, and she got worried.

"Dad, is Mom all right? Tina and Jeannie?"

Her father chuckled and Kelsey's eyes widened. She needed to be sure that she was talking to her father, so she told him that she wanted to have a video chat with him. He acquiesced and soon they were connected. It was her father all right!

"Dad, you're scaring me," she said.

"I have some people who are rather impatient to talk to you, but I won't let them for now. This is a quick one, girl. We're all coming to you for Christmas."

"Dad, what do you mean by we?"

"Your mother, sisters and I are coming to Dallas. Now the jet is about to take off and that's why I won't let you speak to these chatterboxes of mine." And the phone went dead.

Kelsey sat there staring at her own handset as if she was dreaming.

"What just happened?" She asked out loud. Quin was just walking into the kitchen and heard her.

"Are you now talking to yourself, my love?"

She quickly shared the news with him. "If we hadn't had the video chat, I would have said that someone was impersonating my father."

"I told you that Christmas brings miracles."

THE RANCH CAME to a standstill when four black Hummers drove into the homestead. Kelsey was so excited. From the moment the plane had touched down nearly an hour ago, she'd been on the phone with her sisters. They told her that they were just as surprised at the change in their father.

When the large vehicles stopped, her father emerged from the second one. He turned and held out his hand and her mother also soon came into view. She raised her face upward, and Kelsey could see that her countenance was different.

"Mom, Dad," Kelsey ran to them and for the first time in years, her father hugged her.

"Oh, my child, please forgive me," he said, tears in his eyes. "It's been a long journey, but I'm glad that I've found my family and got them back."

Kelsey looked at her mother who mouthed the word, 'later' to her.

Lunch was prepared by Buck Knerr's wife's restaurant, so Kelsey got the chance to take her mother and sisters to her room. She hoped her father would be fine with Mr. Randolph and his sons.

"Well, Ma, curiosity won't let me wait any longer," she said. "What's going on and what have you done with the man I knew as my father?"

Eleanor Brooke threw her head back and laughed. "Oh child, let's just say that the God we serve still does miracles."

"That's for sure, and Quin said the same thing just two days ago. Now talk."

The four women made themselves comfortable on Kelsey's bed. Then her mother told her story.

"After the three of you left, I decided that I didn't want to go on with the kind of life I was living. So, I marched to your father's office and told him that I wanted a divorce."

"Mom, you didn't," Kelsey's eyes were wide.

"I did. You see, over the years I played it cool because I never wanted my children to feel that they came from a broken home. The good thing was that your father never used physical violence and I let him feel that he was winning. But on that day when I told him I wanted us to go our separate ways, I saw him break down and it shook me."

"Are you sure we're talking about the Mr. Jonathan Brooke that we all know?"

"Yes, Kelsey, one and the same. Let's just say we took three days to talk things over. You see, your father never thought he was good enough for me because he never finished college and I'm a highly qualified and skilled neurosurgeon. He allowed his ego to dictate to him and nearly destroyed our marriage. We came away as different people. We still have a long way to go and are undergoing marital counseling, but I have my husband back, the man I fell in love with twenty-seven years ago."

"Mom, I'm so happy for you."

"And what's going on with you? I expected to hear that you were married by now."

Kelsey told her story, "And Quin loves me," she finished. "He…" Before she could say anything more, her phone rang. It was Quin and he was informing them that lunch was served.

Lunch was a happy affair, and when the plates had been removed and dessert was being served, Quin rose to his feet.

"May I please have everyone's attention?" All eyes turned to him. Quin was nervous as he approached Kelsey's father. "Sir, please allow me to fulfill all righteousness by asking you face to face for your daughter's hand in marriage."

Kelsey's mouth fell open. "Shut your mouth dear," her mother said teasingly. "Are you surprised?" Kelsey nodded. "Your young man called your father last night and told us that he couldn't propose to you before officially asking for your hand in marriage."

"He did?" Kelsey squealed.

"Yes, my dear," her father said. "And I told him that your mother and I wanted to meet with him face to face so we can find out what kind of person he is. We also wanted him to do the asking in your presence just in case you were being coerced or forced into a situation you didn't want."

"Oh Dad!" Kelsey stared at her father. He'd come a long way and it was as if a new man sat in his place. Quin was right, nobody was bad, it was just the paths they chose in this life that made them turn into terrible people. Her father had changed so much.

"Well girl, should I say yes to this young man?"

"Yes, Daddy."

"Do you love him, and do you feel that he'll make you happy all the days of your life?"

"Yes, I believe so," Kelsey's eyes didn't leave Quin's.

"Good. Then, Quinten, you have our blessings," Kelsey saw her father take her mother's hand. "We gladly hand over our daughter to you."

"Thank you, Sir, and I promise to cherish Kelsey all the days of my life."

"We'll expect nothing less from you, Son."

And before their parents and siblings, Quin went down on one knee. Kelsey joined him and when he slipped the ring onto her finger, she finally accepted that miracles still happened on Christmas Day. Her once tyrannical and domineering father now sat holding hands with his wife. He was now a born-again Christian who was ready to make up for all the time he'd lost. And here she was, now engaged to the man of her dreams and who she loved so deeply.

On his part, Quin was thinking about his father's words. *Make new memories on Christmas Day.* And as he held the woman he loved in his arms, he knew that this was a bright new day for all of them. Their future would be filled with wonderful new memories.

"I love you so much, Quin," Kelsey whispered.

"And I love you more, my darling, Kelsey."

And Abner Randolph looked at his eldest son with tears in his eyes. He wholly approved of the young woman who'd changed his son and he knew that were she here, his wife Barbara would have approved too.

Then his eyes slowly drifted towards Waylen, his second born and a thoughtful look entered them. This was a stubborn one too and took so much after Barbara. Finding him a bride was going to take stealth and cunning for he was highly suspicious in nature, like a skittish mare that trusted no one.

Then he smiled as he thought about the conversation he would be having with Sally-Jo the next day when he visited Barbara's grave for his private moment. There was really nothing impossible on this earth, and if he'd gotten Quin to give his heart to a woman and commit to her, Waylen wouldn't be a problem.

"Thank you, Lord," he whispered then turned to join in the merrymaking.

WAYLEN'S UNTAMED PERFECT MATCH

PROLOGUE

"*Mommy, I'll be good. Please come home,*" *the fourteen-year-old boy sat in the rose garden planted just a year ago. His head was on his knees while his lanky hands were wrapped around them. He rocked back and forth, chanting the same words over and over again.*

"*Mommy, I'll be good. Please come home.*" *If only his mom would come back home. She'd been gone since Christmas Day a year ago and he missed her so much. This was all his dad's fault. If dad hadn't taken mom to that place and left her there, she would be back by now. He felt rather than saw the person who came to sit beside him and even without turning around he knew that it was his father.*

"*You took mom away,*' *he whispered painfully.* "*Go and bring my mother back.*"

"*Waylen, my son,*" *Abner reached out a hand towards his son.* "*Please...*"

But the boy jerked away and gave his father a look that nearly broke the man's heart. "Don't touch me, I hate you," the fourteen-year-old shouted. "I want my mommy to come back. Go and bring her back home."

"Waylen, we've talked about this," his father's voice was gentle but firm. "Mommy is in heaven and one day we'll see her again."

"No," Waylen turned a tear-streaked and very red face toward his father. "You took her to that place and she never came back. Go and bring my mother back home."

Abner sighed and bowed his head, feeling deep sadness descending on him. Does it ever get better, he wondered. His wife had been dead for a year now and the pain of losing her only seemed to get worse with each passing year. His five sons were all he had now and he didn't know how he would get through this. They all missed Barbara, but Waylen was his greatest concern.

The boy had withdrawn into himself and the past year had been very tough for Abner as his sons struggled to come to terms with their mother's untimely and tragic death. Barbara had fallen off her horse on Christmas Day while riding to visit her friend and she'd lain in the ditch for hours before Quinten, their oldest son, found her. Barbara had breathed her last in Quinten's arms and it was as if he was the only one who got to say goodbye to his mother.

The other boys were still in denial, and Abner tried as much as he could to tell them about death, but lately he'd been feeling overwhelmed. At least his sons had him to comfort them; that's when he wasn't completely drained. But who was there for him? This past year had been terrible, and he was only beginning to stand on his feet once again. The guilt of having left his oldest son, Quin, to take care of his siblings and ensure the household was running ate at him.

"Thank You, Lord, for Mrs. Brian, his housekeeper and the woman who'd taken care of his sons during his darkest hours. Quin had even had to learn how to drive at fifteen so he could drop his siblings off at school, and it was just the mercies of God that not once had he been pulled over by the cops. Perhaps it was because he was a Randolph, or even his physique at fifteen had been that of an eighteen-year-old.

In any case, Quin and Mrs. Brian had held the fort at home while the estate manager had ensured that the ranch didn't crumble to the dust. Still, things had been really tough for his sons during the first few years after losing their mother, and Abner acknowledged that. Hardly a week went by than Abner had to go to school to sort out one issue or another. Either it was Quinten, his eldest, talking back at the teacher or Waylen sitting motionless in class, reacting to nothing at all. Or it was Kendrick beating up another student. Or Maynard and Callen playing tricks on teachers and students alike. His sons seemed to be out of control, and he felt overwhelmed. If only Barbara was here, she would know what to do.

But now he had to deal with his most sensitive son. "Len, I don't know what else to say to ease your pain." Waylen turned his head slightly and saw tears pouring down his father's face, which didn't surprise the fourteen-year-old. This past year he'd seen his father weeping so many times; sometimes openly, others secretly. He felt deep shame for lashing out at his father and felt that his mother would be disappointed in him.

"I miss her so much," he sobbed. This time did not resist when his father reached out and pulled him into his arms.

"I know son," Abner choked up, holding his son close.

IN SEARCH OF ADVENTURE

It was the last day before school broke for summer holidays. Twenty-four-year-old Hazel Singer groaned as she rolled over in bed. Everyone called her odd because unlike everyone else who was looking forward to the long holiday ahead, Hazel was lamenting that there would be ninety days of nothingness. It was the same every year, ninety days of boredom unless she had a holiday planned, which wasn't that often. Hazel hated it when school closed for the long holidays.

It wasn't that she had no family to go to. Her mother begged her to visit them in Boston every year, but Hazel always came up with different reasons not to go. She loved her mother but couldn't stand her stepfather and his four children, all of whom were younger than she was.

Hazel's father had died in a road accident when she was in her first year of college. She'd loved her father so much that the first year had been tough, but her mother had been there for her. She'd even considered deferring a full year of college but her mother refused to allow her to do that and encouraged her to carry on with her studies.

"Your father would want you to get your degree," her mother had said. "He was very proud when you made it to college, and to honor him, you need to complete your degree within the normal time. Deferring may create a vacuum in your life, and then you'll find that you don't want to go back again. Please my daughter, do this for me and stay in college."

Her mother's words had made much sense to her, and she promised to return to school. Those were the days that they would huddle together on their large couch looking at photos of her father. They would talk late into the night just remembering him, sometimes laughing, and other times weeping for their deep loss.

In the second year of college Hazel began to notice changes in her mother. For one, she put off wearing dark clothes or 'widows' garb,' as she referred to them. She also got herself a job at a law firm despite Hazel's father having left them comfortably off. Not many months later, she announced that she was in love with her widowed boss, and he had asked her to marry him.

Hazel was livid. She couldn't understand how and why her mother had moved on so quickly. For a long time she'd even refused to meet Mr. James Webster, her stepfather. When she finally did, she'd thought he was condescending because he always seemed to mock her for having chosen teaching as a career. Mr. Webster always had negative comments about teachers and it really angered her, though for her mother's sake she always kept silent. His own offspring were in college or high school. All of them had chosen different engineering fields and, like their father, looked down on Hazel's career, which they termed lowly and inconsequential. To get back at them, Hazel refused to take part in any of their family activities, always feeling like an outsider.

In the end, because she noticed that the ensuing tension was taking its toll on her mother, she chose to stay away. After her marriage to Mr. Webster, her mother moved into his house. Hazel found herself a small apartment as their house was put up for sale.

And that was how it had been ever since. She missed her mother but couldn't stand the arrogance her stepsiblings portrayed, feeling that they were better than she was. And the few times she'd visited her mother in her new home had been wasted, according to her. Her mother's new family didn't allow them time together, for either it was her stepfather demanding his wife's attention or else it was the children wanting Hazel's mother all to themselves and pushing her away.

Her cellphone rang, and when she picked it up to check who the caller was, she groaned out loud even as she received the call. "Hazel?"

"Good morning, Mom." Hazel forced herself to get out of bed, tucked her phone between her right shoulder and cheek as she quickly made her bed.

"I know you're closing today and was hoping you would come and visit us since it's such a long holiday. We all miss you so much and your stepfather and siblings have been asking about you." Hazel rolled her eyes because she doubted that her mother's family were sincere in their sentiments toward her. But she made her voice pleasant so as not to offend her mother.

"Mom, you have a good memory," Hazel moved to her wardrobe to pick out her clothes for the day.

"Not really, I've been counting the days until schools closed. Your father..."

"Stepfather, Mom" Hazel pointed out as she chose a long flared black skirt and a lilac chiffon top. She liked dressing simply because her middle school darlings were a very active and boisterous lot, all thirty of them. Yet even with all their childish cheekiness, she loved each and every one of them and wasn't averse to frolicking about with them. They were her world and made her job very fulfilling. It always amused her when some of them asked her to marry their fathers so that she would become their mommy.

Quite a number of the fathers in her school were young, handsome, rich and nice people. It saddened her that the statistics showed that many of the students in her school came from broken homes. Others had lost one parent or the other and some even both parents. She rarely had any issues with the female parents who were busy trying to balance their families with their careers. It was the fathers who sometimes made her wish she could hide. Hazel wasn't in love with any of them. It wasn't that she was against marriage; far from it! Hazel believed that out there was a man who was just right and perfect for her. He would be godly, responsible and yet fun loving too. A well balanced man who would never see her rising star as a threat to his own ego. She'd seen a few of her colleagues' marriages head for the rocks when the women decided to pursue further education and rise in their careers. That wasn't what she wanted for herself and she often felt that the wealthy men especially, only wanted trophy wives. She wasn't anyone's trophy to collect, no Sir!

"Hazel!"

"Sorry, Mom, please can we speak later? I have to get going now," she said. "I need to get to school early today because there's so much to do as we break for the long holidays."

"Please say you'll visit us," her mother begged. Hazel hated it when she did that for then she would feel pressured into accepting the invitation and they would all end up being miserable.

So, she hardened her heart, "Mommy dearest, can we please not do this right now? I have to go."

"Only for a few days."

Hazel sighed inwardly, "Mom, I can't promise, but I'll see what I can do."

"It would make me so happy if you come. I love you."

"I love you too, Mom. Now I really have to go," and before her mother could say anything else Hazel ended the call.

Then she sat down at the dressing table and sighed. She knew that her reluctance to go to Boston made her mother sad, but she didn't like all the pretense that went into her being in her mother's home. The strain was too much, and the last time she'd been there, her stepfather had even invited a couple of young men and introduced them to her. Stiff necks was what she'd thought of them, men whose idea of having a wife was one who bowed to their every whim.

Hazel shuddered as she thought about becoming a man's doormat, to be controlled and never listened to. One of her colleagues had to quit teaching because her husband and his mother had insisted on her being a stay-at-home mother. Kendra was frustrated and the last time Hazel had seen her, the once-vibrant woman had been bitter and angry.

"That will never be my portion," Hazel muttered as she completed her grooming, picked up her bag and walked to the door. She loved her one-bedroom apartment because it was all hers and she didn't have to share it with anyone. As she locked the door, she waved to her next-door neighbor, a middle-aged woman who liked to tattle. Before Mrs. Chandler could get into one of her long narratives, Hazel dashed away, preferring to take the stairs because then she wouldn't have to share the lift with her nosy neighbor.

All through the day as she helped the children with their final school projects, her mind was on the days ahead. What was she going to do with herself for three whole months?

Hazel repeated her thoughts to her good friend Sally Jo later that afternoon when she passed her office. She placed a large bag of goodies on Sally Jo's desk. "I come bearing gifts so go ahead and enjoy." She walked to the large windows that overlooked the park. Sally Jo really had a beautiful view of Denver City.

Sally Jo didn't waste any time and dug her hand into the bag. She pulled out a box of very expensive chocolates. "Oh wow! These are really fancy."

"Mr. Foster of Foster Investments sends me a box every two weeks or so," Hazel made a face. "The man doesn't believe that a woman can reject his advances. His twin daughters are so adorable, but I'm not about to become their third stepmother in four years," she shuddered. "Honestly Sally Jo, why is it that marriages don't last these days?"

"For one, there's what I call lack of commitment to run the course of the marriage. Social media, the Internet and television have made marriage look like it's easy work and people blindly stumble into the institution hoping for happily ever after," she sighed. "Then challenges arise and the people begin to tell each other and themselves that they made a mistake. If you ask me, many marriages could be saved if only people would grow up and realize that it takes commitment and perseverance to have a wonderful marriage. Life has ups and downs and in between, and if couples are willing to deal with the different seasons of their marriages while working together and not against each other, eventually they get the happily ever after they seek. But sadly, most only last a year or so before the cracks begin to show in their blissful union, and rather than patching them up, they decide to call it quits."

"Makes much sense to me," Hazel agreed. "I feel really sorry for the little ones in such unions because they suffer the most when their homes break up. I see a number of my students facing such tough times, and it breaks my heart. Many of them come from very wealthy families but they rarely see their parents. The husbands and sometimes wives are high-profile, career-minded people, so it's the nannies who take care of the children. I'll never have children unless I'm ready to be a full-time mother."

"So, at some point in your life you'll resign and become a stay-at-home mom or something?"

"Well, for a while until my children are old enough to go to school. That's why I'm praying that when the time comes, I'll have my three children within four or five years so I can bring them up together and then once they start school I can then go back to work."

"I pray the best for you but sometimes it's tough for women when they lose their husbands either through divorce or death. They have to become the breadwinners and so they have to rely on nannies to help with the children. Not all women like to leave their children for others to raise, but situations force them into that."

"I hear you and I'm sorry for sounding so pompous and sanctimonious. I have a couple of single mothers who are really doing a good job with their little ones. One even took a lower paying job and had to really cut down on her family expenses just to be there for her children."

"Why?"

"She's a surgeon and the long hours meant that she was always away from her children. After her husband passed away she decided that having all the money in the world and ruined children wasn't worth it. So she took a position that pays so much less but she's always there for her children. In fact, this past year she's been the class parent for my class, and we've had so much fun. The woman knows how to organize class functions and trips and she gets along with everyone. I wish all parents could be like her. Mrs. Granger is very cooperative and her children are really doing well."

"She's one of the exemplary ones," Sally Jo bit into a fat chocolate. "These are really world class."

"Just be careful not to ruin your teeth. At some point I had to stop consuming those goodies because of all the sugar," Hazel sat down on the couch. "Can I get a coffee from this office? I'd love a very milky and frothy cappuccino right now with two sugars."

Sally Jo nodded, "I'll ask my assistant to step out and get us some coffee from Starbucks. Our coffeemaker decided to take a break on us and I haven't had time to find another one to replace it." She made a call to her assistant and placed the order for coffee. "Hazel, what will you do with yourself for ninety whole days? Or have you planned a trip somewhere?" She pushed the box of chocolates aside and found an apple in the bag. "I hope this is clean," Hazel nodded and Sally Jo happily bit into the fruit. "Much better and healthier," she pronounced. "So, ninety days of doing nothing with yourself, huh?"

Hazel thought about her mother's invitation but that wasn't something she was considering doing. "I don't know whether to consider them as ninety days or so of pure and utter bliss or of terrible boredom." Hazel kicked her pumps off and stretched out on the long couch. "I could lie here forever."

"Woman, I hope you realize this is my office and a place of business, not a health spa," Sally Jo said in mock anger. "I know that the holidays have begun for you but not all of us are that lucky."

"It's not like anyone is likely to walk in," Hazel said dismissively. "Many people are still working and communicating remotely because of the Corona virus. I know that your clients are no exception. Instead of offering me a drink, here you are glaring at me."

Sally Jo laughed, "Dear Girl, Linda will soon bring you some coffee. But I must say that you, Hazel Singer are actually a sight for sore eyes. I've been going out of my mind and talking to myself. Most of my staff, my assistant included, decided to work from home and only come in twice a week. I'm actually lucky that Linda came in today or else we would have had to go out and get the coffee ourselves. I pray that everything will soon go back to normal and we can return to working five days a week as before."

"For now, why don't you also work from home then? If most of your clients are online then you can work from anywhere."

"I did work from home when everyone else was doing so. Now that the world is opening up again, things have to get back to normal, and one or two clients have started dropping in. So someone has to be here at all times."

"I hear you," Hazel said. "I was so happy when school resumed after the long period of being on lockdown. Sitting at home wasn't fun at all and it gave my Mom the best reason to keep asking me to visit them in Boston."

Sally Jo looked at her in surprise. "Are the two of you still at it? I recall how it used to be when we were in college and your mom would keep calling and begging you to go home."

Hazel sighed, "I love my mom and miss her a lot when we're away from each other. It's her family that I can't deal with."

"Hazel, as long as your mother is happy and her new family fulfills her, let her be. At some point you're going to have to accept them."

Hazel sat up, then rose to her feet as Linda walked in with their coffees. They both thanked her and Hazel carried hers back to the couch. "Don't get me wrong, Sally Jo. I know Mr. Webster and his offspring make my mom happy. But I'm no longer a child to be tugged along to their family functions all the time. What makes matters worse is that Mr. Webster always asks me when I'll be bringing a man back home," she clicked with her tongue. "The last time I was there he brought by some two gentlemen and introduced them to me. Those men pestered me so much on the phone that I had to block their numbers. I don't know why my stepfather doesn't understand that it's not every woman in the world who just lives for marriage alone. Some of us want to do great things with our lives before we take that step."

Sally Jo rested her elbows on her desk and leaned forward. "Is it that you're averse to marriage or something?"

Hazel blew over her coffee, then took a sip. She licked her lips in appreciation of the tasty coffee. "I believe that one day I'll eventually fall in love and get married. Believe me, this term alone I received three whole proposals from the fathers of my students. And of course, Mr. Foster's standing proposal which always comes with the chocolates."

"Didn't any of them catch your eye?"

Hazel shook her head, "They're all very wonderful men, and I see it from the way they're prepared to do anything for their children. But I feel that something is missing. What if all that those gentlemen are looking for is someone to mother their children?"

"Like you say your stepfather did to your mother?"

"Exactly! All Mr. Webster wanted was a mother for his children and my poor mother thought that she'd found true love again."

"Hazel," Sally Jo's voice was gentle. "Not every widower with children is simply looking for a woman to replace their mother. Some are genuinely in love and the rest follows."

"I'm yet to be convinced of that. But enough of the story of my life and my family. I have ninety whole days of doing nothing. Before Covid invaded our lives, a couple of us at school had planned on visiting Thailand. Sadly, we've put paid to that holiday because it doesn't feel safe anymore," she looked around the office. "Maybe I should come and work for you," she grinned at her friend. "The Corona virus didn't stop your cowboys and cowgirls from looking for love now, did it?"

"Far from it. You wouldn't believe it but these past two years have seen Hitch Your Wagon Romance Agency gaining so many new clients. People took to Internet dating with much gusto and I'm very thankful to the Lord for that."

"Truly the Word of God can be trusted. He giveth His beloved food even in famine. While the world was groaning under economic uncertainties, firms like yours were growing."

"Glory be to Jesus," Sally Jo raised her hands in the air. "But we still faced many challenges with our clients. Honestly, some of them are really difficult to please."

"Really? I've never known you to be fazed by anything, Sally Jo. You're one of those people I say have conquered the world and still going strong."

"Thank you for the compliment but be that as it may, once in a while I get very odd clients. You see, I have this really nice client in Texas who has five sons and he loves them all very much. But the young men are averse to marriage and that's a matter of great concern to their father. He even calls them his wild sons."

Hazel frowned slightly, "Wild as in being involved in debauchery and wanton living, doing drugs and abusing alcohol?"

Sally Jo shook her head, "Far from it. The Randolph boys are all gentlemen. They're all born again and respect women very much. Yet no one will mention anything like marriage to them and get a positive response. Their father refers to them as wild because no woman has as yet tamed them, well apart from the first son. Last Christmas, by the grace of God, I managed to get him a really lovely woman to marry."

"That sounds interesting. Wild men that need taming, huh!"

"It is interesting, especially given that Quin had no idea that his father was setting him up. The ranch advertised for a mechanic and by chance one of my clients was a mechanic. Mr. Randolph immediately gave her the position and she went to Texas. The ranch is on the outskirts of Dallas, and the area is referred to as Cedar Hill. Kelsey was perfect for Quin and they got married and are really happy. Now Mr. Randolph wants me to get his second son married as well."

"That shouldn't be too hard now," Hazel said in an encouraging tone. "If the young man is anything like his older brother, it should be smooth sailing for you since you're acquainted with the family. What?" She asked laughingly as Sally Jo shook her head. "Most siblings behave in almost the same way especially when it comes to matters of the heart. Boys will tend to be attracted to women who are like their mothers while girls look for men who have qualities that their fathers possess. Of course, that's not always the best way to go about it, but such is life."

"That sounds like a stereotype."

"But almost true, nonetheless."

"Well in the case of the Wild Sons of Randolph Ranch, you're way off the mark. Waylen Randolph, the second son, is the total opposite of his brothers. According to the dossier his father sent me, the gentlemen is a perfectionist."

"Pshaw!" Hazel waved a hand dismissively. "There's no such thing as a perfect man."

"I didn't say he's a perfect man, it's just that he's a perfectionist. With this particular gentleman everything has to be just right. Nothing must be out of place or else he'll have a panic attack. According to Mr. Randolph Senior, Waylen drives everyone around him crazy with his taxing and sometimes unreasonable demands. The poor father is worried and in despair because he fears that no woman in her right senses will ever attain to the high standards that Waylen has set for himself and everyone else around him."

"So you're looking for a woman who is also a perfectionist for this man?"

"On the contrary. His father wants me to find a woman who will help tone down Waylen's perfectionism. By the way, this said gentleman wasn't always this way."

"What happened to him?"

"Mr. Randolph, the father told me that Waylen used to be very outgoing and fun loving. But now he's a very rigid and strict man. What's more he never raises his voice, never loses his temper and if there's trouble of any kind, he chooses to walk away rather than face a confrontation. According to his father, Waylen is lucky because his four brothers are always here to defend him or else he would be taken advantage of and bullied mercilessly."

"That dude sounds like a wimp to me."

"No, not a wimp, but a man who's repressed his emotions. Mr. Randolph fears that he's like an active volcano that seems dormant on the outside yet is boiling in the center, just waiting to erupt. Mr. Randolph fears that one day Waylen will erupt and destroy everything around him."

Hazel felt excitement begin to rise up within her. "That sounds like quite a challenging person," she told Sally Jo.

"Well, Mr. Randolph says that Waylen's brothers call him a robot, but of course, behind his back. The old man has been praying that a woman would come into his son's life and shake him out of that condition. Taming the perfectionist is how his father puts it and I feel for the old man. All he wants is for his sons to marry, settle down and give him lots of grandchildren."

"You say Waylen Randolph wasn't born that way? Perhaps people didn't notice that trait before."

Sally Jo shook her head, "According to Mr. Randolph, Waylen used to be playful and cheeky just like his brothers but all this changed and he became whatever he is now after his mother's death."

"That's really sad. It reminds me of those middle school students of mine. Now it's clear that something happened that turned Waylen Randolph into the perfectionist that he is right now.

Sally Jo nodded, "As I mentioned, Mr. Randolph said that the changes in his son were very subtle and he didn't realize whatever was going on because he, too, was grieving the loss of his wife. Things got worse when Waylen went to Stanford. He's a very good lawyer but refused to go into practice at all. Instead he settled to do all the legal work for the ranch, which is quite a waste of his skills. Whenever there's any litigation to be done and court has to be attended, Mr. Randolph gets a lawyer from outside because Waylen will never go before a judge to present a defense or even sue."

"It's really that bad?" Hazel was shocked. This was worse than she'd thought.

Sally Jo sighed deeply, "My only question is, where can I find a woman who will draw Waylen out of his acquired lifestyle and take him back to who he used to be?"

"What qualities does he seek in a wife?"

"Hazel, Waylen has no idea that his father is searching for a wife for him. That's one of the conditions that Mr. Randolph gave when he contracted me to do this job for him. None of his sons should find out that they're being set up for marriage. If they as much as suspect a thing, their emotional walls will go up so high that no one will be able to bring them down again."

"So all you know about this gentleman is what his father has told you?"

"Yes. And I need to find someone who is that total opposite of Waylen."

"If the death of his mother is what led him to being such a perfectionist then don't you think that he needs someone who understands psychology and how to deal with those who have survived trauma? The man is hurting and needs healing before love can take over."

Sally Jo had a hopeful look in her eyes, "Hazel, you sound like you know what this new client is all about. Why don't you go out there now that you have nothing to do for the next ninety days? I happen to know that one of your minor subjects was Child Psychology.""Waylen isn't a child and the knowledge I have may be of no use to him in this situation. How old is he?"

"Twenty-seven, but believe me, dear friend, all human beings retain that childishness in them even when they grow old. I believe that you can use this situation as one of your case studies. Please let me send you out there and tame this man so he can have proper balance of his life."

"Is it really right to take Waylen to be a specimen of research? He would be greatly offended if he ever found out."

"Then we have to make sure that he doesn't find out that he's a case study. Consider this to be my contribution to society. If we can get Waylen to loosen up and return to his old jolly nature, then one day some lucky woman will have him as a husband without her struggling to fit into his perfect life."

"Sounds like an impossible task to do and I don't think I'm the right person. Besides, you find love for cowgirls and cowboys and I'm neither of those things."

"Waylen is a cowboy searching for love even if he doesn't know or acknowledge it yet. No one said cowboys can't marry women who've never lived on a ranch. It's all about adaptation just like in the pioneering days when people left the east to go and settle down in the west. Who knows, you could end up being a cowgirl and settle down in the west."

"In your dreams!"

Sally Jo's eyes narrowed. "Or are you afraid that you'll get there and fall in love with Waylen? Is that your fear?"

Hazel threw her head back and laughed out loud. "No, a thousand times No. There's no way that I can fall in love with your client. But come to think of it, your idea sounds like fun and maybe it's just what I need to keep boredom away for these three months. Will I earn any money?"

"Hazel Singer! You sound so mercenary. Don't you ever want to fall in love?"

"What? It's not like you want me to go out there as a wife. It's all about helping a man change his character or habits, so if you ask me, it's a job to be done. Love has nothing to do with it."

"Never say never," Sally Jo slid a thin file over to Hazel. "Look at his photos. You have to admit that Waylen Randolph is a devastatingly handsome man."

Hazel opened the file, and the large glossy facial photo that she saw made her heart nearly skip a beat. Waylen was really handsome, with his blue eyes and thick, dark and wavy hair. The next photo showed Waylen in a tracksuit and looking like he'd won the Athlete of the Year Award. Then she shook her head when she noticed Sally Jo giving her a contemplative look.

"I love my life too much and the freedom it gives me and so love is way out there in the future. But I'm up for this challenge so that Mr. Waylen Randolph can one day find himself a good wife. This will be nothing but a job to me, and if you pay me well, be sure that I'll deliver fantastic results to you."

Sally Jo observed her friend and nodded. "Name your price then, so I can make all arrangements for you to go out to Texas. But remember, don't be too obvious about it. The secret to this mission succeeding is secrecy." Hazel named a figure much lower than Sally Jo would have expected. "Done!" She cried out happily while secretly praying that her friend would find love with Waylen.

Hazel was such a good soul even if she was most times full of jokes and mischief. But she was exactly what the stoic and strict perfectionist needed to have his world shaken out of its false foundations.

Once all arrangements had been done, Hazel left to go home and pack. Sally Jo sat back in her seat and chuckled softly to herself. "Oh Hazel, I dare you to resist Waylen Randolph," she said under her breath. "May something good come out of this even if you think it's all a joke."

"Miss Manning, it's good to hear from you even if I wasn't expecting it to be so soon."

"Mr. Randolph, I've asked you countless times to call me Sally Jo. Anyway, I'm calling because I have a candidate for Waylen."

"Really? What kind of a woman is she? I hope you won't send me someone my son will trample down and crush with his rigidness. That boy makes even tough men and women shake and I wouldn't want some timid and fragile girl traumatized by the whole affair with Waylen."

Sally Jo laughed out loud. "Timid and fragile? Sir, those aren't qualities I'll ever attribute to Hazel Singer. This is a woman who deals with middle school students and subdues them, if you know what I mean."

"She's a schoolteacher?"

"Yes, but a very intelligent one at that."

"Sally Jo, our mission must be secret and I don't see how a school teacher will help our cause."

"Waylen is a lawyer, right?"

"Yes, but what has that got to do with anything?"

"Does he have an assistant that works for him?"

"Yes, a nice girl called Penny. I still don't understand where you're going with this."

"When was the last time Penny took some days off?"

"Well from what I heard Waylen mentioning, Penny's sister is getting married next month so she'll be taking two weeks off work."

"Why don't you give her three months' leave with pay immediately? Planning a wedding is time and labor intensive, and I know that she'll appreciate the time. With her gone, it will create a vacancy and Hazel can come and fill it so as to get close to Waylen."

"You're a very smart young woman," Abner couldn't stop smiling. "I'm sending for Penny right away and the girl actually deserves a crown for putting up with my son for this long without losing her mind. Yes, this will be the perfect ploy to create room for your young lady. I just hope she's someone who can do some office work. Even if this is a ploy, the ranch still has to run and as our legal representative Waylen has much work to deal with on a daily basis."

"Don't worry, Hazel is as smart as they come and she'll make a good office assistant though you need to brace yourself for a few surprises."

Abner laughed out loud. "Just as long as she won't burn my ranch down, I'm game for anything."

"Good! I sent her home to pack and put things in order because her school just closed today. She should be arriving in Texas tomorrow. Have someone pick her up or better still arrange for an Uber to bring her to the ranch."

"That won't be a problem at all. Please just let me know when she's in the air so we can be ready for her. And Sally Jo?"

"Yes, Sir?"

"Thank you so much once again. I look forward to doing more business with you."

"Always a pleasure, Sir."

IN THE MIDST OF CONFUSION

Twenty-seven-year-old Waylen Randolph stared open mouthed at his assistant of two years. He couldn't have heard her right.

"Close your mouth before flies pile inside it," Callum, his youngest brother, said as he walked into the office they shared. "Penny, what is it that has your boss gaping at you like a fish out of water?"

"I only informed Waylen that I'll be taking three months leave so I can deal with some pressing family issues. I didn't think it would be such an issue for him."

Callum waved a hand in front of his brother's face. "And that's what made him this dumbstruck? Dear Penelope, you just broke my brother."

"That's what I fear could have happened," Penelope Ryder mumbled as she packed her stuff into a small box. She was really excited because now she had enough time to plan her sister's wedding which was coming up in a month's time. Mr. Randolph, God bless his kind heart, had given her three months' leave with full pay and even added a generous bonus. She'd been ready to take leave without pay but Mr. Randolph had insisted on her getting all her benefits.

"That's for putting up with my son without being tempted to strangle him from time to time," Mr. Abner Randolph had said. Penny knew that her boss's father was up to something but since she would still be able to return to her position after three months she didn't bother delving into whatever was going on. Besides, who was she to question her good fortune? Why look a gift horse in the mouth?

"Penny," Waylen's voice sounded strained. "How can you leave me in the lurch like this? I thought you'd applied for two weeks' leave to be taken sometime next month because of your sister's upcoming wedding."

Penny shrugged, ready with her answer, for Mr. Randolph Senior had warned her that Waylen wouldn't let her go so easily. "I'm sorry but something pressing came up and I need to deal with it. When I happened to mention it to Mr. Randolph Senior, he approved of my leave and gave me the three months that I need."

"What am I supposed to do without an assistant?" Waylen turned to Callum. "Callum, you're the one who deals with all our human resources matters. Surely, can't you adjust Penny's leave? She could take bits off at a time."

Callum raised his hands in the air as if in surrender. "Sorry Bro, but my hands are tied on this one. See, when Penny asked for leave, I was hesitant to grant it to her so she went to dad and he approved it. You and I know that once Mr. Abner Randolph approves of something not even the Supreme Court of America can overturn it," Callum winked at his brother. "But don't worry, I'll find someone to stand in for Penny for the next three months."

"It had better be someone as good as Penny because I'm not ready to break in a new person."

"Break in?" Callum laughed. "For goodness sake, big brother, assistants aren't the wild horses that you're used to taming. I believe that with proper guidance and instructions you'll be able to manage with one of the other interns. We have six of them in residence; three ladies and three gentlemen. Surely, one of them will be suitable for you."

Waylen's lips tightened. "This is not fair and I'm not happy at all. Penny is my assistant and common courtesy dictates that I be informed when she has to be away from her duties. You people can't just wake up one morning and decide that I don't need my assistant." He glared at Callum. "I hold you responsible for this because you're supposed to have my back since you're in charge of staff welfare."

"Go and tell that to your father," Callum's tone was dry. "Leave Penny and me out of your discontentment. This poor girl has been slaving away for you forever, and she needs a break," he winked at Penny who grinned back at him. "Penny, see you on the first day of September and stay safe."

"Yes, Sir," Penny saluted Callum, picked up her handbag, and when she would have lifted her small box of personal items, he beat her to it.

"I'll get that for you."

They left the office, and Waylen moved to the door to watch as they walked away. He couldn't believe that his assistant was practically dancing beside Callum, as if she was happy to be leaving, and for such a long time. Was he really such a taxing boss?

"Yes, you are," Maynard his younger brother answered him a few hours later when he complained to him about it as they took coffee in the kitchen. "Waylen, you make people cry even without raising your voice at them. Good thing is that Callum is in charge of our human resources and staff welfare or else we wouldn't have anyone working for us."

Waylen looked at his brother and bit his lower lip. Why didn't his father and siblings understand him? He liked things done neatly, carefully and right on time. He couldn't abide untidiness, slothfulness and carelessness. But from the way Maynard sounded it was as if he was some cleanliness and control freak.

"But it's not fair for dad to have approved of Penny's long leave without first running it by me. Penny is my direct assistant and I should have been consulted on this matter."

"Well, dad is our overall boss, and besides, I don't see why you think Penny is the only one who can work for you. Three months is a short time, and before you even blink, Penny will be back. Issues like these are why we have six interns on the ranch at any given time. Those smart men and women are always ready and willing to step up and help in any department. Give one of them a chance to learn from you. The days will fly past so fast you won't believe that ninety days will be over just like that," Maynard snapped his fingers.

"And some intern will have driven me mad long before then."

Maynard chuckled, "Bro, Penny is just a mortal like the rest of us. She's prone to weaknesses and also needs time away from her taskmaster."

"But she's the only one who understands me and how I like things to be done."

"Well, you need to get used to the idea of not having her around. Keep an open mind so you can work well with someone else. Stop being so rigid. And so far, you've been very lucky because Penny, for the past two years that she's worked for you, has never once fallen ill. Let the girl go and have some time to rest so she can return when she's quite fresh and rejuvenated."

"How did I ever survive without her before, and what will happen now?" Waylen sounded like a lost little boy and his brother nearly pitied him. But then Maynard hardened his heart. Like everyone else, he missed the old Waylen and wanted him back. This shake up should be good for him. Getting Waylen out of his comfort zone might make him loosen his rigid stance. But one thing Maynard knew, interesting times lay ahead and he couldn't wait to see how his brother would cope.

"You drive everyone around you crazy, you make both interns and professionals weep. Penny, bless her heart, is from a military family, and her father is a very strict man. That's how she's been able to cater to your every need and whim without breaking down. Now you have to adjust to working with someone else. Or you too can take three months' leave and return when she does."

"Don't be crazy! How do you expect me to take such long leave and do nothing?"

"Then be prepared to work with a new assistant and smile about it."

Waylen sighed deeply, dreading the days ahead.

A SIGHT TO BEHOLD

"*A*nd who, if I may ask, is that creature standing out on the porch?" Waylen walked into the living room where he found Quin and Kendrick playing cards. "Quin, have you seen the person on the porch?"

"Huh?" Quin gave his brother an absentminded smile. "That question belongs to dad, I think. I heard him saying something about a new intern joining us or something like that. Could be the person you're talking about." He went back to playing cards.

Waylen shuddered as he thought about the woman who'd walked up to him a few minutes ago and greeted him. She'd been dropped off by an Uber. So shocked at her appearance had he been that he'd not responded to her greeting and instead hurried into the house. It was rude and poor manners as his father would say, to leave a visitor standing outside, but in this case, he believed he was justified in doing so.

"Len, you need to deal with whoever it is," Kendrick said. "Can't you see that Quin and I are busy?"

"Let me handle this," Quin tossed his cards upside down onto the table. "And don't you dare peek at my cards." He walked toward the door.

"Hello? Is anyone home?" Hazel stepped up to the front door, which was standing wide open, and a man suddenly appeared, startling her. "Sorry, I just arrived," she smiled at the big man who, from the photos Sally Jo had showed her of the family, she knew to be Quinten Randolph, the first son of Mr. Abner Randolph. "I'm looking for Mr. Randolph."

"All the men who live in this house answer to that name," a pleasant feminine voice came from behind Hazel. She turned around to find a really beautiful woman walking up the porch steps. So this was Kelsey Randolph, Quin's wife! The family photo in the file back in Denver had been taken on her wedding day but it didn't do her justice. This was one beautiful woman! "I'm Kelsey and that big one over there is my husband Quinten Randolph but we all just call him Quin. Then his brothers are Waylen, Kendrick, Maynard, and Callum, all of them Randolphs, as well as my father-in-law, Mr. Abner Randolph. So which particular one would you like to see?"

"Mr. Abner Randolph," Hazel said, then frowned slightly. "Who was the rude man I found on the porch when the Uber dropped me off? He didn't even respond to my greeting and just left me standing outside," she said indignantly. "Such poor manners."

Kelsey chuckled softly as she took Hazel's hand. "Do come into the house, please. If you're the new intern then maybe you need to speak with Callum who handles all matters to do with staff." Of course, Hazel knew that, courtesy of Sally Jo, but she feigned ignorance as she entered the house. It was really beautiful but she would have time to admire it later. Her eyes went to Waylen and she glared at him.

"Someone has to pay the Uber driver," she said. "I was informed that my fare would be settled once we got here."

"And who told you that?" Waylen scowled. He didn't like the woman's brashness.

"That information was in the email that was sent to me instructing me to report to this ranch for my three months' internship. Hurry up if you don't want to add waiting charges to the fare."

"Waylen, go and pay off the Uber guy," Quin instructed as he slid a hand around his wife's waist. That's when Hazel noticed the slight bump and smiled. "And after that, please show our new intern…"

"My name is Hazel Singer."

All eyes turned to her and Hazel wanted to laugh out loud at the varying expressions on their faces; from shocked to curiosity and even slight admiration on Kelsey's face. The game was on! Sally Jo had escorted her to the airport and on the way there had given her instructions about handling the family which she was putting into play. *"Be brash without being rude,"* she'd been advised. *"Add sassiness where required and don't be afraid of anything because Mr. Randolph is aware of your arrival and the role you'll be playing."*

"Well Miss Singer, as I was saying, Waylen will show you to the hostel."

"Why can't Kelsey do it?" Waylen couldn't believe that his brother was giving him such a degrading task. Showing an intern to the residential quarters was far beneath him. "Or better still, why don't you call in one of the maids to do that?"

"Really?" Quin stared pointedly at his brother. "I didn't ask you to hold Miss Singer's hand while you show her to the hostel. Do you want our guest to think that we're rude and inhospitable people?"

Waylen's lips tightened but he nodded curtly, "Very well then, Miss Singer, let's get your bags from the car."

When Waylen saw Hazel's three suitcases his eyes nearly popped out of their sockets. He travelled a lot and was used to seeing people—especially women—with matching sets of travelling cases. But none of this woman's luggage pieces matched the other. And even as he carried the two larger cases, leaving her to bring in the smaller one, he nearly groaned out loud.

As they approached the ladies' hostel he was glad to meet one of the other interns.

"Daisy, would you please show Miss Singer to her room? I'm sure the housekeeper prepared it and informed all of you that a new intern would be joining us."

Daisy batted her eyelashes at Waylen, and Hazel was tempted to roll her eyes in derision. The young woman was clearly besotted with Waylen. But to be fair to her gender, Hazel admitted to herself that Waylen Randolph was one of the most handsome men she'd ever met. So no woman could be blamed for being attracted to him.

"Yes, of course, Waylen," Daisy replied but barely spared Hazel a glance. Her attention was wholly on Waylen.

"Thank you," Waylen placed the two cases in the small lobby in the hostel. "I'll be taking my leave now."

"So soon?" Daisy looked disappointed. She placed a hand on Waylen's arm and cast a cold look at Hazel. "Will you be there for the dance at the bunkhouse this evening?"

Waylen nodded, "But of course, you know that we all have to be present."

Daisy clapped her hands happily, "Then I book at least three dances with you."

"Sure," Waylen nodded at Hazel. "I hope you have a pleasant stay with us, Miss Singer."

"Thank you."

After a brief nod at Daisy, Waylen left the two ladies.

"Come along and I'll show you to your room," Daisy said ungraciously. "I have a dinner and dance to prepare for. Mr. Randolph expects us to have dinner with the family at least three times a week. Breakfast and lunch are taken in the kitchen and dinner four times a week. But on Sundays, Wednesdays and Fridays we have dinner with the family. We have to dress up formally," Daisy looked at Hazel's mismatched outfit with much disdain. "Such dressing won't cut it.

Hazel smiled to herself. The young woman, and even Waylen, had no idea that she'd been voted the best dressed student in college twice and even at school, the other female teachers sought to emulate her outfits. But she was here on a different agenda so no fashion sense would come into play here. She was supposed to make Waylen Randolph as uncomfortable as possible, so she had to make sure that none of her outfits matched.

Once Daisy showed her to her room, she quickly brought in her luggage and settled down, being mindful that since it was Wednesday, she would be having dinner with the family.

Her bedroom was done in soft blue and reminded her of being at the beach. She decided to rest for a while before finding her way around the ranch.

A CLASH OF WILLS

"What do you think you're doing?" Waylen didn't bother to hide the irritation he was feeling. "Stop counting on your fingers like a kindergarten student. Use a calculator if you have to," and he pushed one toward her, but she ignored it and continued counting on her fingers.

"My mother always told me to count to ten before losing my temper," Hazel gave Waylen an innocent look and he felt like screaming. This woman was testing the limits of his patience and he clenched his fists.

Hazel saw the clenched fists and smiled inwardly. Finally, she was getting a response out of this stoic fellow.

It was her third day on the job and she silently sent a blessing to Penelope who had withstood this man for two years. And now she was on leave for the next three months. Lucky girl!

Being away meant that she didn't have to deal with Waylen's idiosyncrasies. But Hazel told herself that she was here to do the job of taming this perfectionist.

These had been an interesting three days. From the moment she'd been ushered into Waylen's office she hadn't stopped smiling. The shock and horror on her boss's face when his father, accompanied by Quin and Callum had told him who'd be working as his assistant until Penny's return, was priceless.

"You need an assistant, and who better than Hazel for the task?" Mr. Randolph had said. "Miss Singer here assures me that she's a very fast learner, so there shouldn't be any problem with the two of you working together. She has experience in office management, so I don't foresee any trouble."

"But father..."

"Waylen," Quin broke in. "Since Penny will be gone for the next three months, you surely need an assistant. We all know that you can't really work with any of the other six interns, so Hazel it is."

Waylen had accepted her grudgingly and his instructions were given either by email or via WhatsApp chats, as if he couldn't bear to be in the same room with Hazel. Not that she minded much because it gave her the chance to read up and familiarize herself with the running of the ranch.

"Hazel!" Waylen barked. "Are you even listening to me?"

She raised her head and gave him an innocent smile. "I'm sorry, could you please repeat what you just asked me?"

Waylen's jaw tightened momentarily. It was as if this woman existed for the sole purpose of vexing him. What kind of bad luck had befallen him that he had to be landed with this odd woman?

"Never mind!" he muttered as he reached for a file and opened it. The best thing to do would be to ignore her.

"Mr. Randolph," Hazel's voice interrupted him. She'd risen from behind her desk and was standing in front of his. "What would you have me do now?" She stood there looking like butter wouldn't melt in her mouth but Waylen didn't trust her.

"Sit down at your desk and be still and silent," he roared at her and Hazel scampered to her seat. He saw her lower lip trembling and groaned inwardly, feeling very guilty. He'd never raised his voice to Penny or any other servants and workers on the ranch. Why did this woman push him to the limits?

"I'm sorry," he said and she nodded, reaching for a magazine. She bent her head over it, pretending to read.

Waylen wondered what his new assistant was thinking because she was silent for so long until the quietness began to grate on his nerves. Surely that old magazine couldn't be all that absorbing!

"What are you reading?" He asked. Hazel merely shrugged and didn't bother looking up. She knew that her actions would irritate the man and she wasn't wrong. "It's only polite to respond when spoken to," he said.

"I was told to sit down, be still and silent," she said without raising her head. "That's exactly what I'm doing, Sir."

Waylen was about to say something when the door opened and his father walked into the office. It was as if he picked up on the tension in the room.

"I hope all is well in here," Abner smiled at Hazel. "Are you settling in well?"

"Yes, Sir, and thank you for giving me this chance. I promise that I won't let you down."

"I'm the one who should be thanking you since you're doing Waylen a favor. No other intern will work for him."

"Dad!"

"I hope my son isn't giving you a hard time," Abner said, ignoring his son. Waylen was irritated because his father was talking as if he wasn't present.

"No Sir, we're getting along as well as we can." Hazel was enjoying the frustration on Waylen's face.

"Would the two of you stop talking about me as if I'm not present?"

The door opened and Callum walked in. "Hey Hazel, would you be my date this Saturday when we have Karaoke night at the bunkhouse?"

"Sure," Hazel said without hesitation, giving Callum a dazzling smile. "Is it a formal or informal event?"

"Why do you ask?"

"Because I need to know what to wear. I wouldn't want to show up in the wrong attire and embarrass you."

Callum laughed, "Usually it's just the youngsters on the ranch attending the event so dress casually. However, jeans and tee-shirts aren't allowed because we try to make people look cool and neat, not shabby."

"Fantastic idea," Abner clapped. "I like these social gatherings because it gives all you youngsters the chance to mingle, and who knows," he winked at Hazel, "You might just catch the eye of a dashing cowboy."

"Dad, I'm her date on Saturday, you all heard her saying it," Callum protested. "No other dashing cowboy will be eyeing her, that's for sure."

"And I know she'll be perfect," Abner walked to the door. "See you around then."

The door closed behind Abner, and Callum once again turned to Hazel. "I have a feeling you'll be the most beautiful woman at Karaoke night. There's some dancing too with a local deejay so come prepared to have fun."

"You can count on that."

Waylen found himself wanting to toss his brother out of the office. But they shared the space and Callum had every right to be here.

"The two of you need to understand that this is an office and we're still within working hours. Settle down and work."

Callum made a face that caused Hazel to giggle and her whole face lit up.

"She never smiles at me like that," Waylen thought to himself. And come to think of it, even Penny never smiled much around him. The other interns, save for Daisy who liked to flirt, usually gave him a wide berth. So it irked him that Hazel was splashing all her smiles at his brother and he didn't like it at all!

ALL IN THE DETAILS

"Hazel, what's this?" Waylen tossed a file onto her desk. "What kind of nonsense is this?"

"Stop shouting at me," Hazel's lower lip trembled.

"I wasn't shouting," Waylen said and then took a deep breath. He realized that his voice was raised. "Look, I'm sorry but I won't condone this kind of work."

"Are the figures wrong?" Hazel wiped her eyes.

"No, but..."

"Is everything as it should be?"

"Yes, but..."

The door opened. "What's all the shouting about?" Maynard entered the office. "Waylen, I could hear you from three doors down."

"I don't know why he keeps shouting at me and yet all the work I do is perfect."

"Perfect?" Waylen's voice went up an octave higher and his brother grinned at him. "What is perfect about your work when this piece of paper looks like it has just been saved from a cow's mouth?"

"Oh, the man has jokes now," Hazel stood up and held her hands akimbo. "You wanted me to compute all the figures of the calves that have been born in the past week, and I did just that. Why are you now shouting at me?"

"Aaargh!" Waylen threw his hands in the air. "Woman, you're impossible and you're driving me crazy!"

"Man, you're driving me nuts!" Hazel countered as she swept out of the office. Much as she was tempted to slam the door behind her, she had great respect for Mr. Abner. The best place to go and cool her temper was at the corral. On any given day two or three new horses underwent training and she loved watching as the cowboys coaxed, begged, cajoled the horses into obeying their instructions. The well-behaved horses would then be rewarded with treats like apples and carrots.

Back in the office Maynard ducked as a folded newspaper came flying at him. "Wipe that smug smile from your face, Maynard," he was told.

"I can't help smiling," Maynard started laughing. "My brother, this one got you good! Even Penny on her worst days never elucidated even a warning from you. Now this young lassie has you screeching like a fish wife at the marketplace," another folded newspaper followed the first one and Maynard caught it neatly.

"Transferring aggression to a third party is a crime," Maynard mocked. "And that's what you're doing to me. I could sue you but then you're my lawyer."

"Maynard, don't you have an office to go to? Now get out of my office."

"Oh, I'm done for the day and had come to find out from Hazel if she would speak to Daisy to be my date on Karaoke night."

"Go and get your own intern to send," Waylen growled. "Hazel isn't your messenger."

"Oh, someone's getting all territorial," the door opened and Callum walked up to his brother. Waylen drew back. From past experience he knew that his brother was about to upset him. "Boy!" And to annoy him further, Callum reached out a hand and ruffled his hair. "You're doomed!"

"Get away from me," Waylen slapped Callum's hand away as Maynard laughed on the other side of the office. "What's wrong with the two of you? This is an office and it's during working hours. Cut your nonsense out."

"Well Bro," Callum walked to Maynard and high fived him. "You sound like you don't like the idea of my going to Karaoke night with Hazel. So do you want to be her date? All you have to do is ask her nicely."

"Will you just shut up! Go to the dance or Karaoke or even to the moon, see if I care."

Once again Callum high fived Maynard. "The man doth sound jealous," he drawled and the two of them laughed. "Sir Waylen, keep your boots on, Cowboy."

"Don't give me that look, Maynard."

"What look?" Maynard tried to put on an innocent face but Waylen wasn't buying it.

"Would the two of you leave right now, please? I have a lot of work to do and you're being nothing but a distraction."

Waylen looked at his brothers who didn't seem much bothered by his order. Callum even powered the laptop on his desk and soon the two of them were talking about cameras. Callum was an amateur photographer and his work was really good.

"This one seems better than the other. It's a Nikon Z mirrorless camera," Callum was saying.

"No, someone told me that the Sony Alpha series is the best."

They argued good-naturedly about the different cameras and Waylen struggled to ignore them. But their arguments got more heated, and Waylen struck his fist on his desk.

"Stop that at once! The two of you should know that this is my office and I have lots to do. Carry that laptop to the living room and have your discussions there."

"Sorry," Maynard said.

But Waylen's concentration was broken and he knew that he wouldn't be able to do anything else for the rest of the afternoon. So he rose to his feet and walked to the door.

"I hope the two of you are satisfied now that you've distracted me from my work. You can have the office now and eat it," he hissed at his brothers and walked out, ignoring the laughter that followed him. In years past he would have knocked the heads of the two numbskulls together but they were too old for him to do that anymore. They were so irritating, and he grumbled under his breath as he walked away from his office. He was feeling too restless to watch any television so he decided to go to the corral and see how far the cowboys had gone with breaking in the new horses.

There was a particular mare he was interested in. She was about eighteen months old and was already showing signs of becoming a prize race horse. The only problem with the yearling was that she was highly strung and skittish and one of the cowboys had even commented that she had a wild look in her eyes. That was never a good trait in a horse because she could easily get unhinged and injure someone.

As he walked toward the corral he noticed Hazel leaning against the wooden fence. She was concentrating so hard on whatever was happening inside the corral that she didn't even turn around as he drew closer to her.

"Do you ride at all?"

Hazel was startled when she heard her boss's voice from so close. Truth be told, her mind hadn't been on the horses at all but on whatever was happening to her. She couldn't explain the feelings that were developing within her. It was hard to believe that she'd only been here for less than two weeks but it felt like she'd been here for ages.

"Hazel?"

"Sorry," she gave a nervous laugh. "I've never been on a horse at all. Well, apart from the wooden ones at the fair when I was a child."

Waylen looked at her in surprise. "Seriously? Then you're missing out on a lot of things," he told her. "Riding is wonderful, and especially if you're able to get out there and let the horse have its head."

"The horses are so big," she pointed at the two in the corral. "They're terrifying, and I wonder how women even have the courage to get on one."

Waylen smiled, "My mom was one of the most skilled horsewomen I've ever known," he found himself saying. "She could swing a lasso and rope a calf within minutes. She was the one who taught my brothers and me how to ride right from when we were six months old and could sit upright in the saddle."

Hazel held her breath because Waylen never spoke about personal matters and especially nothing to do with his mother. From the little she'd gathered from the other interns, Mrs. Randolph had died about fifteen years ago after falling from a horse. While Hazel had no further details, she knew that the matriarch's death had brought a great deal of pain to Waylen and his brothers.

"Mom rode in rodeos even when she was pregnant. My dad tried to get her to stop but it was as if he was snuffing the life out of her. When he realized that mom was unhappy if she wasn't around horses, he let her be."

"You must miss her a lot," Hazel ventured to comment in a quiet voice.

"Does it ever get easier?" He turned, and she saw the deep sorrow in his eyes. "Will I wake up one day and realize that I've stopped feeling pain about my mother's absence from my life?"

"It never goes away," Hazel turned to look at the horses once again. "And contrary to what people say, it doesn't get easier. But we manage to live through the pain. I lost my dad when I was a teenager and I still miss him. Every single passing day is a reminder of what I lost when he died."

"I'm so sorry for your loss."

"I'm sorry too," Hazel said. Then she straightened up. "I have to go to the kitchen and help out with dinner."

Waylen smiled and nodded, watching as Hazel hurried away. He couldn't believe that he was feeling bereft of her company. What was wrong with him? He also couldn't believe that he'd opened up to her when he'd never done that with any other woman. In spite of her shabby appearance, Hazel was so easy to be around, for she made no incessant demands outside of work.

"Well, what do you know," he muttered as he watched her walking back to the house, entered the living room and disappeared through the hallway door and was soon out of sight.

ABNER WAS WATCHING his son who had no idea that he was under scrutiny. He felt a smile tagging at his lips when he saw Waylen's eyes following Hazel to the house until she disappeared out of sight.

These past few days had been very interesting and reports kept reaching him that Waylen was behaving very oddly. "The poor fellow has no idea that his life is changing."

THE ROSE GARDEN

*I*t was as if he were watching something emerging out of a pod in a science fiction movie. Something strange yet so fascinating that one couldn't get their eyes off it. Waylen stared, not believing what his eyes were showing him.

"What happened?" He asked in awestruck tones as he moved to the large living room window that looked out onto the porch.

"Our Hazel sure cleans up nicely," Abner chuckled softly, liking the look on his son's face. The young man had no idea that his life was changing right before him. But his father said nothing more.

Quin walked into the living room. "What are you two gawking at?" He joined them at the window.

"Your brother can't seem to get his eyes off his beautiful assistant. And I must say that the transformation is just amazing," their father said.

"Oh!" Quin turned to grin at Waylen. "I can see that you're gaping at Hazel. Make sure you thank my wife for that transformation."

"What?" Waylen wasn't paying much attention to his brother because all his focus was on Hazel who was entering the back seat of Kelsey's car.

"I said, thank me later," Quin deliberately dragged his words as if he was speaking to one who was dull of hearing. "Kelsey did Hazel's makeover and even loaned her one of her dresses. So you need to thank me for transforming your woman."

Waylen grunted, "She's not my woman," he scowled at his brother who simply grinned at him. He was wondering where his sister-in-law was taking Hazel. Callum walked in just then and joined them at the window.

"Oh, I see the girls are going to town to find outfits for Karaoke night," he answered Waylen's unspoken question. "If that's how Hazel looks when she's going on a shopping excursion, I can't wait to escort her to Karaoke night on Saturday night."

Waylen found himself folding his fists and wishing he could punch his brother, unaware that his father was staring amusedly at him. He moved away from the window and sat down on the couch, fuming inwardly.

"Waylen, who's your date?" Callum asked over his shoulder. "And don't give me that look for saying that your assistant is my Saturday night date. You had plenty of time to ask her yourself, but..." he shrugged. "Your loss, Bro!"

"Shut up!" Waylen roared as he rose to his feet seething with anger. "What's wrong with you, Callum?"

Everyone turned to look at him, shocked at the outburst because they were witnessing behavior that was strange for Waylen.

"I'm sorry, Bro, I didn't mean to offend you," Callum said.

"Whatever!" Waylen said dismissively as he stomped out to the porch and sat on the top step. He needed to ride out so he could clear his head. As he rose to his feet again and walked toward the stable, he noticed two teenage laborers gawking at him.

"What are you staring at? Do you get paid to stand around gawking at nothing?" The two young men, sensing that the mood was tense, scampered out of Waylen's way.

KELSEY WAS GIGGLING as her husband's driver drove them out of the homestead. She was scrolling through her phone and kept giggling.

Hazel wanted to roll her eyes because she knew that her friend was reading text messages or WhatsApp chats from her husband. Kelsey acted like a schoolgirl with her first crush. They were both seated in the back seat. Then Hazel berated herself for projecting envious thoughts toward the woman who'd treated her so kindly from the first day she stepped on the ranch. It was quite true that she envied Kelsey the beautiful relationship she had with her husband. If ever there was a couple that was deeply in love with each other, Kelsey and Quin were it.

She'd noticed how they could barely spend much time apart. Though Kelsey still worked in the garage as a mechanic, it was more of a supervisory role because she was expecting their first child. And Quin made sure that even if he was working out on the range, for he preferred the outdoors, he would return home for lunch and dinner, all his focus on his wife. Kelsey glowed because of her husband's love.

"You're rather silent," Kelsey put her phone back into her small purse. "Sorry that I had to answer Quin's texts."

"That's all right."

"No, it's not all right, and I apologize for my rudeness. But my husband was making me laugh with some of his comments. He says Waylen was gaping at you when we left the house and he nearly bit Callum's head off."

"But why?"

Kelsey turned her whole body so she was facing Hazel, giving her an incredulous look. "Are you being serious right now?"

"Kelsey, what is it?"

"It sounds as if Waylen is quite jealous of his brother."

Hazel shook her head, "That can't be right. Why would Waylen be jealous of Callum? All I know is that they're always arguing about one thing or the other."

"What?"

"Yes," Hazel sighed, "Sometimes our office sounds like a battlefield. When Waylen isn't scolding me for something, he and Callum are busy arguing. At least most of the time Callum defends me to Waylen."

"What?" Kelsey screeched.

"Oh yes, hardly a day passes by that those two aren't arguing. Sometimes the office atmosphere becomes so tense that I have to escape to the kitchen just to get away. I would have expected Kendrick and Waylen to be the ones arguing as followers tend to do that a lot."

Kelsey laughed out loud. "My dear girl you seem to be the catalyst in all this. Waylen has never raised his voice to anyone to my knowledge, and certainly not to a woman. This all seems to have started with your arrival. In the past he's always walked away whcn a situation seemed to be more than he can handle. Now I see that he's giving as good as he gets."

Kelsey's words made Hazel very uncomfortable. She didn't want to be the reason why the two brothers kept having their arguments. "I hope those arguments have nothing to do with me."

"Well, let's just say that Waylen seems to have been searching for something which even he isn't sure of."

"Enough of all those men and their issues," Hazel wanted the topic changed. She turned to look outside the window. This was her first time to go to Cedar Hill and she was captured by the beauty of the town.

Hazel instructed the driver on where to drop them off. "You can do anything you want," she told him. "We should be done in about three hours."

"Yes, Ma'am."

"And here," Kelsey handed him some bills. "Fill the tank and then also have lunch on us."

"Thank you, Ma'am."

Kelsey got out of the car first, then Hazel followed suit. As the latter stood on the pavement, she was struck by how clean the town was.

"Wow! I never knew that a town could be so clean. The road looks like it has been scrubbed with soap and water. I wish Denver could be this clean."

"Oh, so you're from Denver, right?" Hazel nodded. "I've never thought of asking you where you're from, and now it turns out that you're from Denver. It's a small world after all," Kelsey sounded excited.

"Why would you say that?"

"Because I, too, come from Denver. As a matter of fact, I was sent here by someone. Maybe you've heard of her."

"Who?"

"Sally Jo. Her name is Sally Jo Manning and she runs a marriage agency called Hitch Your Wagon Romance Agency. They have a good online presence too."

Since Hazel didn't want to admit that it was Sally Jo who'd sent her to Cedar Hill, she feigned ignorance. "I'm not sure that I've heard of this lady of whom you speak. Why?'

"Like I said, she's the director of one of the best marriage agencies in Denver, possibly the whole of America."

"That's interesting."

"To be fair, she's very discreet. Do you know that Quin had no idea that his father was setting him up to fall in love and get married? I came in as a mechanic and believe me, the number of times Quin and I clashed," Kelsey shook her head as she laughed, then blushed when Hazel gave her a knowing look. "Stop giving me that look. You've seen how handsome my husband is, well all those Randolph men are quite something else."

"You can say that again," Hazel agreed. Give credit where credit is due!

"Mmh!" Kelsey stopped outside a large boutique. "Which of those men do you find the most attractive, well apart from my husband, of course?"

Hazel laughed and shook her head. "Sister, I'm not falling for that one. You're setting a trap for me and I refuse to fall into it. But to answer you, all of them including your husband—and even your father-in-law—are exceptional men. I'm surprised that apart from Quin, the others are all still single. Are the women in Cedar Hill blind?"

"Those men, and I include mine among the number, are quite stubborn and hard headed. My father-in-law calls them the wild sons of Randolph Ranch. But that's not to say that they're not gentlemen. They respect women very much and I know they got that from their late mother, even if she died when they were still young. They don't live careless lives of hopping from one woman to the other, or else the ranch would be swarming with women of all ages coming and going. They're all very careful never to get any woman's hopes up." Then Kelsey gave Hazel a thoughtful look. "You and Waylen would make a really suitable couple."

"What?" Hazel spluttered even as her face turned red. "Stop embarrassing me in public, Kelsey."

"Oh yes, you're the first woman I've seen standing up to that stubborn brother-in-law of mine. Waylen is such a perfectionist that his brothers, according to Quin, call him a human robot. The other interns are quite intimidated by him. Yes," Kelsey nodded, "Waylen it is. Now let's get you that outfit that will knock that man off his feet," and she opened the boutique door and pulled Hazel inside.

"Kelsey!"

KARAOKE NIGHT on Randolph Ranch was something Hazel had never experienced before and her eyes glowed as she took in the fancily dressed cowboys and cowgirls. Kelsey had talked her into buying a knee-length black leather skirt that came with a waistcoat and scarlet long-sleeved blouse. She even added knee-length one inch pure leather sole boots.

"That will knock that brother-in-law of mine out of his own boots," Kelsey said as she pushed a large-brimmed felt hat onto Hazel's head. "All you need now is a whip and a gun and Calamity Jane has nothing on you."

Much as she's protested when Kelsey had settled the whole bill, she'd swallowed when she saw the receipts. The outfits were designer and cost an arm and a leg.

And now she was glad that she was dressed so fancily because as soon as she stepped into the bunkhouse that had been converted into a dance hall, all eyes turned toward her. Callum swaggered over to her, looking like one of the cowboys in a few western movies that she'd watched. He tipped his hat at her. "Howdy Ma'am," he held out his folded arm and she slipped her hand into it. "Come, I'll introduce you all round even if you know many of the fellows here."

Hazel felt a prickling sensation at the back of her neck like someone was watching her, and when she turned, she found Waylen's eyes fixed on her. She stumbled slightly and Callum immediately righted her.

"How did you manage to create so much space in the bunkhouse," she asked Callum when he had her seated at a table for two. A waitress immediately came over, and she was someone Hazel didn't recognize.

"It's easy because all we had to do was push back the partitions," he pointed at the walls. "We had someone design this place so that it can serve as a hall or partitioned rooms. We carried the beds into the storeroom outside and then created this space. Do you like it?"

"It looks so fancy, not what I would have expected, and it comes complete with waiters and waitresses."

"That's right," Callum smiled at the waitress. "We not only hire a DJ, but Uncle Buck's restaurant staff as well. Cindy, we'll have everything on the menu and a Sprite for me. What about you, Hazel?"

"Plain water will do for me since I avoid carbonated drinks just before bed since they give me heartburn."

"You heard the lady," he nodded at Cindy.

"Yes, Sir," the waitress tucked her notebook in her pocket and left to prepare their order.

"Don't look now but Len is on his way over," Callum said.

Hazel shrugged, "It's a free world," she said. To her surprise, Waylen pulled up a chair to their table even though it was small.

"What are you having?" He asked, looking around for a waiter or waitress. He spotted one and waved him over.

"We chose everything on the menu," Callum said. "That means a large platter that you're welcome to share with us."

"I'll just ask for Seltzer water then," Len said. "How are you finding our Karaoke night, Hazel?"

"So far so good," she said, wishing he wasn't seated so close to her. The man's presence in the office made her almost have palpitations and now here he was up close and she smelled his expensive cologne. Daisy sashayed over and practically draped herself all over Waylen and Hazel wanted to push her away. Then she berated herself for her reaction. After all, it was a free world and Len wasn't even her date. So she ignored the two and turned to Callum who was watching whatever was going on with an amused smile on his face.

Waylen did all he could to extract himself from Daisy, who was acting all possessive, and he didn't like it at all. He was annoyed that Hazel was practically ignoring him even though they were seated at the same table.

"Daisy, I promise to dance with you later, but as you can see, we're about to have our dinner," he pointed out, uncaring that he was being rude. "This table is too small to handle four persons so I suggest that you return to your table."

"I could pull up another chair," Daisy pouted.

"No," Callum said forcefully. "This table can't hold four because it's made for two people and a third is even a tight squeeze," he stared pointedly at Len who ignored him. Len laughed inwardly. No one was going to take him away from Hazel.

The moment she'd walked into the bunkhouse he'd felt as if all breath had been knocked out of him. And he noticed that the other males reacted to her presence in the same way and felt like shouting at them to get their eyes off his woman.

His woman? Now where did that come from? So as not to reveal his thoughts he turned to Daisy who was still lurking around their table. "Let me walk you back to your table, Daisy," he rose and took her arm, thereby forcing her to move with him. He was gone for only a few minutes and returned just as Cindy brought the order.

Hazel's eyes widened. "This is a lot of ribs."

"Enjoy yourself," Callum said as he reached for a hot towel and cleaned his hands. His companions did the same.

Hazel felt her face flaming at the attention Len was giving her. He picked out the choice pieces of meat for her and placed them on her saucer. Then he kept asking her if she was all right and attending to her every need.

"Hey," Callum protested at some point. "You're taking my date's attention away from me."

Len's response was to glare at his brother, who raised his hands in surrender. "I'll leave as soon as I'm done with my dinner," he told them, and much as Hazel tried to get him to stay, he refused. "Three's a crowd," he grinned good-naturedly at her. "We came here to have a wonderful time so please have fun."

And for the rest of the evening Hazel set out to have as much fun as she could. She needed the memories for those days when she'd be back home in Denver, all alone in her apartment. Somehow the idea of going back to Denver filled her with despair and she finally realized that she'd fallen in love with the West, just as Sally Jo had predicted.

TROUBLES OF THE HEART

*T*his wasn't supposed to happen, Hazel told herself as she dressed for work on Monday morning. How could she have let her guard down and allowed Len to creep into her heart?

"This isn't good at all," she mumbled, wondering how she was going to face Waylen after the brief kiss they'd shared in his mother's rose garden the previous day. What must he be thinking of her?

It all started on Saturday during Karaoke night at the bunkhouse. Waylen had pushed his way to their table and Callum had laughingly surrendered. And it had turned out to be a fantastic night where he got Hazel to sing 'Just the two of us,' by Bill Withers and Grover Washington Junior. And Hazel had blushed through all the catcalls and whistling, relieved when Kendrick grabbed the microphone from Waylen and sent them off the stage.

And on Sunday morning, Waylen had been waiting to drive Hazel to church—even though the ranch van ferried the other employees to church, and it was what Hazel had used since her arrival. Len had insisted on driving her.

And he even sat next to her in church. As they sang in church, sharing a hymnbook, Hazel was still blown away at his strong baritone.

Immediately after the service, Waylen had taken her for lunch, which was a quick affair as he didn't want to stay out too long. Hazel expected that once they got to the ranch, he would bid her farewell and disappear. To her surprise, he'd asked her to walk with him in the rose garden.

"Every time I come here I feel comforted," he said as they strolled through the neat rows of rose bushes in various stages of flowering. Some bushes had closed buds while others were opened all the way. To Hazel it was a most beautiful scene and the sweet scent of roses filled the air. "My mother planted this garden on Christmas Day, sixteen years ago. She said it was her way of showing how much she loved us. And then a year later, exactly on Christmas Day, she went away."

Hazel frowned slightly when Waylen said that. From his words one would be excused for thinking that his mother had walked away from the family, yet she knew it wasn't so. "I'm so sorry for your loss," she said.

"Mom loved spending time in this garden, and whenever I wasn't in school or helping out with the horses, I would come here, and she would tell me stories. Until she left me," his voice dropped to a whisper.

"Waylen…"

"I remember that day like it was yesterday," his voice was so full of sadness that Hazel wanted to weep for him. "Mom prepared a beautiful Christmas Day lunch for us, and we were so happy. Everyone was laughing and joking and then something happened." He sighed. "Mom got so angry, and she jumped onto her horse to go and clear her head, as she said. She liked riding to visit her friends but that day she didn't come back."

Hazel felt deep compassion for Waylen. It was now becoming very clear to her that he'd never quite come to terms with his mother's death. According to his words, his mother had just left.

"It was something I did that made Mom leave me behind." They got to a small bench at the edge of the garden and Waylen sat down first. "Maybe if I'd made my bed like she asked me to, or cleaned my room, then she wouldn't have gotten so angry with me on that day."

Hazel sat down on the bench, careful to leave some space between them. In her experience as a child psychologist, she knew that when someone was pouring their heart out the last thing they needed and in many cases wanted, was any kind of physical human contact. Most people would prefer that someone listened to them without touching them in any way. It always worked with her students back at school. So she also remained silent. It was clear Waylen needed to unburden himself, and she gave him the chance to do so.

"Me and Kendrick were playing in the living room after lunch, and we accidentally knocked into the Christmas tree. Suddenly ornaments were flying all over the place and some fell and broke. Mom was really furious because most of the ones that were destroyed were family heirlooms and were one of a kind." Waylen blinked rapidly. "Mom was shouting, and dad told her that he would find her new ones to replace the ones we'd smashed. But she said they were irreplaceable and rushed out of the house. She rode away and never came back." He bowed his head. "I should have been a good boy because I'm older than Rick. So, I cleaned up and waited for Mom to come back home. I wanted to tell her that I would give up all my allowance money and find ornaments on EBay or Amazon to replace the ones I destroyed. And I kept the house clean every day but Mom never came back home."

"Oh Waylen!" It finally dawned on Hazel why her boss was so fanatically neat. He was waiting for his mother to come back so she wouldn't be angry with him again. Hazel took Waylen's hand and was surprised when he didn't pull it away. "Wherever your mother is she knows you love her and didn't mean to make her angry. It was an accident, and those happen a lot, especially with children around, and I should know. Your Mom also knows that you've been a good person through the years. She'd be very proud of the fine man you've turned out to be."

"If only she'd come back home that Christmas Day, she would have seen how clean the living room was." He pulled his hand away, bowed his head and ran his fingers through his hair. "Why didn't she come back?" He turned tear-filled eyes to Hazel. "Why didn't my mother come back?"

"Waylen," Hazel forced herself not to break down. She placed a light hand on his back. "When my father died I thought my world had ended. I was his princess and he promised that he would always be there for me." She paused to see if she had his attention. He inclined his head slightly and she was encouraged to carry on speaking. "I was in my first year of college, and that was the first time that I was going away from my parents. Little did I know that when I bid him farewell at the airport, it would be the last time I would see him alive."

"What happened to him?"

"My father died in a road accident, but I was comforted that I still had Mom. I thought she would always be there for me, too," Hazel shook her head, letting the pain wash over here.

"Did your Mom also die?"

"No," Hazel blinked rapidly. "My mom couldn't stand the loneliness while I was in college, so she got herself a job at a law firm. It wasn't like she needed the money, because my dad left us comfortably off. In no time, Mom fell in love with her boss who was a widower, married him and moved to Boston when he decided to relocate and take over his family business."

It was Waylen's turn to offer comfort and he took Hazel's hand. "Do you see your mother often?" She shook her head. "Why not?" He was quite surprised that she didn't want to be around her family. During their darkest hours when their mother had left, he and his brothers had held each other and his father had been there for them. Being around his family was what had kept him sane all these years.

"She chose her new husband and his four children and there was no room left for me in her life."

"So she doesn't want you to visit her family in Boston?"

"No, she's always asking me to go and spend holidays with them but I can't do that."

"I don't understand."

"My mother betrayed my father by getting married again barely one year after his death. I wanted to defer for a year in college and stay home with her, but she wouldn't let me do that. Then later I understood that I was cramping her style, and she wanted to move on with her life."

"Do you really believe that?" Waylen asked in a quiet voice. "Did you ever consider how lonely your mom must have been after your father's death? When my mom left, my dad was never the same again. I know that he's also waiting for her to come back and that's why he's never moved on."

"Waylen..."

"Your father died and that freed your mother to find love again. You were in college, and being alone must have been really tough on her."

Hazel bowed her head as Waylen's words sank in. She'd never really thought of it in this way and suddenly she felt very guilty for being angry with her mother.

"I was so angry with my mother for moving on so quickly," Hazel said. "It didn't occur to me that she was so lonely."

Waylen chuckled softly, "You're not alone in that reaction. I didn't speak to my dad for months because I blamed him for everything. Of *course, I blamed myself too but in my little mind I was thinking that dad should have stopped my mom from leaving home and going away. I'm ashamed to say that even now I still blame my father, but I'm not as angry as I was then."*

"Look at us," Hazel wiped her eyes. "We're such sorry people." She smiled at him. "Thank you for opening my eyes to my mom's feelings of loneliness because I'd never thought of it in that way. I need to call my mom," and she pulled her cellphone out of her purse and dialed her mother's number.

"Hazel, this is a surprise," her mother's soft voice brought tears to her eyes. "You've never once called me. I hope you're all right."

"Mom," Hazel's voice broke on a sob. "I'm so sorry. Please forgive me for the way I've pushed you aside," she sniffed. "I'm sorry that I was so angry with you after you got married again. Please forgive me, Mom."

"Oh Hazel! You don't know how I've longed to hear you say those words. I'm also very sorry for making you feel like I abandoned you."

"You didn't abandon me and I know that Dad would have wanted you to be happy. I love you so much and I would like to come and visit you soon."

"You're always welcome to visit, dear."

"Thank you."

Hazel sat there in silence when the call was over. She felt like a huge stone had crumbled and been washed away and her heart felt so much lighter.

Waylen stared at Hazel for a while then took her hands in his. "Are you all right?"

She nodded slightly, "I'll be all right in a moment. I never realized just how much bitterness was inside me until just now when I spoke to my mom. I put her through so much."

"She sounds like a wonderful person."

"That's for sure. My mom is raising four children who aren't hers, and they love her as much as she loves them."

"Hey," Waylen drew her closer and before she knew it, his lips were on hers. It was a brief kiss and then she pushed him away, jumped to her feet and fled.

And now as she thought about the incident of the previous day, a cold sweat broke out on her brow. She was the world's biggest idiot! Now she'd gone and stupidly fallen in love with her boss! Hazel Katlin Singer had gone and fallen in love with Waylen Randolph.

"This can't happen," she murmured. "This wasn't supposed to happen at all." Then she recalled Sally Jo's words and felt really foolish. She'd confidently told Sally Jo that there was no way she would fall in love with Waylen and life in the West, yet that's exactly what had happened.

But she was also realistic enough to understand that the brief kiss in the rose garden didn't mean anything to Len. They'd both been caught up in the moment as they talked about their losses and the kiss just happened. The last thing she wanted to do was make a fool of herself, and she would do everything she could to ensure that Len never found out how she felt about him.

"I feel like an idiot," she told herself. "And the sooner I get out of here the better for me."

BROKEN HOPE

*A*bner glanced up from the kitchen table where he was working on a crossword. His attention had been broken when angry footsteps came toward the kitchen from one of the inner bedrooms. When the person appeared in the doorway he saw that it was his second son.

"Waylen, how is..." his question trailed off when Len stomped past him and opened the back door. A moment later he slammed it hard and Abner winced. His once mild and stoic son now seemed to be even more volatile than his four brothers put together. It was as if Waylen was making up for lost time. And it was all because of Hazel.

Abner wondered if he should go after his son. Then he shrugged. Waylen was old enough to work out his own issues. He purposed that he would only step in if things got out of hand. But for now he would hold his peace.

Callum walked into the kitchen a few minutes later. "Dad, what's up with Waylen?"

"Why do you ask? Abner put his crossword aside and gave his son a distracted smile.

"He looked like someone stuck a bee in his bonnet."

Abner shrugged and went back to his crossword. "The young man is of age, why don't you go and ask him because he can speak for himself?"

"Dad, didn't you see how upset he was?"

Abner sighed and raised both hands in the air, "Oh no!" his tone was filled with mockery. "My twenty-seven-year-old son is throwing a tantrum, and I'm supposed to care."

"Dad, you don't have to be sarcastic," Callum was grinning. "I'm almost one hundred per cent sure that all this has to do with Hazel."

Once again the crossword was briefly forgotten as Abner sat back and folded his arms across his chest. "Do tell!"

"I don't know what it is, but I promise to find out and share."

"Good. Go and be your brother's keeper and leave me to finish my crossword before Mrs. Brian thinks that she's beaten me again. Shoo!" Abner waved his son away and Callum left, laughing hard.

Waylen was really angry because he'd come upon the gift that Callum had bought for Hazel. It was a fluffy white teddy bear that had 'I love you' sprawled on its chest.

"Who does he think he is, buying gifts for Hazel?" He was still muttering when he got to the office. Before he could open the door he heard Hazel laughing. She was talking to someone, and he wondered who it was; then a few seconds later, he realized that she was on phone because of the one-sidedness of the conversation.

"Just make sure you credit my account with the money we agreed on, dear girl. My work here is nearly done and I want to come home now," Hazel was saying.

Unaware that her conversation was being listened to, Hazel didn't bother to lower her voice. She was speaking with Sally Jo who'd called her a few minutes ago.

"Hazel, Mr. Randolph hasn't called to tell me anything about your time being up."

"That's because it isn't necessary. You sent me down here, and my ninety days will soon be over. At least let me get a brief holiday away from all this and be fresh for my students when they report back to school in September."

"How can I tell whether your mission was successful or not," Sally Jo argued. "I need to hear from Mr. Randolph himself."

"My dear girl, why don't you place a call to Mr. Randolph and ask him? The man you sent me to tame is now easygoing and less of a perfectionist. My work here is done and I want to come home. Actually, I'd like to visit my mom before school reopens."

"No, Hazel," Sally Jo's tone was full of suspicion. "I sense that something else is going on with you. Out with it."

"Truly there's nothing, my work here is done."

"Wait a minute," Sally Jo said. "You went and fell in love with your mascot," she said wonderingly.

"You don't know what you're talking about," Hazel stated, glad that no one was in the office to witness how red her face was.

"Au contraire, Mademoiselle! Love is in the air and I hear wedding bells in the near future. My cowgirl at last!"

"Shut up! You really are a dreamer. But on a more serious note, I think it's time for me to come home. I know I have something like three weeks left on this assignment but I'm done here."

"All right then, I'll do you a bank transfer as soon as I've spoken with Mr. Randolph. But are you sure you don't want to stay on? After all, the ranch is quite a lovely place for a holiday, and one of these days I may just fly down there. Mr. Randolph told me that he has an open invitation for me and I should feel free to take it up whenever I'm ready."

"Don't be deceived by the picturesque beauty of Randolph Ranch. Everyone has to pull their weight around here and we all work very hard. It's no walk in the park."

"Ah well, anyway, let me see what I can do in the next two days."

"Please," Hazel pleaded. She couldn't wait to get out of this place before someone discovered her secret.

"Well I have to go now," Sally Jo said. "I have some people waiting on me."

"Bye then, and I hope to hear from you soon."

Hazel stared at her phone after the call was over. She prayed that Sally Jo would come through for her before she made a total fool of herself and everyone found out that she was deeply in love with Waylen. She couldn't face the humiliation of being mocked.

Waylen was a very intelligent man, and if she continued being around him, she might just give into her weakness and let it slip that she was in love with him.

WAYLEN FELT a sharp pain in his chest at Hazel's words. Now he had a true picture about her! She was nothing more than an opportunist, and he would drive her off the ranch as soon as possible. He felt betrayed and wanted to rush into the office and confront her. Let me see her deny everything, he thought. But then he realized that he was very angry and likely to speak words that would wound for a long time.

Over the years his father had taught them that it was better to remove oneself from a confrontation and especially if self-control couldn't be exercised. *"Be very careful to never spew out words that could break someone's heart, no matter how angry you are. The Bible allows for us to get angry but then we're urged not to sin because of that anger."*

So he took deep breaths to calm himself down.

THE CONFRONTATION

*A*s soon as she was done with the call with Sally Jo, Hazel decided to finish up the filing she'd been doing. It wasn't much, and she expected to be done in a short while. Then she heard the heavy tread of cowboy boots coming toward the office, and the door opened.

When she turned around, she found Waylen standing there, and a smile began to form on her lips before she remembered that she needed to act very cool toward him. But his rugged handsomeness took her breath away and she was glad that in about two days' time this torment of beholding his face would soon be over.

"So this was all a game to you?" Waylen walked up to his desk. When she looked into his eyes she realized that he was really angry.

"What are you talking about?"

"I heard you on the phone talking to someone. So you were paid to make me easier going and less of a perfectionist, right? Is that what you came out here to do?"

Hazel paled and stared wordlessly at Waylen. She had no defense because he was right.

"Deny it," he demanded. "Deny that you're here just to squeeze money from my family."

"It isn't like that," Hazel said lamely.

"I heard you bragging that you've tamed the perfectionist, and I take it that you were referring to me, right?"

Waylen sounded so hurt that Hazel felt her heart breaking. "Please believe me, it isn't what you think."

"Enough with your lies."

A loud clap of thunder startled Hazel and she jumped. Lightning followed and suddenly the skies opened and the rain came down hard. Hazel quickly shut the windows and drew the drapes as Waylen switched the office lights on.

"Talk now," Waylen ordered.

"What do you want me to say?" Hazel nervously twisted her fingers.

"So you're nothing but a materialistic woman," Waylen hissed. "So you came out here to trap me, right? Wait until my father hears about this. He'll send you packing because he hates mischief of any kind."

"I didn't come here to cause any mischief."

"Really? So what do you call this then? Someone paid you to change me and turn me into a different person?" Hazel remained silent. "You can't even deny it."

"No," Hazel said. "I won't deny it because it's true. I took on this assignment as a challenge."

"So you're not even an intern?"

"No, I'm a teacher and we're on our long summer holidays. I needed somewhere to go when school closed so I came here."

"How?"

"Through a friend who found out that Randolph Ranch usually offers positions to interns."

"So this was all a game to you?"

Hazel shook her head. "Not all of it and that's why I'm leaving now."

That shocked Len. "What do you mean you're leaving? You signed an agreement to be an intern and my assistant for ninety days and that period hasn't come to an end yet."

Hazel shrugged and wiped her face with the back of her hand, "There's no point in me being here any longer."

"So you want to take the cowardly way of running away from the messes you've made?"

"What mess have I made? What do you want from me?" Hazel cried out. "I've admitted that I came here to change you and so I can no longer continue working here."

Waylen shook his head, "I could charge you with fraud."

Hazel's heart skipped a beat. "Why would you do that? I never received any salary or allowance from you."

"No, but someone else is paying you to be here," his eyes narrowed. "How do I know that you aren't some corporate spy who came out here to steal our secrets and sell them to the highest bidder?"

Hazel stared at him in shock. "What?"

"Oh yes, or do you think there are no corporate spies in the ranching world?"

"You really are paranoid," Hazel bristled and her voice was filled with indignation. "Tell me what kind of secrets do you think I would steal from you?"

"You tell me since you're here under false pretenses. If I get the law involved, then you'll be in a lot of trouble."

"Get the law involved if you want, because I'm innocent of your paranoid accusations."

"Just know that if the law gets involved you can be sure that even your career as a teacher will be over."

"Are you threatening me?"

"It's not a threat, my dear girl but a promise because I intend to get to the bottom of this issue."

Hazel felt her hackles rising. She couldn't believe that this man was accusing her of being a corporate spy. Even if she was here under false pretenses it didn't give him the right to hurl baseless accusations at her.

"I'm done with all this," Hazel said and waved her hand which accidentally swiped the files off her desk and sent them flying in all directions. "You think it's been easy working for someone who behaves like a control freak?" She moved to Waylen's desk and swiped all the contents to the floor, narrowly missing his laptop. "I'm already in trouble so I might as well do my worst," she hissed. "Do you know how much I've had to endure from you just to remain sane?" She moved over to the bookshelf.

"Hazel, please don't," Waylen stared in horror at the mess on the floor.

"Watch me," she said and swiped the books off the shelves. "Deal with your mess and bring in the army to arrest me for all I care. I won't allow you or anyone else to intimidate me." She walked to the door. She spotted more files on Callum's desk and these joined the rest on the floor before she opened the door and walked out, slamming it hard behind her. Waylen felt as if his teeth had all be loosened from the vibration of the slammed door.

He heard footsteps hurrying down the hallway as he stared in dismay at the mess in his office.

"Breathe," he told himself, struggling not to hyperventilate. "This is just a small mess and you can make things right."

The door opened and he turned to find his four brothers standing there.

"What happened in here?" Callum was the first to enter the office and he stared in shock at how it looked. He turned his eyes to his brother. "Did a tsunami sweep through here?"

"Bro," Maynard followed, carefully stepping over some files. He moved to the center of the office and placed his hands akimbo and surveyed the mess. "Who did you offend?"

"Hazel must have done this," Kendrick said, a large grin on his face. "You go, Girl!" And for his words he got a file tossed at him by Waylen.

"I'll gladly rearrange your face for you," Waylen growled. "How can you stand there cheering on a person who's made a mess of my office?"

"What did you do to Hazel," Quin was the only one who wasn't smirking. But neither did he express anger.

Waylen wondered that none of his brothers, not even Callum who he shared an office with even bent down to pick up a single file and place it in its rightful position.

"Congratulations my brother," Maynard actually clapped his hands.

"Why?" Waylen was puzzled at his brother's words.

"That you're standing in the middle of a messed up office and you're not having a panic attack. In the past, had something like this happened you would be lying prostrate on the floor and hyperventilating, almost giving yourself a heart attack. You've come a long way, Bro."

And Waylen realized that his brother was right. For surely, had it been in the days past he would now be clutching at his chest while struggling to breathe. But now, apart from the initial slight discomfort he'd felt as Hazel tossed the files and books on the floor, he was all right, one hundred per cent normal.

"Oh yes!" Quin walked up to Waylen and slapped him on the back. "Our foundling has come of age."

"People, people," Callum called out. "Stop with all that. We need to find out why Hazel who is such a timid and docile creature would go on a rampage."

"Timid? Docile? Are you out of your mind to refer to that whirlwind like that?" Waylen glared at his brothers. "Don't ever use those adjectives to describe that woman. See," he waved his hand around the office. "Is this the work of a timid and docile woman?"

"Yes," Maynard said without blinking. "Even a kitten when cornered will show you its sharp claws. You must have provoked Hazel, and the only way she could deal with matters was to go on a rampage. This is all your fault and I will defend her to the highest court in the world. You brought this upon yourself, brother."

"Why do you people act as if I'm to blame here?"

"Because we know you very well," Rick picked up a file and placed it onto the nearest desk, which happened to be Callum's.

"That doesn't go there," Waylen stepped forward and snatched the file and placed it on Hazel's desk. "It belongs here." For the next few minutes, Waylen's brothers started picking up files and books and placing them at random spots and at first Waylen kept hopping from side to side around the room and correcting the errors. Then he suddenly stopped moving and started laughing.

"I see what you guys are doing," and he actually tossed a book back on the floor.

"Is it working?" Quin grinned and picked up another book which he placed on Hazel's desk.

"I get it," Waylen said. He really did! "You're trying to get me to have a panic attack. This is all a test, and I see that now."

"But your actions prove that you're now cured of your idiosyncrasies. Well, perhaps not all of them but this is a good start." Maynard said. "Now, if you want us to help you clear this office up then you need to tell us what you did to Hazel."

Waylen sighed and then decided to tell his brothers everything. "I just found out that Hazel was paid by someone to come out here and change me, as if I'm oil in an engine," he fumed. "Who does that?"

"Hazel did and we commend her for a job well done," Callum said. "That woman is a saint, if you ask me. Penny is a saint too."

Waylen couldn't believe that his brothers weren't showing any signs of anger toward Hazel, not even Callum whose files were all over the place. "How can you stand there and justify that woman's actions? She took money from someone to work on me and that hurts."

"Ah!" Quin nodded. "You're offended and feel like she sold you out."

"Precisely!" Waylen agreed.

"Bro," Kendrick sat on the edge of Callum's desk. "Even if the woman was paid to change you, what's so bad about that? We've all missed our fun-loving brother who right under our very noses turned into a control freak. We're happy to have you back."

"I never went anywhere. I've always been here."

"Physically yes, you've been here all the time. But emotionally and psychologically," Maynard shook his head. "All of a sudden, you changed into this unbearably neat person and I think I know why."

"Huh?" Waylen gave him a blank look.

"Do tell," Rick encouraged.

Maynard sighed, "Do you all remember the day Mom died?" His brothers nodded except for Waylen. "Rick, you and Waylen were playing near the Christmas tree and almost brought it down. You caused such a mess and Mom got so upset." A solemn air descended on the office. "She rode out a few minutes later and never returned home alive again. That's the day Waylen started changing."

Waylen was startled. He hadn't realized that anyone, least of all his younger brother had noticed.

Maynard was still speaking, "Many times after that I would hear you crying and begging Mom to come back because you'd cleaned up some mess, tidied all our rooms including dad's, washed up and all that," he shook his head. "Suddenly you couldn't bear to see any mess or anything that was out of place. That habit grew subtly until it became almost impossible to be around you again."

Waylen was struck with remorse. "I didn't realize that my actions were affecting you all. Why didn't you stop me, and however did you all put up with me for all these years?"

"Everyone grieves in their own way," Quin once again placed a hand on his brother's shoulder. "We love you and were praying that this would get better and the real you would emerge from that cocoon you'd placed yourself in. Dad told us to give you time, and we did all we could to help you because each time you were faced with any kind of mess you would have a panic attack. But for the past few weeks I've noticed some considerable changes in you and I'm happy."

WAYLEN WAS worried when supper time came around, but Hazel didn't put in an appearance. Being a Wednesday meant that the interns had dinner with the rest of the family, and none of her peers had seen her in a while. One of them even went to check in her room, but it was empty.

"Where do you think she could be?" Waylen asked Callum. "Do you think she's left the ranch?"

"Someone would have seen her leaving and besides, with all that rain I don't think she could. She must be somewhere around and we'll find her."

"But what if she's running away from the ranch because of what happened earlier?" Waylen felt guilty. After spending a few hours with his brothers as they tidied up his office, he acknowledged that he could have handled things better than he had. He was afraid for Hazel because it had rained hard and she was out there alone in the cold and dark. If one of the cowboys had seen her, he would definitely come to report. But as it was, no one had come to the door. What if something bad had happened to her?

"Brother," Callum said. "If Hazel has run away then it's because of how she feels about you." This was said when dinner was over and the interns had left for their respective dwellings.

"What are you talking about?"

Callum made a face, "Even a blind donkey can tell that Hazel is in love with you. I saw how she looked at you and how she behaved whenever you were around. That's how our Kelsey here did when she began falling madly in love with our big brother."

"Callum, I'll get you for this," the previously silent Kelsey pointed her dessert fork at him. "Just you wait."

"The truth must be told, dear sister," Callum looked at all his brothers. "Tell me that I wasn't the only one who noticed Hazel's behavior whenever Waylen was around. And see what a good influence Hazel has had on our hitherto robotic brother. Oh yes, and Karaoke night when this dude snatched my date from right under my nose and behaved all possessively toward her. Then the song they sang," his eyes grew dreamy. "All those signs point to someone being in love, or two someones."

The others, including Kelsey, nodded in agreement.

Waylen rose to his feet. "I have to find Hazel and make things right with her," Callum's words had struck a chord in his heart and it was filled with warmth that he couldn't explain. It surprised him that none of his brothers made a move to join him. "Is no one coming with me to search for Hazel?"

"She isn't lost," their father walked into the dining room. "Sorry I'm late for dinner but Buck insisted that I join his family for theirs. I heard most of what you people have been saying."

"How?" They all looked at him in surprise and Quin held his phone up. Abner pointed at his eldest son. "Quin called me so I could listen in." He turned to Waylen. "You created the mess so go and clean it up. And make sure you bring my girl home or there'll be trouble for sure."

"Dad, even you?"

"Go and get a horse from the stable and ride out in search of the poor girl. She must be very cold, alone and frightened out there."

"You people are no help at all," Waylen grumbled as he walked out of the dining room. He grabbed someone's trench coat then left the house, making his way toward the stable.

The moment he entered the stable he sensed that Hazel was somewhere in there. He hoped she was safe and hadn't been kicked by one of the horses, though the ones in the stable right now were young, months-old foals that hadn't yet learned to kick people with their hooves.

THE FAINT SCENT OF HAZEL'S ROSE PERFUME GAVE HER AWAY. "HAZEL?" HE CALLED OUT AS HE ENTERED THE BRIGHTLY LIT STABLE. HE DIDN'T WANT TO STARTLE THE FOALS LEST THEY BEGIN MAKING TOO MUCH NOISE, BUT HE NEEDED TO FIND HER QUICKLY. SHE'D BEEN OUT IN THE COLD FOR TOO LONG AND HE NEEDED TO BRING HER HOME WHERE IT WAS SAFE.

HAZEL THOUGHT she was dreaming when she heard Waylen calling out to her. She'd fled from the house, and in her haste, hadn't realized that it was still raining heavily. All she'd been thinking about at the time was how to put as much distance between her and Waylen as possible.

Then she'd slipped outside the stable and fallen, getting the breath knocked out of her and scraping her knees and elbows which weren't protected. Because of the rain, there was no one to help her, so she'd dragged her muddy self into the stable, seeking the warmest place to wait out the rain.

None of the cowboys came in and she knew that it was because of the rain and also, they had to eat their dinner. She knew that someone would eventually come, but it would be much later when the final lockup was being done.

"Hazel?" The voice sounded urgent.

"Over here," she croaked. She was thirsty and her knees and elbows hurt. She was also cold and hungry and all she wanted was a hot bath, some food and then bed, in that order.

Waylen heard Hazel's voice and rushed toward it. The moment he saw her bedraggled form he fell to her knees before her. "I'm sorry," he saw the blood on her knees and elbows. She was also covered from head to toe in mud but he didn't care.

"My darling," he said, rising swiftly and easily scooping her from the ground. "You really had me worried. Don't ever do that to me again."

"You'll soil your white shirt," Hazel squealed and tried to get away. "Put me down, I can walk."

"Woman, be still," Waylen roared as he strode out of the stable. He paused long enough to shut the door, then headed for the house. He burst through the front door, leaving his family gaping speechlessly at him.

"Kelsey, I'll need your help please," he said as he made his way to one of the empty guest rooms.

"Your shirt," Kelsey pointed out when he'd gently placed Hazel on a chair and knelt down to pull her canvas shoes off.

"That doesn't matter," he waved his sister-in-law's concerns aside. There were more important matters to be dealt with, and a filthy shirt that was probably completely ruined anyway, was the least of his concern. "Please help Hazel to clean up. I'll get her something to eat and then go to the hostel and get her things. This is where she'll be staying from today."

"Very well," Kelsey hid an amused smile.

Waylen moved swiftly out of the room and found his brothers and father in the living room where he'd left them.

"You need to change out of that shirt," his father told him. "It is probably ruined forever, and it's very expensive."

Waylen shrugged, "It's just a shirt and doesn't really matter. Hazel is safe and that's all that counts. I'm going to make her something to eat; then I'll go to the hostel and bring her bags so she can stay here with us from today."

"Your suggestion is a good one, but you need to get cleaned up before you handle any food. I doubt that Mrs. Brian will let you anywhere near her utensils with you looking like that," Quin said.

Waylen was surprised to catch a gleeful look on his father's face.

$$\sim$$

Hazel woke up and got the sensation that someone was watching her. She opened her eyes and the first person she saw was Waylen. He was fast asleep in the chair next to her bed and he looked so peaceful that she was loath to wake him up. But she needed to use the washroom, and as soon as she moved his eyes flew open. He gave her a lazy and sleepy smile.

"How did you sleep?" He asked her.

"I slept well," she replied. "Please don't tell me that you spent the whole night in that chair."

"I actually went to my room but then couldn't sleep for a long while and tried to read. Then I decided to come and check on you and then fell asleep in this chair." He rose to his feet and stretched himself out. "Are you hungry? Last night you didn't eat much supper."

"I need to freshen up first," she said. "And yes, I'm very hungry."

"Go ahead while I head for the kitchen to rustle up something for you to eat since it's just about four in the morning."

"I don't have anything else to change into."

"Check the closet," Len said on his way out of the bedroom. "Your clothes are all in there."

"Why?"

"Because from last evening this will be your bedroom until further notice."

HER FAVORITE MAN

Hazel was having a wonderful time. Waylen made her feel so beautiful all the time and also shy. His gaze each time it lit upon her was so intense that she felt as if he was reading all the secrets of her mind, not that she really had any.

Two days after the office incident, he declared his love for her before his father and brothers. Then in the evening he asked to take her out for dinner and their destination was a very exclusive and expensive restaurant. She felt underdressed but was glad that she'd worn one of the dresses she'd brought with her.

"You look so beautiful," Len could barely keep his eyes off Hazel. How hadn't he noticed just how beautiful she was? Then he chuckled to himself; of course, her mismatched outfits had made him think that she was an untidy dresser.

"Thank you," she said shyly as he handed her into the passenger side of his Jeep Wrangler. The car suited the man, Hazel thought. She still couldn't believe that Waylen Randolph had declared his love for her. This man was hers!

"I must admit that you really got me with your dressing when you first got here," he said when he joined her and started the car. "Was it all deliberate?"

"Well, I had to get your attention and keep it," she replied with a broad smile on her face. "I needed to pull you out of the place you'd taken yourself and so I decided to become an eye sore."

"It doesn't matter anymore because now all I see is your beauty."

"Stop," she held her palms to her cheeks which were really red and warm. "You'll make me have a big head with all your praise."

"You deserve to hear it and even more," he said. They fell into companionable silence, each lost in their own thoughts. Hazel was thinking about Sally Jo and how she would react to these latest developments. She knew that her friend would laugh her head off and tell her, 'I told you so,' as many times as she could.

Waylen was thinking about how blessed he was to have this beautiful woman in his life. He acknowledged that before her arrival life had been dreary, but she'd spiced it up. And she was his!

Hazel didn't find it odd that the restaurant Waylen took her to seemed to be half empty. Corona virus had really dealt adversely with businesses and many were just starting to pick up again. But she liked the cool and serene atmosphere with soft music playing in the background. Since it was well lit she could clearly see the other diners, and one or two waved at Len.

"This is a nice place," she said as he seated her, then took his place opposite her. This particular table was meant for only two people, and Hazel wished she could tell her mom all about it. They spoke every day, and the bond between them was growing. Hazel longed for the day when she would introduce her mother to the man who'd captured her heart. Her father would have approved of Waylen.

"What are you thinking?" Waylen saw the faraway look in his beloved's eyes.

Hazel blinked and focused her eyes on him. "I was thinking that my father would have approved of you. It's sad that you'll never get to know such a great man; and he, too, missed out on the chance of knowing what a wonderful man you are."

"He lives on in you and the wonderful memories you have of him."

Hazel asked Len to select what they would eat, and after about half an hour of soft chatting their meal arrived. She'd noticed that Len loved potatoes in any form and tucked that information in her mind.

As they took their dinner Len kept feeding her with his fork and she tried to protest. A blush climbed her cheeks when once again, he reached forward with his fork in his hand and a piece of well-done steak at the end of it. She was aware that they were receiving interesting looks from the other diners. But Waylen didn't seem to care.

"Open up, my darling," he said and she obediently parted her lips and received the offering. "Good girl, now I'm waiting for you to reciprocate."

"Waylen," Hazel protested, blushing even more as her eyes went around the well-lit restaurant. "People are looking at us," she even spotted a person holding their cellphone up, no doubt to snap a picture of them. She knew that Len and his brothers were like celebrities in Cedar Hill and she was sure that their photo would soon be posted online.

"Let them look," Waylen said, looking quite unconcerned. "I want the whole world to know that I've found the one my heart sought and yearned for."

"You're making me blush," Hazel whispered.

He gave her such a tender smile that it brought tears to her eyes.

Once dinner was over their dessert plate was brought. "Do you feel that?" Waylen asked Hazel.

"Feel what?"

"This special moment," he smiled again and Hazel's eyes widened when the O'Jays' classic music suddenly filled the air. It was her father's favorite band and music and the song that was singing made her blink rapidly because she felt nostalgic. She'd listened to this song with her father so many times and it had even been played during his burial.

"Forever Mine

All because you're my kind

Aw baby

I got what you want, you got what I

Want,

An' we were made for each other..."

Waylen rose to his feet and held out a hand. "May I please have this dance, my lady?"

Hazel felt really shy and the atmosphere in the restaurant had changed to one of expectancy. Then she saw the waitress who'd been serving them approach their table with a large cake which she placed on the table.

It was white and decorated all round with red roses. There was a single long stem at the center of the cake.

"Oh, the cake," Waylen sat back down.

"What's going one?" Hazel put a hand to her throat. The lights suddenly went dim and a spotlight was focused on their table. "Waylen?"

"My darling," Waylen left his seat again and went down on one knee. "Just as the O'Jays are singing, you're that someone that I've been hoping, praying and looking for all my life. You're the best blessing I've received and since you came into my life you've changed me in ways I would never have imagined."

"Oh Waylen!" Tears of joy pricked at the back of her eyes.

"Hazel Singer, will you please be mine forever? To have and to hold from this day forward?" Waylen took the single stem stuck at the center of the cake and that's when Hazel noticed that it was artificial. He turned the rose and a beautiful gold ring glistened.

"Save something for the wedding vows," Hazel heard Callum's voice and blinked in surprise.

"Say yes, girl, and put my boy out of his misery," Abner's voice also rang out.

"Yes," Hazel held out her left hand and Waylen slipped the ring on with trembling hands. Then he rose to his feet and helped her up. There was loud applause, catcalls, and whistles; then the lights came back on. That's when Hazel noticed that Waylen's whole family was there, including Kelsey who was securely tucked by her husband's side. Even their cheerful housekeeper, Mrs. Brian, was present as were the other interns.

"How?" Hazel looked up at Waylen, her eyes quite dazed.

"Kelsey, Callum and Maynard arranged all this," he drew her close. The music was still playing softly in the background.

"How did you know that I love the O'Jays?"

"Easily," Waylen grinned at her. "You hum their music all the time and this particular one is even the ringtone of your cellphone."

"Observant man."

"That I truly am, especially as far as you're concerned."

~

"WOULD YOU PLEASE COME WITH ME?" Waylen asked the next day as they were in the office. It was just after lunch and work was slow.

"Sure," Hazel answered without hesitation. She still couldn't believe that she was engaged to this handsome and charming man. It felt like a dream but the ring on her finger said otherwise.

She was surprised when Waylen held her hand and walked with her to the rose garden. He pulled out a pair of scissors from his shirt pocket and cut out nine beautiful white roses that were just budding.

Then he led the way to the small hill which was about a mile away from the house. Hazel had been this way once before with Kelsey.

Waylen pushed open the small gate to the family cemetery, still holding Hazel's hand.

"I've never been here before today," he said as he walked toward his mother's grave. "For sixteen years I haven't been here. When my Mom died, I didn't want to accept it and for years I kept hoping and praying that she would walk through the door and come back to us. I told myself that for as long as I didn't see her grave she was still alive out there in the world and would one day return home," he sighed tiredly. "It's been torture all through, and I thought that if I was clean and kept everything in pristine condition then my Mom would come back, and she would be happy."

"My darling, I'm so sorry for all the pain you've been through."

Waylen turned to Hazel and drew her close with one hand. "Thank you for walking into my life and turning it upside down. Thank you from bringing me to this point where I can finally deal with the pain of my mother's death and let go."

Hazel felt the tears in her eyes.

"Today I can finally bid farewell to my mother and move on. I know that she's in heaven and one day we'll meet again. But for now, I'll strive to be a son she would be proud of. Hazel, I promise I'll be the best husband in the world to you, and when the Lord blesses us with children, the best dad ever. Also, I'll take my position as the priest and head of our family and always bless and pray for you and our children."

"Thank you," Hazel was really humbled by the heartfelt prayer.

"Now please help me lay these flowers on my mom's grave. I never did it all those years ago and finally I can say goodbye." They placed the roses in one of the vases provided, for there were several of them sunk into the marble surface. They observed a solemn moment.

"Why nine stems?" Hazel asked as they made their way to the small bench and sat down.

"One for each member of the family. That's dad, mom, the five of us and then you and Kelsey. As the family grows we'll keep adding the number of stems. And now I understand when

Mom said that the rose garden was her gift to let us know that she loved us so much."

They sat in silence for a while, and Hazel was glad that finally her man was letting go of the past. Now he could move ahead and be who the Lord had designed him to be.

"Farewell, Mom," Waylen rose to his feet and held out a hand to Hazel. He blew a kiss toward his mother's grave and finally, after sixteen years, he felt deep peace within him and knew that it was partly because of the woman who was standing by his side.

It was also mostly because of the love he knew the Lord had for him, a patient kind of love that allowed him to grieve without falling apart all these years. "Thank You Lord," he murmured.

EPILOGUE

"*D*ad?" Hazel slowly approached her stepfather. She'd never called him anything other than Mr. Webster or 'my mother's husband.' She saw the startled look in his eyes then the shimmering of tears. "Dad, would you please walk me down the aisle today?" She asked him shyly.

"Yes," the distinguished man choked on the single word.

"I'm so sorry that I haven't been a good daughter to you all these years. You see, I thought you'd come to take my mom away from me. I felt abandoned and held a grudge against you. Please forgive me." She smiled at her mother and stepfather who both looked stunned. "You've made my mom so happy and I finally acknowledge that you never came into our lives to take my father's place. God brought you into our lives to stand in for my father and you've done so without complaining or grumbling, even when I was being very difficult. Thank you so much, Dad, for making Mom so happy and for being the father I needed even if I didn't know it at the time."

"Oh, Child!" Suddenly Hazel was caught up in the warm, fatherly embrace of the man she'd hated for so long. "I forgive you and also ask for your forgiveness for being indifferent to your pain. I should have done more to make you feel that you're part of the family. Can we start again?"

Hazel nodded, tears in her eyes. "I'd like that very much."

Mr. Webster beamed like the proud father he was as he walked his eldest daughter down the aisle. He made a silent but heartfelt promise to his predecessor that he would never again turn his back on this girl. She was a special daughter and he was happy that finally they would be the family his beautiful wife had always prayed for.

Once he'd handed Hazel over to Waylen, he joined his wife on the front row seat which was reserved for the parents of the bride. He turned to his wife as she slipped her hand into his and gently squeezed it, sending him a message that he understood without a single word being spoken.

Throughout the wedding service, Hazel and Waylen only had eyes for each other. The minister, wise man that he was, kept the sermon short and sweet.

"You may now kiss the bride," the minister announced forty-five minutes later.

Waylen held Hazel's face in his palms. "These hands of mine will hold and cherish you and our children forever, my darling. Hazel Randolph, I love you so much."

"I love you too," Hazel said shyly.

During the reception Waylen noticed that his father was walking away. He watched as his parent made his way toward the small hill in the distance, and he knew that he was going to visit his mother's grave. He smiled as he thought about the conversation he'd had with his father just the night before.

"It took me this long to finally let go of Mom," he told his father as the two of them sat in the den. "From the day Mom died, I blamed you for taking her away from us. Dad, I'm so sorry for the way I acted toward you. Please forgive me."

"There's nothing to forgive, Waylen. My son, you don't know how I've longed to hear you say that you've finally accepted that your mother isn't coming back to us. It was hard watching the five of you grieve in your own different ways, but you concerned me the most. Your brothers slowly came to terms with what had happened, but you never seemed to move on, and I was so worried about you. Just to ease your mind, I also struggled with losing your mother and it took me time to come to terms with her death. Barbara was such a vibrant and wonderful woman and no single day goes by that I don't miss her."

"Is that why you've never thought about remarrying?"

Abner nodded slowly. "Barbara was my heart and I've never moved on past her. While I know that a number of women have showed a lot of interest in your aging father through the years, I could have moved on if I wanted to, it just didn't feel right."

"Why didn't it feel right, Dad?"

"I gave all my love to your mother, and it wouldn't have been fair to any other woman to compete with that. Women are to be loved, adored and cherished; and since it's not possible to offer that to another, being single is the best thing for me."

Len smiled at his father, "For years we always hoped and prayed that you would marry Mrs. Brian," he said and his father laughed. "Why are you laughing, Dad? Mrs. Brian has always been there for us and she loves you."

"She loves me like a friend," Abner said. "She only recently lost her husband and I happen to know that she's still grieving for him."

Len nodded, "The foolishness of children. We would talk about the two of you getting married so Mrs. Brian wouldn't have to leave us."

"I'm glad that you boys had someone who stood in for your mother. I wouldn't have managed all by myself because I was hurting so much. Mrs. Brian is a wonderful woman but she's just my friend."

"It's nice to have someone to talk to and especially about issues that can't be discussed with anyone else. Hazel really understands me and I'm amazed that the Lord brought her to me. I didn't even know I needed her until she got here."

"That's how love is," Abner said. "We can go for years without it and think that we're all right, until that special person comes into our lives and takes their rightful place there. That's when we realize *what we've been missing all along. But just know that I love you so much, and all has been put behind me."*

"Thank you so much, Dad. I've lived with this guilt, and your forgiveness has freed me now."

And now as he danced with his new bride, Len agreed with his father. For years he'd lived without the desire to have anyone in his life, until Hazel came along.

"You're thinking deeply," Hazel said as she swayed in her husband's arms. "And you look rather pensive."

He smiled down at her, "Please forgive me for letting my mind wander. I just saw dad going toward the cemetery and remembered the conversation we had last night. I hope he'll be all right."

"He's a strong man, he'll be all right."

"Now that I've found you, I wish everyone in the world would find their God-ordained spouse and be as happy as I am. I really wish my father would find love again. It hurts to see him being so lonely."

"Dad doesn't strike me as being lonely," Hazel said. "There are people in the world who prefer their own company but are never lonely. And he has us now and soon Kelsey and Quin will give him his first grandchild, then you and I will add to his joy. Dad will be all right."

"I pray so," he pulled her closer. "I love you so much and could dance forever with you in my arms."

"Thank you for loving me and I promise that I'll always love and honor you."

ABNER RANDOLPH WAS A REALLY happy man. His second son had just married a wonderful woman who reminded him in so many ways of Barbara.

"Thank You, Lord," he said as he placed two roses on his wife's grave. He'd grabbed these from one of the vases placed all over the house and homestead. Flowers from the garden his wife had planted years before and which bloomed all year round. "Dear Lord, thank You for restoring my son and giving him a good, virtuous and godly woman as his bride."

Then he sat down on the small bench and took his phone out. "Two down, three to go," he texted, then sent the message off to Sally Jo.

Then he leaned back and intertwined his fingers behind his head, a smile on his face. He would join his family soon to carry on with the wedding celebrations, but for now this was his peaceful place.

KENDRICK'S BRIDE ON THE RUN

PROLOGUE

bner Randolph looked at his fifteen-year-old son who stood with his fists folded as if in readiness to fight. Kendrick, his third one born and the middle child, was one who worried him. They had barely spoken on the ride from school to the house. Abner worried that if he opened his mouth to speak, he would begin yelling at his son, and that was something he didn't want to do. It was Kendrick, left alone in the living room with his angry parent, who broke the tense silence.

His brothers, traitors that they were, had all disappeared to their rooms. So he was left to face his angry father alone. The cane still hadn't appeared, and Kendrick was relieved. But to be fair, his father never brought out the 'rod of correction' before listening to a person's side of the story. After which he would point out the person's sins and explain the disciplinary measures to be taken.

In that respect his father was so much better than his mother used to be. Tears filled his eyes as he thought about his mom. He missed her

271

so much. She'd died five years ago on Christmas Day itself, and he missed her every single day.

"What's going on with you Kendrick? Why do I have to come to school every few days because you've beaten someone up?"

Kendrick took a deep breath and faced his father, "Dad, believe me, I never go looking for trouble."

"So what you're saying is that trouble always comes looking for you?"

The teenager nodded, "You could say that, Dad." Kendrick's voice was hoarse because it was on the verge of breaking. "If you ask anyone at school, I never start the fights, Dad. But I have to defend myself whenever those fights start."

"That much I gathered from the principal, but do you have to engage in every scuffle?"

Kendrick noticed that his father looked quite exasperated but still he made no move to go and bring the rod of correction from his bedroom. This was a thin bamboo rod, and Kendrick had felt its effects a few times in the past. But lately his father seemed to have stopped bringing it out and instead chose to speak to the boys whenever they did something wrong. That, however, didn't mean that his other disciplinary measures were any less effective. The withholding of one's weekly allowance was enough to make Kendrick and his brothers careful about what they did. Also, mucking the dung from the stable and repairing fences by a certain period of time were tasks no one wanted to do, and especially not when it was some form of disciplinary action.

"Dad, I only do it to protect the weak students from the bullies at school."

Abner shook his head, "Rick, I know you mean well but I don't like the way you're going about this. One day you could get into trouble, get badly hurt, and there'll be no one to help you then. Your principal says you usually get away with this because your brothers are always there to back you up. What of the day when none of them will be around and you have to face more than one bully, what will you do then?"

"Dad, as I said, I'm not a troublemaker and never provoke anyone unnecessarily."

"But my problem is that you still get into fights at school. What will it take to make you stop doing these things, Rick?"

"When all the bullies at school are eliminated."

Abner sighed tiredly, "My son, the self-proclaimed champion of Cedar Hill Public School."

Rick shrugged, not caring if his parent was commending or mocking him. One thing he knew clearly was that he would never stand by and do nothing when someone bullied a woman, a child, or any weaker member of society.

INTO THE LION'S DEN

en Years Later

"I think someone put something in the water around this place," Kendrick complained looking at his two older brothers Quinten and Waylen, or Quin and Len as they preferred to be called. Both had gotten married within months of each other and they looked all loved up. In addition, their goofy smiles often irritated him—and especially Len who was just two weeks into marriage with his previous office assistant.

This was a woman who'd nearly driven Len mad with her untidiness because his brother had been a fanatical neatness freak. For years Len hadn't come to terms with their mother's death, and his character had changed drastically from an outgoing person to when Hazel had come in as a replacement for Len's office assistant who'd taken a leave of three months to deal with personal matters. At first it had seemed as if the two could barely stand each other, but wonder of wonders, they were deeply in love now and married, and as happy as they could be.

"Dear brother," Hazel, Len's new bride called out, a cheeky smile on her lips. "Why would you say that?"

"It seems as if everyone in America and their brothers are getting married. Someone must have spiked the water that people are drinking. This ranch should be renamed Randolph's Love Ranch. I thought inviting Simon to visit would be a good thing. Then the fellow gets here and reunites with his college love. And to punish me further, the fellow has now made me his best man. He says it's the best way to thank me for having found his lost love and reuniting them again. What nonsense the man speaks," Rick's voice was filled with disgust. "Now I have to go to Denver for another wedding, the third in just six months. Three whole days in that crowded city is my punishment for being a Good Samaritan. I should never have played arbitrator; now all this is on me." He glared at his brothers and their wives who were laughing hard. "It's not funny at all."

Unknown to the twenty-five-year-old man, his father was seated on the large couch in the living room. Rick, his brothers, and their wives had just finished dinner and were still dilly dallying at the dining table. Abner's ears perked when his son mentioned that he would be travelling to Denver. He could barely contain his excitement because that was Sally Jo Manning's city. The young woman had been instrumental in

276

finding wives for Quin and Len through her agency and the two were deeply in love with their wives. Hitch Your Wagon Romance Agency was based in Denver, Colorado, and Sally Jo was in the business of finding spouses for modern-day cowboys and cowgirls who were searching for true love. What better way to have his son meet up with one of the women from the agency? He knew that Rick was drawn to the weak and helpless and that was the information he needed to send to Sally Jo.

So, the next day, a warm Wednesday afternoon quite rare for November, Abner made his way to the family cemetery. This was the one place he was sure that his conversations couldn't be eavesdropped on. Every time he needed to think or make private calls, he came to the cemetery.

There were house servants and other laborers coming and going all the time in and around the house, not to mention his five sons and two daughters-in-law. So, whenever he needed time out, it was to this place that he chose to recourse.

On this November day the place was peaceful and quiet, and for a moment Abner rested his head on the back of the stone bench and closed his eyes. This was bliss, and for a moment his thoughts took him back in time when they'd selected this spot to be the family cemetery. It was his grandparents who'd chosen the spot because it stood at the edge of the homestead. The copse of trees provided natural shade as well as obscured the cemetery's view from the house.

"Death is the doorway to eternal rest in Christ and what better place for one to have their remains interred than among these beautiful

trees?" His grandfather had said. "It's not too near the house to make people weep each time they see the graves of loved ones, yet neither is it too far for one to easily access it when they need to."

His parents had agreed, and thus this spot became the family cemetery. His grandparents and parents were buried here, lying side by side. He missed them all so much and opened his eyes to look toward their graves.

Five graves covered in green marble and standing there were reminders of those gone before him. There was a spot next to Barbara's grave where his own mortal body would one day rest.

Abner often thought about his own mortality, and that was why he was determined to see all his sons settled with godly women before that time came. Though there was longevity in his lineage, Abner was also aware of the fact that accidents of all kinds could so suddenly take away the lives of people, his Barbara being one of them. She'd been in the prime of her life when a terrible riding accident took her away from her family fifteen years ago. Yet each time he visited the cemetery, it seemed like he'd buried Barbara just yesterday.

Over the years he'd tried to move on by clearing the bedroom they'd shared of everything that reminded him of Barbara and storing them in the attic. But then something would spark a memory they'd shared and he would find himself up in the attic digging through her things. Then he would carry a few items back to the room and keep them there for a while until he felt that he needed to let go again. Abner shook his head; people thought letting go was easy, but for him it wasn't.

Barbara's jewelry still lay in the vault in the bank, and he knew that at some point he would have to bring it out and give it to his new daughters. But that time wasn't here yet, he told himself. Maybe when all his five sons were married, then he would share his wife's jewelry with their brides. That thought made him smile and feel less guilty about holding onto his dead wife's properties.

The best way to continue his lineage was through his five sons, and he was really happy that in a few months' time he would hold his first grandchild in his arms. Quinten, his first-born son and Kelsey, his wife, were expecting their first child. And now Waylen and Hazel were married.

Kelsey and Hazel were proving to be wonderful daughters to him, and he never stopped praying that his remaining three sons would also soon find themselves good wives.

He leaned forward and dialed Sally Jo's number. She picked up on the first ring as she always did whenever he called her.

"Mr. Randolph, thank you so much for the bonus check," Sally Jo said. "It arrived in the mail this morning."

"You've done very well, and I can say that I'm a very happy man. The young women you sent this way are such a blessing to all of us. My sons are happy and you should see them grinning like fat and contented cats. Even though I've only known Kelsey and Hazel for a short time, they've proved to be suitable and perfect spouses for my sons."

"We always aim to please, Sir, even though Hazel originally wasn't supposed to fall in love with Waylen and remain there.

You should have heard her telling me with all confidence that she could never fall in love," Sally Jo was laughing. "But for some prior commitments, I would have been down there to shout a loud, 'I told you so,' in her face."

Abner joined her, "My dear, destiny can never be denied. When the Lord decides to do something, He does it in His own way even when we humans lean on our own understanding."

"I'm really happy that you're contented with my choices."

"Good, good, and now I have another assignment for you and this one I can say, is coming right to your doorstep."

"How do you mean, Sir?"

"My third-born son, Kendrick is next in line. I won't call it coincidence but the workings of destiny. Rick will be coming to Denver for three days to attend his best friend's wedding. The boys have been friends right from their high school days and attended the same college, being roommates. Then Simon met and fell in love with a lovely woman in college, but before they graduated, they parted ways. Rick found her through Facebook and offered her a position on our ranch. Then Rick called Simon because he knew that the two were still in love with each other. When Simon came here, the two were reunited and now we have a wedding. It's a pity that all of Simon's family lives in Denver or else we would have had the wedding here. But that notwithstanding, Rick is coming to Denver. Would it be possible to arrange for him to meet one or two of your young women? Of course, like the others, this has to be done secretly without him finding out whatever is going on."

"I know that, Sir."

"Wonderful! And one thing about this son of mine, he considers himself to be a knight in shining armor. The kind of woman who will appeal to him is some damsel in distress."

Sally Jo burst out laughing again. "Mr. Randolph, you're quite hilarious. You sound like someone who has just stepped out of Victorian England, Sir."

"Believe me, Miss Manning, I have tales to tell you. Of all my sons it was Rick who had me visiting their school practically every week. Sometimes it would even be two or three times in the same week. And the worst was one semester when I had to present myself to the school for five days in a row."

"Why, what was going on with your son?"

"Like I said, Rick considers himself the deliverer and rescuer of the weak, and champion of the downtrodden. No bully ever went unpunished, not while Rick was in that school. Sometimes he even had confrontations with boys much bigger than he was."

"Oh dear! I hope he never got hurt."

"He never came home with as much as a scratch on him because his four equally idiotic brothers acted as his wingmen all the time. Sometimes I had to pay hefty fines and even hospital bills to appease the parents of the boys who'd been beaten up. And for some reason, the police never got involved and for that I'm eternally grateful. The last thing I wanted was for any of my sons to have police records. The boys were never arrested," Abner clicked his tongue. "Those boys all gave me sleepless nights but the worst of them all was Rick. So if you can find me some young woman who is in the kind of trouble that needs rescuing, she'll appeal to Rick. Unlike Quin and Len who required strong women, Rick's own is different. I think my son loves to be needed."

"I'll do my best to find him a most suitable partner, Sir. If you would email me his full dossier, I can begin to find him the right spouse immediately. How long do I have, as in, when is Mr. Kendrick expected in Denver?"

"In two weeks' time. Do you think you'll have come up with someone by then?"

"Yes, I have confidence that my systems will produce someone suitable. Our current database is quite large and after conducting intensive background checks you can be sure that we have the best. I'll get down to work right away."

"Thank you, Miss Manning. Send me the new contract, and after signing, I'll get it back to you with the check."

"Yes, Sir. Please pass my regards to Kelsey and Hazel."

"Will do."

RICK HAD both hands in his pockets as he strolled through his mother's rose garden.

Coming here at least once a week always brought him so much peace. His mother had planted this garden a year before her death sixteen years ago. At the time they hadn't understood when she'd told them that it was her love gift to them. But now whenever he strolled through the garden, he was thankful for it.

Being the Randolph brother in charge of operations on the ranch, each day he dealt with numerous figures and they all had to be up to date. On any given day he had to know the full number of all the animals on the ranch. They had over eight thousand head of cattle and horses. He had to know how many calves were born daily and how many stillbirths occurred. The living and dead animals had to be computed and figures had to tally on a daily basis. It was hard work and time consuming, but he wouldn't have it any other way. His degree in Operations Management from the University of Delaware came in handy, and he loved what he did, for he had a good head for figures.

Yet even through all that Rick always made time for his family. Their mother's death fifteen years ago had brought him and his four brothers very close. Rick never took any single moment for granted. Each minute that he had his family with him was counted as special. Life was very precious and he did his best to live it in a way that would make his mother proud were she still here. Being the middle child, Rick thought of himself as the peacemaker of the family, not that he and his siblings had too many squabbles. Of course, siblings had their moments of disagreements but for the most part Rick always tried to stop things before they got out of hand.

To Rick, being the peacekeeper among his siblings was like penance for all the headaches and stress he'd put his father through when he was in school. Just thinking about those times his father had to be called to school because he'd gotten into fights and even involved his brothers was enough to make him sweat a little. If there was a man Rick respected with his whole heart, it was his father. The man had been patient with him and his brothers even while mourning for their mother. Not once had his father crossed the line when it came to disciplining them like he'd seen happening in some families.

While his father had had his own meltdown at some point, he'd remained a loving father. And after his father, Rick loved and respected his oldest brother, Quinten, who'd stood in for their remaining parent until he'd been strong enough to hold the family together.

"Lord, You held us together all these years, even when we would have descended into a really dark place," he murmured. "Thank You so much, and may we never forget nor take Your grace and mercies for granted."

After being cooped up in his office for hours, it was nice to be outdoors, even though it was toward the end of November. He could have gone riding, but he didn't feel like going through the pains of saddling a horse. Though there were a number of laborers that could have assisted him, Rick preferred to saddle his own horse. While no one had ever brought this up within his hearing, he always felt that someone had been careless years ago, and that had led to his mother losing her life.

Though he'd been only ten years old at the time, he could recall the sheriff asking for the person who'd saddled his mother's horse on that fateful day. Because the accident had happened on Christmas Day it was assumed that Mrs. Randolph had saddled her own horse since everyone was away from the stables and busy celebrating the holiday. Of course, no one had come forward to respond to the sheriff's queries, and the matter had rested; his mother's death was ruled an unfortunate accident. But for years now Rick had often wondered if someone had made a terrible mistake and been too scared to own up.

Years ago, Rick had heard their father and Quin talking about his mother's tragic accident and how the saddle had slipped off the horse after she got thrown.

"Your mother was too careful to have gone riding on a horse whose saddle wasn't properly fixed," his father had been saying. "She might have asked someone to saddle the horse for her and the person didn't do it properly. But it's been years now and since no one owned up at the time, I believe she may have been distracted when saddling her own horse."

"Mom was always very careful when going riding," Quin had responded. "The one thing she always emphasized was for us to make sure that our saddles were properly fixed and she always insisted on us doing it for ourselves so we could get it right. But as you say, many years have gone by, and we'll never know the truth now."

Those words had troubled Rick for years as he thought about his mother's untimely death. His mother had fallen off her horse and broken her neck, lying injured in a ditch for hours before anyone found her. It was Quin who'd found her, and she'd breathed her last in his arms. Rick had wept for weeks, not believing that he would never see his mother again. But after hearing his father and brother talking about the loose saddle, he preferred to do it himself and trusted no one.

Since saddling a horse involved much effort, he preferred to take a walk in the rose garden instead. Perhaps he would go riding later in the day but for now he just needed to be around his mother's beautiful garden. Over the years, the roses had been pruned and some bushes replaced, but everyone still referred to it as Mrs. Barbara's Rose Garden.

It always surprised Rick that come rain or sunshine, roses always filled the bushes. No matter how many times a week the roses were plucked so as to fill the vases in the house, they never ran out. His mother had planted white and red roses, and they'd all helped on that Christmas Day, exactly a year before her death.

Right now, there was a full-time gardener who tended the shrubs lovingly, and Rick admitted that his mother had been right all those years ago. She'd called this her love gift to her family and that was true. Once a week they all took turns cutting roses and going to lay them on their mother's grave. Sometimes they laid flowers on their grandparents and great grandparents' graves too, but for the most part they did it for their mother.

Rick used the small pair of scissors he'd brought along and cut seven red roses and carried them to the cemetery, placing them on his mother's grave.

"I really miss my mother," he murmured as he sat on the stone bench, feeling deep sadness and loneliness within. "I really wish she was still here to see how far we've all come. Now Kelsey and Hazel have joined the family, and it's a pity they'll miss out on knowing a great woman. Mom would have really loved them."

He raked his fingers through his hair and fought his tears. Their home was changing because of his two new sisters-in-law. Mrs. Brian, their African American housekeeper had done her best to keep things just as their mother had left them. But his father had told Kelsey and Hazel that they were free to make any changes they wanted, even if they would soon be moving to their own houses, which were being renovated. While Rick wished things would remain the same, he was realistic enough to acknowledge that, with the newcomers to the family, a lot was going to change.

He reached for his wallet and opened it, then stared at the small photograph of his mother that he carried in it. It was a portrait photo of her face and shoulders, and she'd given one to all five of them just months before her death. On the back of each photo, she'd inscribed the words, 'A Mother's Love Is Eternal.' He let a few tears escape and allowed himself to feel the pain of losing his mother. There were so many things he would have loved to share with his mother.

Sometimes he wished he had someone to whom he could pour out his heart about his pain, and he envied his older brothers who now had partners. Even Waylen, who'd refused to accept their mother's death for years had now come to terms with it, all because of Hazel. Then he put the thought aside because he didn't want to think about falling in love or marriage. At least, not at this time!

FEARFUL NEIGHBORHOOD

Twenty-four-year-old Willow Jagger cast a scared glance over her shoulder, then breathed a sigh of relief. The man who she was sure had followed her for three blocks was gone. This was her neighborhood and it was the one place in Denver where she felt safe. Even though it was a lower-middle-class neighborhood, the flats were well maintained because the residents had come together and decided that they would take care of their homes. And also, the neighbors always looked out for each other. Since her mother's death, Willow and her sisters has been treated kindly by nearly all their neighbors.

Living on Kings Avenue in Arapahoe County always made Willow feel that they were more blessed than most. Their two-bedroom apartment was on the first floor of a six-apartment complex, and it was ideal for them. The rent was fair and most of their neighbors had been there forever. What she loved most about this place was that it was a multi-racial and multi-cultural neighborhood, and everyone who came to live in peace was welcomed. Willow and her family had moved here seven years ago, but it felt like they'd been here forever.

"Willow," an elderly woman called out to her as she walked toward home. Mrs. Lorna Parks owned the grocery store that was a few yards from Willow's flat.

"Yes, Mrs. Parks?" Much as Willow needed to reach the house and make sure that her sisters were all right, she liked the elderly woman who often gave them groceries for free.

"I have a package for you," the woman led the way into the store and walked to the counter. She reached down behind the counter and brought out a large shopping bag. "You and your sisters need this, though you need to freeze the milk immediately."

"Yes, Ma'am," Willow received the bag gratefully, feeling the tears prickling behind her eyes. Ever since her mother's death eight months ago, the neighbors had showed them so much kindness. Hardly a day went by than someone dropped off foodstuff and clothing for them. Even if the clothes were used and most food nearly expired, Willow never complained. They ate what they could and froze the rest. And she'd taught her sisters to be grateful for everything.

"*We're blessed*," was what she always told her sisters.

So she smiled at her benefactor, "Thank you so much Mrs. Parks. I don't know what we would have done without you and the other kind neighbors."

"Lynn was a good woman of faith, even though that father of yours..." Mrs. Parks grimaced. "Forgive me but it's never good to speak ill of the dead even when they deserve it. It's a good thing he never lived here with you or else things might have turned out another way."

Willow didn't have an answer for the store owner because it was true that her stepfather had been a terrible person. Though he'd never lived here with them since they'd moved here after his death, her mother had probably told Mrs. Parks about life with Vincenzo Alberto. Pushing all those thoughts out of her mind she turned to leave.

"Oh, Willow, some men came by and were asking about you."

Willow's heart gave a sickening lurch, for she had her suspicions about who they might be.

"What did they want? Did you speak to any of them?"

Mrs. Parks nodded, "They came in here and asked about you and the girls, but I wouldn't give them any information. All I told them was that you often shopped around here but I had no idea from which block of flats you came," her lips tightened. "But that big mouth, Dennis Lark was here and pointed out your block to them, even telling them on which floor your house is."

"Why would he do that?" Willow's heart sank. So far, she'd managed to evade Rico Alberto, and he only ever came to the diner or sent his men to intimidate her there. Not once had they come close to her home. But now it seemed like they'd followed her home and she berated herself for her carelessness. And she was angry with Dennis Lark for he had clearly blabbered much to the men.

"You know Dennis now," Mrs. Parks was wiping the counter. "He has a good heart but a very loose tongue. I hope there's no trouble."

"No," Willow said hastily. She didn't want her neighbor prying too much into their lives. Her mother had always warned her to keep a low profile and never attract any attention to herself. There was much going on, and the last thing she wanted and needed was someone, even a well-meaning neighbor, asking too many questions.

It was with a heavy heart that she made her way to their apartment. She prayed that the men wouldn't have had the chance to go to the house and harass her sisters. The girls were still recovering from their mother's death and the last thing they needed right now was to be scared by anyone.

Isabella and Maria were sprawled on the small living room carpet watching cartoons on the old television set they'd owned forever. Willow had noticed that her sisters loved watching cartoons about horse riding and she wished she could afford to take them to one of the ranches in the Denver countryside for a holiday. A couple of those ranches had been turned into holiday spots, but these cost the earth, and right now she was struggling to meet their basic needs.

"One day," she whispered as she entered the house, we'll have money for horse riding lessons and fun." And she fixed a smile on her face so her sisters would feel that everything was all right.

As soon as Willow stepped in through the door, the two girls turned.

"Sister Willow, welcome home," ten-year-old Isabella jumped up and rushed toward her. Eight-year-old Maria joined her, and they took the shopping bag from her and placed it on the floor; then both of them hugged her. Willow felt the tears in her eyes as her sisters hugged her. She loved them so much and would do anything to keep them safe.

"Hello, girls," she kissed them both on the forehead. "I hope you were good today."

"Yes, Ma'am," Isabella reached for the shopping bag and walked to the fridge where she started putting things away. Maria followed her so she could help. "Mrs. Templar came by and brought us two loaves of bread."

"May God bless her kind soul, and all the others too. All that shopping is from Mrs. Parks at the store. Check the labels and expiry dates so we don't waste anything. Whatever is about to expire is what we'll eat first." Willow kicked her shoes off and joined her sisters in the kitchen to begin dinner preparations. "Did anyone else come by?"

"No," Isabella answered. She held up a tub of ice cream, "Mrs. Parks gave us ice cream today," she said.

"That will be our dessert," Willow said.

Once their dinner of spaghetti and meatballs, as well as ice cream for dessert, was over, the three sisters reclined on the old couch and Willow reached for the family Bible which had a place of honor on the small coffee table.

She was still feeling shaken by the man she'd thought had followed her for three blocks and then Mrs. Park's information about the others who'd come to the store asking about her family.

"Today's reading is from the Book of Isaiah, chapter fifty-four and verse seventeen," she said. "Isabella, will you read the scripture for us?"

"Yes," The little girl reached for the Bible. Willow liked it when her sisters read the Bible, and she made sure they took turns doing so. "*No weapon that is formed against us shall prosper.*"

"Good girl, and somewhere else the Bible says that the Lord is our refuge and strength and He is a very present help in time of our need." Willow took the Bible from Isabella, shut it and placed it back on the coffee table. "Do you understand what that means?" The two girls nodded. "Good, and I want you to know that we never have to be afraid of anything."

Willow needed the confidence, and reading the scriptures out loud gave her peace. They would be all right, and as she took her sisters to their room, tucked them in and kissed them goodnight, she whispered a silent prayer for safety. She then shut the door to their bedroom and went to her own.

Before she fell asleep she reaffirmed her promise that she would always keep her sisters safe.

IN THE OTHER room the two girls had only pretended to fall asleep so their elder sister could leave them.

"Bella, are you sleeping?" Maria whispered.

"Not yet," the older girl answered. "I'm worried about Willow. Did you notice anything today?"

"No, why?"

"She looked really scared when she came into the house, but I didn't want to ask her anything because I didn't want her to cry."

"Should we tell her about the men who were at school to look for us? Those two men that we hid from?"

"No," Bella's tone was harsh. "Willow told us never to speak to any strangers and I don't want to get her upset. I just wish we could go away from here so Willow won't be so scared anymore."

"Mmh! How I wish we could go and live on a farm and see animals and ride horses like in the Pony Tales cartoons. Those girls have so much fun, and if I had a horse, I would ride and be so happy."

"Maria you're such a dreamer," Bella said sleepily.

"When I grow up I'll be a cowboy."

Bella chuckled, "You're a girl so you'll be a cowgirl."

"I don't care which as long as I get to ride a horse."

THE DIE IS CAST

"What kind of job can you do, Willow?" Sally Jo leaned forward and placed both elbows on the desk. "What's your career and where do you currently work?"

"I'm a trained chef," Willow answered, "But right now I work at a diner as an assistant cook, but when there's not much work I serve as a waitress," she twisted her lips. "I really don't like it there much."

"What's wrong with working at the diner?"

"Fries, burgers and chicken aren't challenging dishes to prepare. It's better in the kitchen even if all I do sometimes is flip burgers the whole day. What I hate most is those times when I have to waitress. Some customers aren't well behaved and think that the waitresses, especially the female ones are also items on the menu. I don't want all my training to go to waste. I'd rather work in a restaurant in one of the good hotels as a cook and start from the bottom. In that way I'll gain much knowledge and experience."

Sally Jo observed the young woman seated in front of her with keen eyes. Being a good judge of character she had a feeling that Willow was a timid and rather frightened young woman.

Willow was one of those she termed as her pro bono clients, those she'd registered for free. Initially all her female clients in search of love never had to pay for registration but then she realized that some of them didn't trust in services they didn't pay for. That's how Sally Jo had come up with the one hundred dollar registration fees which surprisingly, nearly all her clients paid. But the few like Willow, who she saw were struggling, were registered for free.

Many of the young women who registered online or came in person to the agency were in search of adventure away from their normal lives. Since Hitch Your Wagon Romance Agency specialized in finding true love for cowboys and cowgirls, the thought of living on a farm or ranch out in the West somewhere appealed to many of her clients. Sally was glad that during the lockdown due to Corona she'd had quite a number of success stories. Love was beautiful, and that's what spiced up an otherwise cruel and dreary world.

When Sally Jo had taken over the agency from her aunt, she'd made a promise to herself that everyone who genuinely sought for love would find it through her. What she usually emphasized to her female clients especially, was that finding true love could take time.

"Don't ever be in a hurry," she liked to say. *"It's better to take your time and find lasting love and happiness, rather than allowing desperation to make you settle for much less than you deserve."*

Those who cooperated with her always walked away happy. It saddened Willow that some young women got so desperate that they jumped at the first chance without taking time to get to know the men who showed an interest in them. A few of them had been lucky and things turned around for them, but there were also those who'd come away hurt and bruised and quite disillusioned. Thankfully those were in the minority.

Willow had walked into the agency a few months ago to make an inquiry. At first, she'd thought that it was an employment agency, but when Sally Jo explained what they did, she'd become interested. But then she wasn't able to raise the one hundred dollars for registration. Just as she'd been about to walk out, Sally Jo had felt compassion welling up within her and she'd registered her for free.

In the four months that Willow's name had been in the agency's data base she hadn't made a single match. This was because even though she was simple and of lowly means, she still believed in having the best. And also there was the issue of her two younger sisters. While Sally Jo felt that her clients were rather narrow minded she also realized that everyone had a right to make their preferred choices. According to Sally Jo, her clients who were single mothers often had a hard time finding suitable men, even though she felt that they would make very good wives. But the few success stories gave her hope that eventually all her girls, as she referred to them, would find suitable men and settle down.

Willow noticed Sally Jo giving her a strange look. "Why are you looking at me like that? Perchance, have you found me a suitor who doesn't mind me coming with my dependents?"

"Not really, but I was thinking about your career. A friend who works at the Astrid Hotel mentioned that they're hiring."

Willow gasped and then slowly shook her head, "That's way beyond my league. I don't think I even stand a chance of getting my resumé through their doors. Seven-star hotels with restaurants that have Michelin accreditation don't hire my kind."

"Wow!" Sally Jo stared incredulously at Willow. "I didn't realize that you have no confidence in yourself. Don't you believe that you're just as good as those who work in those Michelin starred restaurants?"

"I do, but I'm also very realistic. I have a Diploma in Culinary Arts from Trinity Community College, and I happen to know that seven-star hotels only employ people who have degrees."

"Not necessarily. There are always opportunities for one to start at the bottom of the pyramid as an assistant chef or cook and then slowly rise."

That made sense to Willow, but the truth of the matter was that she was hoping to find either a husband or a job outside Denver, and if possible, out of Colorado.

Living in Denver was proving worrisome because of Rico Alberto, her stepfather's younger brother. Willow knew that the man not only dealt in drugs but he also ran a prostitution ring. He'd taken over from her stepfather and expanded his operations to beyond Denver. Rico was daily becoming a threat to the three of them.

Until her stepfather's death, Willow hadn't even been aware that he had any living relatives. He'd never talked about his family and neither had her mother spoken much about them.

Vincenzo had died six years before her mother. He'd tripped on the edge of a frayed carpet in one of the seedy clubs he owned, fallen down the stairs and broken his neck. He was dead before the paramedics arrived, and by that time everyone had fled because it was a joint that had been declared illegal due to all the vices that went on there. If there was any evil to be found in Denver, her mother had once said accusingly to Vincenzo, then his clubs were the top of the pile.

The police had showed up the next day at their house, and Willow had heard her mother explaining what had transpired. According to her mother, who also worked at the same club where Vincenzo had met his death, the two of them had been arguing.

"Vincenzo was drunk," her mother had said. "And whenever he got drunk or high on drugs, he picked fights with anyone. He tripped on the carpet and fell down the stairs."

At the time Willow felt that her mother was hiding something, but she didn't want to ask any more questions. She knew that the argument had started at home when Vincenzo had tried to grab her, and her mother had come to the rescue. In spite of her mother's ugly lifestyle, Willow knew that she loved her children. Lynn Jagger had done all she could to protect Willow, including enrolling her for martial arts classes for her own protection. And she'd never let Vincenzo try anything funny with Willow.

In the deepest recesses of her mind, Willow had been glad when her stepfather had died. His presence in the house had begun making her very uneasy because of the way he'd started observing her. If there was a man she'd feared and hated in equal measure, it was Vincenzo Alberto.

The man had turned her once sweet and morally upright mother into a drug addict and forced her to sell her body to his clients to keep him supplied with money. Many times Willow had begged her mother to leave Vincenzo so they could move to another city where she could get help for her drug problem and begin life again. But her mother's addiction to cocaine had made her totally dependent on Vincenzo. It was Willow who'd taken care of Isabella and Maria, made sure they were clean and well fed, and she kept them safe.

Willow's dream had been to become a pharmacist, for she'd loved chemistry and mixing chemicals while in school—at least during the few times she managed to attend classes. But taking care of her often drugged-up mother and little sisters meant that she'd missed many classes and had barely made it through high school.

But for her concern for her mother and sisters, she would have moved to an out-of-state college. It was the fear of one day waking up to hearing that Vincenzo had murdered her loved ones that had kept her in Denver. And even then, she lived in fear and prayed desperately for a way out of their predicament.

And in the end Vincenzo had indirectly caused her mother's death. Two years after Vincenzo's death, her mother had discovered that she'd contracted HIV. That had been a wakeup call and Willow's mother had decided to clean up her life. Willow had wept tears of joy when her mother checked herself into a state-run rehabilitation center. And for the next three years her mother had been drug free, and happiness entered their home once again.

What made Willow rejoice even more was when her mother had followed them to church and given her life to Christ. The disease had ravaged her, and her health had deteriorated very fast. But even while on her death bed, Willow's mother had been very happy and accepted her condition with much peace in her heart. In the end it was a serious bout of pneumonia that had ended her life.

A few days before her death, Lynn Jagger had been very clear about one thing.

"Willow, while I was strong I could keep Vincenzo's people at bay. My fear is that when I'm gone they'll come up with all sorts of claims to get to your sisters. Promise me that you'll do everything humanly possible to keep yourself and your sisters safe. If it means moving away from this town as you always wanted, go ahead and do it for you have my blessing. You've been my rock, my dear child and I'm counting on you to keep your sisters safe."

"Mama, I promise."

"Don't ever trust anyone with the girls or even yourself. I made the mistake of being desperate after your father died and landed in the wrong hands. Willow, you've taught me to have faith in God, so I'm begging you to hold onto your convictions. A good husband will come

from the Lord. Trust no one with your lives and never allow your sisters to visit other people's homes. That's how many little girls get molested and are introduced into terrible vices. Vincenzo mingled with very bad people but I made them stay away from us. Be very careful."

"Yes, Mom."

And just days after her mother's death and burial, Rico Alberto had showed up at the diner, claiming that he was Isabella and Maria's legal guardian, according to his brother's will. Rico had claimed that his mother who lived in Bogotá wanted to see the children.

"The children's grandmother can as well travel to the US to visit," Willow had argued.

"Girl, you better not stand in my way, for you wouldn't like what I can do to you," Rico had growled.

"Isabella and Maria have just lost their mother and I'm their closest living relative. My mother made me their guardian as their closest living relative. Besides, how is it that none of you ever came to visit when Vincenzo and even my mother were still alive. How is it that you've waited until her death to show up and claim to be the girls' guardian?"

Rico had glared at Willow and without saying another word had left the diner. She'd sighed in relief because the other diners had been present.

He'd stayed away for a while, but then recently she'd started noticing that she was being followed. She'd mentioned this to one neighbor, and the middle-school teacher had started walking Isabella and

Maria home on those days that Willow had to go in very early or work late.

Rico had never showed up at their doorstep again, but Willow had feared that it was just a matter of time. And she'd been right, because now his men had turned up in her neighborhood and thanks to Mr. Lark, they now knew where she lived.

Willow knew that Rico's intentions toward her sisters were evil because of his way of life.

"Willow!" Sally Jo's sharp voice brought her back to the present. "Something seems to be wrong, and I'd like you to trust me enough to confide in me. Surely, for the past few months we've become friends."

Willow sighed, "Truth be told, I've been praying that I would find a husband or a job outside of Denver and if possible, Colorado. I wish we could even end up on one of those ranches out in the West, away from the rest of the world."

"Why?"

"Because of my stepfather's brother. His name is Rico Alberto, and he's a really seedy and frightening person." She decided to open up to Sally Jo and told her everything. "My greatest fear is that one day he'll abduct my sisters and that will be the end of them."

"Oh, Willow!" Sally Jo was very compassionate. "I had no idea that you were dealing with such a heavy issue." She was truly shocked. While she knew that Willow had problems, she hadn't envisaged them to be of this magnitude. Being stalked by a drug lord had to be really terrifying and especially since Willow was a vulnerable young woman living alone with two small girls.

"Why don't you just try for the interview at The Astrid in the meantime? I'll be on the lookout for a husband from out of state and even a job."

"Thank you so much, Sally Jo."

Willow's step was light when she left her friend's office and hurried to work at the diner. It was one of those slow days, even if things were picking up after the lockdown. She prayed that the country, and indeed the world, wouldn't go back into lockdown because that had been one of the worst times for them. But for the kindness of their landlord they would have ended up on the streets and homeless. Mr. Joyner had allowed them to live in his apartment without paying a single dollar for rent and especially after her mother fell seriously ill and was bedridden. Even now he took only half rent and Willow knew that at some point the grace period would end and she would have to find a second job to stay on top of things. But until that time, she would keep counting her blessings. She just prayed that nothing drastic would happen to shake up her world, but a few days later the worst happened.

TO THE RESCUE

Only once did Isabella stir during the ride in the ambulance as she was taken to the emergency room. Willow was shaking even though her sister was already on the way to recovery after receiving first aid from the paramedics who'd arrived on the accident scene within minutes. Because of the pain Isabella was in she'd been sedated and now slept through the ride. Willow and Maria sat on the bench at the back of the ambulance while Isabella lay on the stretcher. Willow held both girls' hands and prayed for strength and protection.

She would never forget how terrified they'd all been when her mother's old Ford Escort was hit on the front passenger's side by a drunk driver who mysteriously disappeared after the accident. He'd left his vehicle on the scene and the policemen had run the number plates and discovered that it was a stolen vehicle.

Willow knew that the person who'd crashed into them was one of Rico's goons. The accident had occurred at ten in the morning, and she doubted that the person had been drunk, even though witnesses had claimed that he'd been swaying on the road. This had Rico Alberto written all over it but she couldn't voice her suspicions to the policemen who'd questioned her. She had no evidence to back up her allegations and in the litigious American society, one wrong word could get her sued to the moon and back.

Her cellphone rang when Isabella was in the examination room at the hospital. It was Sally Jo.

"Where are you?" The older woman asked.

"We're at the emergency room at Centennial Hospital," Willow's voice was shaking. "Someone hit my car and Isabella got hurt."

"I'll be there as soon as I can," Sally Jo said and quickly hung up. Willow was glad that she had someone like Sally Jo looking out for them.

The older woman arrived just as the doctor finished explaining to Willow that aside from slight shock, bruises and scratches, Isabella was fine and no bones were broken or cracked.

"You were all so lucky," the cheerful elderly doctor with a kind smile told Willow after examining her and Maria. "Take it easy for a day or two and keep the girls at home. If any of you begin to have nausea or experience dizzy spells, come back to the emergency room."

"Thank you, Doctor," Willow was so happy to see Sally Jo when she arrived a few minutes later.

"What happened?" She waited until Willow had received drugs from the pharmacy, then walked them to her car.

"We were on the way to Uncle Pete's Horse Farm on the other side of town for a treat. The girls love horses, and I've been saving up some money for a day trip to the horse farm." Willow was still shaken by what had happened. "The other car came out of nowhere and rammed into the front passenger side where Isabella was seated. Witnesses said the driver had been swerving all over the road, but after the accident, he disappeared, and it turns out that the car was stolen. My poor Ford is a write-off and because it was so old, I only had third-party insurance on it. So I have no hopes of getting any compensation from the insurance company," Willow felt sad. "It was my Mom's car."

"I'm so sorry about all that and glad that you're all all right and safe. You'll be fine," Sally Jo insisted on driving them home and coming up to the house. She even ordered a large pizza and soda for their late lunch. While Maria and Isabella enjoyed their delicious feast on the living room floor, Willow and Sally Jo sat at the kitchen space. Willow was glad to note that the incident hadn't dented her sisters' appetites. That was one less thing to worry about.

"Something tells me that you're not convinced that it was a drunk driver who hit you."

Willow nodded, and keeping her voice down she shared her fears about Rico with Sally Jo. "I fear that Rico is now taking things too far so he can intimidate us, and he's succeeding. I was so scared when that man crashed into us."

"We thank God that He kept you safe and preserved your lives," Sally Jo said, feeling angry that a wicked man such as Rico could harass her friend and get away with it. She saw the terror in Willow's eyes coupled with helplessness, and for a while she too felt overwhelmed. Then she tightened her lips and decided that she would stand with Willow.

"Mr. Randolph, I may just have the perfect person for Mr. Kendrick," Sally Jo called Abner as soon as she got home from Willow's house. "An incident occurred today to one of my girls," and she narrated the whole story to him. "Willow is really terrified and if there's a way that I can get her and her sisters out of Denver, I'll sleep much better."

"Well, all that depends on Rick and if he notices the girl. But even if he doesn't, I'll be sure to see how I can help. Rick is flying to Denver tomorrow and if you could orchestrate a meeting with Miss Jagger that would start the ball rolling."

"The Champion of the downtrodden responds to damsels in distress, right?"

"Such a scenario is more likely to get his attention than flirting."

Sally Jo was lost in thought for a moment. "I think I may just have an idea of getting him to act the champion when he meets Willow and I pray and hope that it works. That young woman needs a break and I hope this is it."

"I trust in your judgment and I'll also be praying and hoping for the best."

RICK LOOKED at his younger brothers with exasperation. Maynard and Callum were sprawled on his bed with their dusty boots still on. Then he sighed; experience had taught him that no amount of shouting or scolding would move these two hard heads. In any case, he wasn't Waylen, their second-born brother, who until recently had been such a perfectionist and neatness freak.

At least Len was now loosening up a little bit, and it was because of his former office assistant, Hazel, who'd turned his world upside down.

"Bro, I hope you realize that many people meet their future husbands and wives at weddings like the one you're going to," Callum dipped his hand into the large potato chips bag, pulled out a crunchy chip and bit it.

"Will the two of you stop spreading crumbs all over my bed," Rick swiped at his brothers with a tee-shirt. They ducked and ignored his cries. "Honestly the two of you are such slobs and messy creatures. You should go and try that with Waylen or even Quin and see what happens to you dander heads."

Maynard gave a mock shudder, "No thank you. Do you know that I can count on one hand how many times that brother of yours called Waylen allowed me to enter what he termed as his sanctuary? And now that he's married that's a no-go zone for us. Hazel has her work cut out for her with that one."

Rick grinned, "But you'll admit that our brother has changed a lot in the past few weeks that Hazel has been in his life. He's loosened up and doesn't get panic attacks when something is out of place."

"Cut that out!" Callum snapped and his brothers turned to him in surprise.

"What's wrong with you?" Maynard reached for a chip.

"Didn't you hear what I was saying?"

"What were you saying?" Rick folded another tee-shirt and placed it in his valise.

"The two of you aren't hard of hearing. But I was saying that people often find their life partners at weddings."

"What are you implying, you cheeky lad?" Rick walked to his dressing table and sorted through his colognes and shaving creams, picking up the ones he needed and bringing them back to his valise. He tucked them neatly in the pocket provided for the storage of such small items while being careful to stick to the limit allowed by the airlines. "Speak up, young man."

"I'm not implying but urging you to keep your eyes open for such an opportunity. The place will be filled with many single ladies all with stars in their eyes," Callum shook his head.

"What is it with women and weddings and babies? When women attend weddings, suddenly all the single girls begin to prowl for prospective husbands. And when they see a little baby they all want to have one. You'll be spoiled for choice, brother."

"Perish the thought!" Rick said strongly, glaring at his brother for daring to suggest such a thing. "I'm only going to that wedding because Simon begged me to be his best man and not because I want to find myself a female on the prowl."

"Don't you want to meet a girl, fall in love and marry her, then have a permanently goofy expression on your face?" Maynard mocked. "See how Quin and Len walk around with their heads in the clouds. Honestly, those boys behave as if their wives are their high school prom crushes."

"To be fair to them, they did get such wonderful and loveable women," Callum said. "And if you ask me," he wagged a finger at Rick, "This fellow is next on the list." He ducked as a pillow flew at his head. "Believe me, dear brother, there's something in the water around here and love is in the air. It's only a matter of time before you join the band of lovebirds."

"We shall see," Rick said confidently. His younger brothers liked teasing him, but this time he wasn't taking the bait. He loved his new sisters by marriage so much because they adored his brothers and had made them happy. He was really happy that his two older brothers had found love, but that wasn't for him, no thank you!

Having had his heart broken twice while in college, Rick had altogether given up on romance. Both times the girls had been more interested in his wealth than in him as a person and he'd also found out that they had other men on the side. The pain of heartbreak had nearly made him miss his exams both times, and it was Simon who'd drummed sense into his head.

While he respected women and treated them with much courtesy, he didn't think that love was for him anymore. A guy could only take so much heartbreak in his lifetime.

"Someone is deep in thought," Callum said. "Make sure you take enough photos of all the beautiful, single ladies and send them back here. I may just spot a lass and decide that she can become Mrs. Callum Randolph. Concentrate your attention especially on the bridesmaids. Who knows, one of them might just end up to be the damsel that will touch you, our dear brother's hard heart."

"Give it a rest, Callum, won't you please?" Rick was done with his packing. "Who'll be driving me to Dallas Airport?"

"What time is your flight?" Maynard asked.

"I'm taking the red eye because I'd like to be in Denver very early tomorrow morning. Simon said that our suits aren't quite ready and the tailor needs us to go in for the final fitting. I sent over my measurements but he needs to see how well the suit will fit me."

"That means that you need to be at the airport at around midnight."

"Yes Callum. You could drive me out there and spend the night at a hotel instead of driving back alone at that late hour."

"That's a good idea," Callum rose from the bed and brushed the crumbs from his shirt and jeans.

"Carry your rubbish out of my room with you," Rick cried out as his brothers walked toward the door. "Why do I even bother," he muttered.

Callum and Maynard were the untidiest people he'd ever known, and he was glad that he didn't have to share a room with any of them. No wonder Quin and Len never let them into their bedrooms.

"Three days of being surrounded by the frills of all things weddings and single girls looking for husbands," he shuddered. But he would survive it, he promised himself that. And once the wedding was over, he would be on the first plane out of Denver very early on Sunday morning.

RELIEF AT LAST

"Willow, how fast can you get to The Astrid Hotel?" Sally Jo sounded really excited.

"Why?"

"Remember I told you that my friend said they were hiring? One of the positions happens to be that of assistant chef. The same friend has scheduled you for an interview at nine o'clock."

It was six o'clock and Willow was already up because of her sisters. "What?" She squealed. She'd put all thoughts of The Astrid out of her mind because she knew that she stood no chance of even getting an interview, not with her community college qualifications. "How did you do it?"

"My dear girl, it pays to know people," Sally Jo laughed. "How are the girls doing?"

Willow sighed. It was the day after their accident, and she hadn't intended to leave them at home alone. The three of them were still shaken and had all piled up together on Willow's bed. Willow had barely slept a wink since she'd been watching over her sisters as the doctor had instructed, just to make sure that there were no ill aftereffects. Mercifully, the girls had slept through the night.

"They slept very well, but I don't want to leave them all alone. The woman who normally comes in to babysit for me travelled out of town to visit relatives."

"Don't worry about that. The Astrid Hotel has a child-friendly lounge, and the girls are well behaved, so there shouldn't be any problems."

Willow was hesitant, "Sally Jo, thanks for the opportunity but I don't feel comfortable letting my sisters out of my sight, not even for a single minute. Yesterday's incident really scared me."

"Look, let me speak to my friend at the hotel and see if someone can be there to keep an eye on Isabella and Maria for about an hour while you're having the interview."

"My car was wrecked and I don't have enough money for an Uber," Willow blurted out. Her savings were gone after the visit to the emergency room since they didn't have health insurance. She couldn't afford the seventeen hundred dollars needed for medical insurance for the three of them, and that was the cheapest one on the market. She'd also had to maximize her two credit cards, and for the next few weeks things would be really tight for them as her salary would be going to settle that.

Thank God for the tips she received at the diner, but she had to be at work to receive them.

"Don't worry about that. Just let me know when you're ready and I'll scan an Uber for you. But make sure that you're there by around eight thirty."

"Thanks so much, Sally Jo."

WILLOW HAD BEEN to The Astrid Hotel before, back in college. She'd been offered an internship position which had lasted only one month and she'd loved the experience, wishing she could work in a place like this permanently. Now she had the chance to achieve one of her dreams in life and her heartbeat increased.

As promised, Sally Jo scanned an Uber for them, and the girls were excited that even after the previous day's incident they were having an outing.

"We're going to a very posh hotel so please behave for me. I'll be doing an interview and hopefully it won't last for more than an hour."

"We promise to be good," Bella promised and Willow believed her. She often counted herself as being very lucky because the girls were so well behaved. So far they hadn't given her any problems and she prayed that their upcoming teenage years would be free of any kind of trouble.

If she got this position, she knew that it would pay well, and she would be able to afford so much more for them.

"Dear Lord," she prayed as a bellboy opened the Uber door and waited to usher them inside. "Please be on my side and grant me favor with the person who will be interviewing me."

"Willow, this place is for kings and queens," Isabella said in hushed tones as they entered the large foyer. Though her bruises had turned purple, she was her usual cheerful self. "I'm almost afraid to even sit on their chairs."

"Please don't touch or spoil anything," Willow said, and her sisters nodded. "I'm here for an interview, and I don't think it will last that long."

"Will you be working here?" Maria asked. "I hope you will because it's such a pretty place, not like the diner which is always so full. Me and Bella...."

"Bella and I," Willow corrected swiftly.

"Okay, Bella and I will enjoy visiting you here. They even have a playing area for children. Can we go over there?"

"Not right now," Willow said, noting that the playing area was close to the entrance, even though there seemed to be two attendants there. Like she'd told Sally Jo, she wasn't willing to let her sisters out of her sight even for a moment.

The lounge was almost empty and Willow noted that they also seemed to have suffered the effects of the Corona virus. No establishment around the world had gone unscathed from the virus.

Unlike the last time when she'd been here as an intern, it was now silent. At that time the lounge and foyer had been teeming with people and was a beehive of activities. Now there were only a few guests strolling around and, all in all, it appeared rather quiet.

Willow, with her sisters walking by her side, approached the reception desk as Sally Jo had instructed. She found a young man who gave her a courteous smile.

"Good morning, my name is Willow and I'm here for an interview."

"You're Miss Willow Jagger?" The man looked surprised. "You look very young."

"Thank you, and yes, that's me."

"I'm Jude," the receptionist introduced himself. "Please take a seat," he pointed at the sitting area which had very comfortable sofa seats. "Someone will be with you shortly."

"Thank you," Willow smiled at him, then led her sisters to the sitting area. She wondered what her boss at the diner was thinking. It was her second day of missing work, and she prayed that she wouldn't get into any trouble. The last thing she needed was to lose her job, and especially now that she was stretched very thin financially.

"I have to do something about getting us health insurance," she told herself. "If I should get this job, I'm sure there's a staff medical cover." Willow knew that the staff in this hotel were well paid. She could do some extra shifts and make enough money to get health insurance for her sisters.

For a moment Willow felt quite overwhelmed by what lay ahead for her. Bringing up two children on her own wasn't easy. "Please Lord, spare us from any more illnesses or accidents until I can sort out our medical insurance matters."

A smart-looking gentleman approached her. "Are you Miss Willow Jagger?"

"Yes, Sir," she rose to her feet.

"My name is Andrew Langford and I'm the one who will conduct your interview. How you perform today will determine whether you'll be invited for the second and third interviews and then get employed with us," he said.

"I'll do my best, Sir," Willow said and she really meant it. Working here would do wonders for her resumé, and the money would solve many of her problems. She picked up her file and then introduced her sisters. "This is Isabella and that's Maria," she said. "I was told that it's all right to bring them with me since I couldn't get a baby sister at the last minute."

"That's quite all right," he smiled at the two girls, and Willow's heart settled down.

"They'll be all right here, and Jude over there," he pointed at the receptionist, "Will keep an eye on them. Things aren't fast paced so it should be all right. And in any case we're only going over there," he pointed at another sitting area just a few paces away. "They'll be within your sight at all time."

Willow smiled at her sisters and told them in a low voice to remember to be good, then followed Andrew. He was kind enough to allow her to sit on the chair that faced her sisters. She settled down and prepared herself to take the interview.

Andrew gave her another smile to reassure her. He was in his forties and she thought he looked like a kind man, but she was also aware that one had to be very alert during interviews.

"Dear Lord my Father, please grant me favor in this man's eyes and in Your sight. You know how much I need things to change for us."

"Miss Jagger, please relax. This interview is just to help me get to know more about you, confirm your qualifications and have a general idea about your expectations should we offer you the position."

Willow nodded, trying very hard to relax. Andrew was considerate, and ten minutes into the interview, Willow finally relaxed.

The interview was progressing well, and she kept casting glances toward Isabella and Maria and was glad to note that they were sitting quietly and watching cartoons.

Suddenly a man appeared in the lounge and something about him made her uneasy. He walked to the reception desk and then turned to look at Bella and Maria. He reminded her of the man who'd followed her the other day.

"Is there a problem" Andrew noticed that she was distracted and had tensed up.

"Sorry," she gave a nervous laugh. She was relieved when the stranger turned away from staring at her sisters. She told herself that she was just being paranoid and that could cost her this interview.

The man was probably there to meet someone, so she turned her attention back to the interview but still kept a sharp lookout for her sisters.

A waiter walked over to Bella and Maria with juice boxes and cookies on a plate, and Andrew told her that they were with the compliments of the chef.

But before the interview could resume, Willow saw the stranger approaching her sisters.

"Sorry," she didn't want to make a scene when it was probably nothing but she wouldn't put it past Rico to try anything. That man seemed to have ears and eyes everywhere.

"Miss Jagger," the smile faded from Andrew's eyes and Willow's heart sank. She'd probably tanked the interview but at this point it didn't matter at all. Her sisters' safety was paramount and the man seemed to be gesturing at them.

"I'm sorry but I can't continue with this interview," Willow gathered her papers together and rose to her feet. "Thank you for the opportunity but I have to go."

"Miss Jagger!"

But Willow had ceased listening to him. The man had his hand on Maria's head.

"What do you think you're doing?" Willow rushed forward and grabbed the man's hand off Maria's head. She then put herself between the man and her sisters. "What do you want with my sisters?"

From closer range she noticed that his features were Latino and she knew that she was in the presence of one of Rico's men. "Leave us alone."

"Ah, Chica!" He rubbed his small goatee and gave her a look that made her skin crawl. "It's you that I wanted to see, and I suggest that you follow me very quietly without causing a scene. Unless you want someone to get hurt."

Willow noticed the bulge under his coat and realized that he was carrying a gun. No one seemed to be paying any attention to whatever was going on and Willow turned around in time to see Andrew walking toward the lifts.

"We're not going anywhere with you," Willow said in a strained voice.

"Ah, but you are. Rico sent me to pick you and the girls up and take you to his house. I followed you from the house and was surprised that you ended up here instead of that tiny diner where you work. I don't want any trouble so I suggest that you cooperate with me."

"If you don't walk away from us right now I'll scream," Willow said. Surely the man wasn't so daring as to lay a finger on any of them in broad daylight and in a public lobby in full view of those who were there.

"Chica, spare yourself the tantrums and come with me. Either way you'll be seeing Rico today and who knows what his mood will be like? You've given us so much trouble, and I thought that yesterday would have given you warning that he means business."

"I knew it," Willow felt herself getting angry. "Whoever you are, just go and tell Rico that I won't be intimidated by him. I'll go to the police and file a restraining order against all of you."

The man's laughter mocked her. "You're really naïve. Are we supposed to be scared that you'll go to the police?"

"Just leave and stay away from us."

"You know that you won't stay in this hotel forever."

"What's going on here?" Willow turned at the commanding voice and she saw that it belonged to a man who was in his mid-twenties. He was well built and fearless as he faced her bully.

"Nothing that concerns you, young man," the suited stranger said haughtily. "Run along now and mind your own business."

"Miss, is this man bothering you?" Willow felt that she could trust the newcomer. "Don't worry, I'm a guest here. Are you all right?"

RICK WAS GETTING ready to go for the wedding when the intercom in his suite buzzed. It was the reception desk and he wondered why he was being buzzed.

"This is Kendrick Randolph, is there a problem?"

"Sir, would you please come down to the reception? There's something we need you to attend to."

"Sure," Kendrick said, fastening the cuffs on his sleeves. "I'll be right down."

As soon as he stepped out of the lift on the ground floor, the first thing he noticed was a man towering over three young ladies and it looked as if he was bullying them. His instincts immediately told him that all was not well. Forgetting all about his summons to the reception desk he made his way over to them.

"What's going on here?" Rick quickly glanced at the young girls while keeping the tall man within his sight.

"Nothing that concerns you, young man," the suited stranger said haughtily. "Run along now and mind your own business." Rick noticed that the man looked to be in his forties and the bulge under his coat made him aware that he was armed. This was a dangerous fellow and he needed to be very careful in how he handled matters so no one would get hurt, least of all the three girls.

"Miss, is this man bothering you? Don't worry, I'm a guest here. Are you all right?"

"Would you just leave?" The man sounded very irritated. "This has nothing to do with you."

"On the contrary, Sir," Rick stepped forward and to his surprise he noticed that the older girl was in her twenties and not a teenager as he'd initially thought. The other two were younger and the three of them immediately moved to stand behind him as if seeking his protection.

"Sir," he patiently told the bully, "it's clear that there's a problem here. I think I heard the lady asking you politely to leave. You better do it while I'm still being nice."

"Who do you think you are?" The bully snarled. "Be careful not to interfere in matters that don't concern you, for you could get hurt."

Willow was shaking, but she was glad that the newcomer had stepped up to help them. But Rico's man frightened her, and she was afraid that he would become violent, especially since he had a gun. She expected their rescuer to step back at the vehemence in the other man. To her surprise, he stepped forward and got in the man's face.

"Are you threatening me?" He growled.

Willow was surprised when the bully stepped back, even as two security officers from the hotel walked up to join them.

"What's going on here?" One of the security officers asked.

"I noticed that this gentleman was harassing these three ladies," Rick said.

"And he even has a gun," he pointed out and the two guards were immediately alert and reached for their own guns.

"Sir, would you please come with us?" The security men were burly and gave Willow confidence that they could handle the man. The bully tried to protest, but he proved no match for the two officers who quickly disarmed him while patting him down at the same time just to make sure he didn't have any other weapons on him.

Rick turned to the young woman who looked really shaken. She put her arms around the younger girls and drew them closer.

"Are you all right? Did the man frighten you?" He asked. He knew that time was passing swiftly and he needed to be at the church by noon. But he couldn't just walk away now and leave these three without ensuring that they were safe.

"Are you guests at the hotel?" He asked, and Willow shook her head. "Sorry, my name is Kendrick Randolph."

Another man walked up to them. "Mr. Randolph, I understand that there's been a problem. The security officers told me that they had to escort a guest out of the hotel."

"Yes, the man was harassing these ladies and I stepped in to intervene."

"Are they guests here?"

"No," Willow said hurriedly. "I came here for an interview with Mr. Andrew Langford and that man began harassing my sisters. He wouldn't leave when I asked him to, and Mr. Randolph was kind enough to intervene."

"You say you were here for an interview with Mr. Andrew Langford?"

Rick turned to the manager before Willow could answer him. "They're my guests and I would like them taken up to my suite."

"But..." Willow didn't know what to make of these new developments.

Rick smiled at her, "Don't worry, you'll be all right in my suite. I have to attend a wedding at noon, but I'll make sure that someone is there to ensure that no one else will harass you. When I get back we'll see what needs to be done."

But it wasn't the goon who'd left that had Willow worried. It was Rico. Rico's man had just admitted to knowing about the accident the previous day and today he'd followed them from the house all on Rico's instructions. They were no longer safe and who knew what other mischievous acts Rico would get up to. Perhaps they would be safer in this place than at home, for the moment anyway.

"Thank you, Sir," Willow was grateful that for a few hours at least she wouldn't have to worry about Rico and his goons.

"Come with me then," Rick told his guests. Willow and her sisters followed him to his suite which was on the sixth floor of the ten-storied hotel.

As soon as they stepped into the suite, Willow's eyes widened. This was almost ten times bigger than her apartment. The large kitchenette and dining area extended into the living room. She could see an open door leading to the hallway beyond.

The living room was simply but elegantly furnished, and she noticed the paintings on the walls. She didn't know much about paintings, but she could imagine that they were expensive pieces.

"The fridge is well stocked," Rick led Willow to the kitchenette and opened it. "Please feel free to prepare anything for yourselves. I'll be gone for about four to five hours, but you'll be safe here. We'll talk when I get back."

RICK WENT through the process of standing beside his friend as he exchanged vows with the love of his life.

It was a beautiful wedding, he had to admit that, but he couldn't help thinking about the frightened girls he'd left in his suite. Seeing that man bullying them had brought back memories of his school days. At least they were safe now but what would happen to them once he returned to Cedar Hill and left them behind?

From the way that goon had looked, they were in trouble. That kind of man could be vicious and especially because he'd been humiliated. The gun under his jacket had told a story of its own. The three young ladies were dealing with a criminal who carried a weapon, and he wondered what their story was. Well, he intended to find out more from them before he stepped in to help.

"Hey," someone jostled him and he blinked. It was Simon, the grinning groom and he had a wide smile on his lips. "Such lack of concentration can only mean one thing, my friend."

"And what's that?" Rick asked.

"A woman!" Simon whispered. "It's only the effect of a woman that can make a man not notice all the beautiful ladies who are trying to catch his eye."

"What?" Rick looked around and sure enough he caught a few ladies staring at him. One even winked at him and made suggestive gestures. He shuddered inwardly and turned away.

"Tracy's maid of honor has done her best to catch your eye from the very beginning but you've completely ignored her. The last time I checked, you made no mention of having a woman in your life so I'm thinking that this is fairly recent."

"Well, there's a woman but not in the way you think."

"Do tell," Simon looked very interested but Rick wasn't about to tell him anything. In any case, what was there to say?

"Not now. Tracy needs your attention and besides, it's your wedding day. We'll talk about my issues some other time," and he leaned forward and mouthed, "I'm sorry," to Tracy and she gave him a sweet smile.

When he got the chance to step away he reached for his cellphone and dialed the number of the hotel's female security officer who'd been allocated to his suite. He'd made the request on his way out of the hotel and the hotel's operations manager had promised that the three girls would be safe.

"Good afternoon," the feminine voice came on the line.

"Good afternoon. How are things going?"

"All quiet, Sir."

"Any word from my guests?"

"No, Sir. It's been quiet in there all through. I've popped in a couple of times on the pretext of checking up on something, just to make sure they're fine. All is well, Sir."

"Thank you. Please keep an eye on my guests."

"Yes, Sir."

After he'd disconnected the phone, he noticed that one of the bridesmaids was standing close by.

"My name is Angela," she held out a hand and he shook it. "Would you care to dance with me?" She asked.

Rick frowned. While music was playing in the background, he didn't see anyone on the dance floor. "I don't think it's time to dance yet. Please excuse me."

As he made to walk away, she latched onto his arm. "Please stay and let's get to know each other."

Rick gave her a tight smile, "I'm sorry but I already have someone in my life right now."

"Are you married to her?"

"No."

"Then you can't say that you have someone in your life. Only marriage locks a man down."

"Sorry but I really need to go," and he gently disentangled himself and walked away. As the reception went on, Rick couldn't wait for it to come to an end. He had to admit that his mind wasn't really here but on the young woman back in his suite. There was something about her that touched his heart, then he told himself that he was being protective, that's all.

Then he remembered that he'd promised to take photos of the single bridesmaids and for his brothers' sakes he snapped up a few, forwarded them to Maynard and Callum via WhatsApp and then put his phone back in his pocket.

"Will you be joining us for the evening party at the Stardust Club?" Tracy asked. "Moira reminded me that you owe her the best couple's dance."

Rick shook his head, "You know that's not my kind of thing and also, I have a sort of emergency back at the hotel. But you all go ahead and have fun."

"You're no fun at all, Man!" Simon complained, but with a smile.

"I also have an early morning flight, so I think I should begin saying my farewells now."

"Thank you for coming," Simon said.

"It was a pleasure and thank you for the invitation and honor of being your best man." Rick hugged Simon and Tracy. "Make sure that you treat Tracy right, or you'll have all of us back in Texas to reckon with."

Simon nodded solemnly while gently pulling his new bride closer. "I lost her once and will never take her for granted again. You can be sure that she'll be safe with me always and we'll soon visit the family at Cedar Hill."

Rick kept checking his phone to see if the officer had sent him any messages or calls. There were none, and he prayed that Willow wouldn't have left. Even though the officer had assured him that all was quiet he still couldn't help being worried.

He smiled when he thought about his guests and especially the older one. She looked delicate but had stood up to the bully and he found himself admiring her courage.

As soon as it was socially correct, he excused himself and left the reception. He drove his rental car back to the hotel. The valet was there to take the car for parking, and he walked into the hotel lobby. He reached for his phone and dialed his father's number. It was picked up on the first ring.

"Rick, how is the wedding going on? How is Tracy? I hope you took some photos for us to see."

"Well Dad, something came up and I had to return to the hotel before the reception was completely over. Tracy looked like an angel and it was really wonderful. I have loads of photos and even a video of when they were making their vows to each other."

"You talked about something happening, I hope all is well."

"Simon and Tracy were very grateful for the check from all of us. But that's not why I'm calling."

"Is there a problem, Son?"

"Yes, Dad," and Rick quickly told his father about the morning incident. "I even overheard the man threatening the girls, and from the way he sounded, I'm sure he means ill toward them. He was carrying a gun, but the security officers at the hotel disarmed him. My fear is that he may be lying in wait for them as soon as they step out of the hotel. For now they're safely tucked away in my suite with a female bodyguard to watch over them. But what will happen to them once I check out of the hotel tomorrow morning and return home?"

"What do you want to do now?"

Rick ran a hand through his hair. "Dad, I really don't know, but leaving them here to face that man isn't something I can imagine. What if he harms them?"

"Don't they have friends and relatives to look out for them?"

"Well, I haven't had a chat with them but will do so as soon as I get back to my suite. Then I'll call and let you know whatever is going on."

"Oh, so the girls are there with you now?"

"Not exactly, as I said. I left them in my suite as I was going for the wedding. I was worried about them so I couldn't let them leave."

"That's good. Well, have a chat with them, then call me and tell me how we can help."

～

Abner was chuckling as he disconnected his call. He immediately dialed Sally Jo's number.

"Rick told me of an incident at the hotel. Was that your plan and man?"

"No," Sally Jo said. "My man was the person who conducted the interview and I had another waiting to get things in motion. But then he called to tell me that another person had approached Willow and harassed them before he could make his move. But the man was taken away by the security officers. It all worked out well, according to my man, because Mr. Kendrick stepped in. The receptionist, at my man's prompting, called his room and he came down and rescued them."

"Yes, he told me so. They're now in his suite and he sounds like he doesn't intend to leave them behind."

"That's good."

～

Willow had just tucked Bella and Maria in and was doing the dishes when the door opened, and Rick walked into the suite.

"There's someone to do those, you know," he said. "The hotel staff takes care of those things." He smiled as he loosened his tie and took it off. He also tossed his jacket on the back of one of the couches. "Where are your sisters?"

"They've gone to bed, and I'm sorry that we're being an inconvenience to you. Isabella got hurt in an accident yesterday and the drugs prescribed for her cause drowsiness. So I used one of the rooms to put them to bed as we waited for you."

"That's all right," Rick smiled to reassure the young woman. "What's your name?"

"Willow Jagger."

"As I told you before, I'm Kendrick but everyone calls me Rick."

"Thank you so much for your kindness."

"It's my pleasure. Where's the bodyguard?"

Willow turned to him in puzzlement. "I haven't seen any bodyguard around. The only person who was in and out from time to time is Maureen."

Rick chuckled. "She's good at her job if you didn't realize she was your bodyguard."

"Oh!" Willow turned red. "I thought she was your assistant or something." There was a knock at the door and when Rick opened it, the female security officer walked in.

"Sorry, Mr. Randolph, I was on the phone when I saw you come in. It was my boss calling to find out how things were going."

"You've done a good job, and Willow here had no idea that you were here for their security." The two women exchanged smiles. "I'll take it from here. The check for your services will be in your office first thing in the morning," Rick reached for his wallet. "Meanwhile, please have this for your transport or something."

Willow was surprised that he tipped the security officer two hundred dollars.

"Thank you, Sir, and it was a pleasure being of service to you."

After she left, Willow turned to Rick. "Are you hungry?"

"Yes, I really am. Wedding food is usually overrated. Hard, stringy chicken and soggy mashed potatoes was all I had to eat." He made a face and Willow giggled. "But I don't want to bother you. I could always make myself a sandwich."

"No, Sir, I made plenty of food and there's some left over. Let me warm it for you."

Instead of sitting at the dining table, Rick followed Willow and seated himself at the kitchen counter. He watched as she swiftly and efficiently warmed his dinner and served it on a plate.

"Sorry that it's just simple spaghetti and meatballs—because the girls love it."

Rick admitted that even though the meal was simple it was quite delicious. "You know that I could have ordered something from the restaurant downstairs."

"Yes, but your fridge is fully stocked, and homemade meals are healthier and more wholesome."

"You mentioned something about being here for an interview."

Willow joined Rick at the kitchen counter and sighed. She told him all about her meeting with Mr. Langford and how she'd had to cut short the interview. "When I saw that man harassing my sisters I walked away from the interviewer, so I don't think I'll be invited for another one."

"If you're keen on getting the position you were interviewing for, I could put in a good word for you with the Human Resources person. She's a good person and might consider allowing you to take the interview again."

But Willow was shaking her head. "With all that's been happening all I want to do is keep my sisters safe. I know that restaurants in hotels run until late and I don't like to leave Bella and Maria at home alone. We have good neighbors who look out for us, but the girls are my responsibility."

"And what about your parents or any other relatives?"

Willow smiled sadly, "It's a long story."

"Well, it's clear that you're going nowhere tonight, so why don't we move to the living room, and you can tell me all about it?"

"Let me do the dishes first," Willow didn't know how Rick would react after hearing her story.

"Leave them for later," he said. "There's some ice cream in the deep freeze, and I wouldn't mind a few scoops."

Willow brought out the ice cream, which was in a large tub.

"Where do I begin?" Willow asked minutes later when they were comfortably seated in the living room area. She passed the ice cream to Rick who was reclining on the largest couch.

"You can begin wherever you want," he said.

Willow nodded slightly, "Bella and Maria are my half-sisters. My mom remarried after my Dad died and the man ruined her life."

"How?"

"Vincenzo introduced my mother to drugs and then had her turning tricks for him to make money."

Rick closed his eyes and felt pain and anger welling up, but he didn't say anything.

"Vincenzo died when I was seventeen and Mom left us about eight months ago."

"So who was that person in the lobby this morning?"

"After my mother passed away, Vincenzo's younger brother suddenly showed up and claimed that my stepfather had made him Bella and Maria's legal guardian. He says that he wants to take them back to Bogotá, claiming that their grandmother wants to see them."

"That's not a bad idea, I mean if the girls have a grandmother, isn't that a nice thing?"

Willow shook her head. "If I was sure for one moment that Rico's intentions toward my sisters were good I wouldn't hesitate to travel to Bogotá so they can visit their grandmother.

But all the time my mother was married to Vincenzo none of his relatives ever came to visit, not even Rico himself. My mother told me that they never approved of her marriage to my stepfather because they had another woman lined up for him. So, when Rico suddenly appeared, I suspected that he was up to no good."

"The man could be trying to mend bridges and get to know his nieces well."

Willow's lips tightened. "Rico is a drug lord just like his brother was, and he also runs a prostitution ring, and underage girls are his specialty. That's not the kind of man I'd be willing to hand my sisters over to. His brother destroyed my mother's life and I can never trust that family. That's why the best thing is for me to find a job outside Denver so we can move away."

"What do you mean?"

"I'm willing to leave Denver forever so I can keep my sisters safe."

Rick smiled in satisfaction. "Do you really mean that?"

"Yes. I happen to know that the demand for chefs is high all over the country."

WHEN RICK SPOKE to his father later that day, he had no idea that his shrewd parent had already had a discussion with Sally Jo. He mentioned what Willow had said and by morning he had good news for her.

"My father is ready to offer you a position at the ranch."

"What? Just like that?" Willow was stunned. "And what about my sisters? I can't leave them behind."

"You won't have to, dear lady. The position comes with a two bedroom house since you have a family. Our ranch takes in interns for three-month programs, and this is all year round. There's a hostel for the ladies and the young men are housed in the bunkhouse. But if someone has a family, then we provide a family home for them. The position has a probationary period of three months, after which a more permanent arrangement will be made. If at any time you feel that you want to leave all you have to do is work out your notice and then you'll be free to leave."

"Am I dreaming?" Willow half spoke to herself.

"This is not a dream."

"And if I'm dreaming, dear Lord, please don't let me wake up."

Rick laughed but his heart was at peace. He knew that leaving Willow and her sisters behind would have given him nightmares and sleepless nights. Now they would be safe on the ranch.

A FRESH START

"It looks like one of those ranches in the movies," Marie piped, and Rick smiled at the girl's words. He loved his home and if it was up to him, he and all his brothers and their families would live together in this house. But soon Quin and Len would be moving out of the ranch house so they could begin life with their wives.

"Welcome to Randolph Ranch," he told the three as he packed the SUV that Callum had left at the airport for him.

"Willow, you don't need to fear. I've heard of the Randolph Ranch in Cedar Hill and the owners are respectable people. If you're not sure you can look them up on Google."

"I already did last evening."

"And?"

"Like you say, they're a respectable family, but I'm a little troubled that I got the position so easily."

Sally Jo laughed, "Oh ye of little faith! Willow, didn't you just say that the position is an answer to prayer? Why then are you doubting again? Or don't you believe that the Lord can give you good and wonderful blessings? God works in mysterious ways, so take this to be an answer to your prayers."

"Thank you for that. I feel better letting you know where we'll be. And I was actually calling to ask you for a favor. Mr. Randolph is taking us back to the house to pack our clothes and pick up whatever is important; then we'll be leaving for the airport from there."

"Anything for you, Girl."

"I wanted to ask you to meet us at the house so you can help me put my furniture into storage."

"Why? Do you intend to return here some day?"

"I'm just being cautious though I'm hoping that this position will hold for a long time. Being out there on the ranch means safety for Bella and Maria because Rico won't be able to find us there."

"Then make sure you don't tell any of your neighbors where you're going. So that if any of them is threatened by Rico they won't have any information for him."

"You're right," Willow said, thankful that she'd been warned in time as she'd been thinking about sharing her good news with her neighbors. "I'll make sure that when I get to Texas I'll work to the bone so that I'll retain the position for the longest time."

"I'm glad that you're able to take the girls with you."

"That's the main reason I jumped at the chance. My prayer is that Bella and Maria will have a normal childhood like other children. No more looking over our shoulders whenever we leave the house. No more pushing our heavy furniture to secure the door as we sleep. Do you know that for the first time last night I slept like a baby because I knew that my sisters were safe?"

"Well, it's all right. Let's meet at the house then."

"Thank you. Let me inform Mr. Randolph that you'll meet us there."

But when they got to the house, a shock awaited them. The door was locked just as she'd left it the day before but inside was another story altogether. Everything had been turned upside down and Willow stared at the mess in horror. Even the fridge hadn't been spared and foodstuff lay strewn all over the floor, some of it trampled on as if whoever had done this wanted to cause as much damage as possible. She couldn't believe how far Rico had gone this time and was just glad that they hadn't been at home when the destroyers came to cause this havoc. It was as if the person or people had been searching for something and Willow wanted to cry.

"Willow, who did this to our house?" Bella's lower lip trembled. Nothing had been left in its place in all the rooms in the house.

"I don't know," Willow whispered tearfully. "Where do I even start?" She stared with dismay at the mess. She could feel Rick's eyes on her but the last thing she wanted was to answer any questions.

Rick knew even without being told that the man who'd harassed Willow and her sisters at the hotel was somehow connected to the current state of the apartment. He felt so angry and wished he could get his hands on the man, for he would like to show him a thing or two about how to treat a young lady.

"I'm so sorry," Sally Jo put an arm around Willow's shoulders. "Look, why don't you just pick out the few things you want for your journey and leave the rest?"

"But how do I just leave the house in such a mess?"

"You need to go because of your flight this afternoon. And I promise that I'll bring in some people to help me sort everything out and I'll clearly mark and label them. When I'm done I'll forward whatever you need to you in Texas and keep the rest for you in storage."

All through the flight Willow, was silent, and it was her sisters who asked many questions. Rick was both amazed and amused by the two girls because they were very intelligent.

Rick was glad he was taking Willow and her sisters away from their home because of the bad memories. He was still in a little bit of shock at what he'd witnessed at the apartment and knew that Rico Alberto was a very dangerous criminal. Well, he wasn't going to have any access to Willow and her sisters while they lived on the ranch. It was the safest place for them to be and he was happy to be taking them home with him.

"How big is your house, Mr. Randolph," Bella asked. "Does it look like a big hotel?"

Rick threw his head back and laughed. "While it's not as big as a hotel, it's still large enough to house many people."

"Will we be staying here?" Maria piped.

"No, Maria," Willow took her sister's hand. "I'll be working in the big house but Mr. Randolph said we'll have our own place."

"But you'll be coming to the house from school to wait for Willow. Then when your sister is done with her day's work you can then drive home."

"But Willow doesn't have a car," Bella said. "Mom's old car was smashed badly in the accident."

"Don't worry about that," Rick said. "There are many cars on the farm and one will be allocated for your sister's use. She'll sometimes need to go shopping for groceries and all."

"Where is our school?"

"It's on the other side of the ranch and serves all the workers' children so you'll get to make many new friends, Bella."

The two children were happy as they followed Rick into the house. "We'll say hello to everyone; then I'll take you to your house. You have two days to settle down and get the girls enrolled in school then you can start working on Wednesday. Is that all right?" Willow nodded.

THE COWBOY STRIKES

illow's cellphone rang just as she placed a tray of biscuits into the oven. At least Mrs. Brian wasn't here to berate her for taking her call in the middle of work. The woman was very strict about working hours and Willow was very careful not to upset her. She loved working in this large house not only because of the good salary she'd been offered, but the benefits as well. All staff who worked for Randolph Ranch and their dependents had very good medical coverage, so that was one headache off her list. And then the house they'd been given was twice as large as their old apartment back in Denver, and it came fully furnished with all the comforts of home.

Bella and Maria loved their room which had twin beds as well as two desks where they could work. Rick had informed her that it was his father and younger brother, Callum, who was in charge of staff welfare, who'd made all the arrangements for their house to be ready as soon as she'd accepted the position.

The phone rang again and a quick glance at the screen showed the caller to be Rick.

"Hi," she answered with a smile in her voice.

"Hi Willow, where are you?" Rick asked.

"I'm in the kitchen," she answered. "Did you need something, Sir?"

"I told you to stop calling me or my brothers, 'Sir.' Reserve that for our dad."

"I'm sorry."

"Well, I was just calling to find out if you've settled in okay."

Willow frowned slightly, looking around to make sure that she was alone in the kitchen. Mrs. Brian had gone to town, taking Irene, an intern, with her. It was a relief to be alone in the kitchen.

Willow always tried her best to be on good terms with those she worked with. Mrs. Brian was strict but she was also very kind. She ensured that Willow packed some food to carry home with her every evening. And she didn't mind having Bella and Maria in the kitchen whenever the school bus dropped them off so they could wait for Willow. If anything, the kind woman was always ready with snacks for the girls and they loved her.

But Irene was another matter altogether. She was difficult to work with and always seemed to be moody. It seemed to

Willow as if she went out of her way to make life rather unpleasant for her. However, she was careful to only be unpleasant when Mrs. Brian was away from the kitchen.

"Willow?"

"Sorry, Sir...er Kendrick. I'm in the middle of baking biscuits."

"I'm on my way to the house," Rick said and the call got disconnected. Willow made sure that it was on silent and vibrate, then dropped it into her apron pocket. She didn't want Mrs. Brian to hear her phone ringing when she returned. Not that anyone ever called her since she'd changed her number when she arrived in Cedar Hill. Apart from the people on the ranch, the only outsider who knew her new number was Sally Jo.

Rick appeared through the kitchen door a few minutes later and made for the tray of biscuits.

"These smell really good and they look delicious," he bit into one and grunted with contentment. "You're a woman after my own heart," he said as he grabbed a few more and dropped them in his shirt pocket.

"I could pack those in a napkin for you," Willow offered.

"No need because they will soon be gone anyway," Rick looked around the large kitchen. "Where's everyone?"

"Mrs. Brian and Irene went to town to do some grocery shopping. Do you need something?"

"Yes," he looked slightly nervous, which made Willow wonder what was going on with him. He cleared his throat, "It's just that..."

Before he could say anything else the kitchen door was flung open and Bella and Maria rushed in. They dumped their school bags on one of the chairs at the large table and then hugged Willow. They also hugged Rick, a clear indication that they were happy to see him, and then Isabella reached for a biscuit.

"Stop!" Willow's voice rang out. "You haven't washed your hands and that school bus gathers a lot of dust. All the surfaces you touch aren't clean, so if you eat your food with dirty hands, you'll fall sick."

"Sorry Willow," the two girls quickly washed their hands and dried them, then sat at the kitchen table where Willow served them their afternoon snacks of milk and biscuits."

"Do you have any homework today?" Willow asked, and her sisters nodded. "Finish your snacks then get to it as I start dinner."

Willow noticed that Rick was staring oddly at her; then she remembered that he'd been about to say something just before her sisters rushed in.

"Rick, you were saying something before the girls came in."

He shook his head, "It doesn't matter," he muttered, then left the kitchen through the back door once again. Willow got the feeling that he wasn't pleased about something.

"Uncle Rick looks angry," Bella said as she bit into another biscuit. "Willow, did you argue with him?"

Willow wondered at how perceptive Bella was. The child was very sensitive to any kind of tension, unlike Maria who seemed to have her head in the clouds all the time. Even now Maria was happily munching her snacks without a care in the world. Willow sighed inwardly. They'd only been living on the ranch for two weeks but the girls had settled down as if they'd always lived here. Everyone was very kind to them and Willow slept so much better, getting enough rest every night.

"Uncle Rick likes Willow," Maria said and Willow felt her face turning red. Out of the mouths of babes, she thought.

"Willow is nice and everyone likes her," Bella said.

"Miss Irene doesn't like her," Maria licked her lips. "She's always scolding Willow, and I don't like it."

"Enough!" Willow snapped. The girls were talking at the top of their voices and anyone could hear them. "Finish your snacks and do your homework. I need to begin dinner preparations so we can go home before it gets too dark."

RICK WALKED out of the kitchen feeling slightly cross at the girls' interruption. He'd been about to ask Willow out on a date. In the two weeks that she'd been here, Rick had found himself thinking about her all the time. No woman had ever affected him the way Willow was doing. It was as if she were burrowing her way into his heart with each passing day.

He started walking toward his office, then changed his mind and found himself moving toward the rose garden where he cut five red roses with his penknife, then made his way to the family cemetery about a mile away.

To his surprise, Maynard was there, and there were fresh roses on all five graves. His own joined them.

"At this rate we'll deplete the supply of roses," Maynard pointed out. "Dad was here a little while ago."

"For some reason those roses never run out no matter how often we cut them." Rick sat on the bench beside his brother.

"Mom said that the rose garden was her love gift to us, and I now see what she meant. It's as if she's still here tending to the roses."

Rick rested his elbows on his knees. "I really miss her," he said. "I just wish I could see her one more day and speak with her."

"I know what you mean. There are days that I wake up and go to the rose garden to look for her even after all these years," he shook his head. "Sixteen years and it feels like yesterday. I thought that as I grew older my need for her would diminish. But it seems as if I miss and need her so much with each passing day."

"I hear you," Rick said. "Maybe it's because we're now facing new challenges as we grow older and find that we need her good advice."

"You're right," Maynard agreed. The two brothers sat in silence for a while. "I notice that you like going to the kitchen a lot, Rick. Does this have anything to do with our new cook?"

Rick didn't see the need to keep anything from his brother. "What if it is?"

"Then good for you. Willow looks like a good woman though she's very young to have been left with such a huge responsibility of bringing up her sisters."

"It happens when children lose their parents. Don't you remember how it was with Quin after Mom died?" Maynard shook his head. "Dad fell apart, and for a long time it was Quin who held everything together. Mrs. Brian helped a lot too, but Quin took it upon himself to make sure we were always fine. Remember how he would wake us up and get us ready for school. He would then drive us to school even though he hadn't yet gotten his driving license. And he made sure that we were fine until Dad got better. That's how it is with Willow. She's the guardian for those little girls and it's not a responsibility I envy her."

"Whoever marries Willow will find himself taking on such a heavy load."

"The load of a readymade family is never heavy when love is involved. Besides, Bella and Maria aren't toddlers and can take care of most of their basic needs."

"Don't bite my head off," Maynard chuckled. "I've never heard you defending a woman as strongly as you're doing with Willow. Make sure that it's not just out of a sense of responsibility since you rescued them from that person back in Denver. And be careful not to get Willow in a situation where she begins to develop feelings of hero worship for you.

"Believe me, this has nothing to do with feeling sorry or responsible for her. I genuinely like Willow because in a way, she reminds me of Mom."

"Really?" Maynard looked at his brother. "How?"

"She's gentle but also has nerves of steel. You needed to have seen the way she stood up to that bully back in Denver. It was clear that she was scared but she also refused to cower. Just the way Mom used to be."

"I envy you, Quin and Len," Maynard said.

"And why's that?"

"You three have good and clear memories of Mom and how she was. Callum and I sometimes feel that we missed out on a lot of things. All we have are the old tapes and photos with which to remember her."

"Just know that Mom loved us all equally and specially. Can I tell you something?" Maynard nodded. "The three of us used to feel that Mom loved you and Callum more because you were smaller. Do you know that she spent many hours in your bedroom watching over the two of you as you slept?"

"Really? I didn't know that."

"Yes she did. Do you recall that the two of you shared a room, and Mom would read you bedtime stories until you fell asleep?

She would then sit there for hours until Dad came to get her. She loved watching over you as you slept."

"That's touching."

"Now you know," Rick smiled. "Do you know that Quin and Len were talking about their wives the other day and I overheard them saying that Kelsey and Hazel, in their own different ways, remind them of Mom."

"That's really funny. Now you too are saying that Willow reminds you of Mom. I know you've dated a couple of ladies back in college, but I never once heard you saying anything like this about them."

Rick shrugged, "That's because none of them possessed the qualities Mom had."

"And Willow does?"

Rick nodded. "I feel like I just want to be around her even if we're saying nothing to each other."

"Rick, my dear brother, you've been captured," Maynard made a motion of aiming a bow and arrow at Rick's heart. "And Cupid strikes another fellow in the Randolph house again."

APPEARANCE OF EVIL

Kendrick waited until the two men had identified themselves before he stepped back to let them into the house.

"Agent Collins, what can I do for you?" He turned to the man who seemed to be in charge. "I'm Kendrick Randolph. We don't employ any illegal immigrants on our ranch and you identified yourselves as ICE agents, so to what do we owe the pleasure?"

"Mr. Randolph, it's come to our attention that there are two illegal minors living on this ranch. We've come to collect them so we can send them back to where they belong."

Rick's eyes narrowed but he simply nodded. "I'm one of the directors of this ranch and if you don't mind could you please tell me their names?"

"Certainly," Agent Collins said. "Isabella and Maria Alberto from Bogotá, Colombia."

"I wasn't aware that the two girls are illegally in the States."

"We were informed by a reliable source that they live on this ranch and that's why we're here."

"Well, if you give me time I'll bring the girls to you. Please make yourselves comfortable," he led them into the living room where he saw them seated and served with iced water from the cooler in the dining room then left.

As WILLOW PLACED her phone back in her apron pocket, fear filled her heart.

"Are you all right?" Mrs. Brian asked as she placed a huge chunk of sirloin steak on the chopping board.

"Not really."

"What's happened? You look like your worst nightmare is about to come to pass."

Willow raised stricken eyes to the cook. "That's because it is," she whispered hoarsely. "That was Rick. He just picked Bella and Maria up from school and has asked me to go to his father's study. He's never once picked the girls from school and in any case it's still just about two o'clock and their lessons aren't over yet. So this means that something is going on."

Mrs. Brian frowned, "That sounds serious."

"It is, and I'm really scared. What if that man has traced us to this place? I never told anyone that we were coming to Texas.

Rico is vicious and wouldn't hesitate to use force to get the girls. I thought we were safe here, but I guess it was too good to last."

"Don't agitate yourself needlessly, dear Girl. You can be sure that Rick, his brothers, and their father will never let anything happen to you and your sisters. You can trust them to keep you safe."

"When I left Denver I knew that we would be safe on the ranch because I'd planned to never leave this place. How did Rico find us?" For a brief moment Willow toyed with the possibility of Sally Jo revealing their whereabouts. But then she quickly quashed the thought. Sally Jo would never willingly put their lives at risk and it wasn't as if she and Rico had ever met. But what if Rico had somehow found out that Sally Jo had been at their house on the day they left Denver? What if his goons had followed her and forced her to reveal everything to them? She prayed that Sally Jo was safe and as soon as she could, she would call and find out.

"Let me go and find out whatever is going on," she took her apron off then remembered to extract her phone from the pocket.

She found Rick, Bella and Maria in the den.

"Willow," Rick saw the fear in her eyes. "Don't look so scared. All is well."

Willow immediately hugged her sisters and held them close. She would do anything to protect them even if it meant leaving the ranch.

"Why did you bring my sisters home from school this early?" Willow asked Rick as she led her sisters to the couch and seated them on either side of her.

"Because Dad called and told me to do that. But you'll know shortly."

Willow heard footsteps and then the den door opened. Rick's four brothers Quinten, Waylen, Maynard and Callum, as well as his two sisters-in-law Kelsey and Hazel walked in. Then Mr. Randolph ushered in two burly-looking men. As soon as Willow saw the ICE initials on their jackets she felt that it was all over.

"Good afternoon all," the first man spoke even as he and his colleague took out their badges and held them up for scrutiny. "My name is Agent Gerald Collins and my colleague is Agent Peter Trent. We're both ICE agents."

Quin reached for the two badges, studied them, and nodded when he was satisfied that they were genuine, then handed them back to the first agent.

"Gentlemen, how may we help you?"

Agent Collins spoke, "Like I told Mr. Kendrick, it has come to our attention that there are two minors living illegally on this ranch. We're here to take the necessary steps to see them returned to their country as peacefully as possible."

"On what grounds do you make those charges," Mr. Randolph Senior asked and he moved closer to where Willow and her sisters were seated.

"Miss Isabella and Miss Maria Alberto are the daughters of the late Mr. Vincenzo Alberto who was a citizen of Colombia. His wife Mrs. Lynn Jagger Alberto was American, and both are deceased. Because Mrs. Alberto had no other relatives, the children will be handed over to their relatives in Bogotá."

"But the children were born in the US," Willow cried out. "Doesn't that count for anything? They're US citizens by birth and so why would they be taken to Bogotá? And it's not true that they don't have relatives on their mother's side. Bella and Maria are my half-sisters because we share the same mother."

"Do you have any proof of that?"

"I'm their older sister and my mother made me their guardian."

"Do you have any legal documentation to prove that you're related to the girls by blood and also anything showing that your mother appointed you as their legal guardian?"

Willow's heart sank. Back in Denver when she'd been packing whatever they would need she'd noticed that her mother's personal file wasn't where it was supposed to be. When she would have searched for it, Sally Jo told her that she'd find it and send it over. What if Rico's people had found it first and now had the girls' birth certificates as well as other important documents that could be used against them?

Len raised his hand, "Miss Jagger, don't you have any documents?"

Willow shook her head.

"The late Mr. Vincenzo Alberto was born in Colombia and came to America as an adult," Agent Collins said.

"While that may be so, my mother was an American citizen. Doesn't that count for anything?"

"While we don't dispute that there's the whole issue of guardianship, if the law is to be followed, then these children are wards of the state since Miss Jagger can't provide any documents to show that she was appointed by the court to be their guardian. The children have living relatives in Bogotá, and it's only right for them to grow up over there. When they're of age they may return to the United States."

"I'm their family," Willow said forcefully. "And I'm ready to go to any court in the world to fight for my sisters not to be taken away."

"We'll be forced to arrest you if you try to stop us from taking the children away. They're illegal immigrants."

"Please don't refer to them as illegal immigrants because they were born in the US, and one of their parents was an America citizen even though she's dead," Waylen got into his lawyer mode and Rick smiled. He could see how terrified Willow was and wanted to comfort her. If she lost the girls she would be devastated and these officials seemed bent on taking them away. He wasn't going to allow that.

So he pulled Willow aside, "Do you have any of your mother's documents? Anything at all like a marriage certificate that shows she was married to your sisters' father; anything that would help."

362

Willow frowned, "That's probably what Rico's people must have been searching for when they tossed the house. Mom had a file that contained all her documents, but I didn't see it when we were packing. Sally Jo said she would search for it and send it over. But what if those men found it first?" Something troubled her greatly, "I have a feeling that Rico is behind all this. But how did he even know where to find us?"

"It was me," Bella said tremblingly as she overheard their conversation. "I called Anita my friend and told her the school I go to and where we are. I'm sorry," she burst into tears and Willow took her into her arms.

"No Bella, it's not your fault," she comforted her sister. But Willow's heart sank at the words. Anita, Isabella's friend had a Colombian father who must have overheard the girls' conversation and asked questions. Then he must have told one of Rico's goons and the information reached Rico. Like Rico, Mr. Moreno was a troublemaker and a petty drug peddler who often got into scrapes with the law. If he was offered a few dollars he would sing like a lark.

Agent Trent cleared his throat, "We have documents proving that the children's father obtained citizenship for the girls in Colombia since he was planning to return home just before his death."

"Bella and Maria have never been to Colombia so how can that be?" Willow stared helplessly at Waylen.

"I need to make a phone call," Len said.

"As do I," Mr. Randolph said. "Please give us a few minutes to get all this sorted out."

"An hour at most," Agent Collins said. "We need to get going."

"Yes, Sir."

As Len and Mr. Randolph left the office, Rick followed them out.

"Sally Jo, Willow's friend back in Denver might have a file with all documents that can help this case. I think I have her number here," he browsed through his phone and was glad when he found the woman's number. He'd exchanged numbers with Sally Jo when Willow had mentioned that she would be forwarding some important items to them in Cedar Hill. Now he was glad that he'd taken it. If she had the file that Willow had mentioned then all this would be resolved as quickly as possible. After giving the number to Len, he returned to the den to ensure that the ICE agents didn't harass Willow in his absence.

Abner chuckled softly to himself. Of course, he had Sally Jo's number but he wasn't about to let that fact be known to his two sons just yet.

It took Waylen and Mr. Randolph an hour to return, during which time Willow thought her world had ended. Waylen looked triumphant as he entered the office carrying a file.

"Agents Collins and Trent, I've just received documents via email which you can go ahead and verify. Mr. Vincenzo Alberto, father to Bella and Maria was a naturalized citizen of the United States of America. According to the last records when he was alive there's no mention anywhere that he revoked his citizenship either willingly or unwillingly. This therefore makes the girls full American citizens."

"And what's more," Mr. Randolph came into the office again, "I've obtained a stay from a judge in Cedar Hill to stop you from removing these children from this ranch until further notice."

Willow watched in disbelief as the two agents quickly acquiesced and she was glad of the backing Rick's family had given them. Had she been alone she was sure the men would have thrown all manner of legal jargon at her to completely confuse her. Then they would have taken the girls away from her and she was sure Rico was waiting to pounce on them.

While she didn't condemn the agents for doing their work she was thankful to see their backs as they got into their vehicle and drove away.

Len turned to Willow, "You dodged a bullet on that one, but I would advise you to immediately apply for guardianship for your sisters, and we'll all help you with that. The sooner this is done the better for you." He held up the documents. "Your friend in Denver was able to email these documents to me. She found the file among the stuff you left in your house, and she'll courier it to you immediately, so we can begin to process your guardianship and make it legal."

"Thank you all so much," Willows eyes filled with tears of gratitude. The nightmare was over for now and she was going to do as advised. Sally Jo had come through for her, and she was glad her friend was all right and that it wasn't through her that Rico had found out where they were.

But she had another fear. Rico now knew where they were. What would stop him from trying something else? They could never be safe on this ranch.

Rick noticed the strained look on Willow's face. "All will be well, Willow. You don't need to worry."

"But Rico now knows where we live and what's to stop him from trying something else now that tipping ICE off didn't work out."

Rick put an arm around her shoulders and led her out of the den. "The girls will be all right with Dad. I need to talk to you."

He led her to the rose garden and saw her seated on the narrow bench. "I know you're really scared but I want you to stop being afraid. I won't let anything happen to you and the girls."

"Why are you doing this? What if you get into trouble?"

He gave her an intense look, "Willow, I'm in love with you and will do everything humanly possible to keep you safe."

BREAKING NEWS

Willow stared at Rick in shock. "What did you say?"

"That I've fallen in love with you."

Willow started shaking her head. "No, please don't say that, Rick. It's not fair," she said angrily. "Please don't say that to me again."

"Willow, I'm not joking. I love you very much and want you to be my wife."

"Please," she covered her ears with her hands but Rick pulled them away. "You can't love me, it's not possible. I'm not worthy of being loved by you."

"What do you mean you're not worthy of being loved by me? Willow, if there's anyone who deserves to be loved, it's you, and my heart knows what it wants."

"You don't understand," she dashed the tears away but more took their place. "You're Kendrick Randolph, and I'm a nobody."

"Don't ever say that about yourself. Everybody on earth is somebody, and they're precious."

"I haven't told you all about my background," she sniffed. She didn't want to give herself any false hope that this wonderful man could love a person like her.

"My dad died when I was thirteen and Mom just fell apart. She was very vulnerable at the time and when Vincenzo Alberto started paying attention to her, she fell hard for his cunningness and sweet tongue. At first he was very charming, and just a year after my father's death they got married. All was well for three years or so, and during that time Bella and Maria were born." She fell silent and turned aside to look at the birds which were chirping and calling out to each other as they flew from one rose bush to the other.

Rick waited, knowing that Willow carried a heavy burden inside.

"I didn't notice it at first because I was busy with school. After Bella was born Mom seemed to be tired all the time and I had to help take care of the baby. The same thing happened when Maria was born and I began to fear that my mother was terminally ill."

"What was wrong with her?"

"Vincenzo had started injecting her with small doses of cocaine and he slowly turned her into an addict. I had no idea that while I was at school that man would drug my mother and then bring men into the house to sleep with her for money."

Rick was shocked that a man could do that to his own wife. But then he remembered what the pastor had once preached to them, that the natural man's heart is exceedingly wicked and full of evil, and the only way it can be redeemed is if a person is born again.

"By the time I realized what was happening, my mother was a total wreck and an addict. She was completely dependent on Vincenzo," she was weeping silently. "I think that sometimes the truth is right there in front of us but for some reason we choose not to see it. I blame myself for my mother's descent into addiction. Had I been paying more attention it wouldn't have happened."

"Willow, you can't blame yourself because you were just a child trying your best to keep your family together. Adults often do things that they hide from young ones in their homes. It's not your fault at all."

"I should have been more observant. Instead I would look for any excuse to leave home because I didn't like Vincenzo and that made my mother become more dependent on that man."

"I'm so sorry," Rick tried to take her hand so as to comfort her but she pushed his away.

"I'm not done," she said. "That man began to creep me out and I would find every excuse not to be at home. Then one day he didn't come home from his club and the next thing I knew was that he was dead. According to what people were saying, he and Mom had a fight at his club, and he tripped and fell down the stairs, breaking his neck. For some reason Mom wasn't arrested. After Vincenzo's death, Mom went downhill for a few months because her supply of coke was gone. She became very desperate and sold nearly everything we had to feed her habit."

Rick closed his eyes and felt deep pain within. He couldn't imagine what Willow must have gone through.

"I got fed up and one day just put my foot down," she wiped her tears. "I gave my mother an ultimatum, either to change or I would take Bella and Maria to an orphanage and then disappear. That was her wakeup call, and a few days later she admitted herself into a state-funded rehabilitation center. She was there for about four months during which time I had to stop going to school and find a job to support us. But she got clean and came back home and even got a job. We moved out of Vincenzo's house to the apartment, and we were really happy there. My mom was sober once again and determined to be a loving mother to the three of us. She was a hard worker and her job paid well, so life was coming together for us again," Willow sniffed and fell silent for a moment. "All was going well, and I even made plans to go back to school, but then Mom started falling ill again. At first I thought she was back on drugs again and was so angry with her. But then one day I came back home from school to find out that the neighbors had rushed her to the emergency room after she collapsed in the house. After intensive tests were done, my mom was found to have contracted HIV, and it just broke her.

Vincenzo's wicked ways had landed my mother in that problem. She struggled to stay normal but I could see that she was really scared. The good thing was that she gave her life to Christ and that made it easier to bear the load. I read all I could about HIV and AIDS and got more and more depressed."

Rick shook his head, "Reading about diseases on the internet can lead to a person's mind exploding. There's so much misinformation out there. Only a qualified and professional doctor can provide the right diagnosis and any other information a person requires."

Willow laughed and it caught on a sob. "That's what I realized, but all I wanted was to find a cure for my mother so she wouldn't have to die."

"With proper treatment, nutrition and social support, many people are living healthy lives with HIV."

"I did all I could for Mom, and for a while she was responding well to treatment, and we were hopeful." Willow bit her lower lip. "Then nine months ago she just went down and for a full month she was really sick. In her final days I had to take care of her because we couldn't afford a full-time nurse. Between taking care of my sick mother and my sisters it was just too much and I was so exhausted. One day I made a serious mistake and there was an accident."

"What happened?"

"I was so sleepy, and while I was handling some of Mom's things, I pricked myself with her pair of scissors. I got prophylaxis for HIV exposure but I've never gone for any other tests after that because I'm so scared. What if I got infected?"

"Weren't tests carried out after you got the prophylaxis treatment?"

"The doctor said the initial tests showed that I wasn't infected, but I had to take the drugs for twenty-eight days. After that I would know my status after being tested again but I've never dared to go and find out."

Rick reached for her hands once again, and through she tried to resist, he held her, and she wept on his chest. It felt so good to finally let go and just lean on someone else. She'd carried this heavy load for so long that it had really weighed her down. But now she felt as if the weight was crumbling and being washed away.

"Willow, you're agitating yourself for no reason at all. Didn't you tell me that you worked at a diner?"

"Yes," she said in a small voice.

"Aren't you supposed to go for food handler's medical examinations from time to time?"

"Once or twice a year," Willow agreed.

"Then don't you think the clinical officers or medical personnel would have alerted you to the fact that you have a contagious disease?"

Willow thought for a moment then felt deep relief. She'd never had any symptoms of having contracted HIV but now she felt that she owed it to herself to get tested.

"We can go and get tested if you want, not that the outcome will change a thing about how I feel about you."

"Are you sure?" Hope flared within her heart.

"Willow, I thought I was contented with my life before I met you. When my elder brothers Quin and Len fell in love and got married, I teased them mercilessly. But deep down I felt lonely and envied them. I was heartbroken twice while in college and steered clear of relationships after that. I was afraid of giving my heart to someone and then having it broken again," he chuckled softly. "Then you came into my life and bam! There I was, head over heels in love with you, and it only gets deeper every day. I love you so much and one thing is for sure. You complete me and my life is so much richer and fuller."

"I don't know what to say," Willow felt very shy but elated at the same time. Rick loved her and she loved him too. The burden of wondering if her feelings were one sided was now over.

"Willow? Please say something. Don't you have feelings for me at all?"

"You mean you still love me after all I've told you about my mom and her life and how things have been? Also, we don't know for sure what my HIV status is right now."

"Like I said, nothing changes, my love. And as for your mother, she was the victim of a wicked and cruel man who used her for his own selfish gains. From what I've deduced, your mother was a strong woman who wanted the best for her children."

"I just wish she would have lived to see this day."

"Don't think about that because then the pain will never go away. Consider that your mom's time had come, and she was ready to go to her Maker. Didn't you say that she was born again?"

"Yes. While she was in rehab, she met a nurse who was born again and she started thinking about accepting Christ as her Savior. That's what made her time in rehab bearable. And she was so happy through the pain. When she came home she started going to church with us and finally made the decision to give her life to Christ. I was so happy."

"So be happy that she's in a better place. When your mom accepted Christ as her Savior she became a new creature and that's what gave her joy in the midst of pain."

WILLOW NODDED, "My mom even forgave Vincenzo and all the men who took advantage of her," she felt angry. "I didn't understand how she could do that. Those wicked men don't deserve anyone's forgiveness."

RICK GENTLY RUBBED Willow's shoulder. "Your mom was a woman who understood that all human beings are just frail and limited. Forgiveness is maintaining allowance for the humanity of men and understanding that we've all sinned and fallen short of the glory of God. By forgiving all who hurt her, your mother extended mercy and grace to them. That's why she died with so much peace. Forgiveness frees us from the prison of holding onto the hurts others have given us."

WILLOW PULLED AWAY and covered her face with her palms. She hated Vincenzo and his kind very much for wasting her mother's life. But Rick was right. Hatred weighed a person down, and she was tired of hauling the heavy load around with her.

"Will you help me?" She asked Rick.

"In which way?"

"To learn how to forgive Vincenzo, Rico and everyone who destroyed my mom's life."

"Yes, I'll walk with you through it all, and what I want you to know is that it's all right to be angry. But the important thing is to know what to do with that anger. God will never require us to be perfect. All He wants from us is sincerity and brokenness. None of us can ever sustain the flawlessness that meets God's standards. So be kind to yourself and know that a contrite and broken spirit are all that our Master requires from us."

WEDDING BELLS

"Another mighty oak goes down!" Abner winked at his third son. The young man looked so happy; not for the first time Abner wished that Barbara, his late wife, was still here to see all this.

His heart swelled at how his sons and their wives had all come together to make this wedding successful.

"Today Willow is locking me down forever," Rick winked back at his father. "And I must say that I quite love these shackles."

Everyone standing around the newlyweds laughed. The church service had been brief, and when they'd stood face to face before the altar, the minister of God and the congregation, Willow had known that she was truly blessed.

Though many people had turned up for the wedding, everyone seemed to just fade away and it was as if it was only the two of them left on earth.

376

When the minster finally pronounced them husband and wife, they'd both wept with joy.

Rick pulled Willow close for the slow dance to the timeless love song by Diana Ross and Lionel Richie.

It was Willow's mother's favorite song and when she was young she'd watched her father and mother dance to it numerous times before his death.

When they'd been choosing the song for their first dance as husband and wife, Rick had picked on this one.

"My darling," Rick breathed into her ear. "I want to share all my love with you and no one else will do."

Willow picked up the next lines of the song, "And your eyes, your eyes, your eyes, they tell me how much you care, ooh yes."

And together they said to each other, "You will always be, my endless love."

A loud cheer broke out and it was Maynard and Callum who shouted the loudest.

Abner was holding hands with Bella and Maria who had taken to calling him 'Grandpa.' They danced in their small circle and he felt tears prickling at the back of his eyes. These children now belonged to his family forever.

Just the previous day, Sally Jo had called with news that had made them all remain silent with shock for a while.

"Rico Alberto was found shot to death by one of his numerous women," she'd said.

Later that day Abner had found Willow weeping on the back porch of the house and wondered what was going on with her. "Has anyone offended you?" He asked her.

"I just feel so guilty," she sobbed.

"Why?"

"When you gave us the news about Rico's death, I felt such deep relief and happiness. The fact that he'll never come to trouble my sisters and me again makes me happy, but then I'm feeling guilty that I'm celebrating someone's death. Does that make me a bad person?"

"No, it makes you human," he chuckled. "We all feel relieved when our nemesis is eliminated. Otherwise we wouldn't be human. But the important thing here is to learn to forgive those who have offended us. My daughter, remember that forgiveness is for us who were offended and we need it more than those who offended us. When we forgive we're set free."

Abner turned his granddaughters round as his eyes went toward where Quin was standing holding his pregnant wife in his arms. Waylen had Hazel in his arms, too.

"Thank You, Lord."

"Grandpa, are you crying? " Bella asked him. "Are you sad?"

Abner chuckled and blinked back the tears. "I'm crying a little but they're also tears of happiness. I wish your grandmother was here to celebrate with us," his phone vibrated and he looked at the message from Sally Jo.

"How is it going?" She'd texted.

"Three down, two to go. Expect a hefty bonus," he texted back and then switched his phone off. "Now my darlings, where were we?"

Once again he took the girls' hands and then put all his concentration on dancing with his new 'granddaughters.'

MAYNARD'S SCARRED
SECOND CHANCE BRIDE

THE RECLUSE

Twenty-three-year-old Celine Bourne battled the depression that was trying to overwhelm her as she sat alone in her dimly lit bedroom. Apart from being the place she rested her weary head every night, this room had also become her sanctuary and prison both at once. It was her sanctuary because in here she could hide away from the world and all its mockery; and her prison because she longed to leave it but felt caged in because of her current condition. The invisible bars of fear kept her locked up, and for her, it was definitely life imprisonment because she didn't imagine ever being free again.

It was hard to believe that she'd once loved the outdoors where the sun would gently kiss her face and bring laughter to her heart. The outdoors had been her friend, and she'd loved hiking and jogging to keep fit and stay in shape. But now she embraced darkness like a close friend and the only outdoor space she stepped out to was her grandmother's small backyard where no eyes could pry and look on her disfigured face with revulsion or pity.

How had her dreams gone so wrong, she wondered as tears filled her gentle gray eyes? Her right hand went to her face, and as she touched the rough skin, a sob broke through her lips.

"Cece?" The soft voice made her quickly wipe her face. "Why do you keep doing this to yourself?" Mrs. Judith Bourne entered her granddaughter's bedroom and sat down on the bed. The room was semi-dark, and the only light came from a dim bedside lamp. "Cece, my love, you can't continue crying and hurting yourself like this every day. You'll make yourself ill."

"Nana," Cece felt her grandma's loving arms around her, and she leaned into her strength. "I'm so sad, Nana. My life is as good as over, and I've been asking myself why this had to happen to me. What wrong did I do that my whole life had to be wasted like this?"

"Stop that at once," Nana's voice broke, and as she held her granddaughter close, she felt her pain. "You still have so much going for you. This world still needs you even if you can't see things clearly right now. But one day, you'll smile again—and that's a promise."

"Oh, Nana," Cece hated seeing her grandmother so distraught and forced a smile on her lips. "You're the best grandmother in the world. What would I have done if I hadn't had you? My life would have ended three years ago."

"No, my love," Judith gripped her granddaughter's shoulders firmly but gently and then turned so they were facing each other, and looked into her face. "You're one of the strongest women I've ever known, and you would have kept going. You are your father's daughter and nothing can ever take that away."

"I feel so lost, Nana. My peers are getting married and having children. They're advancing in their careers or finding love and settling down to have sweet babies, but look at me. Look at my face, Nana, I look like a monster, and no man will ever want me," her voice broke. "I'm sorry Nana, I didn't mean to make you sad."

"Cece, don't ever say those horrible words about yourself. Despite those scars, you're still a very beautiful young woman. The Lord is faithful, and when the time is right, He'll bring you the right man—one who'll see your inner beauty and love you in spite of those scars."

Cece shook her head and scoffed lightly. She rose to her feet and moved across the room, then turned to face her grandmother. "Nana, thank you for always cheering me up, but I feel like I'm a lost cause. The last thing I want is for a man to marry me out of pity."

"Your man won't pity you. He'll adore you, and I know that soon he'll come into your life. Those scars will fade in his eyes because a real, loving man will never focus on your physical beauty alone."

Cece smiled sadly. Her grandmother tried her best to always cheer her up but she knew that her face wasn't what any man would want to wake up next to for the next fifty years of his life. She was ugly, and ever since the incident, she'd never looked at herself in the mirror. After spending months in and out of hospital, she'd returned home and begged her grandmother to burn all her previous photos. Any magazines that had her pictures as an upcoming model had perished in an inferno, as had all her paraphernalia that had to do with her dead career.

The small comfort she got in all this was that her attacker had been arrested just days after the ugly incident. What had shocked Cece was that the woman who'd sprayed acid on her face was just an acquaintance.

"Don't think about it," Nana's soft voice broke through her musings. "Your clenched fists tell me that you're still very angry and replaying the ugly scene over and over again in your mind."

"Marion ruined my life," Cece blinked rapidly. "All I ever did was mind my own business. We weren't even in the same line of work and it isn't as if I was her rival in any way. We didn't even move in the same circles so I don't understand why she hated me enough to do this to me. I'll never forgive her, and I'm glad that she's rotting in prison."

"Cece!"

"Nana, that woman destroyed my life, and she should pay for what she did. The seven-year sentence she was given is too little."

"Calm down, Cece," Nana rose to her feet and approached her. She took her hand and led her back to the bed. "Your anger is quite justified, and no one will ever fault you for seeking vengeance. But remember that holding onto the pain will build bitterness within your heart. You can't continue to live like that, my child. It will destroy you."

Cece's lips tightened. Why couldn't her grandmother understand her pain and all she'd been through? This was the rest of her life and she felt justified in being angry that someone had chosen to destroy it without any fault on her part at all.

Even though Marion was behind bars, the seven-year sentence would soon be over, and she would return to her family and normal life. She would probably find a man to marry her and live happily ever after. But Cece had no one else apart from Nana.

"I know you don't want to hear this, but I'm asking you to forgive Marion."

Cece didn't want to argue with her grandmother, nor did she need any sermons preached to her. The seven-year sentence for Marion wasn't enough, according to her. Three were already over and she would soon be out if she was paroled. No, Marion should have received a life sentence for her crime. After all, she'd sentenced Cece to a lifetime of loneliness and misery. What caused Cece many sleepless nights was the reminder that her grandmother wouldn't live forever. One day Nana would die and be gone and she'd be all alone, no one to care about her and keep encouraging her when her emotions hit rock bottom, which they often did. She'd have no husband nor children on whom to lean, and that thought made her anger toward Marion fester even more. No, Marion didn't deserve either mercy or forgiveness.

"Cece?"

"I hear you Nana," she found a smile on her lips. "It's time for me to go to bed."

"Tomorrow is Sunday," there was hope in Nana's voice. "There's a visiting pastor at our church, and you might enjoy his sermon."

Cece shook her head, "I'll just follow the church service online, Nana. I don't want people to keep staring at me, so it's better for me not to appear in church." Months ago she'd given in to her grandmother's persuasion and attended church. It had been a really trying time because people didn't even pay attention to the sermon; instead, they kept staring at her face until it got too uncomfortable, and she rushed out, vowing to never return. Never again would she put herself through such trauma, not even to please her grandmother.

Nana Judith sighed, feeling her granddaughter's pain. She wished Cece would come out of the shell she'd built around herself and live again. Nana knew that somewhere out there was a man who would love Celine unconditionally. But how was the man supposed to find her when she kept herself hidden and locked up like a recluse?

LEGACY OF THE PAST

$\mathcal{M}$aynard Randolph could already tell that his mood was about to be ruined. The twenty-four-year-old made his face expressionless even as he observed the woman who sat across from him at the kitchen table. Why hadn't he come in for his breakfast earlier than this? Then he would have avoided this meeting.

Miss Doris Keller was the newest intern to come to the ranch, and though she'd only been here for a couple of days or so, she'd managed to offend the usually long-suffering housekeeper. Mrs. Brian was a very patient woman, and Maynard should know. She'd brought him and his brothers up when their mother passed away nearly sixteen years ago, and it hadn't been easy for her. Taking care of five teenage boys who were mourning the death of their mother had taxed her to the limit. Some of their escapades made Maynard cringe inwardly as he thought about the past, but Mrs. Brian had remained patient and loving all the while. She'd told them she was aware that they were all acting up because of grief but she would be there for them, and she'd never once let them down, nor acted as if their actions were hurting her. This woman was a saint! Yet she could barely stand Doris Keller.

In their adulthood, Maynard and his four brothers had wished their widowed father would take Mrs. Brian as his wife after she'd lost her own husband. They'd noticed that their father liked her company, yet their relationship remained purely platonic.

"I'm so thankful for this chance to be an intern here at Randolph Ranch. All my followers on Instagram and Twitter are so eager to know what happens on a ranch, and I have so much to share with them. Do you know that I have over fifty thousand followers?" Doris batted her eyelashes at Maynard, making him very uncomfortable. "They would love to see me standing with some real handsome cowboys; maybe I can find one or two who can pose for some shots with me."

Maynard looked around, all the while hoping that Mrs. Brian would walk into the kitchen. Or his sister-in-law, Willow, who loved baking in the afternoons. He couldn't understand how he'd ended up alone in the kitchen with Doris Keller. Though he'd finished his breakfast, it was out of politeness that he stayed to keep her company as she ate her own scanty breakfast of two thin slices of papaya fruit and a glass of orange juice. Maynard shook his head, how did an adult survive on such a meager breakfast serving?

"There's a lot to learn while you're here, and you'll receive all the help you need, but you'll need to respect other people's privacy before posting anything about them on social media," he was careful to stay on his side of the table, thus keeping as much distance between them as possible. "By the way, what's your degree in?"

"Veterinary medicine," she said, smiling broadly. Maynard admitted that she was a very beautiful woman to look at, but from his brief interactions with her in less than two days, he'd quickly realized that her beauty was only skin deep. She was very shallow because all she ever talked about was the latest fashions and having a large following on the various social media platforms. It was as if all Doris existed for was to be seen by the world. "I'm nearly done with my studies; then I'll be free to look for a permanent position at a ranch like this one. And I'll be called a doctor even though I don't have to spend so many years in training like those people who treat human beings. Dr. Doris Keller," she preened, raising her phone to take a selfie. "The world is waiting for my unveiling, and just imagine if I should get a more permanent position on a ranch such as this one."

"That's good," Maynard said, ignoring the hopeful tone of her voice. He didn't think that a socialite such as Doris would enjoy working on a ranch of this magnitude. Randolph Ranch was one of the largest in Texas, and the amount of work that went into running it on a daily basis was vast. There was no time for joking around or seeking one's personal glory. All the men and women who worked here full time knew what was expected of them if the ranch was to continue prospering. There was no time for idle chat or social media attention seeking. "What you need to do then is familiarize yourself with all the work that our resident vets do. Dr. Matthews oversees all vet services and matters to do with the animals, and his assistant is Dr. Kildare. You'll no doubt be spending a lot of time at the vet clinic, so the sooner I take you there so you can meet them, the faster things will begin to move. And after your graduation the world will be at your feet. Vets are in high demand all over the world, and especially well-trained ones."

"I've already met those two gentlemen," Doris flipped her hair. "All they do is run around with the animals. Do you know that they refused to allow me to take photos of them treating some of the animals?"

"That's the work of a vet," Maynard said. "What did you think you would be doing on this ranch as a Veterinary intern? And like I said, please respect other people's privacy. This is a working ranch and everyone takes their jobs very seriously, Miss Keller. Please note that this chance you've been given is one desired by many others out there."

"I didn't mean to sound ungrateful for this opportunity," she said hurriedly as if she knew that her words could get her into a difficult situation. "What I mean is that I believe there's more to being a vet than just chasing after cows and their calves."

Maynard frowned slightly, 'I'm sorry that you're getting the wrong impression about this ranch and what our vets do here. The vets don't spend their time chasing after cows and their calves as you put it."

"No, please don't get me wrong, but I think things can be modernized a little bit. It would be nice to get permanent employment on this ranch because I was reading on the internet that it's one of the best ranches and it is very progressive and prosperous, and I have so many new ideas to share on how things can be even better than they are right now," she jumped to her feet took off the large trench coat she was wearing and Maynard's eyes widened slightly. Doris Keller was dressed in a mini skirt and very high heels; clothing more suited for a photo shoot rather than working on a ranch. He wondered how to get her to change her outfit which was very inappropriate for working around normal young males.

Randolph Ranch did its best to keep all the workers safe, but they also needed to cooperate to ensure their own wellbeing. Apart from Doris Keller's outfit being unsuitable for working with animals, it was also offensive and suggestive. It would also be very disrespectful for her to show up to work dressed like this because chances of her causing a huge distraction were high and everyone needed to be alert at all times, especially when working with animals. Anything small could spook them, and having men ogling interns instead of paying attention to their work could be very dangerous. Maynard was relieved when the outer door opened and the housekeeper walked into the kitchen.

Mrs. Brian looked at the plates on the table then raised her eyebrows at Maynard. He gave her a sheepish smile then gathered the dirty dishes and carried them to the sink where he proceeded to wash them.

"Mrs. Brian, you remember Miss Doris Keller, don't you? She's one of our newest interns who is aspiring to become a vet. I was just about to show her where she can find Dr. Matthew's clinic. She's been telling me that she has some new ideas to share about how to improve things around here."

"Is that right?" Mrs. Brian's eyebrows went up. "Once again, welcome to Randolph Ranch, my dear, but I suggest that if you're going to be working around the animals then you should consider your mode of dress."

"I'm sorry?" Doris gave Mrs. Brian a sharp look. Her chin jutted out stubbornly as if she didn't care for what she was being told. "What's wrong with what I'm wearing?" Doris looked down at her outfit and then draped her trench coat on the back of a chair.

"Girl, don't give me that look as if I don't know what I'm talking about. For the duration of your time here you'll be wading through sludge and muck, and your shoes look like they cost a pretty penny, not to mention how uncomfortable they will make you feel amid all that filth. This is no office job, you know. If you step into a heap of manure, your shoes will be ruined forever. Also, you don't want to get bitten by any gnats which like to land on exposed skin. Some bites can be very painful."

The scowl cleared from Doris's face. "Oh!" She looked down at her shoes. "I brought a pair of boots with me. Let me just go and change into them and also put on some pants," she gave Maynard a dazzling smile as she swayed out of the kitchen, Mrs. Brian shaking her head slowly.

"That one looks like trouble," the African American woman muttered. "Be very careful when you're around her. She reminds me of a hungry shark I once saw on Discovery Channel."

Maynard chuckled, "Believe me, Ma'am, I plan on giving her a wide berth and won't let her anywhere near me." He said as his brother walked into the kitchen.

"I heard that. Who are you planning to give a wide berth, brother?" Callum Randolph grinned at his brother. "I hope it's not me."

"Keep your hat on, little brother. I meant the new intern, Miss Keller," Maynard said. An idea suddenly popped into his head. "She'll need you to sort out all her welfare and HR details," he tapped Callum on the shoulder, "Tag, you're it. That lady now becomes your responsibility," and before his brother could protest, Maynard fled from the kitchen.

He needed to check on a few of the new calves and foals as well as the old horses which could no longer work. He decided to take a shortcut through their largest barn that housed nearly fifty dairy cows.

"What's up, Maynard?" Bill Concher, one of the ranch's longtime cowboys hailed him.

"I'm just passing through on my way to checking on the new calves," he said. The barn had fifty stalls and the new mothers and their calves were housed here until they were ready to be moved to the main herd.

Due to the vast acreage of the ranch and the number of animals they owned, these were separated into four distinctive herds on different sections of the property.

"We lost two calves and a foal last night," Bill said as he joined Maynard. "Perhaps you can begin by checking on these animals; then I'll accompany you to the next barn."

"Good enough," Maynard said as he looked around for a coverall. It was mandatory for anyone working around the animals to be well clothed and shod. He quickly exchanged his everyday boots for a pair of mud boots.

"What happened to the little ones that died?" Maynard began inspecting the stalls for any black mold, which was a health hazard for the animals. Randolph Ranch was run on very stringent health standards both for the people and animals on it, but mistakes occurred occasionally, and as one of the shareholders, Maynard took no chances with safety. Black mold was not only very dangerous for animals but for the men and women who worked on the ranch, too.

"The mothers refused to nurse them and then left them exposed to the cold."

"That shouldn't have happened," Maynard said. "Who was on duty last night?"

"I was here and believe me, we did all we could to keep the little ones warm. Dr. Matthew said he'll perform autopsies to make sure the calves and foal weren't exposed to any diseases that might harm the rest. He said he suspected that their lungs hadn't fully developed even at the time of birth and that could have caused their untimely deaths."

Maynard nodded, "Keep me informed if any other calves look sick. And make sure the heating is sufficient in all the stalls at all times. Winter is fast approaching, and the weather is threatening to be worse than last year, so we have to be very watchful."

"Yes, Sir."

Maynard inspected all the walls to ensure that the insulation was sound and there were no cracks or exposed wires that could be hazardous to the animals and laborers.

"What did you do with the carcasses?" Maynard asked.

"Dr. Matthew is yet to dispose of them since he's conducting autopsies on them. If they're healthy they'll be used in the preparation of feed for the dogs and if not they'll be burnt and the ashes buried."

"See that it's done so we don't have any kind of outbreak due to poor handling of the carcasses. How many other cows and mares are yet to drop their little ones?"

"About forty cows and ten mares when I last counted two days ago. We're keeping a close eye on them."

"Well, the Met Department predicted that this winter might be worse than last year, but we're hoping that it won't be so. But then again this is Texas, and anything can happen."

"We'll do our best to keep all the animals safe, Maynard."

"Well, I think I've seen enough for now, but Quin might pass by later for a more thorough inspection. I also need to see Dr. Kildare about some of the very old horses. Would you perchance know of his whereabouts?"

"The last time I saw him was about three hours ago when he said he was going to assist Dr. Matthew with the autopsies of the dead animals."

As usual, after his main duties on the ranch, Maynard made his way to his Ford Bronco, which was parked in the main garage. He needed to visit the newest building on the other side of the ranch. He drove the five miles, while thinking about more ways to improve his latest project.

Randolph Restorative and Recreation Center was Maynard's brainchild and he felt deep satisfaction as he parked in the lot close to the building. It was just slightly over three months old, and he knew that it would have to be expanded at some point. But for now, it housed thirty animal stalls on the ground level and the offices on the second floor.

Since it was after five o'clock, the main receptionist had left, and there was a guard sitting in her place. The man rose and saluted him as he walked past and entered the main arena where one or two people were to be found. As a rule, the main arena closed at five p.m., and the animals were taken back to their stalls for the night. All patients and counselors also had to leave by five because most of them lived off the ranch.

"How were today's sessions?" Maynard walked up to a sandy-haired man who was in his early twenties. He was putting away some equipment in the bins meant for that purpose.

"As well as always, though attendance was down to half today. I think many patients stayed away because it was so cold."

"Any incidents that need my attention?"

The young man shook his head, "No, Sir."

"Thank you for the good work, Andy. I'll be up in my office for a few minutes. Please let Morgan at the front desk know this in case he needs to lock up."

"Will do that."

Maynard used the stairs instead of the lift that had been installed just for emergency purposes. He didn't intend to stay for long because he wanted to play some indoor games with Bella and Maria, his nieces by marriage. They were actually his sister-in-law, Willow's, small siblings but calling them in-laws sounded very odd.

He walked to the window of his office that overlooked the arena. The building was circular though one end opened up into the fields where most therapy sessions were held. With the weather getting colder, the sessions would most probably have to be held indoors, and he hoped that the horses, most of which were used to the outdoors, wouldn't kick up a fuss. They would just have to try things out and see what happened. Like the barns on the ranch, this place was also kept spic and span, and the highest safety standards were observed to keep both people and animals safe.

Maynard sighed as he walked to his desk and sat behind it, his eyes immediately going to the large framed photo of his parents mounted on one wall. It had been taken on their tenth wedding anniversary and they both looked so happy, not knowing that in just a few years' time all that would change. Life, he thought, was so unpredictable.

"Oh, Mom," Maynard sighed deeply. He missed his mother so much. At the time of her death, he'd been eight years old, and for years her absence had grieved him. Not much had been explained to him at her burial, but as the years went by, he began to understand more about death and eventually accepted that she was gone forever. Yet the pain of losing his mother would never completely go away.

It was his own deep pain and grief that had birthed the idea of this center years ago, though it had only become a reality about three months ago. At first, it had been just an idea in his mind, but then he'd realized that there was something very special about horses. Maynard loved riding but he also cherished the time spent just grooming the horses as they stood in their stalls. While his elder brothers preferred working with younger and more spirited horses, Maynard had found satisfaction dealing with the older, aging ones. Being around the old animals always made him feel better. So, when he began thinking about opening this center, he'd spoken to his father and two older brothers Quin and Waylen about not putting the old horses down unless they were truly too old or too ill to live.

Maynard had used his own pain to set this place up so those who were hurting could receive much-needed help. This had all come about because a few years ago one of his father's old cowboys had once told him that horses were very good listeners.

Carter had found Maynard weeping in one of the barns because he was remembering his mother. It was Christmas Day, and he should have been celebrating with the rest of the family, but he'd stolen out of the house to grieve for his mother who'd lost her life on such a day years before. Maynard had mixed feelings about Christmas because as a child it had always been one of his best days, yet also one of the worst.

"Horses are special creatures who you can whisper your deepest secrets to, and they'll never tell anyone, nor betray you," Carter had walked up to him and pretended not to notice his tears.

"Will they really hear me?" Maynard wiped his tears and turned to look at the man who he always thought was as old as the ranch itself.

"Yes, Maynard, God has given horses special abilities, and they're able to listen to people even if they can't answer back. They're silent listeners to any conversation you may wish to have with them, yet you'll always walk away feeling as if all your burdens aren't that heavy anymore."

And Maynard had found that to be true. Over the years after that, he'd had many conversations with his favorite horses while riding or grooming them, and like Carter had said, it had been very comforting.

Even now he still shared his pain with the horses, though now he could do it at any time of the day if he so wished. Those conversations had kept him sane—especially given the recent trauma in his life.

Three years ago, Maynard had returned home from a trip to New York, deeply in love with a woman he'd met at LaGuardia Airport when their respective flights were cancelled and the planes grounded due to a heavy snowstorm.

Celine Bourne! Maynard sighed as he reached for the gold chain around his neck. He'd gone to New York to celebrate a friend's graduation and on his way back he and several other passengers got stranded at the airport due to a heavy snowstorm that saw several flights, including his, grounded.

Not wanting to get agitated because of a situation he had no control over, Maynard decided to buy a magazine to while away the time until the skies cleared and he could go home. As he walked toward one of the newspaper stands, someone bumped into him.

"I'm so sorry," the soft voice said as he steadied the slender woman who'd stumbled into him. "The heel of my shoe snapped and thanks to you, I'm not lying face flat on the floor," she giggled softly. "Imagine the shame of it all!" Even wearing very high-heeled stiletto ankle boots she was still a few inches shorter than he was.

Maynard's gaze went down to the shoe which was now heelless. Then he raised his eyes, looked into her beautiful gray eyes and was lost forever. Hitherto, Maynard had only heard about love at first sight and scoffed at the poor souls who claimed to have been struck by it. But on that cold January fourth morning, Maynard Randolph had lost his heart forever.

What surprised him was the answering dazed look the young woman gave him. She was so beautiful that his breath caught in his throat and he found himself going down on one knee to help her get her other boot off.

"I have a pair of sandals in my purse," she said breathlessly and with trembling hands pulled a wrapped package from her large leather handbag. Maynard reached for the package, unwrapped it and helped her into the one-inch heeled sandals, then picked up the boots. "Thank goodness Nana taught me to always carry an extra pair of shoes or sandals in my handbag."

"What do we do with these?" Maynard indicated the boots.

She gave him a sweet smile, "I'll take them home and after they're repaired they'll go to a friend who just loves them. Mandy has always told me that if I got tired of these boots she'd gladly take them off my hands." And after wrapping them in the same polythene bag, she slipped them into her purse. "Now I'm good to go," she gave him another dazzling smile.

"Come," Maynard said breathlessly, not daring to believe that she was real and all this was happening to him. "We need to find somewhere to sit," he said as he led her to the Delta Airlines Sky Lounge since he was flying business class on the airline. "My name is Maynard Randolph, a resident of Cedar Hills in Texas. What brings you to New York on such a terrible day?"

The young woman smiled, "I was here for a winter photo shoot," she said. "My name is Celine Bourne but my work name is Cece Bourne, a model by profession," Celine looked at her phone. "My Nana will be so worried because I haven't called her in hours. My cellphone went off and I can't find a free power outlet."

"Sorry about that but as you know, ninety-nine percent of all flights out of LaGuardia have been grounded, and I guess everyone is trying to charge their phones so they can let their families know that they're safe. Does your phone use a power bank?"

"Do you have one?"

"Sure," and after they sat down next to each other on a cozy lounge settee, Maynard asked for her IPhone which he then connected to his still-full power bank. It was a rule by his father that before embarking on any journey, all phones and power banks should be well charged. Maynard also acted as Cece's personal bodyguard when it became clear that she'd been recognized by some of the other passengers in the lounge.

But Maynard saw none of Cece's fame as a fast-rising model. Instead, he saw a humble and meek woman who hadn't allowed fame to go to her head.

"Someone raised you right," he told her at some point.

She gave him a sweet smile, "That's my Nana, my father's mother."

"Where are your parents?"

She looked really sad. "They died in a car crash when I was ten, and it's been Nana who brought me up since then."

"I'm so sorry for your loss," he said, thinking about his own family and how blessed he was to have them even if his mother wasn't there anymore. "Do you have any siblings?"

Cece shook her head, "I'm an only child, as were both my parents, so no immediate cousins or uncles on either side. My Nana has a few distant relatives, though these aren't in our lives at all." She looked at him. "What about you? Do you have any family?"

"Four brothers and a dad. Three brothers are older than me. We lost our mom twelve years ago when she fell from her horse and broke her neck."

"That must have been so horrible."

And the hours passed swiftly as they sat and talked about every topic under the sun, but love. Both were shy to broach the subject that was staring them in the face. Maynard knew that he'd found his soulmate! When morning came and the airport was declared to be back in full service, the two were reluctant to be separated.

"Here," Maynard took off his gold bracelet engraved with his name and slipped it onto Cece's wrist. "It's slightly big for you but if you take it to a goldsmith, it can be adjusted to fit."

"Thank you," Cece admired the masculine bracelet on her wrist. "I'll have it adjusted, then wear it for the rest of my life," she gave him a sweet smile, then took it off and put it inside her purse. "I wouldn't want it to fall and get lost." She then reached behind her neck and took off her gold chain with the Star of David pendant and placed it around Maynard's neck. "Please remember me," she said in a soft voice and Maynard nodded.

"I could never forget you even if I wanted to." He touched the chain. "This will be here for the rest of my life." Then he gazed intensely into her eyes. "We can make this work," he said passionately, then suggested that they exchange contact information. "And I promise that as soon as I can, I'll be coming to Denver to visit you and your grandmother. Then I'll invite the two of you to visit our ranch so you can experience Texas first hand."

"We'd like that very much."

Since his flight was an hour after Cece's he made sure that he walked her to her boarding terminal, and they exchanged a brief kiss, which left them both shaken. Then Cece walked through the door and was soon out of sight but not out of his mind.

Maynard returned home floating on a cloud, and for the next four weeks they called, texted, and even sent email messages to each other. Not a single day passed without them declaring their love for each other and how much they longed to meet again.

But then suddenly Cece couldn't be reached. Her cellphone number, he was informed by the operator, was no longer in service. His emails too, went unanswered, and the few letters he sent through the postal address she'd given him were returned to him unopened and clearly rubberstamped 'Addressee Unknown.'

Maynard sighed and put his head on his desk. That was how he'd found true love and lost it in four weeks and even now, three years later, he'd never gotten over Cece. He doubted that he would and was just glad that his father wasn't putting any pressure on him to find himself a mate. His three older brothers had found love and were now happily married, and Maynard wondered if he was destined to be alone for the rest of his life. While he envied them slightly for having found their soulmates, he wasn't ready to give up his dream of seeing Cece again.

"One day I'll go to Denver to look for Cece again," he said, as he thought about the unfruitful trip he'd made three years ago to look for her. The address she'd given him had belonged to a used-car lot, and no one there had ever heard of her. Dejected and sad, he'd returned to Cedar Hill to ponder his misfortune.

"Lord, how could I have found love and then lost it?"

If only he knew what had happened to Cece! The internet provided no answers, as most sites he visited only highlighted her past successes and were dated three years ago and before. Nothing about her was ever mentioned from the time he'd met her and he wondered how such a famous young woman could have just dropped out of sight. It was as if he'd dreamed up her existence.

"Cece," he rubbed the pendant on the chain she'd given him and which he'd never once taken off. "Where are you? Why did you leave me?"

The pain of loving and losing Cece coupled with his unending grief over his mother's death had led him to found this center and push his dream into this reality.

"S ally Jo?"

"Yes, Mr. Randolph?"

"You've done such a good job with my three sons and I'm so happy. Now we have two left."

"Yes, Sir."

"Maynard is my second-last born and I believe he's ready to settle down now. He's only twenty-four but possesses a maturity that often astonishes me. Do you know that as we speak, his idea of setting up a restorative center finally became a reality? The project is up and running? We had the honor of opening it officially about three months ago."

"That's really good news, Sir. Congratulations to the young man, and I wish him well."

"Yes. Maynard came up with the idea of using our old horses to heal people's hurts. It's been only three months since we opened, yet I'm already receiving reports of how successful the venture has been. Every single day we get twenty to thirty people, both adults and children, coming to spend time with the horses and our counselors. The good thing is that the horses are enough to go round and then some."

"I really need to come down there for a visit. Good things are happening on Randolph Ranch and I think I need to see them for myself."

"You have an open ticket waiting for you to decide when you'd like to visit us. Just let me know when you're ready, and I'll do whatever is needed, so you can see for yourself how successful you've been at finding good and godly wives for my sons. Please find Maynard someone who will be with him for the rest of his life."

"I promise not to disappoint you, Sir."

"I trust you, Miss Sally Jo."

HOPE FOR TOMORROW

"What did you just say to me?" Maynard stepped back sharply, moving away from Doris Keller's outstretched hands. He stared at her warily because it was clear that she was up to no good. "Would you care to repeat what you said to me?" He reached for his cellphone. "Just to be on the safe side, I'm recording our conversation."

She paled slightly but was clearly undaunted. "Why are you acting as if you're unaware of this thing that's between us?" She asked coyly. "There's no need to record anything because we're all adults here and I feel that I can speak to you about my feelings without any fear. I like you a lot, Maynard, and you should know it by now. Or do you think I've been hanging around you all for nothing?"

"Miss Keller, it's quite inappropriate for us to be having this conversation," he told her, while eyeing the door and hoping that someone, anyone would walk in through the door. How had this woman cornered him when he had taken great pains to stay out of her way? From the moment he'd realized that she was making romantic overtures toward him, he'd been careful to keep his distance from her. And whenever it was unavoidable that they should meet, he also always made sure that there was someone else around. "The last thing I want is to become the subject of one of your social media posts. Make sure that it doesn't happen or I'll be very upset."

Usually he was careful not to get caught up in Doris and all her drama. But today he'd been very busy in his office and she'd somehow slipped in. The last thing he needed was any kind of trouble or a lawsuit being brought against him for allegations of inappropriate behavior toward a subordinate. Maynard and his brothers were very careful around all female staff and especially the interns for fear of being accused of impropriety of any kind. A few people they knew, and others they'd read about, had fallen victim to unwanted advances from their employees both male and female and had gone through hell when lawsuits were brought against them.

Newspapers and the media were full of employers who'd been set up or placed in compromising situations by their employees. Of course, some were genuine cases of people being harassed by those in higher positions of authority but many others were false. But by the time the false cases had been settled, good people's reputations lay in ruins and some even had their careers destroyed.

His lips tightened and his eyes became cold and hard. When he spoke, his tone was very chilly. With a socialite like Doris who liked posting everything on social media, he had to be very careful and not take any chances. She was trouble all right, just as Mrs. Brian had said weeks ago.

"Listen and I'll only say this once, Miss Keller," he hissed. "I don't want any trouble from you or anyone else, so I'll politely ask you to leave my office at once." He waved his hand in the air. "There are CCTV cameras all over this office and I have my recording here, just in case you're out to make trouble for me. And I'm putting it on record that I've warned you not to post anything about me on your various social media platforms or I'll sue you for invasion of my privacy."

To his satisfaction, Doris took a hasty step toward the door. "I'm sorry," she'd turned white. "I'll leave."

"Next time you try anything like this again, I'll have your internship revoked and a report sent to your college to complain about your inappropriate behavior."

"I'm really sorry," her eyes teared up. "It won't happen again," she said and rushed out of the office.

Maynard breathed a sigh of relief. He was going to have to be more careful because women like Doris Keller never gave up until they'd landed someone in trouble. And he also remembered the adage, *'Hell hath no fury like a woman scorned.'*

While for now the young woman might seem intimidated because of his warning, he knew that she would probably come up with some way of getting back at him. It might not be immediate because she had her internship to consider, but at some point, he was sure she would try something to hurt him for having rejected her. And to protect himself further he was going to have to write out an incident report and give it to Callum as the HR person and also Waylen as his lawyer, for legal purposes. The last thing he needed or wanted was any kind of lawsuit catching him unawares. One couldn't be too careful in this day and age of social media when people no longer respected others' privacy.

There was a brief knock at the door and Callum walked into his office without waiting for an invitation.

"What's up, Maynard? I just met Doris Keller on my way out and she looked rather shaken up."

Maynard passed a hand over his face, "That girl is trouble and I'm just about to write an incident report for HR and the legal department. I'd like you to place her on caution and if need be, forbid her from coming anywhere close to me."

"That's rather harsh, don't you think?" Callum draped himself on one of the easy chairs in the office. "What's the poor girl's offence?"

Maynard quickly told his brother about Doris's unwanted overtures. "I told her that there are cameras all over the place just in case she's thinking of making trouble and I also recorded our conversation on my cellphone. That's when she bolted out of here."

Callum made a clucking sound with his tongue. "That's dangerous. All the contracts that the interns sign have a clause which forbids them from getting romantically involved with any of their supervisors or those above them in any way. It seems as if most of them overlook that clause, and that could create all manner of problems for us."

"Well, I'll do my report and give both you and Waylen copies just to cover myself, and if possible maybe we should give the young woman a copy as well."

"Why?"

"So she's aware that her actions may have consequences. I want to cover all bases that she can use as loopholes just in case she wants to retaliate because I rejected her advances." He grimaced. "I don't want to end up on one of her social media pages with a huge banner of a lawsuit hanging over my head."

"I get you," Callum nodded. "Go ahead and do what you must."

SALLY JO LOOKED at her watch and sighed. Traffic was rather heavy today because of the rain. It was drizzling slightly, but it seemed as if everyone was in a rush to get somewhere and so there was a lot of chaos on the road. She was going to be late for her counseling session and if there was anything she hated, it was being late and keeping people waiting.

"*Always respect other people's time even as you expect them to respect yours,*" was the personal maxim she lived by, and she always tried her best to honor it. This was important because of the kind of work she did and especially when it came to volunteering as a counselor. Time was of the essence when dealing with someone going through a difficult situation and any delays could have adverse effects. So she always tried her best to be early whenever she was going to be providing any counseling to patients. This was her way of giving back to society for the good she'd received in her life.

The Corona virus pandemic and the whole world being on lockdown as a result had made Sally Jo aware of the number of mental challenges that very many people faced. She'd also realized that there weren't enough counselors to deal with the cases that were rising every single day; hence, her decision to become a volunteer counselor. While the world was opening up again and life was slowly returning to normal, people suffering from mental health issues still needed a lot of help.

Trauma Caregivers Anonymous or TCA as she always referred to the support group of which she was a part, was a church-based organization that had been formed slightly over three years ago, and according to Sally Jo, it was very timely indeed. The main objective of the group was to provide support for caregivers of trauma victims. Sally Jo was a volunteer counselor and she had two sessions each week, working mostly with women who were caregivers for family members or friends. Some of the stories that the caregivers told were really heartbreaking, and it was only recently that it was realized that they too needed support to deal with their own kinds of trauma.

Taking care of a loved one through their pain or as they faced their last days on earth was traumatizing, and the number of incidences of caregivers suffering nervous breakdowns was on the rise. Organizations like TCA were doing their best to provide support for the caregivers, and sometimes they even helped them walk away from the situations without feeling guilty of having abandoned their charges. Of course, in such cases, TCA provided alternative caregivers on a temporary basis until the primary caregiver was well enough to resume their duties.

"We learn something new every day," Sally Jo murmured as her eyes went to the small clock on her dashboard. "Oh dear!" She was going to be very late and she blamed herself for not properly scheduling her time today. Her staff were only beginning to return to work physically, and things were a little hectic at the office, hence the confusion. She took a moment when traffic was at a complete standstill to send off a text message to her colleague to cover for her and only relaxed when she got a message back that simply said, '*K.*'

Traffic moved along slowly, and by the time she got to Penuel Interdenominational Church in downtown Denver where the counseling sessions were always held, thirty minutes out of two hours had already gone by. That left her with only one and a half hours, and when she entered the room, she was relieved to find her colleague deep in session with the almost thirty attendees. So she slipped into the back and sat down to listen.

When the session was over, Sally Jo noticed that one of the attendees was still seated as others moved forward to get refreshments that were usually served, while some picked up their bags and left.

"Mrs. Bourne?" Sally Jo knew her because she'd been coming to these sessions for the past two years, though she'd never once shared her experience. "Are you all right?" Sally Jo moved to sit on the same row with her but left a chair between them.

Mrs. Bourne shook her head, "I feel so tired," she whispered, "And helpless. I've been coming to these meetings for months now and I feel so weary."

"I'm so sorry to hear that you're feeling so helpless and weary," Sally Jo said sympathetically. "Is there anything I can do to help?"

Mrs. Bourne was silent for a while; then she sighed and let her eyes roam around the room. The few people left were gathered in small groups as they partook of the snacks offered. No one seemed to be looking their way, and she relaxed visibly.

"I lost my son and his wife in a car accident about thirteen years ago and my granddaughter came to live with me. I'm her only close living relative," she paused. "Cece was and still is the sweetest and gentlest girl. She came to me when she was ten and we've been so happy together. Cece never gave me any trouble even through those terrible teenage years."

Sally Jo nodded to show that she was being attentive.

"When Cece turned seventeen she was discovered by a modeling agency and they promised to do everything they could to make her a success, and they kept their promise," tears gathered in her eyes. "For three years, my granddaughter's star shone and kept rising. She was about to break onto the international scene in a big way but her dream was cut short."

"I'm sorry, what happened?"

"A jealous acquaintance sprayed my darling's face with acid."

"Oh no!" Sally Jo was horrified. She knew that the world of showbiz and especially modeling could be brutal but she'd never thought it could get so bad and end up with such a horrible physical attack on someone. Rumors and besmirching of names and reputations was common among the world of the famous, but acid spraying was the height of wickedness.

"Cece turned just in time or else she would have lost her eyes. But the acid splashed all over her face and destroyed the left side of it and burned her hair and scalp. Cece was in and out of hospital for almost a year. Many skin grafts were done but she lost her flawless looks," Nana's voice broke on a sob. "For three years now, my granddaughter has lived like a recluse, never leaving the house. The only time she goes outside is as far as the backyard to get some sunshine. Her life is passing by, but Cece won't listen to me. I've seen people with terrible disfigurements walking and living in the open. Of course, some ignorant people are cruel and mean and stare with revulsion and say nasty things about people living with various disfigurements. That's what Cece can't deal with, and she even made me take away every photo and picture of her when she was what she terms 'normal.' To me she's still so beautiful, but she says that she's a freak and doesn't want anyone staring at her as if she's part of a circus."

"I can't begin to imagine the kind of pain your granddaughter went through, Mrs. Bourne. She's blessed to have you taking care of her and loving her."

"But it's not enough," Nana cried out desperately. "Cece has so much love to give but with the way things are going, she'll end up alone as a bitter old maid. I won't be around forever and I fear that when I'm gone my darling will lose herself completely. I don't want that for my beautiful girl. She believes that there's no man in the world who can ever look at her face and love her again."

"Again?"

Nana nodded, "Three years ago, just a month before the terrible incident, Cece returned from a photo shoot in New York and told me that she was in love. She'd met the most caring and loving man who'd taken care of her at the airport when they were snowed in. They seemed to be in love and I was happy because he was a Christian as was my granddaughter. She spoke so highly of him, and coming from Cece, that was really something because I'd never heard her mention anything as much as a boyfriend in her life before. Male friends she had in plenty but none of them was ever close enough to her for her to begin building a relationship. So the presence of this young man in her life was a welcome relief. But as soon as the horrible incident happened, she stopped taking his calls or responding to his emails. That was the end of that budding relationship and I know that hurt her more than anything."

"I'm sorry to hear that the man broke things off with Cece after the terrible incident."

"He wasn't the one who broke things off. Cece just ceased from having any contact with anyone apart from me. I know that even to this day, she misses him but is afraid that if he finds out that she's flawed, he won't love her again. So that was the end of that."

"What about plastic surgery? You mentioned that skin grafts were done to her face, didn't those help at all?"

Nana nodded. "Skin was taken from various parts of her body but eventually the surgeon said that only full plastic surgery would do it. But there were too many hospital bills and all the money we had ran out. Her father had left her a trust fund which matured when Cece turned twenty-one, but all that money also went toward her treatment. More than the physical wounds, Cece also had to undergo countless psychological assessments and treatment for depression. It's been so hard, and I don't know what to do anymore," her voice dropped to a whisper. "This is like a nightmare that just won't end."

"I'm so sorry to hear that. Would it be all right if I came by the house to have a chat with your granddaughter? Do you think it would help?" Sally Jo really felt for Mrs. Bourne. The poor woman looked completely exhausted, and that was one of the signs that she as a counselor looked out for when dealing with a caregiver. The fatigue and hopelessness spoke of a person who was fast reaching the limit of endurance.

Nana shrugged, "You can give it a try, but I won't promise you that she'll speak with you or even appear in the open. No one has ever seen her since her last hospital visit two years ago. Well, we had a legitimate reason for keeping her friends away during the Corona lockdown but she wouldn't even pick their calls. My granddaughter turned her back on the world and embraced a life of loneliness and despair. Eventually people gave up trying to reach Cece and all friendships and acquaintances faded away. Now she sits in her dark room, not even opening the drapes, and she has no one else, just me. I've tried to tell her that out there is someone who will love her but she doesn't believe me."

Sally Jo laid a reassuring hand on the woman's arm. "Mrs. Bourne, my grandmother used to say that when all else fails, prayer is still there. I'll be praying for the two of you. When can I drop by your house for a visit?"

"I wish I could say that we could go even now," the woman looked hopeful and Sally's heart went out to her.

"Unfortunately, I have another meeting this evening or I would have come to see her today. Why don't we make it tomorrow afternoon, say at around three?"

When Sally Jo visited Mrs. Bourne the next day and met her granddaughter, she was quite surprised.

"You're Celine Bourne," she exclaimed. "I don't know how I missed it when your name as Cece Bourne was all over the papers at some point. You took the world by storm and I followed your successes, always rooting for you until you suddenly dropped out of sight." She stared at the young woman but not because of the scars that marred her face, but because she now recognized who she was.

Cece smiled sadly, finding Sally Jo to be someone she could trust. "Hi, yes I'm Cece Bourne, but that part of my life is all gone now. Please don't look at me like that."

Sally Jo laughed self-consciously. "I'm sorry I got carried away by being in the presence of an icon. Forgive me for staring at you so much."

"Please don't call me that," Cece whispered as she covered her face. "I don't want any pity from you."

"Cece, the last thing I feel is pity. On the contrary, you're a strong young woman and I'm filled with admiration."

Cece gave her a lopsided smile. "What can I offer you? Tea or coffee or juice?"

"A glass of room temperature juice will be fine," Sally Jo answered. Then she realized that Mrs. Bourne had slipped away. She waited patiently until she was served the juice she'd asked for, by Cece herself. They sat in silence for a brief moment.

"How do you know my Nana?" Cece asked. "When I saw you coming into the house with her I feared that she might be ill or something like that."

"No," Sally Jo chuckled softly. "We attend a class together at the church and she shared with me about you. Never in a million years would I have guessed that you're the famous Cece Bourne. I'm so sorry for all you went through after that horrible attack."

"Thank you," Cece twisted her lips. "I don't even know your name."

"Pardon my manners, or lack of them," Sally Jo grinned. "I'm Sally Jo Manning and I sometimes work as a counselor. But I own a marriage agency."

"That's nice. Perhaps you can speak with my grandmother. I'm really worried about her especially these past few months. She looks so weary and sad and I don't want her to be that way."

Sally Jo nodded, "I'm glad you've noticed that your grandmother is sad. Mrs. Bourne shared her fears with me and her greatest cause of anxiety is you."

"Why would you say that Nana is worried about me?"

"She's afraid that since you no longer go out or meet with friends, you'll end up as an old maid, all lonely and in despair."

Cece sighed, "I'd really love to go out again, visit the mall, go dancing and just run around in the park. I'd really love to step into the world again but the last thing I want is for people to regard me as if I'm a freak. And neither do I want to meet with people who will look at me with pity in their eyes. I've seen many lovely and loving couples breaking up because they can't withstand societal pressure when one of them has a disfigurement or suddenly becomes disabled. Even well-meaning friends and family only make matters worse. Sometimes I feel that it would be best if they just locked themselves away from the world and lived on their own. Society can be so cruel to them, and after many or even just a few years of marriage they're unable to take it anymore and have to part."

"Cece, from my experience as a counselor I can tell you that there are good men and women out there who shut their ears to any negativism. Have faith and don't give up at all."

But Cece was shaking her head. Why couldn't this well-meaning woman realize that life wasn't that easy for someone like her? "I wouldn't want to put myself out there and end up in pain, and why should I put a man through that and have him end up in pain because we have to part? He may just feel pity and force himself to overlook what people are saying, yet inside he begins to resent me."

Sally Jo observed Cece, "There are people in this world who don't care about a person's outward appearance because they treasure whatever is in the heart. I believe that you can find such a man but you have to go out." Cece was shaking her head. "I could teach you how to do your face up in such a way that the scars won't be noticeable. I took a course in reconstructive make up and with the right tools you'll look as good as new. But I'd also like you to consider accepting yourself as you are. The real you isn't what people see on the outside, but what's inside of you."

"Maybe in future when I'm old and gray and it doesn't matter anymore, then maybe I might think of finding someone who won't care so much about my looks," Cece said. "But for now, I just want to be normal, though I'm really scared of being rejected."

"We'll take it one day at a time and see what happens."

"I'm willing to try anything to make my grandmother smile again. She hasn't been doing much of that lately."

Her words gave Sally Jo hope and she left with the promise that she would be back soon.

A LISTENING EAR

a ***Few Days Later***

For a long while, Celine said nothing, not even calling out his name, for she felt as if this wasn't real. They stared at each other, both of them battling different emotions.

It was Maynard who broke the silence, a gentle smile on his face.

"You're the very last person I expected to see here on this ranch and I still think that I'm dreaming. How have you been, Cece?"

She gave him a shy smile, her heart pounding. How had she ever thought that she was over this man? "I've been well," she said. "You're also the last person I expected to ever see again."

"Why?" Maynard whispered and the question was quite loaded.

Cece looked away because she didn't know what answer to give Maynard. Then she noticed the photos mounted on the noticeboard in the foyer and moved toward them. But Maynard wasn't done with her and followed, standing beside her.

"I won't pressure you, but at some point, we'll have to talk about what went wrong between us," his voice was low so those moving around wouldn't hear. "See these photos? They're like our trophies," he smiled. He wanted her to be at ease. "When this center first opened and we got our pioneer patients, we really didn't know if they would stay on."

"Why?" She turned to him with a slight frown on her face.

"We had just one volunteer counselor and she could only come in twice a week. The rest of the time we relied on the bond that horses and people make. It wasn't easy but eventually things picked up and here we are now. I'll take you round so you can meet the horses since the patients have already left. As of now, we don't have too many patients, so we have allocated one horse for two patients."

"How many patients are there?"

"Currently we have fifty of them but they don't all come in at the same time. Our sessions run for four hours, so we have three per day and since the patients come in on alternate days, the counselors are able to work with smaller groups of eight to ten people each. Sundays are the only days we don't open the center."

Cece was quite impressed. When Sally Jo had told her about a position at a Restorative Center in Dallas, the last place she'd expected to land was on Maynard's home ground. She still felt like she was dreaming and wondered what her Nana was doing at this moment. They'd parted ways down at the ranch house. Not that she was worried about her Nana or anything, for the elderly woman made friends very easily.

After her talk with Sally Jo, Cece had become very curious about the Rejuvenating and Restorative Center in Dallas where animals were used as part of therapy to help people with psychological and emotional traumas and how they went on to heal better.

"Since your grandmother is your primary caregiver, she'll also be welcomed on the ranch," Sally Jo had said.

"We wouldn't want to impose and I guess it must be quite an expensive program if boarding facilities are also provided," Cece had said.

"Not really. I happen to know the owners and they owe me a favor. The question is, would you be interested in going down there for a few days just to check the place out?"

Cece had laughed when Nana jumped at the offer. She felt that she owed her grandmother a holiday. "Anything that will get my Cece out of the house is good. When can we leave?"

Sally Jo also laughed, "Please give me a couple of days to make arrangements for you. Once the owner clears things up, you can leave immediately."

As soon as Sally Jo had announced to them that she'd secured the spot for Cece at the center, it seemed as if new life was injected in her grandmother. Nana had run around and packed days in advance, much to Cece's amusement. But she wasn't sorry that they had come because for the first time in a while, she'd heard real laughter and seen genuine happy smiles on her grandmother's face. Some things were worth making the sacrifice for!

And now here they were. They'd touched down at Dallas Airport at eight that morning, and to their surprise, someone was waiting for them. The man had a plaque with both their names on it.

They were received by Mr. Abner but she'd not connected him as being Maynard's father. After they settled in, her grandmother being given a room in the main house and she being taken to the hostel, she was informed of her place of posting.

A further surprise awaited her when one of the cowboys drove her to the center—and the first person she met was Maynard Randolph, her long-lost love. She'd never forgotten him, and her hand had immediately gone to the bracelet that she'd had adjusted and worn ever since he'd given it to her.

"Cece, I seem to have lost you," Maynard was waving a hand in front of her face. "Where did you go?"

"I'm sorry, I got caught up in the events of the past few days," she turned back to the noticeboard. Maynard took his time telling her about each of the photos.

Once they were done he took her around the center and introduced her to the few people who were still there. Cece was quite impressed by the facility and the equipment. "It's fairly new but I'm hoping that the work we do here will change the lives of many people. It wasn't until the project was up and running that I realized that so many people are hurting—and what's worse, in silence."

Cece nodded because she could relate. But for her Nana, she wouldn't have come here.

"The work you're doing is very remarkable and noble," she said.

"We still have need for counselors and if I recall our conversation three years ago, you mentioned that you were in your final year of college, studying to become a psychotherapist."

Cece bit her lower lip. "I wasn't able to complete my undergraduate degree," she looked away, not wanting to see disappointment in Maynard's eyes. At the time, he'd praised her highly for not just relying on her modeling career like many had and when they washed out or got replaced they had nothing else going for them. He'd encouraged to reach out for more so she would always have something to fall back on should her career as a model end by choice or by chance.

Three years ago, Cece had listened keenly as he'd spoken about the various awards and credentials he'd gotten right from high school and at the time he'd been considering going back to school to get his Masters Degree in Behavioral Sciences. But he hadn't mentioned opening up a center such as this one and she was really impressed at what he'd managed to achieve in such a short time, while she'd hidden away from the world.

"Cece, I'm losing you again," Maynard took her hand and led her out of the building and to the well-manicured field beyond. He walked toward an old mare at the far end of the fenced field. "This is Big Bess, and she's been around since I was a child," he said, placing her hand gently on the horse's head. "She's one of the horses my mother often rode, and she's a really good listener," he grinned at her. Cece laughed in disbelief. "It's not a joke. This lovely lady horse has a way of making people feel better after speaking to her. She'll never reveal your secrets to anyone but God. Try it and see."

"Now?"

"Yes, no time's better than the present. I need to check up on a few things with some of the workers and I promise not to take long. Talk to Bess and make friends with her."

Before Cece could say anything else, Maynard walked away. She stood there with her hand still on the horse's head, glad that she wasn't that short, so the animal wasn't towering menacingly over her. She stared at Maynard's retreating figure until she felt a gentle nudge on her shoulder. She turned around and laughed softly.

"Dear Bess, you know how to grab someone's attention," she knew a little bit about horses and how to handle them. Years ago, she'd done a modeling photo shoot on a ranch in New York and received a crash course in horse handling so she was careful to stay within the horse's sight. "You're such a beautiful creature," she moved to the animal's left side. The old mare neighed as if she understood the compliment she'd just been given. "Maynard says you're a good listener." Cece felt a little foolish talking to an animal. But she noticed two other people standing close to horses and seemingly having conversations with them.

"Well, I don't know what to say to you today," Cece told the mare. "Maynard seems to think that chatting with you will help in some way even though I haven't told him much about anything."

Cece found herself pouring her heart out to the mare who stood still with her head slightly bowed as if she were listening keenly.

Cece laughed softly and glanced at her watch after some considerable time had gone by. "I can't believe that I've been standing here for half an hour talking to you." She rubbed the horse's neck. "Maynard was right, you really are a good listener and I feel so much better," and she really meant it. "Thank you, Big Bess. You're my darling." The horse responded with a soft neigh and Cece laughed again. She felt like she'd just emerged from a satisfactory counseling session even if her counselor hadn't spoken a single word back at her.

From his outer office window, Maynard observed Cece as she stood in the field with Big Bess. From the moment they'd met again he'd felt like she was really carrying a weight within her.

He'd also noticed that she'd lost the vibrancy that had been present three years ago. The heavy make up on her face puzzled him because it was something she hadn't needed three years ago, not with her flawless skin. Then there was also the absentmindedness, as if she were lost in a world of her own.

Something was going on with Cece and he really wanted to find out whatever it was. That was the reason he'd left her with Big Bess, and also to control his emotions because he was afraid that he would have broken down before her. He'd really missed her and seeing her again had been overwhelming. Maynard was honest enough to admit to himself that even three years and the lengthy absence hadn't diminished the love he felt for her. What had pleased him so much was seeing the bracelet he'd given her and how it rested comfortably on her wrist like it had been there for a very long time.

He touched the chain around his neck and found himself wishing that he could take her in his arms and tell her that whatever she was going through, he would always be there by her side and she didn't have to suffer alone.

"But what seems to be the problem?" he wondered. After half an hour he noticed that Cece was now looking around as if searching for him. That was ample time for her first session with Big Bess and he was sure that she would want to do it again.

"I'm coming to get you, Cece," he murmured as he locked up his office. "Forever my heart and my home."

SILENT HEART

Celine heard all about the dance to welcome new interns and staff at breakfast the next morning. It was coming up in a few days and she wondered what the experience would be like. All the other interns were very chatty about it and she got curious. The last time she'd been to any social gathering was three years ago, just a few months before her accident. She found herself feeling excited about what her Nana would say, living again.

"I hear that we all have to dress up for the dance," Doris Keller was saying. "Imagine dancing with all those handsome cowboys," she batted her eyelashes. "I've my eyes on the leader of the pack and I can't wait to be in his strong arms," her expression turned dreamy.

"Doris!" Susan Rowan, another new intern shook her head at Doris. "Be careful of your words for they can land you into a lot of trouble. Didn't you read through the contracts we signed? We're not supposed to fraternize with our superiors at all."

"Susie, if there were no rules to be broken then there would be no law courts and people like judges, advocates and magistrates would be out of jobs," Doris scoffed. "Don't be so weak and scared all the time; live large and take risks. I'm only saying it as it is. This is my second dance since I came to the ranch a month ago. They are held every month since interns are coming and going every month. Let me tell you something, you haven't seen anything like handsome cowboys in their jeans, plaid shirts and Stetsons dancing on the floor. There's so much fun going on. And who knows? You might catch yourself a handsome cowboy who will walk you down the aisle," she wagged a finger at Susie. "But don't you dare lay eyes on my man."

"Doris, please stop this," Susie looked slightly uncomfortable. "You shouldn't be saying things like that. Someone could overhear the conversation and land us into trouble."

Cece wondered who Doris Keller's man was. Even though she'd been here for less than forty-eight hours, she'd quickly realized that Doris Keller didn't like her, but she had no idea why.

The kitchen door opened and two young girls entered the kitchen.

"What do you want?" Doris snapped at them and Cece found that to be rather rude and uncalled for. She didn't understand why Doris was being hostile to the innocent girls. So she smiled and approached them.

"My name is Celine or Cece," she told them.

"I'm Isabella or Bella and this is my little sister, Maria," the older girl, who was about twelve, said. She glared at Doris then turned her back on her and gave Cece a sweet smile. "We're on our way to wait for the school bus down the road and came to collect our snacks. Grandma Tamara always has them ready for us."

The inner door opened and a beautiful woman entered the kitchen, followed by a handsome man who was holding her hand.

"There you are," the woman said as soon as she spotted the two girls. "I hope you haven't been up to any trouble. Have you taken your snacks yet?"

"Willow, this is our new friend and her name is Cece," Maria chirped while pointing with her finger.

Cece hadn't yet met Maynard's brothers but she could immediately see the sibling resemblance. They had the same eyes and dark hair. And as if thinking about him conjured him up, Maynard walked into the kitchen through the outside door.

"We've got quite a crowd in here this morning," he said and smiled at Cece while ignoring Doris. "Willow, Rick, this is my friend, Cece."

Willow laughed out loud, "Maria was just doing the honors when you walked in." "Ah, Maria!" Maynard placed a hand over his heart. "A lady after my own heart! But now that I'm here may I please continue with the introductions?"

"Yes, Uncle Maynard," Maria slipped her small hand into his, and Cece realized that the little girls were members of the family.

"Thank you, dear," he turned to Cece. "This beautiful woman you see here is my sister-in-law, Willow, and this dude is my brother Kendrick, or we call him Rick. He's Willow's husband and I still can't understand how he could have gotten so lucky with her."

"Watch it, Bro," Rick growled. "My wife loves me more than anything in the world."

"Yeah, yeah," Maynard said dismissively, but Cece could see that he was jesting. "These two beautiful little ladies are Willow's sisters, Bella and Maria." He turned around and noticed the other people in the kitchen, so he was forced to continue with the introductions. "You've probably met Doris Keller, Susan Rowan and Patricia Clover who are all interns in various departments on the ranch. Doris is an aspiring vet, while Susan is an HR specialist working in Callum's office where her main duties involve dealing with staff welfare. Patricia works with Waylen in the legal office. Folks, this is Cece Bourne. She's a psychotherapist and will be working with me at the Restorative Center."

"Why does that name sound so familiar?" Doris stared at Cece until she felt slightly uncomfortable.

"Doris, Cece is new, and I doubt that you know her," Willow said, then winked at Cece who was grateful for the interruption. She didn't want anyone delving too deep into her affairs and bringing up what she wanted to remain hidden.

Cece noticed that Doris looked angry because Willow had defended her, but before she could say anything else, the door opened again, and her Nana walked into the kitchen followed by Mrs. Brian.

"Who gave the whole lot of you permission to turn my sacred kitchen into a meeting room," the African American beauty gave a mock scowl, and the two girls giggled. "Only you two darlings are allowed to run free and wild in here. The rest of you, vamoose," the woman said, clapping her hands and shooing everyone out. "Mrs. Bourne wants to prepare breakfast and she can't do it with all of you hovering around the kitchen and getting in her way."

"Mrs. Brian, I only came to get Cece so we can go over some things as I won't be at the center till much later in the afternoon," Maynard said. "I need to give her instructions on what needs to be done today in my office at the center. We'll be in my office here at the ranch so please holler when breakfast is ready."

"No way, go to the dining room and wait over there," Mrs. Brian instructed. "I don't have time to come looking for you and I know that once you immerse yourself into your work, you'll forget to feed this poor girl."

"Yes, Ma'am." Maynard turned to Cece. "Shall we move to the living room?"

"I'll come with you," Doris said quickly. Cece wasn't bothered by Doris's forwardness but she noticed that Maynard didn't look happy when the woman insisted on moving closer to him.

"Out with you all, except Bella and Maria who have to go to school. I need to get their snacks ready so the bus won't leave without them. I'll call when breakfast is ready."

Cece hadn't yet had the chance to tour the huge mansion, and when Maynard led her into the dining hall, she was quite impressed. The large rectangular table could comfortably sit twenty people. Maynard led her to the center of the table and pulled out a chair for her. Before he could take the seat next to hers, Doris slipped into it, forcing him to sit on Doris's other side since Susan was already seated on Cece's other side.

Cece got to meet Maynard's other brothers and their wives as they streamed in one by one. Mr. Randolph nodded at her when he came in and took his place at the head of the table.

As they took breakfast together, Cece was struck by how close Maynard was to his brothers and their wives. She greatly admired the three women who were the newest additions to the family. From the attention they received from their respective husbands, it was clear that they were loved and cherished.

Abner Randolph sat at the head of the table and looked like a proud father beholding his offspring. Cece didn't get a single chance to speak with Maynard because Doris dominated his attention as she was seated between them. Since Cece didn't want to look like she was competing for Maynard's attention she turned to speak with Susan, unaware that Mr. Randolph's eyes rested thoughtfully on her.

THIS WAS one of those days when the family gathered to have breakfast together. Even though Quinten, Waylen and Kendrick had moved out of home after they got married, Abner still insisted on the family sitting down for breakfast together twice a week, on Wednesdays and Saturdays, and everyone was happy to honor his request.

Abner felt such deep longing within as his eyes rested on the empty seat on the opposite side of the table from him. That seat had remained unoccupied no matter how many times he'd had the table changed and rearranged. It had been Barbara's spot and no one ever sat there, not even when they were invited to do so. It was a place of honor reserved for his dearly departed wife and the mother of his five sons.

This particular table was new, having been brought in about two weeks ago. His family was growing, and soon he would have to bring in an even larger one. Good thing was that when he'd built this dining room he'd had a large family in mind. There was enough room to fit in a thirty-seat dining table, but that would come later.

They were in the deep of fall, and work was a bit slow, so Abner wasn't in much of a hurry to get everyone out there to their respective duty stations. Usually he frowned on sluggishness but not today. He just wanted to enjoy his family being around him. His eyes rested on his sons and new daughters-in-law and he felt deep happiness within. This was the doing of the Lord and he felt really blessed. When the idea to find wives for his sons had come to him slightly over a year ago, he hadn't known where to begin from.

Then his good friend Dustin 'Buck' Knerr had introduced him to Sally Jo Manning, a young woman in Denver whose great grandmother had been responsible for finding wives for people in the West at the time. It was Sally Jo's ancestor who'd found wives for Buck's own great grandfather and his brothers then.

Sally Jo ran a marriage agency called Hitch Your Wagon Romance and specialized in helping cowboys and cowgirls find true love, the Biblical way.

Abner's three daughters-in-law, Kelsey, Hazel, and Willow, had all come to the family through Sally Jo, though their husbands really had no idea, well, apart from Quin, his eldest son. Abner had no idea if the other wives had shared the secret with their husbands.

Abner's eyes rested on the young woman who'd come in just the day before with her grandmother. Sally Jo had called him about two weeks ago and told him about a lovely young woman who'd been through a terrible incident in her life.

"When we last spoke, you mentioned that Maynard's center was up and running," Sally Jo began.

"That's right. Randolph Restorative and Recreation Center is up and running."

"Social media is blowing up about it," Sally Jo said laughingly. "You know that whenever anything about Randolph Ranch is mentioned anywhere and I get to hear of it, I'm all over it. I have made myself family so anything happening down there catches my attention and I've done a lot of reading about the new center."

"Well Sally Jo, you're the daughter I never had," Abner said and really meant it. "Even before a year is over, my three sons already have wives. Not only are the young women beautiful to behold but they have hearts of gold and my sons are really happy, Sally Jo. Three of my wild sons have been tamed and my heart is bubbling with happiness. Now I just have two more to go."

"Yes, Mr. Abner. That's why I'm calling you. You said Maynard is next in line, right?"

"Yes."

"Good! I may have someone in mind for him and her name is Celine or Cece Bourne who I met through her grandmother."

"Really?"

"Yes Sir. I volunteer as a counselor for Trauma Caregivers Anonymous or TCA as we refer to the organization in short. That's where I met Nana Bourne, a wonderful woman whose granddaughter has been through so much and it's really affected her too."

"I'm really sorry to hear that."

"Nana lost her only son thirteen years ago in a car crash. Mr. Bourne and his wife perished on the spot and left a ten-year-old daughter at the time. Nana brought Cece up and at seventeen the girl became a model. But her dreams were cut short in a very brutal way."

"What happened?"

"Celine, or Cece as her grandmother lovingly calls her, was about to break into the international scene when a jealous rival sprayed her beautiful and flawless face with acid."

Abner shut his eyes and felt deeply for the poor young woman.

"By the grace of the Lord, Cece didn't lose her eyesight, but her face was badly burned, and one side of her head is badly scarred. Numerous grafts were done but being in and out of hospital for a whole year depleted their finances so the poor girl couldn't have proper surgery done to reconstruct her face. She became a recluse and hasn't stepped out of her grandmother's house for three years."

"That's really sad. How old is this girl?"

"She's only twenty-three. She was twenty when the tragedy happened. I met her and discovered that she has such a tender and gentle heart even through her suffering. I suggested that she should come to the ranch where she can join the healing program Maynard has running. It took quite some convincing but I believe this will be good for her."

"Well, I'm glad Maynard started the program because we get new inquiries every single day, and so far we've seen quite a number of otherwise hopeless cases being helped," Abner fell silent. He took a deep breath. "While I felt that Maynard got inspired by the loss of his mother to begin the center, I also feel that something else happened that pushed him to this. That was about three years ago."

"What happened?"

"My son returned from a friend's graduation in New York and for a month he was like one walking on air. There were numerous late-night calls and laughter and we all believed that he'd found love, but he wasn't saying anything at all. Then suddenly a month later, everything stopped and Maynard began moving around like his heart had been broken. To this day, I have no idea what could have gone wrong, but I believe that the young man has been nursing a broken heart ever since. This girl you mention might just be good for him. Two wounded souls can help each other to heal."

The moment Abner had met Cece and Nana the previous day, he knew that the young woman would be good for Maynard. He could already see the spring in his son's step and had a feeling that it all had something to do with Celine 'Cece' Bourne. Well, time would tell.

Cece suddenly felt like she was being watched and quickly raised her eyes which met those of Mr. Abner Randolph. She didn't know much about Maynard's father save what had been told her three years ago.

Mr. Randolph had lost his wife at a time when his sons needed her the most. Cece saw the sadness in his eyes and wished she could walk up to him and say something that would alleviate his pain. But since she was too shy to do so, she gave him a smile instead. He smiled back and then his oldest son who was seated at his right hand said something to him which made him turn and they broke off eye contact.

Cece took the time after that to observe all the family members one by one, and wondered what each one's story was. With her little knowledge of psychology, Cece had a feeling that the love the three brothers shared with their wives had been born out of pain.

"I wish I could understand each one's story," she thought to herself. Maybe that would also help her through her own process of healing. It was said that sharing one's pain with another who'd experienced the same thing or something similar really speeded up the healing process.

"Ready?" Maynard spoke from right beside her, startling her. She hadn't noticed him rising from his place at the table.

"I'm done here," Cece looked down at her plate, shocked to find that she'd cleared all her breakfast. Usually she had a slice or two of toast and milky tea or coffee only and she was done. But today she'd managed to polish off some bacon, scrambled eggs, baked beans and three slices of toast. When her Nana had served her the food she'd protested that it was too much but she was surprised that she'd finished everything and her plate was clean. "Let me take my plate and cup to the kitchen first," she said.

"We all carry our own dishes to the kitchen," Maynard told her. "But Willow and Mrs. Brian reign supreme in the kitchen and they mercifully absolved us from the task of washing them."

Once Cece had cleared her place at the table she followed Maynard to the kitchen, wondering why it wasn't built in the usual way like most American homes. She would ask Maynard about it later since she was used to the open plan where only a counter separated the kitchen from the dining area.

She bid her Nana farewell and walked out of the kitchen with Maynard.

"Would you like to see my office here at the ranch?" Maynard asked, pleased that Doris hadn't followed them out. The woman was persistent, he had to give her that, and had dominated the conversation at the table.

"You mean you actually have two offices?" She recalled his comment before Mrs. Brian had sent them out of the kitchen.

"Yes, though the one at the restoration center is only used part time. My main job is here at the ranch and I'm in charge of the maintenance of all equipment and machinery. So don't mind all the junk you'll find in my office."

"Well, a workman can't be separated from his tools, so who am I to complain?"

They were laughing as they walked toward Maynard's office, which was in one of the smaller barns, both unaware that Doris Keller was standing at the window watching them, an angry look in her eyes.

"I meant to ask you why your kitchen is closed up unlike most other large American houses I know."

"It's actually an open plan space, but my father had rolling partition walls fixed. If there's need for the area to be opened up, all we have to do is move the partitions to one side of the room to create an open space. But for the most part we keep it closed, especially during the cold seasons. In late spring and early summer the walls are rolled back because of the heat. You'll see it when the time comes."

"That sounds very fascinating," Cece wondered if she would still be here next summer.

"Well, this is a large ranch and there's a lot of construction going on because we're still growing, and adjustments are being made to the buildings all the time. You'll get to see what we do when the weather is fairer. Right now, we've halted all renovations except to people's homes."

A WINTER TO REMEMBER

*D*espite all her attempts to fall asleep, that sweet bliss eluded her and Cece sat up in bed. She switched on the bedside lamp. It gave a soft glow and she leaned her back against the headboard and sighed.

Why was life so complicated? She was sure that if she hadn't had the accident then she and Maynard would have moved forward with their relationship and maybe they would have ended up married by now. But after her accident she'd been in physical and psychological pain for a whole year and beyond. All thoughts of being in a close relationship with Maynard had fled from her mind as she fought for her life and sanity. Thinking about the horrible incident always brought Marion to mind. While they hadn't been friends, they hadn't been enemies either. Marion was a year older than Cece and they'd moved in totally different circles.

Because of Cece's faith and Nana's strict but loving upbringing, Cece had led a very quiet and simple life. Her world had revolved around college, her growing career, church and home, leaving no time for the social scene to which most of her peers resorted.

Her counterparts at work often attended parties in the homes of very wealthy men or high end clubs but Cece had never felt the need to go. First, she felt that it was disrespectful to go and indulge in alcohol and other vices which her Nana disapproved of. The only parties she attended were harmless birthdays and baby showers or wedding receptions but even then she always left if things looked like they were about to get out of hand.

In short, hers and Marion's lives only crossed when they worked together on any products together, which wasn't that often. Marion was strictly a face model who only paused for facial shots to showcase hair products, make up and sometimes jewelry. Cece on the other hand, was a runway model whose main commission was to showcase different clothing labels. Only once in a while was she called upon to do facial shots, but even then it was never anything that would bring her in direct contact with Marion. They exchanged greetings and pleasantries whenever they met but weren't at all close.

So to this day, Cece still didn't understand why Marion had chosen to spray her face with acid. When Marion got arrested after the dastardly act and been questioned, she'd given the prosecutor a vague answer. She was charged with causing grievous bodily harm and at the time Cece was in hospital fighting for her life so she hadn't had the chance to appear in court and question her attacker. The main question on Cece's mind whenever she thought about Marion was 'why me?' What did she ever do to Marion to warrant such a horrible attack? More than once, Cece had thought about going to the prison where Marion was serving her sentence just to ask her what wrong she'd done to her. But each time she thought about meeting her attacker face to face, her whole body broke out in a cold sweat.

Seven years was what Marion had received as her sentence for the crime and in just four she would once again be out and free to go on to live a normal life. Or she could be paroled before she'd served her full sentence, but that would only be if Cece spoke up well for her, which was something she would never do. Marion had the chance of getting out and living a normal life, yet for Cece life would never be the same again. No man would want her if they ever saw her real face devoid of makeup.

In the past she'd only used very light makeup to enhance her looks even though Nana had often told her that she didn't need all that paint. But now she had to layer up to hide the spots and groves caused by the acid and the scars due to the many grafts which discolored her face.

At the time she'd met Maynard in New York three years ago, her face had been devoid of make-up and he'd said that she was the most beautiful woman he'd ever seen or met. Now she wondered if Maynard would still regard her as being beautiful with the tons of makeup she had to apply on her face.

Could a handsome man like Maynard Randolph give her a second look if he ever discovered the ugliness she was hiding under all that makeup? And she now knew that Doris Keller had her eyes on Maynard. Doris was a very beautiful woman who used very little makeup. Cece couldn't hope to compete with such beauty and felt really forlorn.

In any case, even if a man like Maynard looked her way, it would probably be out of pity and nothing else. The last thing Cece ever wanted was to become the object of anyone's pity.

She lay down on her side and allowed the tears to fall. Thankfully she had the room to herself so she could cry for as long as she wanted without having to explain anything to anyone, not even Nana.

She was in love with Maynard Randolph and that would never stop. In her darkest moments while she recuperated she'd often longed to hear his loving voice soothing her and had silently cried for him. Many times, she'd hoped he would one day show up at her grandmother's house and save her from the deep and dark despair, but he'd never come.

She'd switched her phone off permanently as soon as she was discharged from hospital and never looked at any of her emails. When Nana had brought her the letters that Maynard had sent by post she'd refused to take them, begging her to return them unopened.

Cece had never thought that she would ever see Maynard again. And now that she had, the pain of loving and not having him was more intense because she didn't think that he or any other man, could love her beyond her scars.

He'd never loved a woman the way he loved Cece, but he sensed her withdrawal as soon as he tried to get close to her. It hurt him to think that the precious moments they'd shared at the airport three years before hadn't made an impression on her. Yet he was sure that at the time she'd been sincere in her feelings for him and maybe she still felt the same way. Why would she still wear the bracelet he'd given her? He refused to give up hope that Cece still loved him even if they'd been apart for all this time. True love never dies, he told himself. He had to believe that or else he would descend into despair.

But one thing was for sure, Maynard was determined to win Cece's heart once again and he wasn't going to accept no for an answer. This time he wasn't letting her go.

"Why do I get the feeling that you've been avoiding me," he asked her two days later after cornering her at the edge of the field where she was tending to Big Bess.

"I'm not avoiding you," she said in a low voice. "The center is very busy, and you know it."

"You don't even take lunch breaks," Maynard complained. "It isn't healthy for you to skip meals, and especially not when you're working so hard."

"I don't skip any meals, and Nana wouldn't let me go without any of my meals. She always packs me lunch. Now that I'm no longer a model I don't have to watch what I eat."

Maynard leaned against the fence and folded his arms across his chest. "That's something I've been meaning to ask you. Why did you suddenly stop modeling?"

Cece's heart began beating very fast but she had a ready response for him. She shrugged nonchalantly, "I grew up and realized that I couldn't be a model for the rest of my life. New and younger models are stepping onto the runway every moment, and with time I was going to be declared obsolete and archaic, so I got out when I could. There's nothing as sad as an old model trying to compete with fresh young ones for the few spots at the top."

Maynard's eyes narrowed, "Was that the real reason or are you just giving me an answer that you've prepared in advance in case the question ever came up?"

"I don't know what you mean."

"Cece, this is me, your Maynard," he said, leaning slightly forward. "Remember what we shared three years ago and how open we were with each other even though it was the first time we'd met. Why won't you share the truth with me?"

Cece turned away, "You're reading too much into things," she said.

"No, I'm not, and you know it. Something happened three years ago that made you drop out of circulation and it seemed as if you'd vanished from the face of the earth," He shook his head. "Your phone became permanently switched off, you never answered your emails nor even read them and you sent my letters back without opening them. I thought we'd started something beautiful, but then all of a sudden, you just vanished and there wasn't even any mention of you on the internet. Only old videos and photos could be found, nothing that mentioned where you were or what could have happened. At one time I thought," he choked then cleared his throat, "I even thought that you might have died, but then I knew that I would have felt it right here," he touched his heart. "You're my soulmate, and I would have known. Yet you went into hiding and I couldn't reach you." He reached under his shirt and brought out the chain. "This is what kept me hopeful, and I knew I would one day see you."

Cece swallowed. "You didn't search for me hard enough," she found herself saying. She couldn't believe that Maynard had kept her chain for all this time. It made her feel some hope within, but he was only seeing the well-made-up and covered version of her, not the actual person beneath the mask. What would he say or think when he did?

"What did you say?"

"Nothing," her face warmed up.

"You think I didn't do anything to find you, including travelling to the address you gave me in Denver?"

"What?" She was shocked at this revelation.

He gave a bitter laughed, "Yes, the address that turned out to be nothing but a used-car lot. Yet all the letters I sent there somehow found their way back to me unopened."

Cece bowed her head, "That was the address my agent suggested I should give anyone who asked. You see, a few colleagues and friends of mine who are models had a lot of trouble with stalkers, so my agent said I should never give out my true home address. The used car lot belongs to my agent's husband so it was easy to get my mail from them."

Maynard nodded, "I see clearly now," he straightened himself and let his hands drop to his side. "There I was thinking that we were building something good that would last for the rest of our lives. We spoke by phone three times a day for a full month, we texted and chatted and occasionally even exchanged emails. Yet you still thought of me as a person you couldn't trust enough to share your life with." He shrugged. "I'm sorry that I assumed too much when clearly you weren't on the same page with me."

"Maynard..."

"Sorry," he raised a hand up. "I won't ever bother you again, Cece," and he walked away. Cece was shattered because she knew she'd deeply wounded him. But what was she supposed to have done at the time?

"There you are," Cece turned her head at her grandmother's voice. "I came to bring you some tea and was informed that you were out here with the horses."

"Oh Nana," Cece burst into tears as her grandmother hurriedly placed the small wicker basket she was carrying on the ground and moved toward her, taking her into her warm embrace.

"Child, what's wrong?"

"Oh Nana! I've made a terrible mistake and I don't know if he'll ever forgive me."

"Who?" Nana's brow creased in concern.

"Maynard."

THE REQUEST OF AGES

Celine shivered, but not from the external cold, for her thick warm coat insulated her against that. She shivered from fear and disbelief that anyone hated her enough to want to hurt her by stealing her whole makeup kit.

It was the night of the much-talked-about dance, and she'd been looking forward to letting down her hair and attending it so she could get close to Maynard. She hated the silence and distance between them, and she really wanted to see him so she could make things right.

But now her makeup kit was gone. It was too large a box for her to have misplaced it, and in any case, she never carried it out of her room because it was rather bulky. She had a smaller kit which she carried in her purse each time she left her room for long durations. But this one only contained light face powder and lip gloss, and that wasn't enough to hide the hideous marks on her face.

And she couldn't even get in touch with Nana to ask her to bring back her old kit. Nana had flown back to Denver just the day before to check on the house and other things and the woman always forgot to charge her phone battery. Cece was sure that it had flat lined at some point. Nana would only remember to charge her phone when she needed to use it. The house phone back in Denver had been disconnected months ago when they couldn't pay the bill so there wasn't any quick way of reaching her grandmother. She just had to wait for her grandmother to get back on line, which could be hours from now or even tomorrow.

"What do I do now?" Cece wanted to weep. She'd been hoping to find Maynard at the dance and explain everything to him. Nana had advised her to come clean with him about the terrible incident that had disfigured her face and made her go into hiding for three years.

"If this man means as much as I think he does to you, then you need to tell him the truth, and the sooner you do that, the better. It's always better for him to hear the truth from you than for him to find out in some other way, and especially not through social media for they have the tendency to exaggerate things because sensational news sells."

"But what if he rejects me, Nana?" Cece had asked tearfully.

"Then you'll know that he's not the one meant to be your spouse for life, and you can then move on with your life. But what if he accepts you just the way you are? Don't you think you owe him the respect of telling him?"

"Of what use will it be if he turns his back against me?"

"Cece, you need to give people the benefit of the doubt. You can't continue to live your life in the shadows by keeping people at arm's length. I know that some people will look at you with pity and maybe even revulsion. But you can be sure that there are many others who will love and appreciate you just as you are. It's time you started trusting people again. Don't get me wrong, dear. I don't mean you should trust everyone you see, but you have to sift through humanity and find those who are for you."

But now her makeup box was gone. Could Nana have somehow taken it away so that Cece would begin stepping out into the open without hiding her face? Then she shook her head. Her Nana might be stubborn and straightforward, but she wasn't cruel. This was an act of cruelty, and her Nana would never do that, knowing full well that Cece needed her facial makeup mask to go out in public. But then who had taken her makeup kit?

The only people she'd ever invited into her room apart from Nana were Bella and Maria, Willow Randolph's little sisters. She quickly ruled them out as suspects because they were really adorable and kind. Also, she knew that they would never enter her room without her permission, and in any case, she always kept her door locked whether she was inside or outside the room.

Her cellphone rang, and the caller identity showed that it was her Nana.

"Cece, you haven't called me all day. Are you all right?"

"No Nana, I'm not all right at all," she started crying softly. "Someone took my makeup kit, and tonight's the dance. I can't go out without using it, and now I'm going to miss the chance to speak with Maynard."

"Oh, child! Did you leave your door open at any time?"

"No, Nana. You taught me to always be careful whenever I was around strangers. I locked my room as usual this morning when I was going to the center. But when I got back this evening to get ready for the dance, the door was locked, but my make-up kit was missing. I've looked everywhere for it but I can't find it."

"Cece, listen to me. That make up is only a mask. I know you feel that the scars on your face are something to be ashamed of. They're not. I want you to go to that dance with your head held high. Your scars are what will separate your true friends from your foes."

"But Nana..."

"Listen to me, Cece. I love you so much and would never mislead or give you the wrong advice. You need to live again, and it would please me very much if that life started right this evening. Go and see your man and let him look at the real you, not the one you're trying to be."

"People will laugh at me."

Nana sighed, "Cece, anyone who can rejoice at the misfortune of another is wicked, and believe me, society will condemn them harshly. Be brave and let the world see your beauty through those scars."

But after Nana had assured her that she would be returning to Cedar Hill in a few days' time and hung up, Cece knew that there was no way she'd be attending that dance.

"Waiting for someone, Bro?" Callum walked up to Maynard and put an arm loosely around his shoulder. "The dance is on and many young women are staring hopefully at us. Yet your eyes remain glued to the door as if you're expecting someone else."

"Have you seen Cece this evening?" Even as Maynard asked the question his eyes continued roaming all over the barn that had been converted into a dance hall. Previously, all such functions were held in the bunkhouse, but after Kendrick and Willow's wedding, their father had had one of the old, empty barns renovated and turned into a recreation room.

Everyone had been happy and relieved because using the bunkhouse meant moving the beds and closets to the far end of the building then putting them back again once the activities were over. That was quite tedious work for all concerned. Sometimes the cowboys who lived in the bunkhouse would complain that their properties were missing, but not anymore. The bunkhouse would never again be used as a social hall.

Maynard turned back to his brother. "I'm looking out for Cece because I really need to see her."

"No, I don't see Miss Bourne anywhere. As a matter of fact, I haven't seen her all evening. Do you think she's with her grandmother?"

Maynard shook his head, "Nana left for Denver yesterday and won't be back for days." Just then Doris and Susan walked up to the two brothers.

"May we have this dance please?" Doris held out a hand to Maynard. A slow number was playing and much as he didn't want to dance with the woman, Maynard couldn't embarrass her in public.

"Sure," he said though the smile he sent his brother was tight. Maynard was careful to keep a respectful distance between him and Doris as they danced, though she tried her best to change things. He watched his brother as he danced with Susan, and the two were laughing and having fun, unlike him and his companion who were dancing silently. Normally, Maynard loved dancing but only when he had the right partner. He wasn't having any fun and wondered if Cece would be attending the dance at all. Maybe she was tired and had decided not to come.

"Why do I feel like you're only dancing with me out of politeness?" Doris asked crossly when he'd once again thwarted her moves to get him to hold her closer. "You're making me feel like I forced you to dance with me."

Maynard didn't have to answer her because mercifully, the song came to an end. He led her to one of the tables where there were a few ladies, wives of some of the cowboys, saw her seated and quickly excused himself. He spotted his father who was dancing with Bella and Maria. They were all holding hands in a small circle.

"May I please join your dance circle?" Maynard asked as he smiled at Maria and held out a hand to her.

"Sure, but then these lovely ladies can only be here for two more songs; then it's bedtime for them," Willow came up to the circle. Rick was holding her waist. "I'm rather beat myself so, young ladies," she bent down to her sisters, "Make the most of the last two dances. Hazel and Kelsey have already left, and we should be heading out, too."

"Yes, Ma'am," Isabella was grinning as she led Mr. Randolph in a spin around the dance floor. Maria took Maynard's hand. "Shall we dance, Uncle Maynard?"

"Sure, Sweetie."

Maynard finally found himself having a lovely time as he danced first with Maria then exchanged partners with his father.

"Miss Cece isn't here tonight," Bella said. Maynard had to bend down to hear her above the loud music. "Maria and I went to her room before the dance because she promised to do our makeup and hair. But her door was locked and she refused to open for us. Willow did our hair and make-up, but she's not as good as Miss Cece."

"But you both look stunning this evening," Maynard cheered the little girl on. "Sister Willow did a good job, and make sure that you thank her when you get home."

"We already did," Bella said, "And Sister Willow was very happy, but I still wish Miss Cece could have been here. She was really looking forward to the dance but then we heard her crying in her room, and she wouldn't open the door for us. We told Sister Willow, and she also went to knock on Miss Cece's door, but she still refused to open."

Maynard's heart constricted. Something must have happened to Cece, and he wanted to rush out and find out what it was. He wished he could go to the hostel and beg her to open the door for him. But no males, irrespective of who they were, could access the women's hostel. There had to be some other way that he could find out what was going on with Cece.

"Uncle Maynard?"

"Yes, Bella?"

"The song has ended and Miss Doris is coming this way," the child had a cheeky look in her eyes and Maynard realized that nothing passed this girl by. "She probably wants you to dance with her again."

"Really?" Maynard held onto Bella's hand. "Willow said it's your bedtime so shall we go?"

Bella giggled when Maynard swiftly but subtly turned his back on Doris Keller. "I don't like her very much," the little girl said.

"Don't say such things," Willow had overheard the comment and she frowned. "Anyway, who is it that you don't like?"

"Do..."

"Bella here was just telling me that she doesn't like the cartoon Donuts," Maynard interrupted quickly and gave the girl a knowing look.

"Yes," Bella corrected herself quickly. "I don't like Donuts."

"Why don't you like that sweet cartoon?" Willow asked as she herded her sisters toward the door in preparation for their exit. Maynard followed just so Doris couldn't get to him again. Dancing with her once was quite enough, thank you! And now that he knew Cece wasn't coming, there was really nothing left for him to do in this place.

"Because every time I watch it I get very hungry and just want to bite into a thick and sugary donut, but Mrs. Brian says they make people very fat."

Willow's eyes narrowed as if she didn't quite believe her sister, but Bella gave her a clear and innocent look. "Why do I have the feeling that I'm being played by the two of you?" She looked at Maynard then Bella.

"Willow, can we go home now?" Maria whined. It was clear that after all the evening's fun she was tired.

"Rick mentioned that he wanted to speak to Dad about something," Willow looked around for her husband. "There he is, and it seems like they might take quite some time since Quin and Waylen have joined the party. Now Callum is also making his way over there," Willow sounded quite exasperated. "My dear husband has the car keys," she gave Maynard a sweet smile, "Would you please go and get the keys from your brother for me?"

"Why don't I drive you girls home?" Maynard offered and Willow turned to him with a grateful smile. "Then Rick won't have to look for a lift home once he's done talking to Dad."

"Thank you so much, but I need to let him know that we're leaving, and I don't feel like walking across the room," she said. "Let me send him a text to let him know that you're taking us home."

"Sure," Maynard said. His evening was pretty much ruined, and he didn't want to stay a moment longer. But he also needed to find out if Cece was all right. The only person who could help him was Mrs. Brian but she rarely attended such functions, preferring to stay at the house and bake.

ONCE MAYNARD HAD DROPPED Willow and the girls at their house and ensured that they were all right, he drove out of the cul de sac and stopped briefly to speak to the security guards on patrol around the residential area. All was well and there were no disturbances, so Maynard drove on.

Maynard was always appreciative of their lives and how blessed they were. They had good and loyal workers, and while one or two still turned out to be problematic occasionally, for the most part their staff could be trusted. And he knew that it was because of how his father ran the vast ranch.

"Happy and contented employees will never rob you nor think of harming you in any way. But if you ill-treat the men and women who work for you, then you're asking for trouble," Abner Randolph had told his sons a while ago when he'd been allocating them different departments to head.

So Maynard and his brothers strove to show fairness when dealing with all their staff regardless of their positions. Currently it was only him, Callum and their father who lived in the ranch house, and of course, Nana Bourne when she was around. Mrs. Brian had her own private quarters in the loft of one of the old stables that had been turned into a carpentry workshop.

Previously Mrs. Brian had lived in the cul de sac, but after her husband's death a few years ago, Maynard's father had insisted that she should come and live closer to the house so she wouldn't be so lonely. All her children were grown up and gone from home, so she was all alone.

While Mrs. Brian had agreed to come closer to the ranch house, she'd refused to live in it, saying she didn't want to invade the family's privacy. To compromise, Mr. Randolph had instructed his workers to turn the loft over the old stable into a dwelling for her, since it was nearest to the house. And Mrs. Brian was delighted with the results of the renovation.

Over the years, Maynard and his brothers had secretly wished that their father and Mrs. Brian would get married. The two shared a deep bond, and the boys didn't understand why their father wouldn't propose to her. Mrs. Brian had been there for them ever since their mother's death nearly fifteen years ago. She was more than just a housekeeper and cook, and they wished she would officially join the family.

As he parked his Bronco in the garage with the other ranch vehicles, he wondered if Mrs. Brian was still up. He was hungry and decided to head to the kitchen through the back. He noticed that the lights were on but as soon as he stepped onto the porch, they went off. He waited to see if Mrs. Brian was the one who'd been in the kitchen, for then she would step out and head to her house, but the door remained closed.

After staring at it for a while he realized that someone else had been in the kitchen, not the housekeeper. He decided to find out from Mrs. Brian if she'd seen Cece that evening and was glad to note that the lights in her loft were still on. He used the elevator that he and Callum had installed for the middle-aged woman so she wouldn't have to always use the stairs and was soon standing at her door.

"Who is it?" Mrs. Brian called out from within when Maynard knocked.

"It's Maynard."

"Oh!" He heard the bolts being drawn back, and finally the key turned in the lock, and the door was thrown wide open. "It's been a while since any of you boys came up here looking for me at such an hour. Are you hungry? You actually look like you haven't eaten. Weren't you at the dance? I thought the bunkhouse chef and his team were preparing a sumptuous dinner for everyone."

"I went to the dance but then had to drive Willow and her sisters back home before dinner was served at the dance." He made himself comfortable on her large settee. "I didn't feel like going back there."

"Did something happen?" She frowned.

Maynard twisted his lips, "Cece wasn't there."

"Aha!" She nodded. "Well, I prepared something for Bella and Maria to eat before they went to the dance and I carried whatever was left over. It's lasagna. Can I warm you a plate?"

"Yes, thank you."

Maynard ate in silence, but he could feel Mrs. Brian's eyes on him. She'd served him a glass of lemonade with the lasagna.

"Something is troubling you," she stated. She paused from her crocheting. "I'm making a baby set for Kelsey. She's due at any time now, and I wouldn't want her little bundle of joy to get here and freeze." She pointed at the small pile of crocheted baby items on the seat beside her.

"The things you make are beautiful, Mrs. Brian," Maynard smiled at the woman's labor of love. "Kelsey will be so happy."

"Hazel and Willow aren't far behind," Mrs. Brian's smile broadened. "It will be wonderful to have little ones running around here. Bella and Maria have brought life to the home, but soon they'll enter high school, then be gone off to college. So having newborns around here will be a thing of joy to your father," she winked at him. "We're now looking to you for the next generation of Randolph children. Don't you think it's high time you joined your brothers in their efforts to repopulate Mr. Abner's family?"

"The family is growing," Maynard agreed, ignoring the comment about him. "It's exciting to know that soon Kelsey and Quin will have their child, then Hazel and Waylen as well as Rick and Willow. Dad is really in his element. If only Mom were here to see all this unfolding."

"Maynard, don't make yourself sad. I've been watching you and Cece and feel that the two of you have something beautiful between you. Yet you're both so sad, and it makes me wonder whatever is going on."

Maynard chewed the last bit of his food then rose to his feet to take his plate and glass to the sink. After washing and rinsing then placing them on the rack he returned to his seat.

"We had a small fight a few days ago and I haven't seen nor spoken to Cece since then. She hasn't called nor sent me any text messages. I was hoping to see her at the dance tonight and make things right but she wasn't there."

"You young people are always so impatient and bent on getting your own way at all times. What did you do to Cece? And just out of curiosity, why must she be the one to call or text you? Don't you have a phone and airtime to do it? What if she was waiting for you to do it and on this side you're thinking she'll make the first move? Don't you see that you're wasting a lot of time for nothing? Pride and stubbornness are the killers of any relationship."

Maynard cleared his throat, "This isn't the first time Cece has shut me out, and I was afraid that she would refuse to pick up my calls and that she would ignore my text messages. That's why I thought that if she's really interested in me, she would make the first move."

"Why would a nice, polite girl refuse to pick up your calls at all? Unless you offended her, in which case, I wouldn't blame her for giving you the cold shoulder for a little while. Haven't I taught you young men to treat women right at all times?"

"My relationship with Cece is rather complicated." He rose from his seat and began to pace the floor. "You see, it started three years ago. Cece and I met at LaGuardia Airport where we were both stranded due to a snowstorm and all planes were grounded. You recall that at the time I'd travelled to New York for Tyron's graduation," Mrs. Brian nodded. "That was the first time we met."

Once again Mrs. Brian nodded, then looked up from her crocheting. "I remember you returning from New York with a broad smile on your face and looking like you were walking on air. I suspected that you'd fallen in love, but then just a month later, it was back down in the doldrums for you. What happened? No one ever dared to ask you what had gone wrong."

"Cece was the woman I met at the airport and it was love at first sight for us, at least I thought so. We spoke on the phone every single day after I returned, and when we weren't talking it was texting. Emails made up for when we had so much to say that it couldn't be done by phone. But then one day, Cece just suddenly stopped responding to my messages. She wouldn't pick up my calls and the emails were unread and unanswered. Then her phone went dead. I even sent letters by post but those came back unopened. Finally, I flew to Denver, but the address she'd given me turned out to be a used-car lot, and no one there knew who she was. I never thought I would ever see Cece again until she came here."

"So what's the trouble?"

"Cece has refused to open up about what happened to her three years ago, and I know that it was bad. At the time we met she was fast becoming a household name as a young model."

"No wonder she looked so familiar to me, as did her name. But there's something different about the girl all the same. I used to love reading about her because she's very classy and elegant. But her grandmother didn't drop any hints on who she is. I thought something like that would make a grandmother proud and eager to tell everyone about her successful grandchild."

"That's just the mystery. Cece says she decided to stop modeling because she was growing up, but I have a feeling there's more to the story than she's willing to admit."

"Why didn't you just ask her to tell you what the issue is?"

"I asked and it led to the quarrel we had. I got upset and walked away from Cece. I'm not proud of the way I behaved."

"Cece has a good head on her shoulders and I know that she'll eventually open up to you. But you've got to be patient, Maynard," Mrs. Brian frowned. "I noticed that she uses a lot of makeup, unlike before when I admired her flawless skin."

"Well, this evening Bella and Maria went to her room because she'd promised to do their makeup, but she refused to open the door, and Bella told me that they heard her crying. They even told Willow and she too tried to get Cece to open the door, but she refused. Something must have happened that upset her to the extent that she decided to lock herself up in her room."

"Oh no!" Mrs. Brian put her crotchet aside. "Should I go and check on her?"

"No, it's late and she might be asleep by now. But I'd be most grateful if you did that tomorrow and let me know whatever is going on. Her grandmother isn't here and that's the one person she will open up to."

"Sure."

Maynard left soon after, and just as he got to his bedroom his phone buzzed twice, indicating that he'd received two messages. He quickly opened the chats hoping it was Cece.

"*Celine Bourne isn't the beauty you think she is,*" the first text said. "*See for yourself just how ugly she is. All that makeup is hiding a hideous face.*" The second message had a link to a website and he clicked on it, staring in horror at the pictures that came up. He quickly perused through the caption and turned as white as a sheet. The article was dated the same day that he'd last heard from Cece three years ago. An anonymous number had been used and he wondered who could be so callous as to do something like this. Only cowards hid behind the shadows so they could spread harmful messages about others, Maynard thought.

"*Upcoming model sprayed with acid by jealous rival*," the heading read. The story told of how Cece had been leaving her changing room after a show when the other woman accosted her and sprayed acid on her face.

As Maynard clicked on photo after photo of the horrible incident, he felt his tears falling unchecked. Cece had been through such a terrible time, no wonder that she'd dropped out of sight for three years. These were photos that had definitely been taken and posted by the paparazzi who could be very insensitive about people's lives. Maynard wondered why the paparazzi rarely printed anything about happy families and prosperous homes. All they did was find out the darker side of people's lives and bring these to light, uncaring who got hurt in the process.

There were even photos of Cece as she lay in the hospital bed with her face all bandaged up, then some long-range shots of her scarred face with insensitive captions such as, '*From beauty to a beast,*' and '*The Freak Circus Comes to Town and One Has Been Let Loose.*"

No wonder Cece had hidden away from the world! He couldn't believe that people could be this cruel, but Pastor Manoah often preached that the hearts of men are deceitful above all things, and desperately wicked, and the only remedy is being born again. Only new birth in Christ takes away the hearts of stone and replaces them with hearts of flesh. But society had rejected Christ and so went on in their own ways; no wonder other people's pain became the subject of jesting and cruel jokes. "We're living in a loveless world," Maynard murmured, slowly perusing through the photos, and it became clear to him why Cece now used a lot of makeup on her face. Poor girl, he thought. From having flawless and beautiful skin to the scars that marred her face, not that it mattered to him. She was still the woman he'd fallen in love with three years ago, and nothing would ever change that. Now all he needed to do was make her know that she was loved, cherished and accepted just as she was.

"Dear Lord, please have mercy on us and forgive whoever sent me these horrible messages," he prayed. "Please forgive me for all the times when I too have made jokes and taken lightly the misfortunes of others, either willingly or unwillingly, knowingly or unknowingly."

As he read on, he found out that the attacker was behind bars and paying for her crime. Well, justice had been served but what about Cece? Imprisoning her attacker wouldn't take away the pain she'd suffered physically, mentally, and emotionally.

"Cece," he whispered as he wiped away his tears, "I'll always be there for you and help you heal through this."

CORE STRENGTH

$\mathscr{A}$s he tossed and turned in bed that night, Maynard wished he hadn't opened the link sent to him anonymously. He wondered who could have sent the messages with the link and why the person felt the need to do so. Given the nasty comments, it was clear that it was someone who wanted to hurt Cece. If only he hadn't found out what had happened to Celine three years ago, his heart wouldn't be filled with so much torment. But how then would he have known what had happened to the love of his life and why she'd suddenly stopped communicating with him? Maybe she'd felt that he might be like everyone else who'd turned their backs on her.

He was up very early the next morning and walked to the kitchen. Mrs. Brian was making oatmeal porridge and frying eggs. When she saw the shattered look on Maynard's face, she turned the flames on the stove down and walked toward him, holding wide her arms.

Maynard allowed himself to feel the warm embrace of the woman who had been like a mother to him over the years.

"Maynard, what is it? What happened?"

"It's horrible, Mrs. Brian," his voice was shaky.

"Come, let's go to your father's den and talk about it. Someone will soon come in and continue preparing breakfast."

"Thank you."

The door opened and Willow came into the kitchen followed closely by her husband and also Bella and Maria.

"Willow, please handle breakfast," Mrs. Brian said as she led Maynard out.

"Yes, Ma'am," Willow agreed even as she gave Maynard a puzzled look. She moved to the stove to do what was needed. Rick kissed his wife, then Maria and Bella, and followed his brother and Mrs. Brian out of the kitchen.

Quin, Waylen and Callum were in the den with their father for the usual early morning briefing before going to their various work stations. Maynard greeted his family members, then moved to his father's desk and quickly powered his laptop, typed in the link he'd been sent and showed everyone the horrifying photos and news articles. No one spoke for a while then Quin broke the silence.

"How did you come across these photos? This is one of those links that is so hidden that only computer experts can dig it out. Someone went to great lengths to hide all this, but then someone else also dug deep to get this information out again."

"Someone sent me two messages last night, and I haven't been able to sleep." He read out the text messages and also briefly told everyone how he'd met Cece three years before. "She just stopped communicating with me and I had no idea that all this was happening to her. How Cece must have suffered. That first time we met at the airport, Cece barely had any makeup on, but when she came here, I couldn't help noticing that she'd really layered up. I never thought things were this bad," Maynard studied the photos of Cece after she'd left hospital. "That was such a cruel act. And taking photos from long range means her privacy was invaded time and time again. I can't begin to imagine what that must have been like for her."

"Such an abominable act," his father agreed. "What is this world coming to when young women and men have so much hatred and murderous thoughts toward others in their hearts?"

"That's a really sad child," Mrs. Brian wiped a tear away from the edge of her eye. "What pain the girl must have been in."

"Who? Cece?" Callum asked. "Of course, judging by these pictures she must have been in so much pain. Acid is a terrible weapon to use on someone."

"No, I mean the girl who hurt our Cece," Mrs. Brian said. "That Marion somebody."

"Mrs. Brian, you surprise me," Maynard spoke through clenched teeth. "That woman didn't even get the sentence she deserved. What is seven years when she's completely ruined someone else's life forever?"

"Maynard," Mrs. Brian's tone was gentle. "Hurting people hurt others. Never forget that. Some people can't cope with pain in their own lives, so they lash out and cause a lot of harm to others unless they can get help."

Maynard shook his head, "I don't believe this. You always see only the good in people, Mrs. Brian."

"Which is as it should be," his father put in. "If we're to help our Cece heal, then we can't show anger toward her attacker. *Forgive us our trespasses as we forgive those who trespass against us,*" he finished. "Forgiving others allows the grace of God and His mercy to deal with them as they deserve. As Mrs. Brian said, people who are hurting will more often than not, hurt others."

CECE KEPT herself locked up in her bedroom for three days, praying that Nana would return soon. She'd begged her grandmother to bring her old makeup set when she returned. While it wasn't as elaborate as the gift from Sally Jo, it still had enough makeup in it to help her don her usual mask.

But she wasn't staying a moment longer on this ranch. As soon as Nana brought her the set she would leave. Someone was sending her a warning and the last thing Cece wanted was to get caught up in another person's anger again. She'd received an anonymous text message with a link she'd opened and nearly screamed. All the pain had returned when she saw the old photos of her after the acid attack and while in hospital. But what had hurt the most was the text message that had followed.

"Frankenstein is the only suitable husband for an ugly creature like you. No amount of makeup or masks can hide all that ugliness. If I were you, I would find a cave, crawl into it and hide from the world forever."

That's what had made Cece realize that whoever had taken her makeup kit had done so deliberately so she would be humiliated and shamed.

She ignored all the calls made to her cellphone and Maynard's numerous text messages. But in the deep of the night when the household was fast asleep, Cece crept out of her bedroom and sneaked out to the kitchen to find something to eat.

"When I catch whoever sent those messages to me they'll be very sorry," Maynard spoke to Mrs. Brian. He walked into the kitchen on the fourth day after receiving the ugly messages. "That person isn't fit to be called human because they're clearly rejoicing at another person's misfortunes."

Doris and Susan were in the kitchen. Maynard had his back turned toward the two women, so he couldn't see their reactions. But Mrs. Brian was watching them.

"Someone on this ranch is out to cause trouble, and we can't have such a person staying here. Not only will I fire them as soon as I find out who it is, but the police will also deal with them."

A soft gasp made him turn around. "Oh, Doris and Susan, good morning to you." He walked out of the kitchen.

His father, as well as Quin and Waylen, were in the den. "Mrs. Brian tells me that Cece hasn't been to the kitchen for her meals for three days, but at least she isn't starving. If by tomorrow morning she hasn't opened the door, I'll break it down."

Mr. Randolph nodded, "That's just what your brothers and I were talking about. I'm sure that the person who sent you those messages did the same to Miss Bourne and now she's unable to face the world."

"But I love her more than ever," Maynard cried out. "She's a very special woman, and I want her to know that she'll forever be beautiful to me, scars or none."

"But you said she's not starving, right?" Quin asked. "Who is serving food to her?"

"Mrs. Brian says that every morning she notices that some stuff is missing from the pantry and whatever has been left on the stove is usually also consumed," Abner told his sons. "So I suspect that Cece comes out of her room at night to get something to eat. If you want to get to her, you need to lie in wait, Maynard. Wait until she comes out of her room at night."

As usual, Cece waited until the household had settled down before she crept out of the hostel, praying that the kitchen door wouldn't be locked. She touched the knob and it turned easily and she gave a sigh of relief.

She never dared to switch the lights on for fear of being discovered. Instead, she used the flashlight on her phone. It wasn't bright, but it was enough to enable her to see at least a few feet in front of her.

Cece was also careful never to get any food from the fridge or freezer for then she'd have to warm it using the microwave oven, which was quite noisy. The last thing she wanted was for anyone to hear the noise and come to investigate.

She entered the pantry and brought out the box of cereals and prepared her meal. She was about to sit at the table when suddenly the lights came on. Cece screamed and covered her face, rushing toward the kitchen door. But she ran into a wall and she screamed again.

"Cece, it's me," Maynard said as he held her by the shoulders. She struggled to set herself free, but Maynard refused to let her go, and she finally collapsed in his arms, sobbing in anguish.

"Hush, my love," Maynard held her tenderly, feeling her pain. But when she was eventually spent, he led her to the table. Her hair was covering part of her face, the side that was burned.

"Cece, please look at me," his voice was soft and gentle.

"No," she whispered, bowing her face even more.

"Cece. please," he took her chin, but she pulled away. "You know that I love you so much."

"Stop!" Cece covered her ears with her hands. "Don't say such words to me out of pity."

"I don't feel pity for you, my love, but compassion. Someone hurt you and took away three years of your life. But I'm here now and I know everything, and believe me, your situation changes nothing. I'm still as much in love with you as I was when we first met three years ago."

"You're just saying that."

"No," his hand was firm on her chin. "Look at me and let me tell you something, darling."

Cece was forced to look at Maynard, and she saw only love and tenderness in his eyes, nothing like pity. But she was still afraid.

"You can't love a freak like me," she whispered.

"Don't ever refer to the woman I love in such a manner."

"But it's true."

"Cece, I love you so much; you don't know just how much."

"Even with all these scars?" She stared at him incredulously.

"Yes, I love each and every scar that you carry because they're beautiful to me," he chuckled softly. "Or maybe love is blind, but I don't care."

"You're just saying that," Cece repeated.

"Cece, you've been through so much and I understand why you felt that you had to hide away from the world. But you're the strongest person I know, my darling. Don't let these scars remind you of the ugliness of that act or the pain. Let them instead remind you of how far you've come in life. Be proud of your imperfections for they make you perfect. It hurt me when you hid yourself from me for these past three days. What happened?"

"Someone took my makeup kit so I wouldn't be able to cover the ugly scars. That's why I haven't been able to leave the room," Cece bit her lip and then showed him the text message that she'd been sent. "I don't want people to stare at me as if I'm a freak."

Maynard felt really angry. "Whoever did this to you will be found and you can be sure that no mercy will be showed to them."

"I just want to go back to my Nana," Cece whispered tearfully.

"And I won't let you leave to go and bury yourself away from the world again. I love you, and believe me when I say that all will be well."

"You promise?" The innocent hopefulness in Cece's eyes and voice nearly brought Maynard to his knees.

"I promise."

~

Mrs. Brian had a suspicion about who might have taken Cece's make-up box but she didn't want to look like she was on a witch-hunt. She was glad when two new interns reported to the ranch the next day. None of them knew any of the other girls so they couldn't be accused of being vindictive.

With the help of Linda Hurst and Brenda Frost, Mrs. Brian used the master key to open all the rooms in the women's hostel, all twelve of them. The search led to them finding the makeup kit hidden at the back of the closet in Doris Keller's room, and her lips tightened.

"Don't touch it," she told the interns after she'd explained everything to them. "We, however, need to take photos as evidence of where we found the box. I don't care that this is an illegal search but I want all this done and ended."

"Yes, Ma'am," the two young women agreed.

"Good. Now, not a word to anyone, do you hear?"

"Yes, Ma'am."

THE CROWN OF ROSES

"Celine, I'm asking, no begging you once and for all to admit that you love me," Maynard's voice was earnest and his hands rested lightly on her shoulders. "My darling, please tell me that you love me as much as I love you."

They were in his mother's rose garden where he'd taken her after her makeup box was restored, and she was able to cover her face up.

"Cece, you're everything I ever wanted and prayed for. The Lord blessed me by sending you to me. Three years ago, when you suddenly dropped out of my world, I was heartbroken. I begged the Lord to restore you to me, and when time went by, I nearly lost all hope," he fell silent and Cece felt his inner anguish. "When you walked back into my life three weeks ago, I knew then that I'd never stopped loving you. I knew that the Lord was giving us a second chance, and I was ready to fight for our love. I purposed to win your heart again because I sensed that you weren't the same person of three years ago. Something had changed, but it only made me love you more and want to be there for you."

"Maynard, I don't want your pity."

"I told you it can never and will never be pity that I feel for you, Cece," he turned to observe the roses in the garden then his eyes returned to her face and rested there. "With or without your makeup on, you're still the most beautiful woman in the world to me and I love you so much."

Cece saw the yearning in her beloved's eyes and suddenly felt warmth filling her heart. Then shyness overtook her. She lowered her eyes and wanted to cry; not in pain but with happiness. Was this God's way of telling her that her happiness was here at last, that it was time to let go of the pain she carried deep inside her heart?

"Cece, now that every secret you think you have in your life is out in the open, will you marry me? Will you be the mother to all our unborn children and even those the Lord will allow us to nurture during our lifetime?"

"Oh Maynard!" Tears filled her eyes. "Do you really mean that?"

He nodded, "With all my heart. More than anything in the world, I want you to be my wife, to love and to hold you for the rest of my life."

"Then yes, I'll marry you," she said, half laughing and half crying. "Thank you for asking me." Maynard caught her in his strong arms.

Truly this was a garden of love as his mother had said many years ago.

"I wonder what Nana will say when she arrives tomorrow."

Nana Bourke was ecstatic when she arrived, and Maynard didn't delay but proceeded to ask her for Cece's hand in marriage.

"I've prayed for this day," the middle-aged woman wept unashamedly. "I'm so thankful that God in His mercy has answered my prayers," she hugged her granddaughter and then Maynard. "Seeing you so happy makes what I want to ask you so much easier," she said cryptically.

Cece observed her grandmother with puzzlement. "Nana, what am I missing here?"

Nana sighed and reached into her purse and brought out a letter. "This is a letter from the Parole Board of Denver Women's Correctional Facility."

Cece closed her eyes, feeling like the walls were closing in on her and she found herself on her feet, breathing heavily. When she would have left the living room, Maynard held her back.

"I can never forgive that woman for what she did to me," she hissed angrily. "She ruined my life and never even said she was sorry. Now she gets the chance to be paroled and I'm supposed to do what, celebrate?"

"Cece..."

"Nana please don't ask me to forgive that woman for I won't and I can't."

"It's all right, my Love," Maynard soothed. "I don't want anything to cause you any kind of distress. Let's put this matter aside for now."

"You don't know what I went through because of Marion. My life will never be the same again. Yet now everyone expects me to go the parole hearing and look at her and give her the chance to be set free. How does she expect to come out and carry on with her life as normal when she ruined mine?"

"Cece, it's all right," Maynard said. "No one will force you to attend Marion's parole hearing. I'm here by your side and I won't let anyone force you to do what your heart isn't yet free to do. Take your time and remain calm. Nana is only the messenger."

A FEW DAYS Later

"My darling," Cece couldn't believe that she was now married to the handsome man standing beside her in the Civil Registrar's office.

Because she'd stopped wearing anything but the lightest of make-up, Cece hadn't wanted a large wedding. Of course, her three sisters by marriage; Kelsey, Hazel and Willow were quite disappointed because they'd been looking forward to planning a big wedding for Cece and Maynard.

Her father-in-law was able to soothe all the ruffled feathers because Mrs. Brian and her Nana had also joined the group that wanted a large wedding.

"None of us knows what Cece has been through," Abner said when everyone was in the living room. "I know you've seen the articles and photos as well as the nasty comments. Let's respect her desire and decision to have a very private wedding at the Civil Registry. She's a well-known person, and if news gets out about the wedding, then we may not be able to contain the paparazzi and the nightmare will begin all over again for Cece. But we can have a celebration right here on the ranch after their formal ceremony, right?" He turned to Cece and she nodded. She knew that everyone would do their best to protect her from any outsiders who might try to use her misfortune to sell their stories to the public. "Then it's settled. We'll have a lavish reception here." And everyone was appeased.

Cece knew she could now trust those who were close to the family. She was just getting used to people accepting her as she was and she was surprised at how kind everyone on the ranch was.

They were all angry with Doris Keller when the truth about what she'd done came out. Even though she apologized over and over again, she'd crossed a line that couldn't be undone.

"You may claim to have been jesting, but your actions were cruel and intended to inflict psychological harm to someone who's already been through so much pain," Mr. Abner Randolph's voice was cold,

and Cece had never seen him looking so serious. "Be glad that this is where it ends and Miss Bourke isn't willing to let the matter go further. I pray that you'll change, or else the good things in life will pass you by. A bitter and envious heart only attracts hatred and rejection, and much as your actions have disappointed me, I wouldn't want you to live in dejection for the rest of your life."

Doris had begged and wept as Callum drove her to the airport to take her flight home. No one at the ranch was speaking to her, and Cece had seen the regret on her face. But it was too late, and Mr. Randolph's word was final. She lost her internship, but he spared her the agony of presenting a negative report to her Dean of Students back in college. According to Kelsey, Hazel and Willow, she'd gotten off real easy.

Cece looked around the small room where she and Maynard had just been joined together in marriage and smiled. There were a few other couples waiting for their turn to tie the knot and in her heart she wished them love and wellness and a bright future like she knew was waiting for her.

The compromise they all reached was that a large reception would be awaiting them back at the ranch. Nana, Mrs. Brian and Willow had insisted on preparing a banquet at the ranch and invited as many folks as they could. Cece was also happy because Pastor Manoah would be there to pray for them and bless their union. She'd always wanted a church wedding but given the circumstances, settling for a civil wedding had made a lot of sense.

"Maynard?"

"Yes, my love?"

"What present can I give you for our wedding that will touch your heart?" Cece snuggled close to her husband as they were being driven back home. Callum was their designated driver, for he and Susan had been their witnesses. "If I was the queen of a country, I would give you up to half of my kingdom because I love you so much. You've decorated my life and deserve every good thing to come to you."

Maynard chuckled, "My darling wife, be careful what you're offering," he said. "Some offers may be too expensive for you to fulfill."

Cece sat up and looked into her husband's eyes. "I promise that whatever you ask me for, I'll give it to you. But it has to be something that is humanly possible," she gave him a cheeky smile.

"Anything, you say?" Maynard's heart was pounding.

"Yes. Callum and Susan here are my witnesses that I've made this promise to you on this day of our wedding. May it go down in our books as a memorial day for us and that I gave my husband the best gift of all."

Maynard took a deep breath, "All I want is for you to be happy, my Darling. That's what will bring me so much happiness and it's the best gift you can ever give me."

"I'm happy," Cece said, a sweet smile on her lips. She was loved and she knew that this was special grace that she'd received. Maynard loved and accepted her just as she was, and he'd even told her to think about having the plastic surgery she needed to restore her face again. That was his wedding present to her and he'd told her that whenever she was ready they could schedule an appointment with one of the best plastic surgeons in America.

Dr. Alfonso Barrera had been suggested to them by Mrs. Brian, who knew someone who'd had facial reconstruction done by him after a horrific traffic accident.

But that was something she would look into later, because now all she wanted was for her husband to be happy. And he said that he would be happy if she was.

"I'm happy," she repeated.

"But still in pain," Maynard said softly. "Darling, I want the pain in your heart to be gone for good. And that can only happen when your heart is free."

Cece's smile faded. "What are you talking about?"

"Please forgive Marion and Doris," he said, looking deep into her eyes as he held her face gently in his palms. "They don't deserve your forgiveness for all they did to you. But I want you to know that when you forgive them, you're setting yourself free from the prison of bad memories and bitterness," he said.

It seemed as if everyone in the car was holding their breath. Finally Cece sighed and gave her husband a gentle smile.

"Maynard, if I forgive Doris and Marion, will that satisfy and make you happy?"

"It will be the best gift ever, because I'll know that your heart is free to love me wholly, and when the Lord blesses us with children, them too."

"Thank you," Cece said. "I forgive them and wish them well. I never got to read the letter that Nana brought back from Denver. When is the parole hearing?"

"In two days' time," Maynard said.

"Then we can fly out to Denver as part of our honeymoon and get that over and done with," Cece said.

"I totally recommend The Astrid Hotel," Callum said happily. "Rick and Willow claim that it's one of the best five-star hotels in Denver."

"It's settled then," Cece said. "We'll leave for Denver as soon as we book our tickets and the hotel room."

Maynard took her face between his palms once again and placed a soft kiss on her lips. "Thank you so much for my priceless wedding present."

CECE CLUTCHED onto Maynard's hand as they entered the Correctional Facility where Marion was serving her sentence and had been for the past three years.

"You're not alone," he whispered when they entered the room where the hearing was taking place. They were shown to their seats after Maynard gave out their identities and Cece took a deep breath.

When Marion was brought in a few minutes later, Cece was glad that her husband had asked for this as a wedding present. Forgiveness had set her free and as she finally got to look at the face of her attacker after three years, all she felt was compassion. She loved her husband so much because he was selfless and thought about others.

"Miss Bourne, now Mrs. Celine Maynard Randolph has requested to say something before this board," her lawyer began. Maynard nodded as Cece rose and walked toward Marion, stopping a few feet away because, by law, she wasn't allowed to get too close to the prisoner.

"Many times, I've asked myself why you chose to hurt me like you did," she started in a soft voice. "We weren't rivals, I never did anything to hurt you in any way. But I won't let the pain of what you did to me and the bitterness I felt afterward control my life anymore. Please just answer one question for me," she looked at Marion who couldn't even raise her head but nodded slightly. "What did I do to deserve your hatred?"

"I don't hate you," Marion whispered tearfully. "You weren't supposed to have been in the corridor at that time," she said. "It wasn't meant for you and I'm so sorry."

"What?"

Marion nodded, "Rhonda Whittaker always mocked and taunted me because we were rivals. Both of us were facial and hair models, and she'd stolen my boyfriend, so I was really angry with her. I wanted her to pay for hurting me, and I deeply regret allowing my anger to get the better of me. When you stepped out of the changing room that day, I thought it was Rhonda because I'd seen her entering your changing room."

Cece wanted to scream out in anger. It hurt to know that she hadn't even been the intended target but had just been in the wrong place at the wrong time. For a brief moment she considered running out of the room, but then her feet were heavy, and she felt like she couldn't move. She'd suffered for someone else's mistakes and it wasn't fair.

"Forgive," she heard Nana's voice, Maynard's and all those who wished her well. The saddest part of it all was that she'd heard that Rhonda Whittaker had died while skiing in Switzerland just months after her own accident.

"Marion, anger and hatred can destroy your life and destiny," Cece found herself saying. "I don't know if you heard that Rhonda lost her life while skiing in Switzerland just a few months after, well, that incident?"

Marion nodded, "That was my turning point," she said. "I realized that it doesn't pay to hate anyone. I totally understand if you won't forgive me or even say anything good about me during this hearing. My sins and wrong actions put me here, and this is my penance. Cece, please forgive me and I'm not asking in order to influence your decision before this board. I'm asking for your forgiveness because I need it so my heart will be at peace."

"I don't want to dwell on the past," Cece said at last. "Now I have the answers that have tormented me. Marion, from the bottom of my heart I forgive you today. And if my forgiveness leads to your being set free after this, then I'm truly happy for you and may you find peace after all this."

"Thank you," Marion sobbed.

KEEPING THE PROMISE

Celine was suddenly sobbing in her husband's arms. Maynard gave thanks that his prayers had been answered in a way he would never have anticipated as he comforted her while holding her tight.

The Parole Board allowed them to take their leave once Cece was done giving her testimony because they realized that the experience was still too emotional for her. They would continue deliberating on other factors that would contribute to whether Marion was granted parole or not.

"Thank you," Cece sobbed. They returned to their hotel room and she still felt very emotional. "I never knew that I was carrying such a heavy load in my heart until I came face to face with Marion."

"When we forgive those who have hurt us, we take away their power to continue causing us pain. Thank you for such a wonderful wedding present, my Darling."

"Do you think Marion will be set free?" Cece asked. "Now I feel sorry for her because she will have the stigma of being an ex-convict for the rest of her life. It's a huge cross to bear."

Maynard nodded. "If only people would realize that all their evil deeds have terrible consequences, they would think twice before executing any kind of wickedness on others."

"And Doris lost such a good internship opportunity because of her jealousy and envy."

"She only got what she deserved. I'm glad that my father said that from now on, all interns will be thoroughly vetted before joining the ranch. And what's more, Callum and his HR team will ensure that they read the fine print on all contracts they have to sign. If such envious behavior isn't checked, it could lead to terrible actions and consequences."

"I just pray that Doris and Marion find peace in their hearts."

"Amen."

CECE LISTENED to Maynard's even breathing and knew that he was still asleep. So she slipped out of bed and sat by the window looking out to the well-lit city. It was very cold in Denver, being early December and she found herself longing for sunny Texas.

Her lawyer had sent her a text message last evening informing her that Marion had been released. But as a condition for her release, she was charged to never step foot in the same city or town as Cece while she was there, until the remaining four years of her sentence were over. For Cece that was overkill because the woman she'd seen in the prison was a broken vessel and would never do anything to hurt anyone else again. Marion had paid for her sins and Cece prayed that society would accept her back and allow her to begin all over again.

Cece felt so light within. Maynard sighed and turned in his sleep until he was facing her. She loved this man so deeply and thanked God over and over again for bringing him into her life.

"How long have you been sitting there?" Maynard asked lazily, running a hand through his hair. He sat up and leaned his back against the headboard. "It's freezing and I don't want you to catch cold."

"I haven't been here for long," Cece said. "I just needed a few minutes to give thanks for this second chance we were given, and also to pray for Doris and Marion so they will be accepted into society without any counterattacks against them from anyone. They've learned their lessons and deserve a second and even third chance."

Maynard was happy to see his wife opening her heart to extend the grace of forgiveness to the two women who'd really hurt her. Going forward, he knew that she would continue to heal in her heart, and he'd be there for her all the way.

"Come back to bed where it's warm," he raised the beddings and with a small and happy laugh, Cece joined him.

They gazed into each other's eyes and knew that they'd received such special grace that only a few ever experienced. And they knew that their future would be filled with love and warmth all the days of their lives.

"Sally Jo?"

"Yes, Mr. Abner?"

"You have a special gift for knowing what your clients need and even after all my sons are hitched I'll still find other people who could use your services. Maynard and Cece are married and no better match was made on earth and heaven. The beauty of it all is that they found each other after three years. That's such special grace and thank you so much for making it happen."

"It's always an honor to be of service to you, Mr. Abner."

"Thank you so much, and you know what's coming next."

Sally Jo laughed, "My check?"

"And a bonus too, and then you can now put down the last one of the pack."

"Your wish is my command, Sir."

"Good. I'll send you a detailed dossier on Callum so you can immediately get down to work. There are just a few weeks left to Christmas and my greatest desire is to see him find someone so that come next year, a new era will begin in this family. And just to let you know, my eldest son and his lovely wife were blessed with a sweet baby boy just days ago."

"Congratulations, Sir," Sally Jo said happily. "My special regards to the parents and the baby."

"They named him for Barbara, my late wife, and me. Abner Barry Randolph is my first grandson, and according to his father, the little one is already beginning to look like me," Abner laughed." He couldn't hide the joy in his voice.

"Once again, congratulations, Sir."

"Thank you. I pray that come next year, Little Abner will have many cousins around him. If I remember right, there's a history of twins somewhere in Barbara's lineage, so I'm hoping that one of my sons and his wife will give me a set or two."

"May the desires of your heart be fulfilled."

"Amen, and I'm praying and hoping that you can at least make it to come and be with us for Christmas this year. This has been a very fulfilling journey that you and I started last year. It would be nice for you to come and see the fruits of your hard labor."

"Now that's a good thought, Mr. Abner. Let me run around and rearrange a few things and see if I can come down there for a holiday. But even if I can't make it to be with you and your family for Christmas, there's always the New Year."

"Just let me know and I'll make all the necessary arrangements for you."

"Thank you, Sir."

EPILOGUE

"*T*he bandages come off today," Cece said. "I'm really nervous."

Maynard held his wife's hand in the private room where she'd been admitted for the past three days after reconstructive surgery was done to restore her face.

"Cece, you're a beautiful soul and that's all that counts to me. Are you in pain?" The surgery had taken nearly six hours and he'd been on his knees for most of that time, praying that Cece would come through without any problems at all. When the surgeon had told him that all was good, Maynard had wept in his father's arms. Now the whole family was waiting to receive Cece again, not that they'd loved her any less when she was scarred. They were happy that she'd gotten the chance to get her looks back again.

Cece felt the tightness which the doctor had told her was normal, but so far, she wasn't in pain, and it was because of the anesthesia. So she shook her head slightly. Only her eyes were visible through the bandages. "I know it will come later but I think it's worth it." She fell silent.

"Is something wrong?"

"I don't know," she sighed. "I asked the doctor to leave one little scar and not get rid of it."

"Why would you do that?" Maynard frowned.

"Because I want to remember that even though life can be very unfair, even the ugly can turn into something beautiful. That scar will be a reminder that God's love makes all things beautiful."

"Won't it interfere with your modeling career?"

Cece laughed softly, "I'm not going back to modeling, my Love. I asked Callum and he helped me fill out the forms for college. I'm going back to college to get my degree in Psychotherapy; then I'll be well equipped to work at the Restorative Center full time. Most of my classes will be online but once in a while I'll need to attend lectures and hand in my assignments. This arrangement will help me continue working at the Center so there won't be any vacuum. But that doesn't mean that I won't use my experiences as a model to make other people's lives better. There's so much to be done, and I'll spend a lot of time working with abused women and girls and helping them regain their confidence. Like Pastor Manoah advised, I'll never waste my bad experiences and pain. Instead I'll use them as a means of making the lives of others better."

"You're an amazing woman, my dearest wife."

"No, this is the Lord's doing. Surely, out of the ugly comes the beautiful and that's how I'll always consider my trauma. The devil intended to destroy me and rob me of my divinely given destiny, but God allowed it to happen and then changed my story, and now only goodness will come out of it. I'll do anything to help others and especially abused women and girls, and those who've had terrible accidents that have disfigured them and caused them to lose all their self-esteem. It's going to be tough, but with the Lord by my side, victory is sure."

"Amen."

When Maynard saw his beautiful wife's face with a small scar on the right cheek after the doctor took the bandages off, he wept with her.

"You remain the most beautiful woman in the world."

Cece saw her nearly flawless face staring back at her in the mirror and she knew that unlike before, she would never take life for granted again. Every single moment that she breathed would be used to give thanks to God for His goodness.

CALLUM'S BROKEN BRIDE ON A MISSION

FRIENDLY ENEMIES

"*H*ow did you know that I'd be here," the harsh words startled twenty-one-year-old Leila Solomon. The moment she raised her head to look at the occupant of the hotel room, it was the angry eyes of her cousin Fiona Jordan that she saw. What bad luck, she thought, because this wasn't going to end well for her.

"I promise you, I had no idea that you would be in this hotel room," Leila said, her brown eyes widening when she looked over her cousin's shoulder and saw the man reclining in the bed. He was one of the hotel's regular customers and from what she knew, Bill Romper was married with three children. He and his wife had just holidayed here a month ago with their children, and the moment he realized that she'd recognized him, he turned his face away.

Leila couldn't believe that her cousin would get involved with a married man. What was Fiona even thinking? The man's wife was a nasty piece of work, and Leila feared for her cousin. Mrs. Romper had poured a drink on a waitress who she claimed had been ogling her husband. What then would she do to Fiona if she ever found out about this relationship? This wasn't good at all, and Leila regretted that she'd responded to the summons to provide room service to these two. Or maybe Fiona had no idea that her companion was a married man and she thought about letting her know.

"What are you doing snooping around here?" Fiona hissed. "Or perhaps you're spying for Bill's wife?"

All thoughts of warning Fiona fled when Leila deduced from her words that she was aware that her companion was married. "I work in this place three days a week down in the kitchen and sometimes the restaurant. My supervisor sent me to bring champagne and cake to the room as ordered," Leila pointed at the trolley. "I'm sorry, I didn't know it would be you in this room."

"And you saw nothing, do you hear me?" Fiona's eyes were blazing with anger and hatred. "Do I make myself clear, Leila?"

Leila nodded, "I saw nothing."

"You'd better keep your mouth shut, or else you know what will happen to your wretched father if you say anything to anyone. Learn to mind your own business."

"Yes, Cousin Fiona."

Fiona hissed at her, "How many times have I warned you to never refer to me as your cousin? I don't ever want anyone knowing that we're related. How can I be related to such a wretched creature as yourself?"

Leila bowed her head. Her cousin's words stung, but all she said was, "I'm sorry."

"Get out of here, and if you're expecting me to tip you, think again."

"What's keeping you, darling," the deep male voice floated toward them. "It's really cold in this bed and you've left me alone for a long while. Come back and keep me warm, Baby."

"Coming, Big Daddy," Fiona's voice came out as soft and coy, but her eyes were icy cold as they continued resting on Leila. "One word from you, and you'll be sorry," she pulled the trolley into the room and slammed the door in Leila's face.

Leila stood there quite shaken at what she'd just witnessed. She couldn't believe that her seemingly pious and very sanctimonious cousin was in a hotel room with a married man, of all people. Yet Fiona's mother was always the first to ostracize any girls she considered to have loose morals. Single mothers and mature spinsters in church had it rough with Mrs. Hannah Jordan as she was always accusing them of running after other people's husbands. What would she say if she knew that her own daughter, who was supposedly one of the 'good girls' in church was involved with someone's husband?

Leila shook her head and gave one last glance to the closed door. What was wrong with her cousin? But it was none of her business since Fiona clearly knew what she was doing. Leila returned to her duty in the kitchen where the chef indicated that he wanted her to wash some pots and pans for him.

She hadn't been working for long when she was summoned to the restaurant supervisor's pigeon hole of an office.

"Miss Solomon, I'm afraid that your services are no longer required. Return your uniform and pick up your dues from the cashier for the days that you've worked this month," she was informed.

Leila stood there silently, but she wasn't shocked at all. If anything, she'd been expecting something like this to happen after she'd seen Fiona in that hotel room. So she simply nodded at the supervisor and reached behind her back to untie the apron.

"Thank you, Ma'am."

Leila saw the surprise on the other woman's face. "Aren't you going to ask why we're letting you go?"

Leila gave the woman a sad smile, "I have an idea of what must have happened," she said. "So I won't waste your time, Ma'am."

"Won't you even plead for me to give you another chance?"

Leila remembered what her father had once told her. "*Leila, my beautiful daughter, always remember that you're descended from the great King Solomon through our ancestors from Ethiopia. It doesn't matter how you live now, not enjoying the luxuries that you deserve. My dear child, don't pay attention to this poverty that has been a part of our lives for so long. Always remember that even if we're poor, we're royalty, so you should carry yourself with the dignity and honor befitting your status. How you carry yourself around people is how they'll treat you and never be in a place where you're not wanted."*

Of course, at the time she'd laughed at how mythical her father sounded. He was a dreamer and often told her stories about her ancestors and many times she wondered if they were all part of his imagination, or had they truly taken place? But to make her father happy, Leila always nodded and agreed with whatever he was telling her.

So she purposed within herself to always carry herself with dignity and honor. And that meant that she never groveled nor worshipped any human being. She accorded respect and honor wherever it was due but that was it.

"Leila, I'm talking to you," the woman sounded cross.

"Mrs. Simpson, you've already made up your mind and terminated my services in this place," Leila said in her soft and gentle voice. "It would be useless for me to beg for a position you've already taken away from me. Nevertheless, thank you for giving me the chance to work in this beautiful hotel."

As she spoke, she thought she saw something like regret flash through the woman's eyes. But she wasn't going to stay around here and be humiliated by Leila and her married companion. They were clearly the ones who'd reported her for whatever reason and the motto of this particular hotel, like most work places was that the customer or client was always right. She was sure that the couple were afraid that she might tell Bill

Romper's wife about their illicit dalliance. But Leila was one who had learned to mind her own business, and she never indulged in gossip of any kind. She had other, more pressing matters to attend to.

Once she'd returned her uniform and picked up her final dues from the hotel's cashier, she didn't waste any time hanging around the hotel. She could see the curious looks on the faces of her colleagues with whom she'd worked for close to a year and knew they were eager to know why she'd been laid off. But since she didn't want any trouble with Fiona, she simply waved at them and left.

When Leila got home she left the shopping she'd done in the small kitchen then made her way to her parents' bedroom. A quick glance at the wall clock in the parlor showed the time to be a little after ten in the morning, and she was surprised. It had seemed like the day was long gone, yet it was still just mid-morning.

"Mama, are you awake?" she entered the room which was semi dark because the drapes hadn't been opened.

"Leila, is that you?" The frail voice came from the bed.

"Yes, Mama. Do you want me to open the drapes for light to come in?"

"Yes, dear. I was waiting for Mrs. Finn to come in and do it for me. I'm feeling rather weak today."

"Mama, Mrs. Finn only comes in on Saturdays and Wednesdays," Leila said of the nurse cum housekeeper who'd

514

been such a big help ever since her mother was diagnosed with coronary artery disease two years ago. On other days it was Leila who took care of her mother because her work schedule was such that she was free most mornings. Then, when she went to work in the afternoon, a neighbor would come to check in on her just to make sure she was all right. The system had worked for the past few months. Now Leila had more free time since she'd been fired. "I'm here now and I'll do it," she said, wishing that her lovely mother didn't have to go through this pain.

According to the cardiologist Mrs. Solomon had seen at the time, she needed urgent coronary bypass surgery or else she would be dead within a year. The same specialist had estimated the cost of the surgery to be between forty and fifty thousand dollars, depending on where it was done, but that was money they didn't have. Dr. Fraser had even suggested taking her mother to India, but her father refused. Going to India meant he would have to take long leave from his place of work, and in those months, he wouldn't be earning anything.

Having the surgery in India would cut the cost of the surgery to almost a quarter of the amount Dr. Fraser had told them, but Leila's father wouldn't hear of it.

As the days went by and her mother got weaker and her condition deteriorated, Leila prayed for a miracle. She loved her mother so much, and the thought of losing her because of lack of money made her feel very frustrated. Why were they so poor, and how was it that no matter how hard they worked, nothing seemed to move forward or change for the better?

"Leila, why are you home early today?" Her mother struggled to sit up and Leila rushed to make her comfortable. Mrs. Malika Solomon had once been a strong woman, but the disease had taken its toll on her. Seeing her lying helplessly on the bed, unable to take care of herself as she'd been able before, nearly broke Leila's heart. "It doesn't seem as if you left so long ago. Or did you forget something at home and return to get it?"

Her mother was a dignified woman and Leila had often seen the frustration on her face because she wasn't able to take care of her own basic tasks. She was also very strong in spirit, even if her body was letting her down. She insisted on being told the truth about any updates on her condition or whatever was going on with her husband and daughter no matter how bad things were.

Leila sighed as she sat down on the bed and took one of her mother's frail hands in hers. "Mama, Fiona got me fired," and she told her mother all that had transpired. "That man is married and I know his wife. Maybe they thought I would tell on them."

"Leila, don't mind their business. You're out of that place and I know that the Lord is protecting you from such sights. One day God will remember us," her mother said. "There's no condition on this earth that is permanent, and one day we'll get the miracle we need and have been praying for."

"Amen to that, Mama. Thank you for always encouraging me no matter how tough things get."

Malika smiled at her beautiful daughter. She never ceased to pray for her only child, who'd lived a very difficult life and went without so much, yet not once had she ever heard Leila complaining. Now that Malika was completely bedridden, Leila worked so hard to see that the home ran smoothly and never even had time to see her friends or go out on dates, much to Malika's regret. Like any good mother, Malika often prayed for her daughter to find a good man to marry but with all that was going on right now, she doubted that Leila even thought about getting married. In any case, she would never leave her parents, at least not while Malika was still bedridden. "Poor child," Malika thought. "Lord, please do my child some good."

"Let me get you some fruit," Leila rose to her feet. "I passed by the Farmers' Market and got some. I brought back cantaloupes, clementines, apples and even a large papaya. Would you like them all mixed together, or do you prefer taking a single fruit and then a different one later?"

"Mix them, please, and Leila, thank you."

Once she was sure that her mother was comfortable, Leila went to the kitchen where she cut the fruit into manageable sizes and put them onto a platter with a fork. At least her mother was still able to feed herself though Leila worried that she might one day be unable to do so.

"These are delicious," Malika said as she partook of the fruit.

"Do you need anything else for now?" Leila made sure to place a glass of water on the table beside the bed within easy reach for her mother.

"No, I'll enjoy these. If you need to do something please go ahead. I'll be all right, and if I need you, I'll call out."

"Okay, Mama."

Leila returned to the kitchen to clean up the mess she'd made as she was preparing the fruit for her mother. She'd long ago learned how to buy rejected produce from the Farmers' Market, which was sold at a throw-away price. The Farmers' Market had a section where such vegetables and fruit were sold. Leila would then cut out the still good bits and store them in the freezer for future consumption like she did right now. Her father would also enjoy some fruit when he got home from work. The poor man worked so hard and deserved to get at least one good, well-balanced meal.

"What a life," she sighed. "But my Father God, I'm not complaining, just sighing. I stand on Your promise in the Book of Jeremiah that says You have good plans for our lives, to give us a future filled with hope. As I hold onto this hope, I want to say thank You for this far You've brought us. May we never take anything for granted, in Christ's name, amen."

When Leila's father returned from work that evening dinner was ready, and all she had to do was serve it. They shared the simple meal of roasted potatoes, thick beef gravy with pieces of meat in it and green peas. Her mother had already had her dinner and was sleeping, so Leila quickly filled her father in on the day's happenings. Terry Solomon looked at his daughter with so much love in his eyes. She reminded him of his beloved mother who'd gone to be with the Lord years ago. Leila was a young woman who should be out there enjoying her life, but she'd chosen not to continue with college when her mother fell ill, because firstly, the money wasn't there. And she also helped at home as much as she could.

Leila, in turn, was thinking about the strong man who was her father. In all her life she'd never once seen him without a smile on his face, regardless of the hard life they lived.

Her father was the eldest son in a family of five but sadly, only two of them had survived infancy. Poverty had played a big part in their hard life, and though many people suggested that being an African American was a contributing factor, Terry Solomon refused to accept that.

"The world all over is filled with people going through even worse than we are and they're not African American," he would argue. "Look at India and the poverty that leads families to use animal chips to prepare food they scrounge for. Consider many countries in Asia and the Middle East whose citizens don't even have access to clean water and electricity. We're rich and I refuse to complain about my state. Time and chance happens to all men and I refuse to give up hope. I refuse to blame the color of my skin, for then I'd be saying that the Lord was wrong to create me as I am."

Terry's youngest brother and only surviving sibling had become his responsibility when they had lost their parents while they were both still teenagers. Terry, as the older brother, decided to drop out of school and find a job in one of the big bakeries in Denver. The advantage the two boys had was that the house they'd lived in all their lives was their parents' property and there was no mortgage attached to it.

Terry had scrimped and saved every penny he could just to see his younger brother through school and college. Zeke Jordan had promised that once he made it big as a lawyer he would help his brother complete his own education. He'd promised to repay the big brother who'd given up everything for him.

Leila sighed as she ate her food. Her Uncle Zeke had repaid her father all right, but not as expected. Instead of helping Terry return to school, Zeke had given him a menial clerical position in his thriving law firm. The pay was dismal but thankfully they didn't have to pay rent because they lived in the house her grandparents had left. But her mother's medication took a huge chunk out of her father's wages, and Leila's own little money that she brought in was used to buy the food they ate, as well at pay for utilities.

"Your Uncle Zeke is having some people over for the weekend," her father told her as he helped her clear the table. "Your aunt asked that you go and help with preparations and serving the guests. She mentioned that there would be about twenty or so people so it won't be such hard work."

"Not this time, Papa," Leila said, for the first time feeling that she'd been taken advantage of enough times. It always happened that when her aunt, Fiona's mother had guests, she would go and help, often working herself to the bone. But she wouldn't get paid for her efforts.

"I'm allowing you to carry away the leftover food so why should I pay you as well?" Was what Leila was often told when she asked about payment for the services she'd provided.

"Leila what did you say?" Even her father looked shocked that his usually docile and agreeable daughter was now rebelling.

"Papa," she said slowly for emphasis, "I'm never going to Aunt Hannah's place again to work. I'd rather go and wash clothes for Mrs. Sanjay because she pays me in cash, which we need, rather than do work that has no wages."

"Leila, your aunt might think that I stopped you from going to help her."

"Daddy, please don't trouble yourself. Aunt Hannah is rich enough to hire as much help as she needs, not to mention her four full-time servants. Besides, after what happened with Fiona, I know that I'm the last person she wants to see any time soon."

"If you put it that way, it's all right. At least you'll be here to help your mother out full time. But if you need to go somewhere or do something outside the house please just let me know and I'll ask Mrs. Finn to come and stand in for you."

"Daddy," she rose to her toes and kissed his cheek, "please don't trouble yourself. I'll ask Mrs. Sanjay to allow me to wash her clothes from here so I can sit with Mom. And since I'll be at home, the two children that I mind can also be brought here."

"You're a good girl and I pray that one day the Lord will give you your own home, a better one than this." Terry looked around the small kitchen with a sigh. This house was old, as it had been built by his grandfather. Over the years he'd tried to keep it in good shape but with his wife's illness there wasn't any extra money for repairs.

"Daddy, a good home isn't bricks and mortar, but the love that the people in it have for each other. I'd rather have a man who loves me even if he doesn't have much money, than be like Mrs. Bill Romper whose husband is one of the wealthiest men in Denver, yet her life is full of strife and suspicions all the time."

But Leila had no idea that in just a few weeks' time she would be putting love aside and thinking about finding a wealthy husband who could take care of her mother's medical bills.

THE ONSET OF TROUBLE

"*I* have something to tell you," Fiona's eyes were filled with tears and Callum Randolph stared at her in surprise. Her arrival at the ranch earlier that day had surprised him because he couldn't remember ever meeting her. Yet she'd told Quin and his father that the two of them had shared some very close and intimate moments. Fiona Jordan had just appeared out of nowhere.

His father had said nothing but immediately sent for him and told him to speak to Fiona, and he was curious to hear what she had to day. "What is it you want to tell me, Fiona?"

"I'm pregnant," she blurted out. "I'm carrying your child, Callum."

"What?" To say that he was stunned was an understatement. To his knowledge he didn't even know this woman so how could he be responsible for the child she was carrying? "How and when were we together?"

"I'm eight weeks gone," Fiona said. "Don't you remember what happened eight weeks ago? We met at that wedding in New Jersey and spent the night together," and as if to prove her words she took out a stack of photos and passed them over to Callum. "There are more photos on my phone," she said. "Don't you remember me at all?" She started crying and Callum found himself feeling quite helpless.

Fiona Jordan was a very beautiful woman with flawless chocolate skin and a figure that many women would do anything to have. But Callum felt no attraction for her, not even a little.

"Fiona, I'm sorry that I can't even recall talking with you at the wedding," Callum said. "Are you sure about what you're saying?"

"Are you denying the evidence before your eyes?" She pointed at the photos. "I wish I hadn't given in to your cunning tongue. Did all those things you whispered to me that night mean nothing at all?" She wept. "It's now obvious that all you wanted was to use me and now you want to abandon me and deny that you're the father of my baby."

Callum stared helplessly at the woman who'd just suddenly showed up at the ranch and was now making such serious allegations. He couldn't believe that he could have been with a woman and yet have no recollection of the night in question.

For one, he'd made a vow to the Lord that he would honor his body and remain chaste until his wedding night. Secondly, he never took any alcohol, yet the events of that night after his friend's wedding were rather hazy in his mind. All he could recall was being very exhausted during the late afternoon reception. He hadn't even attended the evening party because as soon as he'd been able to, he'd slipped away and made his way back to his room where he'd passed out until the next morning when he woke up, packed his belongings and left the hotel to return home. But what he knew for certain was that he'd gone to bed alone and awakened alone. As to the photos that showed him and Fiona Jordan sleeping in one bed, he had no recollection. At no point did he remember taking a woman with him to the room.

It was quite a relief when his father and four older brothers walked into the living room. The mood was solemn, and Quin, his eldest brother looked at him questioningly and then back at their visitor.

"This is Miss Fiona Jordan from New Jersey," Callum began.

"No, we met at a wedding in New Jersey but my home is in Denver. I was just there for the wedding, that's all."

"Miss Jordan," Abner Randolph acknowledged the young woman. For some reason, something about her made him quite uneasy and it crossed his mind that she wasn't to be trusted. For a fleeting moment he thought that Sally Jo had sent Miss Jordan over. But then his good friend would never send over someone without first informing him, even though he'd asked her to find Callum a wife like she'd done for all his four brothers. He sat down on the single settee opposite the couch on which she was seated and fixed his gaze on her. "Welcome to Randolph Ranch. As I told you before, my name is Abner Randolph and Callum is my last-born son. How did you and Callum meet?"

Fiona raised a trembling hand to her forehead. "Thank you for the kind hospitality and I'll be happy to answer your questions later. Right now I'm rather tired and feeling slightly ill because of my condition." She turned to Callum. "Could you please show me to the room where I'll be staying?"

"What condition?" Abner feared the worst.

"I'm expecting your grandchild," Fiona said. "Callum will tell you the rest. But for now I need him to show me where I'll be staying until he does right by me."

Callum turned to his father for help because he was still in shock. He knew himself and was very sure that he hadn't been with this woman like she claimed. Yet there was indisputable evidence that the two of them had shared a bed which had probably led to intimate relations. How had that happened, yet he couldn't recall anything about that night?

"Miss Jordan," Abner told her, "Please be patient as your room is being made ready for you."

"My room?" Fiona turned to Mr. Randolph. "I don't understand what you mean by my room is being prepared? Aren't Callum and I going to be sharing a room?"

Abner shook his head, and though he felt disturbed by the woman's audacity, he kept his face expressionless. "All our visitors who are single ladies are accommodated in our hostel. When we get male singles they use the ranch's bunkhouse. Seeing as you and Callum aren't married yet, you'll be staying in the hostel until further notice."

"That's not fair," Fiona started crying again. "I came out here because of what Callum has done to me."

"What has my son done?"

"Didn't you hear me telling you that I'm expecting his child? It's only fair that I should be treated better than this. He'll marry me so he can give my child a name, so I thought we would be sharing a room."

Callum frowned, more convinced than ever that this woman was a stranger to him. The only thing he had to find an explanation to was how the two of them had ended in bed together and there was photographic evidence. He feared that Fiona might cause trouble if she wasn't properly handled.

Waylen made an impatient sound, "The parentage of the baby you're carrying is yet to be proven, Miss Jordan," he said. "I suggest that we have DNA tests carried out before we make any further plans. This news has come as a shock to all of us because Callum never once mentioned that he had a woman in his life."

"The DNA tests can be done after my baby is born," Fiona said.

"No, DNA testing needs to be done now," Waylen insisted. "It's the only way if you want to get married to my brother."

Fiona paled, "Don't you trust me? Do you think I would leave my home in Denver and fly all this way if I wasn't sure about what I'm saying? I don't want to put my baby at risk of any unnecessary procedures. He or she will soon be born and then you can carry out whatever tests you want to so as to prove that I'm telling the truth."

"There's a Non-Invasive Prenatal Paternity test that can be carried out to determine if what you're saying is the truth," Waylen refused to back down, and Callum wanted to hug his brother.

To everyone's surprise, Fiona burst into hysterical weeping. "It's clear that you all want my baby to die," she sobbed. "Why did I have to end up with an insensitive man who is clearly determined to harm me and my baby?"

"Hush," A tall and beautiful African American woman entered the living room and Fiona turned to her. "I'm Mrs. Tamara Brian," she said. Mrs. Brian walked over to where Fiona was. She took her hand and raised her to her feet. "I heard what you said and I'm sorry that you're going through this. Crying isn't good when you're in this condition. Your baby needs you to be happy at all times. Come, your room in the hostel is now ready," she turned to Callum. "Please bring our guest's luggage through." She cast an indescribable look at Abner, then walked the weeping woman out of the room.

Callum didn't move until his brother Rick nudged him. "You'd better do as Mrs. Brian instructed, but as soon as you drop the luggage off, come back here so we can talk about this."

"Thank you," Callum felt slightly better. With his brothers and father present he was sure they would get to the bottom of this matter.

Callum collected Fiona's luggage from the car she'd rented and carried it to the hostel. Since the women's quarters were out of bounds to all males without exception, Callum left Fiona's two large suitcases in the small hostel foyer. He rushed back to the living room where he was glad to find that no one had left. He needed the wisdom and advice of his father and older siblings so he could make sense of everything that was happening.

"Callum, that woman sounded very sure about what she was saying. How did the two of you meet and why is it that you never told us anything about her before?" Quin asked as he made himself comfortable.

Callum sat down and rested his elbows on his knees, held his head in his hands and sighed. "That's just it," he said. "I don't recall speaking to Miss Jordan at any point during the wedding. And I'm know I went to bed alone and woke up alone also. So I have no idea nor recollection of having been with her."

"What do you recall of that night that Miss Jordan claims you were together?" Waylen asked. He was a lawyer by profession and in charge of all legal matters pertaining to the ranch and all staff and family living there. "I need to know how to prepare to defend you in case that young woman decides to bring a law suit against you. Is it possible that you could have been with her," he pointed at the photos on the coffee table, "And something happened to make you forget all about it?"

Callum shook his head, "Deep down in my spirit, I know that I never met Fiona before today, so I couldn't have done what she's accusing me of. Yet there's photographic evidence that we were together. It's all very confusing."

"Son," Abner Randolph rose from his seat and come to sit beside Callum. He placed a light arm around his shoulders. "I don't want you to worry about anything. Waylen is taking care of the legal implications, and your other brothers will stand by you, no matter what. We'll dig deep to find the truth."

"Thank you, Dad," Callum looked at all his brothers and felt hope stirring up within him. This was a formidable team, and he knew that they would stand and fight with him.

"Listen, I don't mean to press you," Waylen said. "But I need you to paint me a picture of what that day was like. Perhaps there's something you might remember that will shed some light on all this."

Callum scrunched his face and dug deep into the recesses of his memories. "The wedding started at around noon, and it took place at the Golden Plume Hotel. It so happened that we'd all been booked into that same hotel. During the reception, which was held in the hotel's ballroom, I recall feeling very tired all of a sudden."

"Were you drinking anything intoxicating?" Quin asked. "Some wines seem mild but can get a person drunk."

Callum shook his head, "You all know that I don't take alcohol in any form, and the wine I take is always non-alcoholic. So there's no way that I could have been drunk because I was only taking grape juice."

"Was it served at the wedding lunch table or by passing waiters?"

Callum tried to remember all the sitting and dining arrangements. "I don't recall taking anything other than water at the dining table. But while we were waiting for the cake to be cut, waiters started serving drinks on trays. I recall asking for a glass of grape juice."

"How many glasses did you take?" Waylen asked.

"Just one, and before the cake could be cut, I suddenly felt very nauseous and tired. So I slipped away even before the cake was cut and went to my room. The next thing I remember was that it was morning. I'd slept for over fourteen hours. And at some point I threw up because in the morning I found a mess on the floor beside the bed."

"Was Miss Jordan there with you when you woke up?"

Callum shook his head. "No, I was alone, and after taking a shower and cleaning the mess up, I left for the airport and returned home. That's as much as I recall."

"So you're sure that at no time did you meet up with Miss Jordan?" His father asked. "If you all noticed, Fiona is a very beautiful woman, and I would have remembered meeting her at the wedding. Yet I don't recall anything, let alone taking her to my room with me. I know that when I escaped to my room because I was feeling poorly, I was alone."

Everyone was silent for a while; then Rick spoke up. "Callum, I'm afraid to say this but you may have been drugged."

"But how?" Callum was perplexed.

"That grape juice that you were served was probably spiked with something. What was done to you is abominable and two things could have happened after that. One, you could have chatted up Miss Jordan and taken her to your room in that state where your mind was altered by the drugs you were given or else she was part of the whole set up and took advantage of your drugged state. Obviously, there was foul play, but how can you prove it when so much time has gone by?"

SHORT-LIVED RELIEF

"Fiona, what are you doing here?" Leila was shocked that the person who opened the large front door when she knocked at Randolph Ranch mansion was her cousin. This was the last place that she would have expected to find her cousin. What was going on?

"I'm the one who should be asking you that question," Fiona looked shaken. "I'm here on personal business and I can't believe that you're also here. I'm beginning to suspect you of having some unnatural and evil powers because you're always popping up in the most unusual places. But if you would know, I'm here to marry the father of my child."

"What?" Leila's eyes nearly popped out of her head. Would the shocks not end? "You can't be serious that you're expecting the child of someone out here. When and how did you even meet?"

"Listen to me, you pesky and interfering imbecile, how and when I met my baby's father is none of your business. If you breathe one word to anyone that you know me, there will be trouble. And if I may ask, why are you here? Are you now stalking me?"

"No, I would never do that," Leila said strongly. "I responded to an advertisement for a nanny's position here on Randolph Ranch, and that's how come I'm now here."

Fiona scoffed at the explanation. "Why am I not surprised?" Her tone was derisive. "You're such a washout, and it's clear that you'll never amount to much. Being a nanny isn't something you fly across the country to do. This is so demeaning, but why am I even bothering since your useless life has nothing to do with me? It's your business since what my mother said is true, Leila. You'll never amount to anything in this life."

Leila told herself not to take offence at her cousin's mean words. This wasn't anything new, for Fiona went out of her way to humiliate and shame Leila whenever she got the chance to do so. She just prayed that Fiona wouldn't cause her any more trouble, especially not when she really needed the money this job would provide.

"Please may I see Mr. Randolph?"

Fiona laughed, "Which particular one? There are six of them on this ranch, so which one do you want to see?"

"Mr. Abner Randolph. The agency told me that I should report to him so he can give me further instructions about my position."

"Oh, that's the old man. Well, he must be somewhere around here."

"May I please come in and see him?"

"No," Fiona frowned at her. "You're nothing but a stranger and I'm not in the position to allow aliens into this house, not when I only just got here myself."

"Oh? How long have you been here then?" Leila was surprised that her aunt hadn't mentioned anything to her mother or father about Leila moving to live in Texas.

"I've been here for a full week now, if you must know. Not that it's any of your business, but I don't want you calling your parents and telling them stories, do you hear me?"

"Yes, Fiona."

"Now wait out here while I find someone who has the authority to allow you into the house. And remember your place." With those words, she retreated and shut the door in Leila's face, leaving her standing on the front porch.

Leila just shook her head and sighed. Her cousin would never change. She wrapped her arms around her midriff and moved toward the edge of the wide porch, leaning slightly against the intricately welded iron railing. She tested it for stability and was surprised to find that even though it looked delicate it was firm and strong.

Randolph Ranch was like being in paradise and she still couldn't believe that she was finally here.

"Lord Jesus," she prayed, "If this is a dream, please don't let me wake up."

Though it was cold and windy, Leila didn't mind. There were well-arranged plants and pretty flowers all around the porch, giving it a warm look. She'd never seen such a large porch; it had two sitting areas with teak seats, the kind she'd only seen in one of the classy hotels where she'd worked. However, the seats had no cushions on them, probably because of the weather, so she couldn't even sit down. Leila could just imagine the whole family spending time out here in the summer. She wondered if the ranch had a swimming pool or if they preferred to take dips in the natural waters. If she got to stay, she would eventually find out where people went to swim because it was the only sport she loved. What lucky people, she thought, having all this beauty around them.

In the distance she could see various buildings and told herself that when she got the chance she would explore this vast homestead. On the way to the ranch, the Uber driver had pointed out various landmarks to her, telling her that Randolph Ranch was one of the largest in Dallas.

"But this area is Cedar Hill; well, it's still part of Dallas. Make sure that you get the most of your visit here because it isn't every day that people are invited to places such as these," the man had said.

Leila had smiled and said she would do her best to enjoy her time on the ranch.

The weather was actually warm at this time of the year in comparison with what she'd left behind in Denver. Even though the sky was laden with dark clouds, it still wasn't as cold as Denver would be in such weather.

And thinking about Denver brought tears to her eyes. She really missed her parents and prayed that her present venture would make her mother's treatment possible.

Leila turned to look at the closed door and wondered if she should press the bell again. According to the instructions she'd received from Sally Jo as she was giving her details of her flight to Dallas, she would be working for the eldest son of the family.

"Mr. Quinten Randolph and his wife Kelsey have a two-month-old baby. Little Abner, named after his grandfather, needs a full-time nanny. But that's just the front you'll be using. You know very well that your intention is to meet Mr. Callum Randolph and see if the two of you can fall in love and get married."

"My purpose for registering with this agency is to find a man who will marry me and help me take care of my parents. Love really has nothing to do with all this. I know that it sounds rather mercenary but I feel that I should be open right from the start. We've had a difficult life and right now my mom needs a very expensive operation."

Sally Jo smiled, "It's never wrong for a woman to look for a man who can provide for her and her family. But I want you to also keep in mind that men also need to be loved, respected and appreciated. I know that many of the clients I've brought together never started out with love, but they respected each other, and with time, love grew."

"So how will I go about getting Mr. Callum to fall in love with me? Do I approach him or what am I supposed to do? Should I begin corresponding with him like it is with other dating agencies?"

Sally Jo shook her head, "His father is the one who's my direct client. Mr. Abner Randolph wants his son to find love, get married and settle down but the boy doesn't seem to be in a hurry to do so. His four brothers have all settled down now and the father expected that it would push Callum to do the same. Your mission on that ranch is to find a way of getting close to Callum without making it too obvious. Hence the idea of you going there as a nanny. Mr. Abner tells me that Callum loves his nephew so much, and whenever he has any free time, he's to be found close to the child."

"If I'll be so busy taking care of Little Abner, how will I make time for my intended? Don't people go on dates anymore? What if he asks me out on a date and I have to take care of the baby?" Leila asked. "Do they all live together in one big family house?"

From the little she knew about ranching families and especially very wealthy ones like the Randolphs, they all tended to live together in one big mansion.

"No, these Randolphs don't live together. I mentioned that Callum's four brothers are married," Leila nodded. "They each have their own homes and have moved out of the family one. It's only Callum who now lives in the main ranch house with his father."

"Does this mean that I'll be living with my employers?"

"No. Mr. Abner prefers that you stay in the women's hostel. So you'll be reporting to work at seven each morning and then leaving at six in the evening when Kelsey returns from work. But during the day, *you'll be expected to take the little one to his mother so she can nurse him. Mr. Abner suggested that between nine and three p.m. you'll be at the main ranch house. That will also enable him to spend time with his grandson. The little one nurses every two hours and hasn't been introduced to anything else. Kelsey prefers to only nurse her son until he's six months old. That means that when you get to their house you'll clean and wash up, then head for the main ranch and spend the rest of the day there, returning at around three or four to settle the child down."*

"It sounds like quite a taxing position."

"Would you want me to find you someone else?"

"No, I'm up for the challenge. I just hope the weather isn't as terrible as it is here because exposing a little one to cold isn't advisable."

"You seem to know something about taking care of a child."

Leila shrugged, "I've had to take many jobs just to help out at home, and babysitting has been one of my favorite ones. The little ones don't have any prejudices or hatred like so many adults do. It's just a pity that most people I've worked for can't afford to pay much. And then again, living on a ranch or farm is something I've been desiring because the fresh air would be good for my mom and help toward her healing. Maybe my prospective husband will allow my parents to visit and stay for a while until my mom gets stronger."

"Though I've never been to Randolph Ranch, I know that it's quite a huge spread. If you play your cards right and end up as a bride, I know that Mr. Abner will be open to you inviting your family from time to time. He's a generous man, and I believe his sons have taken after him. But the important thing right now is to go down there and

prove that you have what it takes to be a good bride. However, there's a condition to your going down there."

"What condition?"

"Callum Randolph must never suspect that his father has arranged all this. He's supposed to fall in love with you without bowing to any kind of pressure. So you'll tell no one of your true mission to the ranch. Let them think that you're going there as a nanny, for that's what Mr. Abner will tell them. The salary they're offering is really good, so you'll need to work very hard and diligently. Kelsey will be relying on you to take care of her little one while she's working."

"Mrs. Randolph works?" That was surprising news since Leila had expected that as a wealthy man's wife, her new mistress would be a socialite or stay-at-home mom by choice.

"All the women married to Mr. Abner's sons are very industrious and hardworking. It would be a plus for you to find ways of making friends with them. Kelsey is a mechanic and works at the workshop on the ranch. Hazel is married to Mr. Waylen Randolph, and she's a schoolteacher. The ranch runs its own school, not only for the workers' children, but those from the surrounding area as well. That's where Hazel works. Her husband is a lawyer." Leila listened keenly, putting the information away for when she would need it. "The third son is Kendrick or Rick. and he's in charge of all purchases and something like that. His wife is Willow, and she's a chef by profession. She and the housekeeper, Mrs. Brian, recently started a business together, preparing and selling snacks to the school, and they also bake cakes for all occasions. When you eventually win Callum Randolph's heart, your wedding cake will be a sure thing. Maynard is the fourth son, and he's the maintenance person. His

wife Celine is studying to be a psychotherapist and currently works at the Randolph Restoration Center."

"What's that?"

"About four months ago, Maynard started a project to help people healing from all kinds of trauma. The center uses old, gentle horses as part of the therapy. Many people find much inner peace by being around these gentle creatures. Of course, the horses used are those that are past their prime and have been retired. Instead of putting them down, Maynard found a way of using them as part of the center, until they get too old or too sick."

"That sounds like a very noble and interesting venture."

"It is, and Mr. Abner told me that even though the center is still in its infancy stage, there have been vast improvements in the lives of the patients who attend those sessions with the counselors and horses."

"I'm humbled that the four women are so down to earth. I know that many women, once they marry into wealth, only think about spending their husbands' money and becoming socialites on YouTube and Instagram."

"Such a pity," Sally Jo said. "So you can be sure that if you want to catch Callum's eye, you'll not go there and become a lazy layabout. It's the reason Mr. Abner suggested that you go as a nanny. Let the man see you as a hardworking woman because he won't accept anything less, especially since he sees how industrious his sisters-by-marriage are. But even then, you should be thinking about improving your own life for the future. What's your given career choice?"

Leila sighed, "I always wanted to be a nurse and would have gone for the necessary training, but for my mom's illness. Her medication costs a lot of money and my father's salary is the only income we have. I try to help whenever I can, but without proper qualifications, all I can get is menial jobs which don't pay much."

"Don't worry," Sally Jo said. "Just do your best and keep hoping and having faith that one day things will be better for you. You could take classes in one of the colleges down there should you so wish."

"When would I do that when I have a baby to take care of full time?"

"Where there's a will, there's definitely a way. With the world on lockdown, many universities and colleges developed extensive online curriculums for their students. You could check out the colleges that offer online nursing courses. The world is at your feet, and you can be anything you want to be. All you need is faith in God and faith in yourself."

Leila gave a small laugh, "What kind of faith is needed to survive in this world? My parents are both born again Christians, as am I, and we pray so much for things to change. But I feel as if our faith isn't doing anything at all, for life continues to be so hard for us."

"Leila," Sally Jo's voice was filled with deep compassion. "I've been a counselor for a while now and I can tell you this: we may feel like our troubles are overwhelming, until we hear someone else's story. Faith doesn't make things easy, it only makes them possible and achievable."

"I just pray that this cowboy will look at me with favor and consider that I can make a suitable wife for him. Then all our problems will be over."

"Man plans but it's God who sees those plans through. That's why it's very important to always have faith and believe that regardless of what you're passing through, God is working for your good."

"You sound just like my father," Leila smiled. "His own life hasn't been easy but I've never seen my father without a smile on his face and a word of encouragement on his lips, not even when things get so tough."

"Your father is one of those giants of faith, and one day, the Lord will remember him."

"Amen, I pray so. It's true that my father is a man of strong faith, or we would have given up by now. It hasn't been easy." She sighed. "His life humbles me, and also the way he loves my mother so much. Even when my mom is so sick and can barely keep anything down, my father is there by her side even after working twelve long hours at his office. He holds her with so much love and tenderness that it brings tears to my eyes. Pa is only forty-four and in the prime of his life. He's a very handsome man, and my mom calls him her Emperor Amha Selassie, after Ethiopia's last emperor. The name sort of fits because Dad bears a striking resemblance to him. According to my father, that's one of his ancestors as we're supposedly descended from the Solomonic Dynasty of Ethiopia." Leila laughed. "To me, it's all just mythical history, but since those folktales make my parents happy and bring joy to their otherwise mundane lives, who am I to judge?"

"You're lucky and blessed to have two such loving parents," Sally Jo told her. "And like I said, one day, things will work out for you when the Lord will remember you all."

And now here she was, waiting to be received by Mr. Abner Randolph, the patriarch of the family. With a sigh she walked back to the door and raised her hand to ring the bell once again.

Suddenly the door opened, and she came face to face with a man who took her breath away. Leila considered herself to be a level-headed woman who wasn't easily swayed by looks. Yet coming face to face with Callum Randolph, for she knew him from the photos Sally Jo had showed her, made her go weak at the knees. In fact, none of the photos Sally Jo had showed her did him enough justice. The man was fine! He was tall and had striking blue eyes and thick black hair that fell to his shoulders, reminding her of one of the cowboys in the Hollywood movies. He smiled and she saw his evenly formed white teeth.

CALLUM THOUGHT he was dreaming when he opened the front door of his father's house and came face to face with one of the most beautiful women he'd ever seen in his entire life. One thought came to his mind.

"The Queen of Sheba!"

"What?" The breathless voice spoke and made him aware that he'd said the words out loud.

He blinked and smiled; then his eyes went to the single piece of luggage at her feet. The battered suitcase told a story of its own.

"Who are you and where did you come from?" He asked. Callum wasn't aware that any new interns were expected. Already the ten internship slots were filled, and his father hadn't mentioned adding any others to the number.

The internship program had been started by his father to help poor and needy students who needed practical hands-on experience as part of the courses they were doing in college. The internships were paid ones, and Mr. Randolph felt that by allowing students who deserved them to earn some money for the three to six months they were on the ranch, he was returning something to society for all the goodness he'd received from the Lord. The internship program was designed such that most of those who passed through it were assured of finding good positions with other ranches, farms or even agricultural organizations when they completed their studies. Callum knew that his father always went the extra mile for the interns, and because he had vast connections, he always got them placed and secured in good positions.

"Sir, I'm here as nanny for Mrs. Kelsey Randolph," Leila forced herself to focus on the business at hand. She wasn't here to ogle this man and make him run a mile in the opposite direction. She would follow Sally Jo's instructions and pray that things would eventually work out between them.

"Ah yes!" Callum nodded. "Quin, that's my big brother, mentioned something about that. We're actually expecting you. But why are you just standing out here in the cold?"

"I..." Leila opened her lips but then Fiona appeared behind Callum and slipped her hand in his arm.

"Here you are, my love," she spoke, and Leila felt as if someone had slapped her right on the face. Earlier on when Fiona had told her that she was here to be married to the father of her child Leila had thought that it was one of the cowboys on the ranch. Seeing her cozying up to Callum was a shock. How had this happened?

How was it that the one man she was hoping to be married to was the same person as Fiona's lover? Could it be true that her cousin was with child by this man?

"My name is Leila Solomon," she forced herself to speak when it became obvious that Fiona wasn't going to introduce her. It became clear that her cousin didn't want anyone to connect them or know that they were first cousins.

"Miss Solomon, welcome to Randolph Ranch. As I handle all matters for staff who work in any capacity on the ranch I'll need you to come to the office and fill out the necessary paperwork. I hope you've had all your Covid shots."

"Yes, Sir, including the boosters."

"Good girl," he smiled, and Leila felt her insides melting. "First, we have to get you settled in the hostel, for I believe that's where you'll be staying. After that I'll take you to meet my father and other brothers, especially Quin, since you'll be working directly for him and his wife." He gently but firmly removed Fiona's hand from his arm.

"Thank you, Sir," Leila made as if to pick up her battered suitcase, but Callum beat her to it. She was impressed at his gentlemanly act. Chivalry clearly wasn't dead on this ranch!

"Let me get that for you," he carried it as if it weighed nothing. "My name is Callum Randolph. I'm sure Mrs. Brian prepared your room since Quin must have told her that you were expected."

Leila entered the house but didn't have time to admire anything since she had to hurry after Callum. "We'll go through the kitchen so you can meet my sister-in-law, Willow, and Mrs. Brian, our housekeeper."

Leila wasn't surprised when Fiona tagged along. From the little she saw as she passed through the large living room, this was a very wealthy family. She'd thought that Fiona's parents' house back in Denver was the highest mark in affluence but now she realized that she was wrong. These people lived like royalty, yet Callum Randolph looked like he was a very down-to-earth man.

When they got to the kitchen, Leila was surprised to find that the housekeeper was an African American woman who looked so much at home in her surroundings. There was a younger woman with her, and the two seemed to share a close bond.

"Willow, Mrs. Brian," Callum called out. "Sorry to intrude on your busy time here but I wanted to introduce someone to you. This is Miss Leila Solomon..."

"Just Leila, please."

"Very well then. This is Leila." Callum gave her a smile that made her face warm up. She noticed that Fiona was giving her an angry look but decided to ignore her cousin for the moment.

"Leila, meet my sister-in-law, Willow, and Mrs. Brian, my second mother."

"It's a pleasure to meet you both," she wondered why the two women exchanged a swift look. "Your kitchen is beautiful."

Willow smiled at her, "Welcome to Randolph Ranch, and we hope you'll have a wonderful time here as one of our interns."

"She's just a nanny," Fiona snapped and all eyes turned to her. "I mean, I heard her telling Callum that she's here to take care of Quin and Kelsey's baby."

"Aah!" Mrs. Brian nodded. "You could do with some feeding, dear girl," she smiled at Leila. "Fiona, why don't you show Leila to the room close to the foyer in the hostel. That's the only empty one and though it's smaller than all the others I hope you'll be comfortable in there."

"Thank you, Mrs. Brian."

"Once you're done, please bring Leila back so I can begin putting some meat on those bones. She could do with a snack before lunch time."

"Let's go," Fiona said ungraciously. Leila knew that she was angry at being sent like an errand girl.

"Thank you so much," Leila said as she picked up her suitcase. Callum shook his head and took it back from her.

"Let me take you to the foyer, even if I'm not allowed to cross the threshold of the women's hostel."

548

DARK LEGACY

*C*allum noticed that everyone had their eyes on him and Leila. He could feel their breath-held gazes, and the silence made him slightly uneasy. He could sense the tension in Leila as well, though her focus was on the baby in her arms.

He'd found Leila and his nephew in the parlor, which his father had converted into a day nursery for Little Abner. Since the child and his nanny were supposed to spend most of the day at the main ranch house, Abner had seen fit to prepare a place for them.

Callum's heart had skipped with happiness when he found Leila alone with his nephew. They'd been joking and standing close to each other with the baby between them when Quin, Waylen and Maynard walked in.

"Please excuse me," Leila said when the tension became too much for her to handle. She grabbed Little Abner's carrier basket and fled to the kitchen, where she found Mrs. Brian and Willow arm deep in flour as they mixed up some dough.

"Do you need any help?" She asked as she placed her charge in his carrier. He was dozing off and made no protest.

"You have your hands full with that little lad," Mrs. Brian came over and tickled the baby's chin, leaving a slight smudge of flour. "Why don't you sit down and watch us as we work?" She used the edge of her apron to wipe the smudge off the baby's chin. "He's so adorable and it's clear that you're doing a good job with him."

"Thank you," Leila said, relieved to be away from Callum and his brothers. The man had caught her unawares as she played with the baby and she found that she couldn't resist him. He was good company and had just started telling her about his family when his brothers had walked in.

Back in the parlor Callum was still under immense scrutiny from his brothers.

"Little Bro, what game are you playing at?" Waylen asked him. "We're still trying to sort out this whole Fiona issue, and here you are already making bull's eyes at Abner's nanny. What's wrong with you? It's a dangerous game you're playing, and you need to stop before things get out of hand."

"We weren't doing anything wrong," Callum protested. "Leila is a nice person, and besides, you all know that I love spending time with the first and only nephew I have at this moment. I'd just started telling her a little about the family when you walked in, that's all."

"You need to be very careful," Quin warned. "Fiona has her hooks in you and with all this mess that's going on around you, the last thing you need is two women getting into any kind of altercation. You really don't want to ruffle any female feathers here."

Callum sighed. The whole Fiona Jordan issue felt like a huge albatross around his neck. With each passing day he got more convinced of his innocence, but Fiona was still insisting that he was responsible for her condition. Yet she was still adamant about having DNA tests done.

"I just wish this whole issue would be over and done with; then I can move on with my life," Callum told his brothers.

Maynard's eyes narrowed, "You seem to like this new girl."

Callum smiled sheepishly, "The very first time I set my eyes on her three days ago when she'd just arrived, I actually called her the Queen of Sheba to her face."

His brothers burst into laughter as his face turned red. He couldn't believe that they were standing around chatting about romance, when just months ago they'd all been adamant that true love didn't exist. Yet his four brothers were now married to wonderful women who they referred to as the loves of their lives.

"This dude is toast," Maynard said. "We thought you were the last man standing and not about to take a nosedive into the world of romance. Weren't you the one who teased me mercilessly when I buckled under the pressure of Cece's adorable eyes? It gladdens my heart to know that you're just a mortal like the rest of us."

"The heart wants what the heart wants," Callum defended himself. "But let's keep it all on the low until we can solve this Fiona mystery. The last thing I want is any kind of trouble, especially if it will affect Leila." Then his eyes narrowed thoughtfully, "Is it just me, or do Fiona and Leila bear a striking resemblance to each other? They could easily pass for sisters or even twins."

His brothers all nodded, but it was Quin who spoke up. "That's quite a relief because I thought I was the only one who'd noticed the similarities in their looks and even the way they carry themselves around. I actually thought I was seeing things."

"Do you think there's any chance that they could be related?" Waylen asked. "That would be very odd, since I haven't seen them acting like they even know or like each other."

Callum shook his head, "I doubt that they are related. Or don't you think they would have mentioned that fact to us?"

"You're right," Maynard said. "I guess it's just a case of people looking alike even if they aren't related at all. Someone said that each one of us has a look-alike somewhere out there in the world. That might be the case with these two."

But Callum was troubled. It was true that Fiona and Leila looked so much alike, yet he detested the former and was deeply attracted to the latter. What was happening to him? Is that what they call falling in love, he wondered.

Leila had been here for less than a week but he found himself thinking about her all the time. What was her story? She looked like a very intelligent woman, and her beauty took his breath away. Her caramel complexion was flawless, and even without any make up on, she was still very stunning.

"Just keep your nose out of trouble until we've sorted this whole issue of Fiona out," Waylen advised his younger brother. "The last thing we want is for there to be any bad blood between the two women. We wouldn't want what happened between Cece and Doris to rear its ugly head again."

Callum nodded. His brother Maynard had married Celine Bourne, a once-rising model whose career had been cut short by a jealous rival. Though it later turned out that Cece had just been in the wrong place at the wrong time, for her attacker had intended to harm someone else. The woman had sprayed Cece with acid, and for three years she'd hidden herself away from the world.

But then she came to Randolph Ranch to find healing at the Restorative Center and discovered that Maynard was the founder of the program. They'd met three years before, just about a month before the ugly incident, and spent many hours together at LaGuardia Airport when their planes were grounded due to adverse weather conditions. After the unfortunate incident, Cece had refused to continue corresponding with Maynard, and for three years they stayed apart.

But as soon as they met again, their love was rekindled. Because of the scars she'd sustained and lack of money for proper facial reconstructive surgery, Cece had to use very expensive make up to cover up the flaws. But then another intern, Doris Keller, who'd had her eye on Maynard got jealous and decided to humiliate Cece. She stole her makeup kit and hid it. It was Mrs. Brian who'd conducted a search of all the women's rooms in the hostel and found the missing item in Doris's room. What made matters worse was that Doris had sent text messages to both Maynard and Cece after uncovering the link to the website that had the information and photos of the whole tragedy.

Unfortunately for her, the tables had turned and she lost her internship position. Cece and Maynard got married and the former was still recuperating from the surgery she'd had after their wedding. Though she was once again the flawlessly beautiful Miss Celine Bourne, she'd requested the doctor who performed her surgery to leave one little scar as a reminder of how life could be so feeble and fickle.

"I promise that I'll be very careful," Callum said. "We don't need any kind of trouble right now."

"Good," Quin said.

LEILA WAS CHATTING with Willow and Mrs. Brian when Fiona entered the kitchen. She had a glass of orange juice in her hand.

"What's going on here?" She demanded, narrowing her eyes at Leila. "I asked you to bring me some cookies and was waiting for them in the parlor but you didn't show up. Then I find you sitting here and chatting your head off like you don't have anything to do."

Willow cleared her throat, "Excuse me, Fiona. Leila isn't your handmaid. You have legs to come to the kitchen and get whatever it is you need. Besides, as you can see, she's fully occupied with watching my nephew. It's not wrong for a worker to take a break from time to time and especially when it comes to taking care of a little baby."

Fiona's lips tightened and she took a deep breath. "You know that I shouldn't be stressed by anything because of my condition. That's the reason I asked Leila to get me something to chew on since my appetite has been very poor lately."

Leila felt ashamed at the way her cousin was behaving as if she was the most important person in this household. She didn't want any trouble from Fiona, who wouldn't hesitate to humiliate her in public.

"I'm sorry," she found herself apologizing and earned herself odd looks from Willow and Mrs. Brian. The two then chose to ignore Fiona and carried on with their chatting.

Fiona stood there with clenched fists, glaring at Leila.

"I need to talk to you," she hissed and Leila nodded.

"Willow, would you please keep an eye on Little Abner," Leila rose from her seat at the kitchen table. "He's sleeping and won't wake up for a while."

"It's even a wonder that the child can sleep at all," Fiona curled her lip in disdain. "Do its parents know that you carry it everywhere like a piece of luggage? I don't think they'll be happy with you when they find out that you're failing at your duties."

"Fiona, that's enough!" Mrs. Brian stopped whatever she was doing and turned to Fiona. "First of all, that child is he and not it. Stop referring to my grandson as if he's an object and not a person. Secondly, that boy is in safe hands, and as you can see, he's secure in his carrier and sleeping very peacefully. Why would you speak to Leila as if she doesn't know what she's doing?"

Fiona pasted on a false smile, "I'm sorry Mrs. Brian. I didn't mean to sound like I was criticizing Leila in any way. It's just that she needs to know that this child is very delicate and shouldn't be handled roughly. After all, she'll be taking care of my own child when he or she is born. I'd hate for her to lose her position because of being careless."

Willow gave Fiona a tight smile, "Your concerns have been duly noted and we'll do our very best to take good care of Little Abner and your child in future."

"Oh Willow," Fiona laughed. "I didn't mean that you should do Leila's work for her. I'll be leaving now," she said. "Leila, come with me."

"Very well."

Fiona walked out through the back door and Leila followed, wondering what her cousin was up to now.

"What was that in there?" Fiona turned on Leila. "You were making quite a spectacle of yourself and embarrassing everyone. Have you no shame? Don't you know your place anymore?"

"I'm sorry," Leila had long ago discovered that arguing with Fiona was a waste of time and energy and she didn't have any of that right now. It was cold and she wanted to return to the kitchen where it was warm, and to be with Little Abner.

"Listen, you better be careful because one phone call to my dad, and yours will be without a job. You know how desperate your father is to retain his job in my father's firm. You know what will happen should your father lose his job. Your mother will suffer, and they'll probably starve to death."

Leila sucked in her breath and decided to overlook all her cousin's insults. "It won't happen again."

"Make sure that you don't go around forcing yourself to be a part of this family. You're not of their class and it would be a shame for them to consider you as an opportunist."

Leila blinked back her tears. "I need to check on Little Abner," she said, turning to walk away.

"Don't you dare walk away from me."

"I have nothing more to say to you," Leila said and walked away. Leaving her cousin staring at her in disbelief.

LEILA WAS DOZING on the chaise longue beside Little Abner's cot in the parlor when she felt a presence hovering above her. Her eyes flew open, and she saw Callum staring down at her.

"I'm sorry," she sat up quickly and wiped her mouth, praying that she hadn't been drooling.

"You looked so peaceful lying there that I was loath to disturb you."

"Did you need something?"

Callum shook his head. How could he explain to Leila that he loved being around her? But he also needed to be cautious of Fiona finding out that he really liked Leila.

"I see that little man is asleep. I was hoping he was awake so I could play with him."

"You really like children, don't you?"

Callum nodded. "We all do. You should have seen us waiting for Kelsey and Quin's son to arrive. This little dude has brought so much joy to the family and I always find myself just wanting to be around him. I envy Kelsey and Quin."

"You'll soon have your own little one," Leila said softly.

"Well, don't you think that I ought to find myself a wife first?" He winked at her. "Babies can only come into the world where there's a man and his wife."

Leila frowned slightly. Callum didn't behave as if he were the father of Fiona's baby. She really wished to know where and when they'd met because to her knowledge, Fiona had never been to Texas. Or maybe Callum had visited Denver and that's how they'd met.

"What about you?"

"What are you asking me about?"

"Do you like children?" Callum asked Leila.

"Of course, they're such darlings and a great blessing to a family. Back at home I used to babysit my neighbors' children and loved the experience. There's so much we can learn from these little ones," Leila reached forward and straightened the blanket that was covering her charge.

Callum couldn't help noticing that Leila's fingers were long and slender and very gentle when they handled his nephew. This woman would make a wonderful mother someday, and he found himself envying the man who would marry her. In contrast, Fiona looked like she would be a hands-off mother, only appearing to show off her baby to whoever cared to watch. She'd even asked him if she could make a blog of the journey of their baby right from the womb but he'd completely distanced himself from the whole process. Of course, Fiona had been really angry but he refused to give in.

Just to make sure she didn't post anything inflammatory on her social media platforms, he'd cornered her into signing a Non-Disclosure Agreement that their lives and the pregnancy would remain secret until they got married. He knew that he wasn't ever going to marry Fiona, but he needed to keep her appeased while he and his brothers carried out their investigations.

What made Callum very cautious was the fact that he had no idea what had happened that night. Just in case he'd gotten careless and done the unthinkable, he was playing it safe so as not to alienate Fiona.

"Did you need something?" Leila's voice broke through his thoughts. "I need to change Abner, then take him to the kitchen for some petting time with Mrs. Brian and later on with your father." She rose to her feet to gather the baby into her arms. He was now awake, and she carried him to the changing table.

"Please let me do that," Callum begged and Leila handed the baby over to him. As she watched him, he carefully and skillfully changed the baby's diaper, disposed of it correctly in the bin and then dressed him in his warm rompers.

"There, see what I can do?" He grinned at her.

"You're really good at doing that," Leila envied the woman who would be Callum's wife and felt slightly distressed that it would probably be Fiona.

"We all got a crash course from Kelsey, including dad, even though he'd done it before with all of us. That woman can be demanding and she made us learn all the basics of child care."

"Which is really good for you because when your own baby comes it will be easy."

"When I find the right mother for my children," Callum muttered. "Come," he spoke up. "Let me walk the two of you to the kitchen."

"Thank you," Leila picked up Little Abner's hand carrier and followed Callum who was talking gibberish to the baby. Little Abner cooed back as if he could understand whatever his uncle was saying. They made such a cute pair, and she wished she could take a snapshot of them, but she didn't have her cellphone with her. She always left it in her room because she didn't need any distraction while taking care of her charge. In any case, it was only her parents she spoke to, and that happened in the evenings when she retired to her room.

Her mother was really happy that she loved her job and even though it had taken quite some convincing for them to allow her to come, now they saw that it was a good thing. First, Leila sounded really happy and also the money she sent home was much appreciated. She hadn't told her parents the real reason she was here because Sally Jo had forbade her from doing so. Her parents would never have allowed her to come if they knew she was searching for a husband without necessarily being in love with him.

But now Fiona was standing in her path to happiness. What was she going to do? Perhaps she should let Sally Jo know what was going on. Callum was clearly off limits, so the agency director would probably need to find her another husband. Yet her heart was set on Callum and she couldn't imagine leaving and never seeing him again.

UGLY CLOUDS

"*I* came here prepared to be a bride right from the start," Fiona's words were icy, and the smile on her lips wasn't a happy one either. "Much as I'm tempted to say something nasty right now, I'll simply tell you that my father is one of the best lawyers in this country. I think you've all heard of Ezekiel Jordan, Esq. If you don't do right by me, you should be ready for a lawsuit of such magnitude that you'll be forced to sell everything you've ever owned to meet the settlement required. Excuse me," she tossed her head back and walked out of Callum's office.

Callum wasn't bothered much by the threat of a lawsuit for he was sure he wasn't responsible for the baby Fiona was carrying. But he also didn't want the kind of scandal that might follow such a lawsuit. The media was a circus, as his father liked to say. Sensational news is what sold and by the time the truth was unraveled, innocent parties have had their reputations sullied and sometimes completely ruined.

Fiona was a woman scorned, and she was reacting in this way because all her efforts to get closer to him were being thwarted on every side. She'd tried to gain access to his bedroom on the pretext of helping with cleaning, but Mrs. Brian had put paid to her plans.

"All my boys are well trained," she'd told a fuming Fiona. "They all clean up their own rooms and have done so for a very long time now. I don't see why you want to do it for Callum."

And then just this morning, Fiona had followed Callum to his office to demand his attention.

"Fiona, I'm rather busy at the moment. Christmas is coming up in a few weeks' time and I need to prepare the staff bonuses and schedule holidays, so I don't have any time to spare," he'd told her. Of course, she'd tried to use her tears to manipulate him, but he refused to give in.

"How are we supposed to bond and get close to each other when you won't even spend time with me?" she'd whined. "We have to think about getting closer for the sake of our baby. Your father won't let us share a room even though we're practically engaged and I need you to give me some of your time. We need to start thinking about names and even buying things for the baby."

"Fiona," he'd held onto his patience as much as he could. The thought of being forced to accept a pregnancy that he couldn't be sure was his left a bad taste in his mouth. It wasn't that he was averse to raising another man's child but it was the way in which Fiona was handling this whole issue. "This is neither the place nor the time for such."

And that's when she'd tossed the threat at him. The more Fiona insisted on getting closer to him, the more convinced Callum was that he was innocent of her accusations. She'd even insisted on them having a counseling session with the pastor, and that was scheduled to take place this evening.

Callum wasn't looking forward to the session, and he wished something could come up that would give him an excuse not to attend.

What bothered him a lot was that Fiona seemed to have it in for Leila. Even Willow, who was usually very mild tempered had complained about it to her husband, who in turn had spoken to Callum about it. According to Willow, any time anyone mentioned Leila's name within Fiona's hearing, she had something derisive to say.

"What's going on with these two?" Callum asked himself. Even if they insisted that they didn't know each other from before their arrival at the ranch, he was sure that they were hiding something.

"Leila?"

"Yes, Kelsey?"

"My father-in-law says he'd like to take Abner to town for some shopping."

"Abner is still too small to be exposed to so much cold," Leila said. "It's getting colder with each passing day. I even wanted to suggest that for now we should stay at home and not have to go to the ranch house every day."

Kelsey shook her head, "That is something I can't change, Leila. Please bear with me. My father-in-law must see his namesake every single day," Kelsey had just finished nursing her son and placed him on her shoulder, gently rubbing his back to burp him. "I also don't like exposing my son to the cold, but Quin says we just have to make sure he's warmly dressed. Since you have a car at your disposal, the exposure to the outside is minimal in any case."

Leila didn't want to argue with her employer. In truth, the reason she wanted to avoid the ranch house was because of Callum and Fiona. Seeing them together and hearing her cousin speaking about their upcoming wedding was breaking her heart.

Kelsey misunderstood her silence, "Look, I'll try to suggest to Dad that he can always come to our house. We could even have it so that you don't have to drive to the ranch house every single day, but on alternate ones."

"That could work," Leila said. She looked around at the neatly arranged nursery. She loved working for Kelsey who was such a considerate employer. She never put any undue pressure on

Leila, and that made her enjoy her job. Little Abner was also such an adorable little boy.

As long as he was dry, warm, and fed, all he did was sleep. He was growing heavier with each passing day and Kelsey said it was because he was well fed. Whenever she couldn't nurse him, Leila would use the milk she'd expressed.

"My man here is growing so big," Kelsey said. "You've been very good for him, Leila," she sighed. "I live in fear each day."

"Why?"

"You're probably thinking about going home for Christmas. What will I do without you? How will I cope?"

Leila laughed, "Kelsey, I only just got here, and I won't be taking leave any time soon. Home is all the way in Denver and I haven't saved any money for a return ticket. Please don't worry about me, for I'm going nowhere."

"It's just three weeks to Christmas Day and we're yet to plan anything for the holidays. We've all been very busy, and no one is even thinking about decorating Dad's house, let alone their own. Ah well, Willow mentioned that Bella and Maria were thinking of finding a Christmas tree for their house, but then they decided that it would look better in dad's house. So at some point, someone is going to have to go into the woods and get a good, tall tree. Callum is the only one living at home now, so Dad insisted that we should all spend Christmas Day together at his place. But no one has even thought about finding decorations or even a Christmas tree. Maybe we should get him to look for the Christmas tree. Out here there's such a huge difference from how things were back at my home in Denver. By the first of December, the neighborhood was already glowing with various decorations. I miss that."

Leila looked at Kelsey in surprise, "Are you telling me that you're originally from Denver?"

"Yes, I am. What about you?"

"Denver born and bred," Leila held both hands up. "The coldest city in the world, according to me, and I'm glad that this year I'll get to experience Christmas away from all that snow."

The two women exchanged a smile.

"It's really interesting," Kelsey said, then looked thoughtfully at Leila. "Perchance, would you be knowing a woman called Sally Jo?" Leila simply smiled. "Your smile says it all. And from what I see, you and Callum need to be given time to find each other."

"Don't say that," Leila felt her face warming up. "I don't want any trouble from my co...er, from Fiona," she quickly corrected herself, hoping that Kelsey hadn't noticed the near slip of tongue. "I understand that she and Callum will soon be getting married."

Kelsey's lips tightened, "Well, that's yet to be determined," was all she said on the issue.

"You don't want to be late for work," Leila reminded her mistress. "Is Abner sleeping yet?"

"He just burped a second time and is now dozing off. Here, have him so I can get ready for work."

Leila took the baby from his mother and held him close. He smelled of powder and baby sweetness and she felt such deep longing in her heart. All her life she'd dreamed of finding a good husband and having her own little ones. But with the way things were, it seemed as if her desires would remain just as dreams because she needed to be practical about the man she would eventually marry. A rich one who could take care of them—and love had to take a back seat.

Finding Sally Jo's website had been an answer to her prayers. Hitch Your Wagon Romance Agency prided itself on finding romance for cowboys and cowgirls who were determined to experience true love the godly and Biblical way. At the time, all Leila had been thinking about was finding a wealthy man who would take care of them, and especially her mother's hospital bills. It hadn't mattered to her if the man would fall in love with her or not; as long as he provided well for them, she was prepared to be a good wife to him.

But the moment Sally Jo had introduced her to Callum Randolph's profile, more than anything she'd wanted him to be the man for her.

Yet now Fiona was here with her claims, and Leila wondered how the two had even met and shared the intimacy that had resulted in her cousin being with child. But there was nothing she could do because she was worried about what Fiona might do to her father. If her cousin got her father fired from his job, her mother would suffer because purchasing drugs would be next to impossible for her father. As it was, the last two paychecks she'd received since coming to work for Kelsey had all gone to her father so he could make her mother's life comfortable. At least, here she had free room and board and so wasn't expected to spend any of her money. She'd learned to avoid her peers whenever they went into town to shop for anything they needed. Of course, Fiona also received an allowance from Mr. Randolph, and whenever she got anything new, she would flaunt it in Leila's face, knowing full well that the latter couldn't afford to spend any of her money.

"Leila, are you all right?" Kelsey's voice brought her back to the present. "Abner is sleeping. Why don't you lay him in his cot, then prepare yourself to go to the ranch?"

"Yes, Ma'am," Leila put the baby down, unaware that her employer was watching her thoughtfully.

Two hours after Kelsey's departure, Leila had finished cleaning and tidying up the room. While that wasn't part of her duties, she felt that helping her kind mistress didn't hurt at all. She ensured that Abner was well covered, then secured him in the baby seat at the back of the Toyota Camry that had been put at her disposal.

Fiona had fumed when she'd found out that Leila had an almost brand-new car at her disposal. What's more, Kelsey had made it very clear that no one else was to use the vehicle save for Leila, so Fiona couldn't even borrow it. That was a small victory for Leila, for she was used to her cousin's bullying. It was as if Fiona felt that Leila didn't deserve any good thing in life.

Mr. Randolph was waiting for her as she pulled up at the front of the main ranch house. He ran down the steps, opened the back door and quickly grabbed his grandson. "Bring his paraphernalia in," he said over his shoulder as he hurried into the house where it was warm.

Because it was very cold outside, Mr. Randolph cancelled the trip to town. "I wouldn't want my little grandson to freeze," he said as he held the sleeping child close to his chest. Leila could see the love in the man's expression and in the way he handled her charge. "Why don't you leave him with me while you go and find out if Mrs. Brian needs you to help her with anything."

"Thank you, Sir," Leila left her charge with his grandfather and walked to the kitchen, passing through the living room. Someone had lit the fire in the large grate and the room was very homey and warm. And the sliding partitions had been pushed back so the dining area and kitchen were open.

It was a busy hive of activity with all four Randolph wives and Mrs. Brian moving around. She'd expected that her own mistress would be in the garage working on cars as usual.

"You all seem to be very busy," Leila smiled at all the women, who acknowledged her. "What's going on here?"

Willow ran toward her with an apron in her hands and wrapped it around Leila's waist.

"We've decided to start preparing for Christmas, and Mrs. Brian has put us all to work. We have cookies and cakes to deliver to four children's orphanages, and we're late as it is."

"So dear girl, pick up a ladle or wooden spoon and hop to it," Mrs. Brian said. "Less of a hen coop in here and more of being busy, girls."

Leila couldn't believe that these four, no, five beautiful women had embraced her into their circle. She remembered what Sally Jo had told her, that it would do her good to make friends with Callum's sisters-in-law.

There was much laughter and teasing until Fiona walked into the kitchen about an hour later. She stood at the doorway, and it was a while before anyone noticed her. As soon as she realized that her presence had been noticed she turned and walked away. Leila's heart sank. From the expression on Fiona's face, she knew she would be getting an earful later.

"HAVE YOU BEEN AVOIDING ME?" Callum caught up with Leila as she was walking to the garage two days later. Kelsey was waiting for her to bring Little Abner so he could nurse.

"I don't know what you're talking about," she murmured as she tried to hurry away. Fiona was somewhere around and Leila wanted to avoid any kind of trouble from her today. The past two days had been very trying with Fiona finding any little excuse to insult her, but she was careful to do it when they were alone.

But Callum was tired of missing the woman he now acknowledged himself to be in love with.

"Here, let me have the little one," he said. Usually Leila walked through the house to get to the living room and so avoid much exposure to the outside. But the sun had decided to put in a rare appearance today, and she'd felt that her charge could benefit from its soft rays.

When Callum reached for the baby, she gave him up without a murmur. It was a relief, for he was getting heavier with each passing day, yet all he fed on was his mother's milk.

"Now you have no choice but to walk with me," Callum said as he held the baby securely in one hand and took Leila's with the free one. He drew her close and she sighed inwardly.

It felt good being held close to the man whose presence made her heart beat like she was sprinting one hundred meters in the Olympics.

"You're so beautiful and your hands are very soft," he said as he slowed his pace. It was as if he didn't want them to get to their destination too fast.

"Thank you," she responded shyly. "We have to get Abner to his mother before he begins howling," she said.

"You're right, and my dear big sister will have my head on a platter if she hears her precious bundle of joy making as much as a squeak."

Kelsey was waiting in the small office she used when nursing her son and smiled when she saw Callum and Leila arriving together.

"I was wondering whatever was keeping Leila because she's always very prompt. Now I know," she teased as she received her son. "Run along both of you, and Callum?"

"Yes, Sister?"

"Show Leila that beautiful rose garden. With the sun gracing us with its presence today it's a bright day outside. I need to spend about an hour with my second best dude," she kissed her son's forehead. "And how are you, my darling?" She was already lost in loving her son and Callum held out his hand.

"Is this a private party or can anyone join in?" Quin walked into the office. "I can see that it's lunchtime for our son," he said, reaching down to plant a kiss on his wife's forehead, then his son's.

"Good to see you, my love," Kelsey reached up a hand and touched her husband's cheek. Then she turned to Callum, and he knew that the two of them wanted what they called their private family time. "Go and show Leila the rose garden. Hurry along now!"

"Yes, your majesty," Callum gave a mock bow.

"I'll get you for this later. Now go," Kelsey ordered, then turned back to her husband.

"You heard the woman," Callum was laughing as he led Leila out of the garage. "Come see my mom's rose garden."

Leila found herself being taken to the garden she'd always admired from afar. She shivered, and Callum wrapped one arm around her shoulder, drawing her closer to him.

"Don't worry, I won't keep you out here for long because it's lunch time and you need to eat. But come and see this," he guided her into the garden with a gentle hand. "This rose garden was planted over fifteen years ago. I was only seven at the time and none of us knew that our mom would be dead a year later."

"I'm sorry for your loss," Leila said. She couldn't imagine losing her mother even at this age. It must have been terrible for Callum and his brothers to lose their mother when they were still very young.

"At the time, I didn't even know what was going on. My mom died on Christmas Day, exactly a year after she'd planted this rose garden." Leila could hear the pain in his voice. "She said it was her love gift to us, and so it is," he plucked a red rose and tucked it in her hair. "I love your hair. Is it natural?" She nodded. He touched it and breathed deeply. "A beautiful rose for a gorgeous woman."

"Please don't say that," Leila moved away from him. "I don't want any trouble."

Callum frowned slightly, "What are you talking about? We're only enjoying the roses in my mother's garden."

"Fiona is carrying your child and she's here to be married to you. The last thing I want is strife of any kind that will affect my work." She took the flower out of her hair. "I need to return right now because, if someone sees us here, they might get the wrong impression. Kelsey will be waiting for me." She placed the rose in his hand.

"Leila, wait..." Callum called out as Leila fled from the garden. He sighed and looked down at the flower in his hand. He plucked the petals one by one until only the stigma was left. Then he cast it into one of the bushes, wiped his hands on his shirt and walked out of the garden.

He was surprised when he immediately bumped into Fiona on his way back to the house. From the furious look on her face it was clear that she'd seen Leila leaving the garden and deduced that they'd been together. Her words confirmed this.

"What were you doing in the garden with that woman?" She demanded.

"Fiona, please, not now," he tried to pass her, but she grabbed his arm.

"You claim not to have time for me but keep chasing that nanny all over the place. She's just a mere servant, and I'm the woman carrying your child. Don't you care about this child at all?"

"Let's not talk about this right now. There's somewhere else I need to be."

"You didn't even honor the appointment I made for us with the pastor. I've asked him to come to the house this evening. Make sure you're there," she said and flounced off.

Leila was in the parlor with Little Abner when Fiona charged in.

"What's wrong with you, Leila? Can't you mind your own business? Why do you want to ruin my life? Are you so detestable that you would deny me of my chance at happiness?"

"What did I do now?" Leila was puzzled.

"I saw you throwing yourself at my man out there in the rose garden. How shameless can you be? Do you know what kind of trouble I could put you in?"

UNHAPPY ENCOUNTER

"*I* feel very sorry for you," the scornful smile touched Fiona's lips. "The absolute, truth is that a nonentity like you can never win the heart of a man like Callum Randolph, no matter how hard you try. He's too refined and classy and you only end up looking desperate and silly by running after him every chance you get. So if you know what's good for you, don't ever speak to him again, or I'll give you trouble that will last throughout all your generations. You know me, and you know what I'm capable of."

"I'm sorry."

"You really don't know what you're up against. Stay away from Callum, do you hear me?"

Leila didn't say a word because she didn't want to get into any further arguments with her cousin. Fiona walked out of the parlor, and Leila turned to the baby who, mercifully, was still asleep.

"I don't want any trouble," she murmured. "Why is this man determined to create trouble for me with my cousin? The last thing I want or need is to lose this job. I've clearly lost any hopes of winning Callum so this job is the only thing I have going for me. Now that Fiona has her clutches on Callum, I have to make sure that I don't lose my job. I just pray that Kelsey will let me work for her for a long time so I can help Papa pay for Mom's surgery."

The salary she was being paid was so much more than she'd ever earned before. She'd worked out how many months it would take her and her father to put down a deposit for her mom's surgery. In six months they would have raised over half of the amount needed, and then she would work hard to settle the balance within a year.

All she had to do was stay as far away from Callum Randolph as she could. Yes, he was the kind of man she'd dreamed of being with for her whole life, but Fiona's words brought her back to reality. Her cousin wasn't wrong. Class mattered in marriage. Money, they say, marries money. She was a nonentity and Callum Randolph, apart from being the son of a very wealthy man, was quite rich in his own right.

What had she even been thinking by imagining that she could win herself a wealthy cowboy while women like Fiona existed? No, her kind only made it in life by working for the wealthy.

CALLUM REALIZED THAT ONCE AGAIN, Leila was doing all she could to avoid him. And even when he managed to catch up with her, she did all she could to get away from him.

"Fiona," he sighed. "A real thorn in my flesh." Why had this woman come into his life? He'd tried all he could to see if he had any feelings for her but to no avail. The only emotions he felt toward her were either pity that she could be so desperate as to try and pin her condition on him, or anger that she was messing up his life. "Lord, please help me and show me what to do."

He'd avoided having a counseling session with the pastor because he didn't want to look like he was a bad person. He had no interest in Fiona at all, and he was tired of trying to pretend otherwise. Fiona was turning him into someone he didn't even know.

Something had to be done or he would go out of his mind. He knew that his family members were all backing him up but the longer Fiona stayed here at the ranch, the more credible her allegations seemed.

Callum prided himself on being a morally upright man, but now he could see the questioning looks on the faces of those around him, well, apart from the immediate members of his family. And the woman wasn't helping matters because she told anyone who cared to listen that she was expecting his child.

He strolled into the kitchen for a cup of tea and found Leila feeding his nephew.

"How is my little man?" He approached the table and sat down.

"Abner is all right," Leila said, feeling very uncomfortable that it was just the two of them alone in the kitchen. She wanted to ignore him, but her parents had taught her to always be courteous even in difficult situations.

"You've never told me anything about your life, Leila."

She shrugged as she went on feeding her charge his milk. He was half asleep but determined not to let a single drop pass him by, and she smiled at the contentment on his face as he enjoyed his meal. "That's because there's nothing to tell," she said. "Please just leave me alone because I don't want any trouble from your fiancée."

"My fiancée?" Callum scowled. "I wasn't aware that I've asked anyone to be my wife."

"Isn't it obvious that you'll end up with Fiona? I wouldn't want her to put my job in jeopardy if she catches you talking to me."

"Did she warn you to stay away from me?"

Leila didn't answer. Little Abner finished his bottle and she placed him on her shoulder to burp him.

"Please excuse me," she rose to her feet. "I need to get Abner home now, before it gets too cold."

"Let me drive you there."

"No," she said strongly. "I'd rather you didn't try to come close to me. In any case, Kelsey will soon be here, so we can drive to her home together. I'm going there to tidy things up in the nursery and prepare for tomorrow; then I'll be back later."

Once Leila had left, Callum sat at the table for a long time.

"You need to deal with this issue at hand before you can take any further step forward," Mrs. Brian came into the kitchen and joined Callum at the table. "When your Mama died, I got the chance to raise you boys, and you've all turned into fine young men. When a scandal such as is going on hits this family, it affects me too. I know my boys and what you can and can't do. I believe that you're innocent, but that young lady is trouble epitomized. Her kind only look out for themselves and I'm sure she's posting everything on the internet for the whole world to see, and she can cause a lot of damage to your reputation. I don't understand this generation at all."

"Mrs. Brian, I just want all this mess to end," Callum said. "Deep down in my heart I too know that I'm innocent, yet Fiona has incriminating photos of the two of us. My brothers think that the drink I was served that night was laced with something that caused me to lose consciousness and that's how I was taken advantage of. But considerable time has lapsed, and even if I went around searching for witnesses as to what happened that night, I don't think anyone would recall much and be able to provide any helpful information. Besides that, people shy away from such situations for fear of being implicated in crimes like these. I can't even remember who served me the drink save for the fact that it was a young man of average build and dark hair. Or it could have been sandy hair, I don't know. The place was crowded and people seemed to be coming and going all over the place. With the Covid restrictions being lifted, everyone was in a partying mood, so the place was packed. And the description of the waiter that comes into mind is that of nearly half of America's male population. I can't even recall if I saw his face or not."

"You sound as if you're giving up."

"Short of a DNA test proving the paternity of Fiona's child, there's really nothing I can do at this time. Dad and Waylen are trying to get Fiona to agree to the procedure being done right away but she's refused. If we try to force her it won't look good at all."

"You may feel like you're caught between the devil and the deep blue sea, but one thing I know is this: the truth always wins in the end. Don't give up on yourself."

Callum rose to his feet. "I have bonuses to prepare in the office. Thank you for the time and I always feel so strengthened whenever we have these chats, Mrs. Brian. Please tell Dad that I won't be in for dinner tonight."

"Really? A hot date or something in the works?"

Callum laughed, "Not really, I'm going to Quin's place for dinner."

"Huh!" Mrs. Brian grinned as she slapped the table with her palm. "Are you sure dinner is all that's taking you to your brother's place tonight?"

"I don't know what you mean," he said with an answering grin and left the kitchen whistling cheerfully.

LEILA HAD FINISHED TIDYING up Abner's nursery when she heard Callum's voice in the living room.

"You're just in time to join us for dinner," she heard Kelsey say. "I already asked Leila to stay. You can then drive her back to the hostel when we're done. I left my car in the garage because it had some issues, so she drove me here. I'll use her car tomorrow morning so you can drive her home tonight."

Though dinner was a lively affair as Callum, Quin and Kelsey chatted about everything, Leila kept her head down and listened in silence, smiling from time to time. Each moment she spent with Callum's family she felt such warmth that it made her yearn to have such an extended family.

What surprised her most about this family was that all the members were down to earth and treated all those around them with kindness and respect. She'd searched them on the internet and been stunned at how wealthy the Randolph family was. Yet one couldn't even tell because they fitted in with everyone.

"Leila are you done?" Callum was standing beside her chair and she blushed when she noticed the knowing looks Quin and his wife were giving them. "Since Kelsey and Quin were so kind as to prepare dinner for us, I think it's only fair that you and I do the dishes."

"Go on now," Kelsey urged and Leila rose to her feet, her face on fire.

"You don't have to be scared of me because I don't bite," Callum told her once they were in the kitchen.

"I'm not scared of you."

"Then why are you always so nervous around me, Leila? You know that I really like spending time with you."

"I know you love your nephew and being with him makes you so happy."

"There's that but I also like spending time alone with you."

PLAYING TO WIN

"*P*lease don't say such things," Leila begged. "It's not right. We can only be friends, and even then, from a distance."

Callum nodded, "If that's what you want, then I'll honor your wishes."

"Thank you."

The drive back to the main ranch house was done in silence. As soon as Callum stopped the car outside the hostel, Leila shot out and ran inside.

"Where are you coming from at this time?" She found Fiona waiting outside her room.

"I work for Kelsey remember? She asked me to help out with something at her house and it took long." She unlocked her door and hoped that Fiona wouldn't follow her inside. But her wish wasn't granted and she sighed as her cousin made herself comfortable on her bed. "It's late and I'd like to sleep because I have an early morning tomorrow."

"You need to watch how you speak to me, Leila. With just one phone call to my father your parents will sink into the abyss of poverty."

Leila bit back a harsh retort. She was tired and didn't want to get into any arguments with Fiona.

"And just so you know," her cousin held up her left hand on which was a beautiful ring. "Earlier today, Callum proposed, and I accepted. We'll be getting married in twenty-one days. Our wedding is right after Christmas Day. So if you ever had any stupid infatuation dreams for my man, give up already. You're not Callum's type and can never be. I think you would do well to find someone of your own class, like maybe one of those poor cowboys out there on the range. That's the kind of class you belong to."

Leila shook her head, "Why do you hate me so much and I've never done anything to you, Fiona? Wasn't it enough that you've gotten me fired from two jobs? Now you're here trying to stir up trouble for me again, yet I've done nothing wrong to you."

"I hate you because you just won't let things be. You keep trying to raise yourself to my class, but you don't belong there. Every time I see you around me, I get angry because if people find out that we're related they'll put me in the same class with you."

"Your father and mine are brothers, Fiona. Nothing can ever change that."

"And that's why I hate you being around me. Your father is just a lazy man who depends on my father for everything."

"Please don't disrespect my parents. I can take any other insults but that."

"What will you do?" Fiona rose to her feet. "Just be sure that as soon as Callum and I get married you're out of here. See this ring? It's time for you to start counting down and numbering your days on this ranch."

Though she was devastated inside, Leila forced herself to smile as if she didn't really care.

"Fiona, you may have that ring on your finger but any woman making wild claims as you are can make a man put a ring on her finger just to keep her quiet. However, the point you need to consider, dear cousin, is this: does that ring stand for true love or just necessity because of the child you're carrying?"

"How dare you talk to me like that?"

"Just please leave my room. I'm tired and need to sleep because I have to go to work early."

"That's all you'll ever be, a servant to the wealthy. Don't let your position go to your head because soon you'll be without it."

"Thank you, now leave my room so I won't have to push you out."

Two days later, Leila was feeding Little Abner in the kitchen when Mrs. Brian came in and told her that she was needed in the den.

It was quite odd because Mr. Randolph had never summoned her to his office before. Whenever he wanted to spend time with his grandson he would simply come to the parlor and then ask Leila to go and help out in the kitchen.

"Is anything the matter? Does Mr. Randolph want to spend time with his grandson? I was just finishing up with Abner's feeding; then I'll take him to his grandfather."

"No, leave the child with me."

That sounded even odder to Leila but she simply handed the child over to Mrs. Brian and made her way to the den. She knocked and was bid to enter. Her heart sank when the first person her eyes lighted on was Fiona. And she had a smug, triumphant look in her eyes.

"Miss Solomon, please come in," Mr. Randolph was seated behind his large desk. Waylen and Callum were also present.

"Thank you," she felt rather uncomfortable and had a premonition that something bad was about to happen.

Abner looked at the young woman seated before him and sighed inwardly. She looked frightened and he felt sorry for her, but this needed to be done, though it left a sour taste in his mouth.

"Miss Solomon?"

"Yes, Sir?"

"A serious allegation has been brought against you."

"What?" She wondered if the accusation had anything to do with Little Abner. As far as she knew, she was always very careful with the baby. "Sir, if it has to do with your grandson then you can ask Kelsey and she'll tell you that I take very good care of him. She's said so herself on many occasions."

Waylen cleared his throat. "We're not accusing you of any wrong doing, Leila. But a matter of concern has come up and we'd like to get to the bottom of things."

"Of course," she said, but her heart was in her mouth. What was she being accused of by Fiona now? She was sure all this had to do with Fiona because first, she was present, and besides, she looked like the cat that had licked the cream. It was no coincidence that her cousin was here in this room. She must have brought a charge against Leila.

"Miss Solomon, did something happen at Quin and Kelsey's house this morning when you drove over to pick my grandson up?"

Leila nodded. "Yes, Sir. Kelsey asked me if I'd been to her bedroom and taken anything from there. She seemed very upset, and I told her that the only time I ever enter her bedroom is when she's present. I only do that when I'm taking the baby to her for nursing or when she wants to hold him. The rest of the time I'm usually in the nursery with Little Abner, or in the kitchen cleaning his dishes."

"Was my son at home this morning?"

"Yes. He wanted to know why I hadn't come to the main house yesterday when Kelsey asked me to. So I told him that it was very cold and you can all attest to that. My car refused to start and I even called the garage and spoke to one of the mechanics there. He said he'd be by to fix the car as soon as possible but it was noon before he showed up. It took him nearly four hours before he was able to get my car to start. I kept calling Kelsey to update her on whatever was going on and got through in the morning. But in the afternoon when I tried to call her again, she didn't pick up any of my calls. The other mechanic who picked up told me that she'd gone to town to purchase some supplies but had left her phone behind."

"Was that all that happened?"

"Yes, Sir."

"Did anyone else come by the house, apart from the mechanic?"

Leila shook her head. "While he was repairing the car I was in the nursery with your grandson. When he was done, I drove to the house so you would have some time with your grandson, but you weren't there, and I quickly went back home before Kelsey got there. She likes to find her son warm and ready for her when she gets home. Is there a problem?"

Mr. Randolph sighed, "I'm afraid so. Yesterday after you left their house in the evening, Kelsey and Quin realized that a huge sum of money was missing from one of the drawers in their bedroom."

Leila closed her eyes and her heart sank. She knew what was coming next. With Fiona present she knew that she was in trouble. Her cousin had found a way of getting her into serious trouble once again.

"Am I being accused of taking the money?" She didn't even look in Callum's direction for fear of the accusation she would see in his eyes.

"No one is accusing you of anything," Waylen said. "But Fiona here gave us some disturbing information. She says that she saw you with a substantial amount of money last night. Or rather, she saw quite some amount in the drawer of your room."

"What?"

"Yes, I saw you putting money in one of the bedside drawers, and I know you don't have such money with you. You told me that you always send all the money you get from Kelsey to your parents. So how is it that you have such a huge amount?"

"Why are you lying against me?"

Fiona sneered, "I knew that you were too good to be trusted, always pretending to be very holy. Mr. Randolph, I can show you where the money is."

Leila shook her head sadly, "You're doing it again. I'm innocent but you're determined to make me be falsely accused."

"I told Mrs. Brian that you're not to be trusted, but she didn't believe me. I saw you hiding the money in your drawer, yet here you are denying it."

"The only thing to do is send someone to Miss Solomon's room," Mr. Randolph picked up his intercom and gave instructions to whoever was on the other side. After about ten minutes Mrs. Brian and Willow entered the den.

"I found this in Leila's drawer just like Fiona said," the older woman placed the bundle of money on the table. "It was right where Fiona said it would be, Sir."

Callum was shocked and he turned to Leila. "What's going on?"

"I don't know," Leila shook her head. "But I've never seen that money before."

"I just know that Leila took that money," Fiona was saying when Callum walked into the kitchen. "The evidence was there for everyone to see."

"Miss Fiona," Callum's voice was hard. "Listen to me and be very attentive," the other three interns looked like they wanted to flee but one look from Callum and they all stayed put. "You're not supposed to be discussing that matter because it's still under investigation. I won't have you going around spoiling someone's name when all you have are allegations."

"But I saw her...."

"Did I allow you to speak?" He gave her a cold look and she shrank. "I won't tell you this again. There will be trouble if I catch you talking about such serious matters to everyone." He looked at the interns. "I believe you all have places where you need to be."

"Yes, Sir," they chorused.

"Then I'll advise you to get there before you land yourselves in trouble."

The interns fled from the kitchen, and Callum walked to the coffeemaker to pour himself a cup.

"You didn't have to humiliate and embarrass me in front of those girls. Now they'll never respect me, even when I become the mistress of this place," Fiona fumed.

Callum laughed shortly, "Don't count your chicks before they hatch, Miss Jordan. You may have been used to treating people with disdain where you came from, but out here we do things differently. We treat everyone as being innocent until satisfactory evidence of their wrongdoings is found. Before that, we don't go around spreading lies and allegations that can't be proved."

"Why are you so determined to believe that Leila is innocent, yet I saw her with my own two eyes?"

"That remains to be seen."

"Are you now calling me a liar?" Fiona demanded. Callum merely shrugged as he took his coffee and sat down at the kitchen table. Mrs. Brian walked into the kitchen. "Mrs. Brian, why don't you tell Callum exactly where you found the missing money?"

"I'm just surprised at the way you're determined to make Leila look really bad," Callum said. "As I said, I won't have you talking about a matter that is still under investigation. In fact what I need to do is get a fingerprints expert to come and check all those bills that were found in Leila's drawer. We might be surprised to find that none of the fingerprints on them belong to Leila," Callum rinsed his cup, placed it on the rack and then walked out of the kitchen through the back door, leaving Fiona staring at him with an uneasy look on her face.

BED OF THORNS

Over the next two days, it seemed to Leila that Callum's attitude toward her changed. He wasn't rude or unpleasant to her but the warmth he'd previously exhibited was gone.

Because of the suspicion hanging over her head, Leila refused to go to Kelsey and Quin's house. Even though Kelsey told her that she didn't believe she'd taken the money, Leila preferred to work from the main ranch house. She spent time quietly in the kitchen helping Mrs. Brian and spoke to no one. Whenever Kelsey brought Little Abner over to the house, Leila received her charge without saying a single word to his mother.

"Do you think she could have done it?" Abner asked Callum. "Miss Jordan says Miss Solomon confessed to her that she was very broke and in dire need of money. Money can tempt even the strongest saint when they're pushed to the limits of their endurance."

Callum twisted his lips, "Dad, I would take everything Fiona says with a pinch of salt. Remember that I'm also being accused of something I have no knowledge of. Do you see the pattern here?"

"But why would Miss Jordan choose to lay such an accusation against her peer? It just doesn't make any sense."

"Fiona is a complicated woman and has her own reasons for being mean. But I intend to investigate and find out what is going on. Deep within my heart I feel that Leila is being set up because Fiona really has it for her."

Abner nodded, "If you can do that I'd really appreciate it. I like Miss Solomon and hate to see her suffering because of the allegations leveled against her which might just turn out to be false. I just pray that she has no hand in the theft of the money even if it was found in her bedroom."

"I need to find her and let her know that we'll all stand by her."

"That's if she's innocent."

"Dad, Leila is innocent, and I'm going to prove it. I'll see you later."

FIONA WAS LIVID. She couldn't believe that the Randolph family was reacting in a way that was totally contrary to what she'd expected.

She had expected the police to be called in to arrest Leila, or better still, that she should be sent packing. But the silly girl was still here and that really annoyed her. She'd seen Callum going to his father's den and followed so she could eavesdrop on their conversation.

What she heard made her a little afraid and angry at the same time. Callum kept insisting that Leila was innocent and he was going to investigate the matter.

"I have to get rid of this girl because she's become a very sharp thorn in my flesh," she hissed.

Callum called Waylen and Maynard to his office a few hours later. "Come and see this," he pointed at his computer screen.

"What are we looking at?" Maynard leaned forward. All he could see was Quin and Kelsey's back door. The video seemed to have been taken in the late afternoon.

"Wait for it," Callum said. As they watched, the figure of a woman furtively walked to the back door and turned the knob. It opened easily and she entered the house.

"Who's that?" Waylen asked, leaning closer to get a better look. "We only saw her back."

"Just wait and see," Callum insisted. The three brothers had their eyes glued to the screen and after about half an hour the door opened once again and the person emerged. She stood on the back patio and raised her face, smiling cunningly.

"I don't believe this," Waylen said. "And she has something in her hands where before when she entered the house, they were empty."

Callum laughed and rubbed his palms in satisfaction. "Got you!" His beloved had been vindicated. Now he just needed to find out why Fiona would go to such lengths to hurt Leila, then level such accusations against her. It was as if Fiona hated Leila and he wondered what could have happened between the two women. To his knowledge, the two of them had met here at the ranch but he wasn't aware of any altercations between them to warrant such strong negative feelings from Fiona.

"We now have proof that Leila didn't take the money from Quin's house. Fiona took the money and then she must have planted it in Leila's bedroom so it would be found and she would be called a thief. This means that Fiona has a very strong case to answer. First, she has no right to be in that house when the owners aren't present. It's clear that she waited for Leila and the mechanic to leave before sneaking in and combing through the house to find something of value to steal so she could plant it in Leila's room. I want her to confess to her crime."

Waylen and Maynard both nodded and it was the latter who spoke. "We need to show this to Dad and also let Quin and Kelsey know about it."

"Right," Waylen said.

"Leila please wait," Callum caught up with her as she walked toward the garage.

"What is it now?" She snapped. "Are you here to make another accusation against me?" "Don't talk to me in that tone," Callum said in a quiet voice. "I'm not your enemy."

Leila felt ashamed and bowed her head. "I'm sorry."

"I know you're feeling very frustrated because of whatever has been happening these past two days. I kept my distance because I didn't want to seem like I wasn't doing anything to find out the truth. But believe me when I say that my family and I have always been on your side."

"I'm innocent and don't want to go to prison," she looked at him with fear in her eyes. "Upon my honor, I never took that money from Kelsey's house."

"I know that," Callum said in such a strong voice that Leila's fear turned to hope in an instant. "There's much that I want to tell you, but first, I need to get you away from this place where no one can interrupt us."

Leila looked down at the ground. "I'm going to get Abner from his mother after his mid-morning feeding," she said.

"I know that. I've already spoken with Quin and Kelsey and she'll stay with her son until we return. Come," he took her hand, and as they walked toward the parking lot, they ran into Fiona. She was standing with two interns and as soon as Leila and Callum appeared, she burst out laughing. It was mocking laughter and the two interns looked at her in confusion. They also looked very uncomfortable when Callum pinned his eyes on them.

"Leila, ignore that woman," Callum said in a low voice. Then he did a surprising thing; he pulled Leila into his arms and planted a kiss on her lips.

Leila thought Fiona would pop a vein. But Callum ignored her and led Leila to a shiny black Hummer. He seated her on the front passenger side and then went over to the driver's side and roared away, leaving Fiona staring angrily at them.

"What did you do that for?" Leila was still shaken by the swift kiss and also curious at what Callum had done and his reason for doing it right in front of Fiona. "You're engaged to Fiona."

"I am?" He gave her an incredulous look.

"She showed me the ring you gave her."

Callum threw his head back and laughed out loudly. "That young woman is quite priceless," he said. "Believe me when I tell you that I've never given Fiona any ring, nor do I ever intend to do so."

"She showed it to me," Leila insisted. "Why would she lie about something like that?"

"Just to hurt you," he faced forward and drove into town, stopping in front of a trendy restaurant. "Please give me a few seconds," he said. He left the car and returned a few minutes later carrying a wicker basket which he placed on the back seat. "I called ahead and asked them to prepare a picnic basket for us."

The delicious aroma of spiced meats and freshly baked bread wafted through the air, causing Leila's stomach to rumble. She hadn't eaten properly ever since the accusation had been made against her and she found that she was really hungry.

"It's not a good day for a picnic," she said. "It's really cold out there," she turned her face toward the window. "I keep expecting it to snow," she said. "I'm sure that Denver is drowning under all that snow."

"We rarely get any snow here in Cedar Hill. In fact, in my lifetime, I think I've only seen it snow three times and even then, it was very light and soon melted away."

"The parks must be freezing."

"I know," Callum said as he started the car. "We'll go to the park but stay in the car. You won't be cold at all."

Just as he'd said, Callum parked in the lot, then turned to Leila. "Before we eat I need to ask you something."

Leila had a vague idea what Callum wanted to ask her so she nodded.

"Why does Fiona treat you so badly and why don't you ever fight back?"

Leila took a deep breath. "Leila's father and my dad are brothers. Dad is the older one. It's only the two of them left in their family."

"I said it," Callum said. "The two of you look so much alike that you could pass for twins. I always wondered how it was so, and yet you both denied knowing each other."

Leila gave him a tight smile, "When my grandparents died, Dad and Uncle Zeke were still teenagers. Dad dropped out of high school so he could work and take care of his younger brother. The agreement was that once Uncle Zeke was done and he got a good job, he would then support my dad to go back to school."

"Did that happen?"

Leila shook her head, "After Uncle Zeke graduated, he met Fiona's mother, whose family was and still is quite wealthy. They set him up, and he eventually opened his own law practice. Instead of sending Dad back to school as they'd agreed, Uncle Zeke gave him a menial clerical position in his firm. Through the years, my father has never risen to any other position. My uncle and his wife humiliate him because of his lowly position, and that has even come down to the way Fiona treats me."

"Why can't your father find work elsewhere?"

"He's too old now, and besides, he has no qualifications like those young graduates have. He didn't even finish high school, so you can imagine how it is for him. He has to stay at his lowly job because of my mother."

"What's wrong with your mother?"

"She has a heart condition that requires her to have surgery or she'll be dead within a year. That's the reason I can't afford to lose my job. I've been sending all the money I receive so my father can put it together with what he has and so we can put a deposit for Mom's treatment to begin."

"I'm so sorry to hear that. But it doesn't explain why Fiona treats you so abominably. Sometimes I feel as if she fears you and so intimidates you so you can't get the better of her."

Leila smiled and decided to tell Callum everything she knew about her cousin. Fiona had put her down one too many times and she was tired of being treated like a doormat.

"Fiona fears that I know too much about her."

"What do you mean?"

"I worked at two hotels, and twice, I found Fiona in the rooms with different men. One was even married and I knew his wife and children. Fiona had me fired each time that happened and charged me to never let her parents know that she was messing up. I got tired of being in Denver where she could get to me and decided to find work outside the state. Little did I know that I would find her in this place after I got the position of Kelsey's nanny."

"What about her pregnancy, do you know anything about it?"

Leila nodded, "About five months ago I was at their house when she was sick. Her mother asked me to go and keep her company, not that Fiona wanted me to, and I found a pregnancy test in her bathroom. The test was positive, and I knew she was pregnant, but I didn't let her know that I was aware of it."

Callum frowned slightly though his heart started beating rapidly. Dare he hope? "Did you say that was five months ago? That would make the pregnancy quite advanced and she's in her second trimester."

Leila nodded, "Fiona is five months pregnant. When I got here and found out that she was claiming that you're the father of her child, I was quite surprised. But then I thought that you'd probably met at some point in your lives," she shrugged. "Fiona travels a lot with her friends, so the two of you could have met anywhere."

Callum laughed, "According to what Fiona claims, she conceived when we met at a wedding in New Jersey two months ago. Actually, I don't remember meeting her, but it so happens that we must have been at the same wedding. All I remember is that I asked for a glass of grape juice during the late afternoon reception, and after that I felt quite exhausted. I didn't stay until the end of the reception and even missed the evening party. I know that I never had a woman with me when I went to my room. The next day I woke up alone in my bed and came home. Then just a few weeks ago, your cousin gets here with photos showing the two of us in bed together."

"Did you take a closer look at the photos?" Leila asked.

"She left copies with me but then took them back. But I know that I was in that bed and she was there with me. How she got there is a great mystery to me."

"You need to get those photos and have an expert look at them. What if Fiona used a Photoshop App to have those photos modified so that it looked as if the two of you were together?"

"I never thought about that at all. Since I have no recollection of whatever might have happened that night, I began to wonder if perhaps I could have done what Fiona was accusing me of. She refused to have an early DNA test done that will determine the paternity of her child. I should have insisted. She also refused to let anyone accompany her to the hospital for her prenatal checkups. But why didn't you tell me all this before?"

"Because I was afraid. Fiona threatened to have my father fired from his position in Uncle Zeke's firm. I didn't want my father to struggle financially, not more than he already is."

"Oh Leila," Callum took her hand in his. "You should have spoken up and spared us all this needless suffering. But thank you for telling me the truth now. I can finally get rid of that woman and get my life back on track again."

WHEN CALLUM and Leila returned to the ranch, he immediately called his brothers to his father's den. He quickly told them all that Leila had shared with him.

"That's the reason Fiona has been mistreating Leila," he said. "And now I think it's time that we showed Miss Fiona Jordan the truth so she can own up to her mistakes." Everyone agreed and Fiona was summoned.

"Miss Jordan it's rather shocking to find out that certain unpleasant things have been going on here on the ranch and these involve you," Abner Randolph wasn't smiling.

"I don't know what you're talking about."

Callum noticed that she looked very nervous because of the two burly men that had joined them shortly before.

"Please meet Detectives John Guard and Simon Leer from the Dallas Police Department. They're here to investigate more about the money allegedly stolen by Miss Solomon. Detective Leer is a fingerprints expert and he's going to test all the bills that were found in Leila's room. Of course, Kelsey and Quin's fingerprints as well as the bank clerk's will be on those bills. Please tell me that we won't find any other surprises," Abner looked straight at Fiona. "I also have here a court order from a judge that compels you to have a DNA test after Callum decided to sue you for wrongful paternity claims."

Fiona seemed frozen.

"If the baby you're carrying turns out to be my grandchild, then I'll pay all damages to you and for emotional stress too. Even if my son refuses to marry you, I'll always take care of both you and the baby. But if the baby turns out not to be my grandchild, then I'll sue you for the trauma, distress, and embarrassment you've caused my son because of the false accusations. Your father is a lawyer, and a big one as you've always told us, and I suggest that you contact him so he can come and stand with you, whichever way this will go."

"No, please," Fiona looked quite shaken. "Don't bring my father into this. I'm sorry for all the things that I've done, please forgive me."

"What exactly are you needing forgiveness for?" Callum wanted her to state everything out loud because he was recording the session. He needed proof that Fiona had falsely accused him and Leila. "And for my protection, I'm recording this conversation."

"I'll speak the truth," Fiona started crying. "It's true that I was at the wedding that day that you were there, but not with you. I was there with my boyfriend who happened to work at the hotel. His name is Frank Plume, and at the time, I had no idea that he was a petty crook. He lied to me that he was the events manager, but I later found out that he was only a bellhop. He'd noticed that you were wearing a very expensive watch and chain. When you asked for grape juice, he was the one who laced it with cocaine. We only wanted you to sleep deeply but not be harmed. I told him to be very careful."

"Really?" Callum glared at her.

"Yes, really. All Frank wanted was to grab your expensive accessories. You see, Frank had access to the master key that could open all the rooms in the hotel. I didn't want to do it, but I had to because I was afraid of Frank. He told me that he only wanted to take your jewelry and leave so I followed him to the room to make sure that he wasn't going to harm you."

"Mmh!" Abner grunted.

"When we entered your room, we discovered that you'd locked up all your valuables, including the watch and chain, in the safe, which he was unable to open. So, Frank forced me to take photos of you lying in your bed, and then he planted some cocaine on the table next to you. His idea was to blackmail you and claim that you were a drug addict."

Callum couldn't believe what he was hearing. "What?"

"I managed to convince him not to leave the cocaine on your table," Fiona said desperately. "Though I had to give him some money so he wouldn't harm you."

"Then how did you end up in the bed with me?" Callum demanded.

Fiona covered her face with her hands and wept. "Weeks before that I'd found out that I was expecting Frank's baby. I thought he loved me and was ready to settle down, but it turned out that I was wrong. All Frank wanted from me was my money and just a good time but without any serious commitments. So, after the wedding, I told Frank that I was pregnant, and he abandoned me. I got desperate and remembered the photos I'd taken of you, using my phone. So, I decided to use the photos I'd taken of you in bed and make it look like we'd been together. I used a Photoshop app."

"Why did you choose me for your evil plans?"

"Because you were the only one who was alone at that wedding. Frank said it was easier to rob and blackmail a man or woman who is alone because there are no witnesses. He hoped that you were a married man so he could blackmail you by threatening to tell your wife everything. But after we went through your wallet and found out that there was no indication that you were married, we decided to drop that."

"So that's how you found out where I was from," Callum shook his head. "Fiona, I promise you that you'll pay for all the distress you've caused me."

"Please no, I've told you what happened. It wasn't me. I'm so sorry that I got so desperate and didn't know what to do. I felt that since you had completely blacked out that night, I could pin this pregnancy on you."

"Lying against another person and pinning your pregnancy on them is sheer wickedness no matter how desperate you are. That's more of a moral thing, but using those photos obtained without my brother's consent and doctoring them to suit your purposes so you could manipulate him into marrying you, is a crime. Also, breaking and entering my brother's house, stealing his money and planting it in someone else's room so they can be accused of theft is another serious offence. This is the time you need to call your lawyer to be present because now there's definitely going to be a lawsuit."

Terry Solomon stood in the doorway of his brother's office and stared at his bent head. He couldn't believe that this man had once been his best friend and they would have done anything for each other.

"Terry, what am I going to do?" Zeke Jordan raised his head. "My whole life seems to be crumbling around me. First, my wife is threatening to divorce me for cheating on her but that's not true. We both signed prenuptial agreements that state that if either of us was caught cheating, the person would lose everything. I've never been unfaithful to Hannah. Then just a few minutes ago I received a phone call from someone in Cedar Hill, Texas, telling me that Fiona has been arrested and is facing charges of blackmail, theft and fraud. Terry, what's happening to my family? Who have I offended for this to be happening to me?"

For the first time, Terry's heart hardened toward his brother. "Why are you asking me all this when we're no longer brothers? Don't you have close friends who can come and give you advice since my counsel has never been taken by you?"

"Terry, please," Zeke pleaded. "You're my big brother and the only one I can count on right now."

"Really?" Terry laughed briefly as he unbuttoned his coat and sat down, something he would never have dared to do before. "So all the ill treatment against me and my family has been because I'm your big brother? With a relative like you, my quota for enemies has been filled."

"Terry..."

"You listen to me for once," Terry's voice was hard and harsh. "I dropped out of school to make sure that you achieved your dreams, Zeke. We had an agreement that when you got a good job you would help me finish high school and go to college.

Instead what did you do, dear brother? You gave me the most menial clerical position in your firm and ensured that whatever you paid me was only enough for me to take care of my family. I couldn't even advance myself by taking evening classes if I wanted to. And over the years, I've stood by and watched in silence as you, your wife and daughter humiliated me and my family. Yet I continued to serve you with diligence and loyalty. My wife fell sick, and you didn't show any brotherly care at all. The medical coverage you placed me and my family on is the barest and can hardly cover the drugs my wife needs. I overlooked all that ill treatment and kept silent, praying and hoping that my brother would open his eyes and see that whatever he's been doing is wrong and very unfair."

"Terry, I'm so sorry," Zeke looked totally ashamed of himself, but Terry wasn't done yet.

"I would have let all that go, but then your daughter, my own niece who I love and treat with so much affection, crossed the line this time. She went down to Cedar Hill where Leila works, stole money from my daughter's employer and planted it in her room so as to get her into trouble." Terry shook his head. "What if those people that Leila is working for hadn't been so kind and understanding? My daughter would now be in prison for a crime she didn't commit and it would have killed her mother. Because I have no money, it would have been impossible for me to find the kind of legal representation that would see her win the case. She would have been allocated a tired and overworked government counsel at law, and things would have really gone badly for her." Terry looked at his brother. "Zeke, all I ever did was love you, and I gave up my own dreams to see you achieve your own. But what

611

my family and I got in return for my goodness is shame, humiliation, and ill treatment." He rose to his feet. "Anyway, I came to let you know that I'm resigning with immediate effect because my wife and daughter need me right now. I stood by all these years and watched your daughter humiliating mine, yet they're supposed to be as close as sisters. You and your wife never said anything to stop Fiona from doing the things she was doing to Leila. When it comes to my child, I've decided that I'm going to ruthlessly protect her from here on out."

"Terry please don't leave me now," Zeke also shot to his feet. "We can work something out. You've been my most loyal and trusted employee and I can't afford to lose you."

"Yet I was the least paid even after working for you for twenty years. All those broken promises that you made to me ended up never being fulfilled at all." Terry laughed. "I'm thankful that this happened because I have finally realized that being your brother is just a lost cause for me. I wish you well, but I can no longer stay here, since I can't count on you. This is where I leave you, Mr. Zeke Jordan."

"I'll pay for Malika's treatment and increase your salary, promote you and backdate all the benefits that you should have enjoyed over the years. I'll even pay for Leila to go to college if that's what you want, as a way of apologizing for my daughter's ill-treatment of her."

But Terry shook his head. "Your kind of generosity expired long ago and I don't need it now. My family no longer needs you because you've never been there for us. Do you recall that I even had to buy your share of the house our parents left us? You wouldn't let me have it for free but demanded your own share of our parents' inheritance. So that house belongs squarely to me, and I'll sell it and get Malika the treatment she needs since you have no claims on it. Good thing was that I got you to sign off on the transfer documents or else you might have turned around and defrauded me of the same. At least, I have documents that will defend me should you decide to become funny. But I'm not staying a moment longer in your firm, and if we never see each other again, I really don't care. You ceased to be my brother decades ago. My wife and daughter are the only family I have right now and can rely on. As for you, Zeke, we can no longer be in the same place because the anger within me might fester, and I might do something I'll regret. This is goodbye from me."

"Terry please, temper your justice with mercy. I'm your brother."

"Zeke, I don't like ending things like this between us but there comes a time in a man's life when he must make choices that will protect his family. I really wish you well in all that you do going forward."

As Terry packed his few belongings into the small removal box, he felt as if he were walking away from bondage. He'd been his brother's minion for years because of fear of stepping out into the unknown but that yoke had now been lifted off his shoulders.

As he walked out of Jordan & Associates Law Firm for the last time, he ignored the shocked looks on the faces of those he'd worked with over the years.

"Leila, on behalf of me and my family, please accept our sincere apologies for the way we've treated you. Please forgive us for not protecting you as we should have," Abner told an astonished Leila. "The investigations Callum carried out have cleared your name and you're absolved of any wrong doing."

"Thank you, Sir," Leila's voice trembled. Could this really be happening? "And where was Fiona in all this?"

"Miss Jordan has been taken to the police station to write her statement for the part she played in accusing you."

Leila sat with her head bowed down and thought about her cousin and the fact that she often got away with wrongdoing. Even now, Leila was sure that her Uncle Zeke was probably in the air flying down here to get his daughter off the hook. That didn't matter at all to her but she was afraid for her parents. Fiona would definitely accuse her of getting her arrested and demand that Leila's father be sacked from the law firm. If her father lost his job, things would be very rough for her parents.

"Please, can you drop the charges against my cousin?" Leila asked.

"Why?"

"When her father comes down to bail her out of jail, she'll accuse me and then get my father fired from his job. Dad can't afford to lose his job because it's all that sustains him and my mother. Please just let Fiona go."

Callum looked at Leila with compassion. "Leila, all will be well, you'll see. But the law has to take its course so that Fiona can learn that it's never a good thing to accuse others falsely. While she thought she had gotten away with her lies, the truth finally emerged and now everything is out in the open."

"I just wish you would release her."

"She'll be released," Abner said. "But only when her father gets here and hears about this issue. Somehow I have the feeling that her parents have no idea that she's expecting a child."

TABLES TURNING

"*P*lease Lord, if this is a dream, let me not wake up," Leila murmured as she looked around her. She was in the waiting room of Dallas' newest and very well equipped medical facility. Rhodes Medical Center was one of the best in the field of research.

Her mother had been flown down here from Denver so she could get the surgery she needed. Callum was covering all the expenses and Leila couldn't believe that her dreams had actually come true. The surgery would take between six and ten hours, and after that her mother would need three months of monitored recuperation. Callum had arranged for her parents to get a house on the ranch and two nurses would be on call twenty-four hours a day to monitor Mrs. Solomon's recovery process.

"It's not a dream," Willow told her. "This is really happening, and we're all so happy for you."

Leila looked at the five women who'd come to sit with her during her mother's surgery. Her father, by special arrangement, was in the theatre with her mother. When Callum had told her that he would pay for her mother's surgery, Leila had wept tears of happiness.

"We've prayed for so long for this to happen," Leila's eyes filled with tears. "And my father and I worked ourselves to the bone, scrimping and saving every single penny we earned. But just suddenly like that," she snapped her fingers, "This has happened."

"*When the Lord turned again the captivity of Zion, we were like them that dreamed. Then was our mouth filled with laughter, and our tongue with singing; then said they among the heathen, The Lord hath done great things for them,*" Mrs. Brian chanted softly.

"Amen," Leila wiped her eyes. Everything seemed to be too good to be true. From the moment her uncle and aunt had flown down to Dallas to take Fiona away, she'd felt like all the burdens of her life had flown away. Callum and Leila had dropped all charges against Fiona, and that was why she was let off very easily. For the first time, Uncle Zeke and Aunt Hannah came face to face with people with more power than theirs, and Leila saw them humbled. They actually drove to the ranch to look for Abner and Callum so they could apologize on behalf of their daughter.

What shocked her most was when Uncle Zeke actually apologized for what Fiona had done to her over the years.

"Fiona is your cousin even if she hasn't acted like it in the past," he'd said. "Please forgive her, and me too, because I overlooked so many things that she was doing to you. And when you see your parents please ask them to forgive me too."

"I thought you saw dad at work every day."

Uncle Zeke shook his head, "Didn't he tell you?"

"Tell me what?"

"Your father resigned from the firm and said he was going to sell the house so he could pay for your mother's surgery. I offered to settle all the hospital bills for your mother but your father rejected my offer."

Leila wanted to shout and tell her uncle that his offer was coming too late but she was too respectful to do that. To get him to go away and leave her alone, she said she had forgiven everything and even promised she would talk to her father so he could return to work, with better conditions of course.

But deep down, Leila was happy that her father had finally walked away from her uncle's oppressive presence. She knew that she was still very bitter toward Fiona. Her cousin had subjected her to so much humiliation over the years, and that wasn't something that could be so easily forgiven and forgotten.

"You look sad," Kelsey said. "I hope you're still not thinking about what happened and how you were wrongfully accused. You know that I always believed in your innocence."

"I know that and I'm very grateful for what you did for me. I'm just praying that my mom's surgery will go well, and she'll come out victorious and healthy again. I miss her so much."

"We've arranged for a prayer chain and Pastor Manoah has mobilized people to pray around the clock for your mother and her total healing," Mrs. Brian said. "Your mother, and indeed your whole family, are covered in prayer round the clock for the next seven days."

"Thank you so much," Leila felt overwhelmed by the outpouring of love that she'd received from everyone around her. "I don't know how I'll ever thank everyone who's been so kind to us."

WHEN THE DOCTOR finally emerged from beyond the theater doors to update Leila on her mother's progress, she was fast asleep with her head on Callum's shoulder and his arm was around her. He didn't want to wake her up because she'd paced the waiting room floor for half the night.

"How is Mrs. Solomon?" He asked in hushed tones so as not to wake Leila up.

"The surgery was a great success and it's the first of its kind since we opened this facility six months ago. Mrs. Solomon is in our recovery room and you can see her after about an hour when the anesthesia wears off."

Leila opened her eyes and quickly sat up when she noticed the doctor standing a few feet away.

"My mom?" She was almost afraid to ask.

"Miss Solomon, your mother's surgery went very well, and she'll be all right."

"May I please see her?" She half rose to her feet but Callum gently pulled her back down.

"You can see her in about an hour's time," the doctor said. "Right now she's in recovery and still very heavily sedated. Your father is in there with her. I'll send someone to get you when it's all right for you to see her."

"Thank you so much, Doctor."

Once he'd left, Leila turned teary eyes to Callum. "What did I ever do to deserve you?" She asked. "In just one day you've changed the whole landscape of our lives, and I feel like I'm still dreaming."

"You're not dreaming, and we thank God who made it possible for all this to happen. My family and I are but vessels of the Lord, and we feel honored to be used to bring this to pass for your family."

"Even vessels can refuse to be used by the Lord and He'll never impose His will on them," Leila said bitterly. "For all these years when my father worked for Uncle Zeke, he could have done something to help my mother have her surgery and things wouldn't have gotten to this point. Uncle Zeke watched us go through so much pain and anguish, yet he had the means and resources to end all our suffering. What angers me most is that he thinks that he can now offer us the world and we'll go running to receive it from him. Where was he when we needed him most?"

"My darling," Callum's voice was gentle. "The Lord makes all things beautiful in His time. Because of all that happened to you, He remembered your family and opened a way for you to come to Cedar Hill because that's where your destiny lay. See it like that. Otherwise how else would you and I have met?"

Leila bowed her head and allowed Callum's words to wash over her. Mrs. Brian had said pretty much the same thing before she and the other four women returned to the ranch.

But how could she let go of the pain that she'd harbored for years? Fiona and her parents didn't deserve her forgiveness. They'd apologized yes, but it was too late. What if her mother had died before receiving treatment? What if she'd never met Callum and what if he hadn't been so generous and kind to them?

Callum could see Leila struggling with her thoughts and remembered what his father had once told him. *"Forgiveness is a gift from one who has been offended. Just like any other gift, this has to be through the victim's good will. Just as one can never be compelled to give a gift, a person cannot be forced to forgive those who have offended them. Allow them to process their emotions and feelings, and when they eventually forgive it will be from the bottom of the heart."*

Callum knew that Leila needed time to process her feelings and emotions, but he purposed to continue praying for her and not stop praying and supporting her until she was completely healed in body and spirit.

CHRISTMAS FORTUNE

*I*t was the night before Christmas Day, and Leila gazed at the beautifully decorated tree standing in one corner of the living room of the ranch house. She couldn't believe just how fast things had gone. There were no gifts under the tree and Callum had explained to her the reason why.

"The year before Mama died we all decided that we would be giving our gifts to the orphanage next door every Christmas time. We buy them and wrap them, but then instead of exchanging them among ourselves, we send them to the orphanage."

Leila never stopped considering how blessed she was to be part of such a loving, caring and giving family. They'd changed her life, indeed the lives of her parents, too, and in such a tremendous way.

Her mother was out of hospital and settled in the house that Callum had prepared for them on the ranch. Due to Covid protocols, her parents lived in controlled isolation. Mrs. Solomon was still very vulnerable after her surgery, and the doctor was very strict about anyone who wanted to visit with her.

Leila spent every single day with her mother even though this had to be done with a glass barrier between them. Leila also had to have a mask on for the duration of her visit to her mother, but she wasn't complaining. Her mom was alive and getting better and stronger every day and everyone was so happy for them.

Callum had actually proposed to her in the presence of his family and her parents. Dr. Miyako, her mother's attending physician had allowed them to enter the house where Leila's parents were staying but on condition that everyone wore a mask and didn't draw too close to his patient. Her mother had wept with happiness when Callum went down on one knee and asked her to be his wife.

That was five days ago, and after the stipulated waiting period of seventy-two hours after applying for a marriage license, they'd gotten married earlier today.

"There's my beautiful bride," Callum came up behind her and wrapped his arms around her. "It's too cold for you to be out here."

Leila turned in her husband's arms and put her hands around his neck. "I needed to do something and I'm glad that you're here with me." She rested her head on his chest. This man had taught her so much in the past few days, and she wondered, once again, what she'd ever done to merit such great blessings.

"Please don't be sad," Callum told his bride. "Tomorrow is Christmas Day and it should be a time of happiness for us. The Lord has answered our prayers, and your mother is recuperating well."

"I'm truly grateful for all that."

"And my father has already spoken to a good friend of his who is a senior counsel at law in a very prestigious firm. Your father begins his new job at the beginning of next year and this comes with so many benefits, including all-inclusive medical coverage for him and your mother. Henceforth, your mother's bills will never be an issue again. The beauty of it all is that the man has law firms in all the major cities of America so your parents get to choose if they want to go back to Denver or stay in Dallas."

"I can't begin to thank all of you for everything you've done for us."

"So you see, my Darling, there's no more reason to cry."

Leila nodded, "That's the reason I came out here to look at the Christmas tree. It's just a symbol that stands for families coming together to share not only presents but the gift of love as well. It's now time for me to forgive Fiona and her parents, or else this beautiful day will be wasted. If I don't give the grace of forgiveness to those who offended me, then Christmas makes no sense at all. Jesus, the Christ, brought salvation and forgiveness to mankind, and if I am going to celebrate Christmas then I too must forgive and let go."

"I'm so proud of you, my Darling. I love you so much."

"I love you too."

EPILOGUE

*A*bner stood at his wife's graveside early on Christmas Day morning. It was a cold day, and he was bundled up and felt quite cozy in his warm clothing.

Callum and Leila would probably be stirring from sleep as would Mrs. Brian. The housekeeper had decided not to travel to Georgia to be with her family these holidays as she did every year. That was because she'd wanted to give Callum and Leila a befitting wedding as she termed it. And she'd gone all out to ensure that their day was really great.

"There's so much to celebrate," Abner turned to find Mrs. Brian approaching him. "I saw you coming out here and decided to join you and remind you of all the good that has happened for these past sixteen years. Barbara wouldn't want you to continue mourning her."

"You always know what to say. And no, I'm not weeping for Barbara. I came here to remind myself that even out of pain can come so much happiness. I lost Barbara sixteen years ago on a day like this one. Yet every Christmas Day after that has been quite a blessing instead of invoking painful memories. My sons started the culture of donating all their Christmas presents to the needy years ago, and to date this still stands. It was Barbara who taught our sons how to be good boys, but you, Mrs. Brian, taught them how to be exemplary young men, and I thank you from the bottom of my heart."

"We thank God for His mercies."

"I don't know what I would have done without you all these years. You held us together and were like a mother to my sons. Last Christmas Day was the beginning of a new era in my family when Quin proposed to Kelsey. This past year has seen all my sons meet and marry wonderful women. All the five wild sons of Randolph Abner have met their matches and been tamed."

Mrs. Brian gave her employer a speculative look. "Why do I have the feeling that Abner Randolph had a hand in all this? Suddenly women were popping up from all over the place and your sons were falling before them like well-coordinated dominoes," she cracked up and so did he.

"I don't know what you're talking about," he protested a little while later when the laughter had died down, but without much conviction.

"All your five daughters-in-law speak very highly and fondly of a certain woman back in Denver where, by coincidence or maybe not, they're all from. This woman's name, Sally Jo Manning, is on the lips of all your daughters. I was so curious about this paragon of excellence, according to the girls, that I looked her up. And voila! The woman runs a marriage agency for cowboys and cowgirls who are seeking for godly spouses. Hitch Your Wagon Romance Agency," Mrs. Brian chuckled softly. "You found your sons wives through the agency and you've done very well."

"And I have no regrets at all."

"And so it should be," the housekeeper agreed. "The Lord led you to the right place to look and brought the women He'd predestined for our boys."

"My life is fulfilled and I have a grandson and many more on the way. This is beyond the prayers I made over my children."

"This woman called Sally Jo needs to be rewarded handsomely."

"Already done! Her check went out in yesterday's mail and that includes a large bonus to say thank you."

"You're a good man, Abner Randolph."

"And you're a good woman, Tamara Brian."

"My darling," Malika Solomon called out softly to her husband who was snuggled close to her in bed. It was Christmas Day in the morning and something was bothering her mind.

"Yes, love of my life?" Terry rose up. "Do you need something?"

"Yes and no," his wife of twenty-two years said. "I've been thinking."

"What about?"

"Your brother," she said and saw his countenance changing. "Terry, I don't want you to continue being angry with your brother. He's all you have."

"I have you and Leila, and now I have a new son and extended family. I don't need a man who couldn't be there for me when I needed him to be. The worst of it all is that Zeke could have helped me become the man I wanted to be but no, his wife and daughter were more important to him. I gave up everything for my brother but he repaid my good with evil. Please don't talk to me about him because he hurt me deeply."

"I know that and I feel your pain but see the grace that we've received. I know you're angry that Zeke refused to pay for my surgery. But had he done so we would never have heard the last of it. Hannah would have broadcast it all over the place and made us look like we're so poor and they are our benevolent benefactors. Instead, the Lord brought us divine helpers and here we are now. Christmas Day is a time for new beginnings and I want you to call your brother."

"What?"

"Yes, please call Zeke and tell him that you've forgiven him. That's the only present I want from you this year, my Love."

Terry thought for a brief moment then nodded, "You know that I was born to make you happy," he grinned at her. "And I can never refuse you anything. I promise that as soon as we're up and I've had a good breakfast, I'll call that good-for-nothing brother of mine..."

"Terry!"

"Just joking, Love. I'll call Zeke, wish him merry Christmas and then tell him that I forgive him. I also need his forgiveness for being so angry at him for a long time; yet I carried on as if all was well."

"The first step is forgiveness and with time I pray that the two of you will be reconciled."

"How does a man repay the Lord who has given him so much grace?"

"By living to serve Him all the days of our lives," his wife said. "Terry Solomon, my Amha Selassie, the first and last emperor of my heart, I love you so much and thank you for the beautiful years that you've given me. Through the good and the bad, you've always been there for me."

"As have you," he said. "You're a beautiful woman and at any time you could have walked away when things got so tough. Yet you stood by me, believed in me, encouraged me, and honored me as your husband," he took her hands and brought them to his lips, reverently kissing each one. "I love you so much, my beautiful African Queen."

"And see how the Lord has blessed our only child with a husband of her own," Malika couldn't help smiling. "I used to worry that Leila would never meet a godly man to marry her but the Lord heard the cry of my heart and answered me even beyond what I could have imagined."

"Now I understand why the Lord tells us to trust Him with all our hearts and minds and lean not on our own understanding. We're so blessed, Malika."

"That we are, my darling husband; indeed we are."

THANK YOU FOR CHOOSING A PUREREAD BOOK!

We hope you enjoyed the story, and as a way to thank you for choosing PureRead we'd like to send you this free Western trilogy, and other fun reader rewards...

Click here to claim your free Historical Western trilogy...

https://pureread.com/western

Thanks again for reading.

See you soon!

LOOKING FOR ANOTHER GREAT ADVENTURE?

*I*f you enjoyed the five wild sons of Randolph Ranch you'll be sure to enjoy the series that inspired the five wild sons stories.

The Seven Sons of Jethro tells the story of long-suffering father, Jethro, and his seven sons. Their stories will have you laughing and crying all at the same time. Each of Jethro's boys has their own character and stubborn ways, but they are no match for Jethro's quest to get each of them married off to a good and godly young lady!

You'll feel like you are right there in the story with the characters.

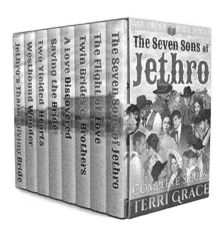

The complete 7 book box set is a real bargain and Free To Read on Kindle Unlimited

Jump Right In and Start Reading The Seven Sons of Jethro Complete Boxset Today

Click here or search Seven Sons of Jethro Boxset on Amazon

OUR GIFT TO YOU

AS A WAY TO SAY THANK YOU WE WOULD LOVE TO SEND YOU THIS BEAUTIFUL TRILOGY FREE OF CHARGE.

Our Reader List is 100% FREE

Click here to claim your free Historical Western trilogy... **https:// pureread.com/western**

At PureRead we publish books you can trust. Great tales without smut or swearing, but with all of the mystery and romance you expect from a great story.

Be the first to know when we release new books, take part in our fun competitions, and get surprise free books in your inbox by signing up to our Reader list.

As a thank you you'll receive this exclusive Western trilogy - a beautiful collection available only to our subscribers...

Click here to claim your free Historical Western trilogy... **https://pureread.com/western**

Made in the USA
Monee, IL
01 October 2023

43792792R00374